Blood and Thorns

Twisted Ever After

Taylor Aston White

DARK WOLF
PUBLISHING

Edited by Enchanted Author Co
Proofread by Kat's Corner
Cover by Estheticah
Chapter art (Paperback) by Jade Dee Visions

www.taylorastonwhite.com
Official Taylor Aston White Newsletter

Playlist

SKIN - elijah
Like A Villain - Bad Omens
Emergence - Sleep Token
Cut the Bridge - LINKIN PARK
Stay - Palaye Royale
Do or Die (Acoustic) - Natalie Jane
PLEASE - Omido & Ex Habit
Red Velvet (With Ari Abdul) - Jutes
Teeth (feat. Diggy Graves) - WesGhost
Obsessed - Jutes
PRAY TO ME - DeathbyRomy, Palaye Royale
Rush - Dutch Melrose, Benny Mayne
Demi God - Architects
Smut - Jutes
Desire - Palaye Royale

Content warning

Blood and Thorns is a dark contemporary romance inspired by the tale of Beauty and the Beast. It contains explicit content, graphic violence, profanity, and topics that may be sensitive to some readers. If any of the below topics are distressing, please proceed with caution. Your mental health matters.

Triggers include:
Graphic gore/death
Extreme torture
Offensive language
· Threats of sexual assault
Attempted rape (not by MMC)
Dub-con
Sexually explicit scenes
Complex Post-Traumatic Stress Disorder
Drugs
Emotional abuse
Mentions of suicide
Mentions of self-harm
Degradation

Historic child abuse (physical)
Removal of genitalia with a knife
Blood play
Knife play
Spiders

*This book is written in British English, including spelling
and grammar.*

For everyone who wants to be chased and then fucked by the big bad Beast.

Sebastian is waiting for you...

Chapter 1
Arabella

I swear, if this guy touched me one more time, I was going to scream. I didn't, obviously. Because I needed this job, and Michael was my boss' nephew's son twice removed, or something equally as ridiculous. He was family, apparently, and since he liked to run the bar as if everyone was one big happy family, he was off limits.

So rather than shoving him like I'd wanted, I forced my smile to look a little more threatening, which apparently translated to *'please, grope me harder.'*

Suzy snickered at me from across the room, clearing up the table while I tried, and failed, to untangle myself from Michael's greasy fingers. I shot her a pleading look, but it only made her cackle harder.

"Come on, cupcake. Just one date," Michael crooned with a slight drunken slur. "I promise you won't regret it. Is it the age thing? It's what... only eight years? What's eight years between two people wanting to get to know each other?"

But it wasn't eight years. He must be in his late forties, which made him almost two decades older than me. Not that age mattered, but it was still a hard pass. But rejection clearly meant little to Michael, because he'd ignored all my protests over the past few weeks since Suzy turned him down. Then there was Rachael before that. I should probably be more offended that I was the last woman in the bar he'd tried to date.

"I have a boyfriend," I lied, finally managing to twist myself away, only for another set of hands to land on my hips, making my skin crawl.

"Fuck off, arsehole," a familiar voice growled, and honestly, if the ground opened up and swallowed me whole, I wouldn't even be mad.

Pulling away, I turned to find none other than my ex, his dark hair expertly styled to frame his handsome face, and those familiar blue eyes looking down at me with a glint I once loved. Now I couldn't stand them, especially when paired with that smirk that seemed to permanently curve his lips.

"Gabriel," I said stiffly, putting some space between us, "what are you doing here?"

"Is that how you greet your man?" he asked, reaching out to grip my wrist.

I didn't fight because I didn't want to make a scene, especially considering I could see my boss hovering in the corner.

Now, the bar wasn't exactly glamorous, but with its dated décor, neon beer signs and dim lighting, it had a gritty charm that I enjoyed. Plus, the patrons usually kept to themselves, coming to enjoy a cheap drink without all the fanfare the more expensive places offered in the city. Gabriel wouldn't usually be caught dead here and had never once bothered to come see me when we were actually dating. Which begged the question why he was here now.

"I was out buying a new watch because for some reason I can't find mine, and I thought, why not come visit the love of my life?" His eyes narrowed in suspicion, even as he continued to smirk in a way that was supposed to be intimidating.

That was the problem with Gabriel: he always wanted everyone to feel smaller than he was.

I swallowed, tugging on my wrist, but his grip only tightened with a sharp chuckle. Up close I noticed his dilated pupils, which made sense with his slightly manic energy. "Are you high?"

His lips tightened into a thin line. "You've been avoiding me, baby."

Disgust roiled through me. "I'm not your *baby*."

"You left me on read." His definitely high eyes narrowed. "And you never answer my phone calls. You've even blocked me on Instagram."

"I got tired of seeing you pose with all those women."

That glint brightened, his mouth curling into a cruel smile. "So you've been looking at my pictures?"

Fuck.

"No," I lied, because of course I'd been secretly stalking his Instagram. Firstly, because I was clearly a glutton for punishment, and secondly, because it reminded me what a sleazeball he was. "It's been three months. I thought you'd have gotten the hint by now."

He licked his lips. "I was only posting those girls to get your attention."

"Gabe, you're hurting me." His grip didn't let up.

"I'm bored of this now. I've given you long enough to get over it."

I scoffed. "Over it? Are you serious?" I finally noticed Lennon over his shoulder, his friend and colleague from the Metropolitan Police grinning with the same chaotic liveliness. Neither were in uniform, which meant they'd been out partying.

"You still reading this shit, Bella?" Lennon drawled, leaning over the bar to grab my latest book and peer at the cover.

I bristled. "I've told you before not to call me that."

But Lennon didn't care, continuing as if I hadn't even spoken. "What's wrong? Reality not exciting enough for you?" he taunted as he flipped through the pages.

Where Gabriel was tall and handsome, Lennon was the opposite. His height was only an inch or so taller than my five foot five, and his nose had been broken one too many times. Not to mention his dark eyes always made me feel on edge, his lingering gaze like hornets prickling my skin.

"She won't be reading much once we're married," Gabriel laughed like I was still his girlfriend and we hadn't been separated for the past twelve weeks. "No wife of mine will have her nose buried in a book."

I narrowed my eyes at him. "Not your baby. Not your wife."

Gabriel's smile slipped, and I recoiled when he dipped his head close enough that his lips brushed against my ear. "You'll always be my baby," he hissed, his breath hot against my skin. "And you *will* be my wife. You'll regret turning down my proposal, but you'll still end up mine. I'll make sure of it."

"Not in this lifetime." Gabriel was a walking red flag, and I couldn't believe I had been blind to it for so long. I'd once loved him, but luckily my rose-tinted glasses shattered when I walked in on him fucking not one, but *two* women at once. "You cheated on me, remember?"

He dared to roll his eyes. "If I can forgive you for stealing my watch, then you can get over those women. They meant nothing."

"I never took your stupid watch." Apparently, the stress

of being a detective constable was reason enough to stick his dick in other women, not to mention his need to party hard.

The drugs I could handle, because I understood addiction and the need to escape. Although my escape was dragon riders, long lost cities, and fairytale endings. I'd even forgiven him for trying to share me with his friends, but clearly cheating was a hard no, because after almost a year together I'd walked away.

Gabriel was a toxic narcissist, and it sucked that it took me so long to see it. He was supposed to be the one who saved me from this life, a man of the law, but instead he'd made it even shittier.

"Once we're married, you'll be enough."

"I didn't take your stupid watch," I insisted again. "Maybe it was one of the girls you were screwing behind my back." I dropped my tone, hoping it came out threatening. "Seriously, Gabe. Get off me."

"Is there a problem here?"

Gabriel's head jerked up to glare at my boss, Chase, who despite being the calmest guy I'd ever met didn't look the least bit friendly. Probably due to the fact he was built like a pro sumo wrestler. He was genuinely a decent guy, and while he liked to ogle the girls, he didn't dare touch any of us. Plus, he let us all keep our tips, which was a bonus.

"No problem." Gabriel finally released me, and I immediately stepped back, my wrist throbbing. "Arabella and I were just discussing something personal."

"Arabella should be behind the bar," Chase snapped, gaze piercing.

"Please, just leave," I urged. "Go get yourself clean. Straighten out your life, and stay out of mine."

Gabriel finally returned his attention to me, his smile unfriendly as his voice dropped to a whisper. "This isn't over, *baby*." He turned, stalking toward the exit with Lennon sneering at me over his shoulder.

With a *thwack* Lennon dropped my book to the floor, making sure to step on it on his way out. With a curse I dropped to my knees, ignoring how the floor was sticky. The cover was ruined, his shoe print marking the picture as well as ripping the paper. Luckily the inside seemed mostly unharmed, even if my bookmark was missing.

"You're not bringing any trouble in here, are you doll?" Chase asked, folding his arms across his chest. His shirt stretched obscenely, the buttons threatening to explode and ping in all directions.

A shiver ran down my spine as I stood. "No."

"You sure?" Chase narrowed his eyes, and I forced a smile.

"Everything's fine."

It wasn't, but Chase didn't actually care. As long as I turned up to my shifts and smiled at his customers, he was happy. His favourite motto being, 'Not my circus, not my monkeys.'

"Sorry about that. It won't happen again," I mumbled, dusting off my clothes.

"Make sure it doesn't," he grunted. "And what did I say about reading behind the bar?" His eyes dipped to my breasts, and I held back a grimace.

I wasn't actively looking for attention, but considering the majority of Chase's customers were older men, the less clothes I wore, the more they tipped.

Was I proud of myself? Not really.

Was I desperate enough to wear low-cut tops, short skirts, and tight jeans? Yes, even if it made me feel uncomfortable.

Hiding the paperback, I returned to serving drinks. On a brighter note, Michael had gotten over my rejection, having swiftly moved on to another patron who had the misfortune of sitting on the stool next to him. So I got lost in serving the regulars, glad that embarrassing encounter was over.

But it didn't take long for my phone to brighten with a notification, and once I'd handed a regular his scotch on the rocks, I risked a look.

> GABRIEL:
>
> You looked beautiful tonight.

I didn't bother to reply, leaving him on read again.

Luckily the next few hours were busy, distracting me from my crazy ex. My phone beeped a few more times, and I ignored every single one.

Gabriel had never been physically violent towards me, but he'd threatened me enough times after a night out with his boys when I didn't do what he'd wanted. So I swore to keep my distance and hoped he eventually grew bored before he could act on those threats.

Ringing the bell for last orders, I finally let myself check my phone.

> GABRIEL:
>
> Not nice to be left on read again, baby.
>
> Last warning, Ara.
>
> Answer the fucking phone.
>
> Fine. I'm no longer being the nice guy.

Chapter 2
Arabella

Pulling my jacket tighter around my shoulders, I stopped at the bus stop directly outside the bar. The glass had been smashed, as had the seats, so I settled for standing in the corner, the sky so dark I couldn't see a single star. Luckily the bus was right on time, and the journey back home wasn't more than twenty minutes.

Being past midnight, Dad's garage was locked up tight, the shutters down to protect his clients' cars inside. We lived in the flat directly above, which was convenient.

"Dad?" I called as soon as I opened the door, grimacing at the stench of beer. Frowning, I entered the living room, only to find him slouched in his favourite armchair with his head resting against his chest. Pulling out my wages, I placed everything on the table beside him. I kept the tips for myself. "Dad?"

"Where... where the fuck have you been?" he slurred, swiping his arm out to push me back. Several bottles stood by his feet, clinking together when he adjusted his leg.

"Working." Just like I did every night.

Dad finally looked up, his eyes bloodshot and his face flushed from the alcohol. "You earn good tonight?"

"I've put the money on the table."

With a grunt he reached for the cash, quickly counting it before throwing it on the floor. "What the fuck is this?" he snarled. "This isn't enough. How are we supposed to survive on this? This doesn't even pay your fucking rent, never mind enough to keep the garage."

I didn't look at him as I picked up the money, placing it neatly back on the table.

"How did your game go?" I asked, already knowing the answer from the amount of empty glass bottles. During the day he ran the garage below, repairing and maintaining cars. At night he liked to hit the poker tables.

"I lost."

No shit.

"How much did you lose?"

Dad chewed on his tongue, taking a moment to reply. "Five grand."

I closed my eyes for a second and prayed for patience. "You promised. You promised you wouldn't do this anymore."

He threw his hands up. "I'm trying, Ara! I promise you I'm trying, but we needed the money, and I thought I'd win."

"Dad, where the hell are we—"

"Do you have a way to find that money?" he interrupted, the armchair's springs squeaking as he repositioned himself. Only then did I realise he'd fallen asleep clasping a half empty beer. Some of the liquid had splashed onto the fabric, and I made a mental note to clean it tomorrow before he realised and blamed me. "If you don't, they'll come after me."

Guilt sunk my stomach. "When do you need it by?"

He licked at his teeth. "Tuesday."

"Tuesday?" I fisted my hands, my blood running cold

with dread. "That's not even a week. How am I supposed to find *five grand* in four days?"

Dad sneered, "This is why I told you to fucking dance; that's where the big money is for someone as useless as you. Not working at that fucking bar. Sometimes I think you're just as useless as your mum."

I flinched. He only ever spoke to me like this when he'd had a drink. Every other time it was like we were acquaintances at best, and strangers at worst.

"I'm nothing like mum," I whispered through the weight suddenly clogging my throat.

She left us broken, abandoned. I refused to be like her.

"You're not even using your education. What the fuck was the point of going off to Uni if all you do is serve drinks? I told you English Literature was a waste of time, not that you even finished the degree." His grip on the bottle shattered, sending liquid and glass shards everywhere. "Fuck, look what you made me do!"

"Stay still." I quickly grabbed the glass, wary of the shallow cut across his palm.

He didn't listen, instead slapping the hand against the fabric on the armrest. "Can you find the money or not? Because if not, then I'm fucked, and you'll be alone."

"Dad, I'll—"

"See, this would never happen if you agreed to marry Gabriel like I told you to!"

That was just another reason I'd declined Gabriel's proposal. He thought he could buy me, offering my father money before even speaking to me.

I'd loved him once, but even before I'd caught the lying prick cheating the idea of being his wife had filled me with dread. Dad had begged me to marry him, and then take the money and divorce. But the idea had turned my stomach.

"I'll get the money," I said, knowing I had no choice.

Dad frowned at me, and I realised he'd aged so much these past few years. His hair was more grey than brown, and his eyes always seemed sunken. Exhausted.

He nodded, seeming pleased by my answer. "Good, you owe me."

You owe me.

For as long as I could remember, he'd always said that to me. Everything I ate, or wore, he reminded me that I'd always owe him. That my life wasn't a gift, as if I had any choice in being born. Then I hit eighteen, and any sort of parental responsibility he felt simply vanished. And now he didn't care, so long as I continued to pay my way.

I dreamt about leaving. Of escaping this life... but I always found myself stuck. Trapped by a twisted sense of responsibility to make sure he was okay. That he ate, that his debts were paid on time, and he didn't get into too much trouble with loan sharks.

At the end of the day, he was still my father, and he'd stayed with me when he could have left.

Just as he'd said, I owed him.

"Don't worry, I know I'll win on the next one." His eyes that were so hard only moments ago had softened. "Trust me, Ara. It'll get better, baby girl. I promise."

I tried to smile, but it came out weak. Dad borrowed money to get into the poker tournaments, but he lost just as much as he won. When he won, he splurged, and when he lost, he'd borrow more. It was a vicious cycle that I couldn't stop, no matter how hard I tried, or begged. He's had his arms broken, and the tip of his pinky finger removed with a pair of shears. His car had been burned to nothing but the frame, and the garage below trashed in warning. But still he borrowed money, and still he gambled.

Grabbing the blanket, I carefully tucked it around him. He'd already fallen asleep, his snores quiet as I gently removed any remaining glass shards, as well as the bottles. After making sure he was okay, I finally climbed the stairs to my bedroom.

It was a converted loft and offered me a little bit of my own space. Tossing my bag on the floor beside my bed, I ducked my head so I could get to my desk. The entire bedroom was small, sloped on both sides so dramatically even I couldn't stand straight. Kneeling by my desk, I shoved my used notebooks to the side, mostly filled with stories and ideas that I knew would never be read by anyone but me.

At one time I had a passion for storytelling, but that died when I was forced to come home from university to find Dad beaten almost to death.

It took three months for him to recover, and in that time the guilt had been crushing. If I'd have been here, it wouldn't have happened. I could've helped. Stopped the situation from escalating to that point. So I never went back.

Ignoring the slight pain in my arm at this angle, I stretched further until my fingers brushed against the box I kept hidden for emergencies. With a thump it fell, and the contents scattered on the carpet.

"Shit." I scooped up the money and watch, taking my time to count every single note twice. It was everything I had, all my tips saved over the last three years. It was my emergency stash, for when I finally got the courage to create a new life somewhere else.

Somewhere I could start again.

Be whoever I wanted to be without guilt haunting me every step of the way.

With shaking hands I placed the money Dad owed on the side, but it wasn't enough. Which meant I was going to have to sell Gabriel's stupid watch, and that left me with nothing. No backup. No emergency fund.

Three years of saving, of dreaming about another life far away, gone to a man who didn't care that I was his only child.

Chapter 3
Sebastian

I glowered down at the dead prick on the table, taking my time to study the way his skin had been burnt away to reveal the muscle and bone beneath. Even those were charred, the stench so thick it'll take hours to clear it from the back of my throat.

Which was just fucking great.

I glanced over at Langdon, who was calmly flicking at his lighter as if he didn't just torture someone to death.

Click. Snap. Click.

You'd think it was a nervous gesture, having to constantly fidget. But in twenty years I don't think I've ever seen the bastard nervous. Burns scarred the strong column of his throat, darkening his golden skin. They were mostly hidden behind the tall collars he preferred, but there were too many to hide entirely.

I knew more scars twisted along his torso and thighs, thicker ones that over the years we've hunted down the best surgeons to help treat. They'd once restricted his movement, and now you wouldn't even know the majority of his body had once upon a time danced with flames.

Pocketing his lighter, Langdon raised his hands. "I

didn't think he'd die so quickly," he signed, upper lip twitching into his signature smirk.

"No shit." I tugged at the mask I wore when on official business. It covered my jaw all the way to my nose, leaving only my eyes free. It was a statement more than a way to cover my face. The mask didn't hide all of my own scars, but it did represent power. Fear. Death.

Not many people were brave enough to risk my wrath, especially when I was known for striking without hesitation. Fear and respect held a symbiotic relationship, which was why this was the first incident to escalate to this point in the past five years.

There were some fools who tried their luck, dealers who thought they could steal, or business associates who believed they could undercut, but they were quickly dealt with. Tossed into the Thames, only to be forgotten. Insignificant lives lost because of greed, or a self-inflated sense of worth.

As you might have guessed, I didn't get to my position by being forgiving.

Which was why I'd come with the full expectation of watching the light die from the prick's eyes, because I could simply not allow someone who dared to fuck with me to live without consequences. I had a reputation to uphold, after all.

"You weren't supposed to kill him until I got here." I craved chaos and blood, but I thrived with control. And Langdon had gone against my orders. It made my skin feel tight, as if straining to contain my bones.

If anyone else had failed, I'd have killed them.

But Langdon had proven his loyalty, as had Caden.

"Do we know what he did with my money?" I asked once I'd calmed down, and the rage I so carefully contained didn't call for violence. Yet, anyway. "Or did you kill Mr Potter before he gave us what we wanted?"

Caden cleared his throat, and I turned to find him pouting. He always seemed to have a faint ticking sound, the watch he'd been gifted by his father, my uncle, so large it was a statement on his wrist. He held a sledgehammer, the blunt edge splattered with blood. Clearly, he was just as guilty as Lang for fucking up my plans.

"Mr Potter kept extensive records," Caden answered, tilting his head and turning the hammer over in his hand. "A little black book of people he loaned the money to, Bas. He even wrote down all the interest rates and profits." He kicked at the corpse, which made the blackened skin split further. "Honestly, I'm impressed with the balls on the guy."

Langdon chuckled, the sound a deep gruff that barely perforated Caden's fucking ticking. "Play stupid games, win stupid prizes," he signed, eyes drifting back to his masterpiece.

"How long has he been skimming off me before anyone noticed?" My empire usually ran like a finely tuned machine, so the fact a rat like this managed to slip through the cracks only pissed me off.

"He was smart about it," Caden said. "Apparently there's been a few times where some money went missing, but it's usually found on the next intake once Dad settled the accounts."

My uncle, a man of little talent except counting money. He wasn't too bad with the stock market either, and while he was a pretentious bastard who believed he was superior because of his aristocratic blood, in reality he was just as low and dirty as the rest of us.

"How much total?"

Caden glanced at Langdon, who was still staring at the body like it was a piece of art. "Three hundred grand."

I blinked, feeling anger prickle through my bloodstream once more. "That's a lot of fucking money to go walking, Cade. There's nothing little about three hundred grand."

Caden clenched his jaw, his fist tightening around the handle of his sledgehammer. "I'll deal with it."

"Uncle shouldn't have waited until that much went missing before informing us."

"I said I'll deal with it," Caden snapped, touchy when it came to his father. It wasn't a secret there was no love lost between me and my uncle. Even though the fucker was technically the one that saved mine and Lang's life.

Not like he'd ever let us forget it, but then again, you couldn't pick your blood.

Red flashed across my vision, followed by an intense pain across my back. Then another. And another.

Il ne m'a pas laissé le choix.

He left me no choice.

My shoes squeaked against the threadbare carpet, breaking me from the memory.

"Bas, you good?" Caden appeared at my side.

I concentrated on the room, studying the wallpaper that had been stripped, leaving spots of exposed mould and plaster. The TV that had been shattered, and there were chunks taken out of the wooden stand. There was no glass or splinters littering the floor, which meant they were already broken before Caden and Langdon had hunted Mr Potter down.

Not that it was difficult. He may have managed to steal money from me, but he wasn't a criminal mastermind. Caden had found him within the hour after he was caught using my name. Which was actually pretty pathetic, as was this poor excuse of a hotel room he'd decided to hide himself in.

Frowning, I realised the black book was sitting neatly on the bedside table. Opening it, I flipped through the pages, the various squiggly lines blurring, causing an ache to pulsate behind my eyes. With a grunt I tossed it to Caden, who caught it with little effort.

"You confident we'll find the names in there?" I asked, watching how Caden read the first page.

He nodded. "Don't worry, we'll get the money back." His chin jerked towards the side. "What do you want to do with Mr Potter?"

I returned my attention to the bed, finding Langdon had moved closer, his body stiff as he stared down at the body with a slight glaze to his eyes.

"Make him disappear."

Chapter 4
Arabella

Another night, another–thankfully–uneventful shift.

I'd called last order almost thirty minutes ago, but there were still two customers left. Luckily, Suzy was subtly convincing them to leave so we could close, my feet aching from being on them for twelve hours straight. Heading towards the back, I grabbed a crate, using it to wedge the door open so I could take the rubbish out to the bin.

The lights outside flickered, giving off a slight whine as they struggled to fight against the impending shadows creeping in the distance. The night air was cool, so I hastily made my way to the shared bins, tossing the bag into the one on the left. It made a racket, and I flinched as a rat almost skittered across my boots.

"Shit!" I jumped back, only to laugh at myself.

It was just a rat. The city was full of them. Literally, and figuratively.

Shaking my head, I turned back towards the door, only for the light above to click off. Sudden darkness eloped me, and I automatically froze. There was no moon or stars to brighten the night. The only illumination was from the streetlamp along the road, which created an eerie glow at the mouth of the alley.

Something shuffled, like shoes on cobbled stones.

It was only seconds later that the light buzzed back on, but not before sweat had broken out along my skin. Glancing around, I couldn't see anyone else, but then something pressed against my shoulder, shoving me so suddenly I staggered forward. My palm scraped against the brick, steadying my fall when a pressure landed on my back.

Rancid breath feathered across my cheek, and I stilled even as the wall bit at my skin.

"Fucking hell. When I found out Morris had a daughter, I expected an ugly cunt just like him."

I stilled in my panic, my pulse frantic at the side of my throat.

"Not something like you, sweetheart."

The stranger's hand snaked down, tugging the hem of my T-shirt out of my jeans. His fingers clawed at the skin beneath, and yet I didn't move, completely paralysed as I tried to calm the growing fear.

"What do you want?" I asked, proud my voice somehow didn't falter.

He licked his lips. "Your Da owes my boss quite a few grand, and Mr O'Connor isn't the one to take kindly to people owing him money, you understand?"

"O'Connor?"

"Aye, your Da likes to play with dangerous people," the stranger snickered. "Now, you either hand over the five grand that he owes, with interest, or... maybe we can come to some sort of arrangement?" With each word he dug his fingers harder into my body.

"Interest? That's bullshit!" I let out a hiss when my head was forced to the side by my hair. The stranger smirked down at me, his gaze like oil over my skin.

"That was before he missed the deadline."

"The deadline's not until tomorrow."

"Change of plans, sweetheart." He released my head but didn't step back. "You should probably tell your Da not to mess with the Irish. He's lucky O'Connor's the forgiving type."

I swallowed hard, my throat bobbing. "I only have the five."

His chuckle was dark, the sound making me want to puke. "You're going to have to take option B then, aren't you?"

The pressure on my back released, and there was a distinctive sound of a belt being pulled through loops. The blood left my face, and I gasped. *No.*

"Wait!" I tried to control my breathing, pressing myself as far away from him as possible. His brow was raised, waiting for me to continue. "How much is the interest?"

He tilted his head. "Ten percent."

Which made it £500. *Fuck.*

He reached for my shoulder, and my panic surged. My head snapped back, connecting with his face hard enough that pain radiated across the back of my skull.

"Fucking bitch!" he cursed, sneering at me with bloody teeth.

"I have your money," I swore, twisting around before he could grab me again. I ran to the bar, kicking the crate away while simultaneously slamming the door shut behind me. I expected it to crack open, for the man to finish what he'd started. But there was nothing but silence, and when I looked out the peephole, I could see him waiting, his belt now buckled.

Tears prickled my eyes, and I wiped at them before anyone noticed.

"Hey, Ara," Suzy said when she found me. "Did you

put the rubbish out? Rachael's just left to catch her last train, and I've finally managed to rouse Joe enough to kick him out."

Wiping my cheeks once more, I turned to offer her a forced smile. "Yeah, all done. You mopped yet?"

Suzy's eyes dropped to where my skin stung, and it took everything in me not to react. "Ara..."

"I just need to finish tidying the bar," I said. "Won't be long."

Suzy's look of concern only deepened. "Yeah, okay."

I waited for Suzy to turn, disappearing into the storage before I started counting out my tips, my stomach turning to ice when I realised I didn't have enough. Not even close. Chest tight, I quickly opened up the register, grabbing the rest and closing it just before Suzy reappeared, this time wearing her coat.

"You ready to go?"

The money felt heavy in my pocket, like I'd somehow stolen rocks and thrown myself into a river. It wasn't the first time I'd had to resort to stealing to pay my father's debts, but the guilt never lessened.

"Yeah, I'm ready."

I winced when I accidentally pulled at the cut on my lip, tasting blood on my tongue. *Next time, I hope you don't pay the interest,* the man had chuckled before backhanding me. My head had snapped to the side, but before I could react, he'd already walked away.

Gazing out the window, I watched as raindrops raced

down the glass, each one desperate to win. I must've been lost in a daze, silently rooting for the ridiculous competition, because when I finally blinked, I suddenly recognised the street outside. The bus rumbled to a stop, and jumping up I stepped out, taking a moment to let the rain wash over me.

It wasn't long before I was soaked to the bone, but I didn't care. My body shivered, and yet I stood for a moment more. My fingers ached from the cold, my hair slicked to my forehead, and still I didn't want to move.

It was a few minutes before I finally made my way home, my keys rattling in my hand. The door opened, and I was immediately greeted by cursing, followed by a crash.

"Dad?" I frowned, wanting to know why he was still awake at 2 a.m. "What are you doing?"

Dad didn't even look up from where he was throwing things into a large cardboard box. A kitchen towel, a mug, and then a lamp. "You're late," he said, grabbing a few of his mechanic monthly magazines. They flew across the room, landing on the heap. "The bar closed at one, and it doesn't take a fucking hour this late to get home."

"I had to pay O'Conner."

"He's paid? Good, that's one less thing to think about." He finally turned, his eyes wild before they settled on my face. "O'Conner do that?"

I tried to smile, but it came out more of a grimace. "I'm fine. It's nothing."

Dad's eyes lingered a moment more, lips pressed into a thin line. "What the fuck are you doing still standing there? Pack. We're moving."

"What? Why?" We'd been here three years, which was the longest we'd stayed in one place since I could remember. The flat may not be much, but it was the only constant thing I had. "I've already paid–"

"It's not O'Connor, Ara. It's... everyone else. People are fucking disappearing, or turning up dead," he muttered, quieter this time, almost as if he was talking to himself before returning his attention to me. "It's not like you bring any fucking money into this house to support us. So it's up to me, isn't it?"

"Dad, we can't leave. You have your business and—"

"Fixing cars barely makes ends meet, and my luck these past few months hasn't exactly helped my game." He dragged a hand down his face, his fingers trembling slightly. "We can hardly make rent, and the water's just been turned off."

"Who else do you owe?" I asked, my voice barely above a whisper.

He stilled, a nerve feathering in his jaw. "Baby girl..."

"Dad!"

"Look, it doesn't matter."

Goosebumps prickled along my skin, and even though I knew I was freezing, heat burned through my blood. "Clearly it does if you're trying to pack the bloody lamp!" It wasn't even a nice lamp. "Can you not borrow the money from someone else to cover until we figure it out?"

"No, I've been fucking marked," he sneered, shaking his head. "No one is lending me shit. Now, go pack or—"

A smash, like glass shattering below.

"Fucking kids again," Dad growled. "Go. You have ten minutes before we're leaving." He didn't wait for me to reply, grumbling as he went to deal with the kids likely trying to steal some scrap.

I stood there, looking at the living room which had been wrecked. We didn't have much to begin with, but Dad had frantically thrown everything into the box. He'd clearly lost his temper at one point, because bottle shards glinted on the carpet.

I thought of my books. Hundreds I'd claimed as my trophies, displayed with pride along my makeshift book-shelf. Then there were my clothes and the silly empty perfume bottles I liked to line up by my bed. I wouldn't be able to pack them all. Dad would want me to use a small suitcase with the bare essentials, and that was it. I was never allowed to pack more, and each time we moved I lost every-thing. Only to have to start again.

Another new city.

Another new job.

The same cycle on repeat.

No. I couldn't do this again. I *wouldn't* do this again.

We'd figure it out. We always did.

Walking to the door, I took the steps down the side of the building towards the entrance to the garage.

"Morris, you've been a bad fucking boy."

I stilled, frowning at the unfamiliar voice coming from inside.

"I don't... I don't know what you're talking about." A smack of flesh on flesh, followed by Dad crying out. My eyes widened.

"You calling me a liar?"

Shit.

I grabbed my phone, quickly dialling 999 and whis-pering for the police.

"Please!" Dad begged. "I didn't know the money belonged to you!"

"Oh, so you *do* know what we're talking about? Funny that. If you'd told us the truth the first time, I wouldn't have had to introduce your nose to my knuckles."

Sneaking closer, I glanced through the gap in the door, finding Dad on his knees. The door squeaked slightly as it opened, and I sucked in a breath. No reaction, so I quickly slipped inside as silently as possible.

There were two men I didn't recognise, both towering over Dad. The blond's smirk held a slight feral edge, and lifting his hands, he signed to the brunet who stood opposite.

"Alright Lang, no need to shout," the brunet chuckled.

Dad glanced between them, blood dripping from his nose. From the angle, it almost appeared broken. "What... what did he say?"

"He said, 'Did you know that eyeballs don't explode? Instead they slowly and painfully melt if held under heat long enough.'"

Dad let out a sob. "Please... I'll find your money."

The man who signed with his hands was tall, with an athletic build and pale hair that was long enough to brush his collar. His translator was an inch or so taller, which had him around six foot four. He was a little wider, stockier, like he enjoyed lifting weights but not to excess, and his brown hair was cut to just above his ears.

The brunet wore a suit, the fabric clearly expensive and perfectly tailored even from a distance while the blond wore black jeans and a dark T-shirt.

I slowly moved around the Volkswagen, keeping to a crouch. The bonnet was up, the engine in pieces by my feet, as were spills of oil. I was conscious of those spots, carefully moving around while the men were distracted.

Coming to the edge, I froze, realising there was a third man.

He leaned casually against the wall, knee bent and his head cocked. He hadn't said a single word, yet power radiated from his large frame. He was by far the tallest, and his shoulders were so wide they strained against the black suit jacket he wore. His hand flexed, as did his thigh when he straightened to his full height.

Fuck.

He still hadn't noticed me, so I slowly moved towards the desk beside the suspended Ford my dad had been working on that morning. My fingers brushed against something cold, solid, and I automatically picked up the heavy metal.

I dipped behind the car, hoping they heard nothing as my foot knocked one of the tools forgotten on the floor.

The big man stepped forward, and the other two stepped back. "Do you know who I am?" he asked, his voice a throaty growl that seemed to weigh the air.

Dad audibly swallowed before nodding. "I... I didn't know it was your money."

"Where is it?"

"I... lost it." Dad's eyes widened when the third man took another strategic step closer, his voice taking on a frantic edge. "But I can get it back, I swear! There's a tournament coming up, and I'll make sure I'll win. I'll pay you back every penny, plus more! You've just got to give me some time."

My fingers tightened on the wrench.

The third man finally reached Dad, standing over him in his black-on-black suit like the grim reaper. That was when I struck, using all my strength to swing the tool. I knew my strength wouldn't do much damage, but it didn't need to. I just needed to distract them long enough for the police to get here.

Pain radiated up my arm, the man turning at the last second to catch the wrench before it could even strike him. Before I could jerk back, he pulled me closer, yanking the weapon from my grip and locking both my wrists in one of his larger hands.

My head automatically dipped back, and my breath

whooshed out in one long, panicked exhale. Eyes of the deepest blue, cold and merciless, glared down at me with a fury laced with cruel amusement.

But it wasn't the rage in his gaze that made me still.

It was the matte black skeletal mask shrouding the lower half of his face.

Chapter 5
Sebastian

Morris Grey was a pathetic excuse for a human being, which wasn't a surprise considering he apparently owed half the city money, including the Bratva, as well as the Irish. Idiot clearly played with people far bigger than him. Apparently, he was a name within the underground poker tournaments, but if I went by his current situation, he clearly wasn't any good.

"Do you know who I am?" I asked, my voice more of a growl as I closed the distance.

I knew he did, recognition widening his eyes before he gave me a jerky nod. "I... I didn't know it was your money."

Rage burned through my veins, barely restrained. "Where is it?"

"I... lost it. But I can get it back, I swear! There's a game coming up, and I'll make sure I'll win. I'll pay you back every penny, plus more! You've just got to give me some time."

I cocked my head to the side, and I was pretty sure Morris just pissed himself. I was surprised the snivelling cunt was still alive, especially once I'd found out there was a price on his head. But that didn't matter, because I got to him first, and no one was going to challenge it.

There was a carefully created truce between the other organisations within the city. They stayed out of my business, and I stayed out of theirs.

One man wasn't worth starting a war over.

The air behind me shifted, and Langdon turned with his gun the same time Caden lifted his hammer. But I'd already moved, catching the wrench that had been aiming for the back of my head and pulling the little assailant tight to my chest.

She was a small thing, having to crane her head back to better meet my angry gaze. Her brunette hair was a wet mess around her face, strands having fallen out of the high ponytail to stick to her damp skin. Her eyes were a warm brown with flecks of gold, and they rounded in fear when they settled on my mask.

"The police are on their way," she said, her voice a husky, quivering sound that didn't match the delicacy of her bone structure.

"Are they now?" My thumb moved to brush along the pulse on her wrist. It thrummed, giving away her fear even as she composed herself.

Thick lips, large eyes framed in black, and the fairest skin that looked as if it would mark so easily beneath the slightest touch. My eyes drifted to the small graze on her cheek, the flesh pink and fresh, and then the slice along her bottom lip.

Her breath hitched beneath my scrutiny, and for some reason that made me want to smirk.

Looking up, I met Caden's gaze. *"Who the fuck is she?"* I asked in my father's tongue. I may now call London my home, but France was the country of my birth, even if I hadn't stepped foot on French soil in almost two decades.

Langdon was the one to reply, his hands moving at a speed that reflected his excitement at the change of events. "There's no name other than Mr Grey on the rental agreement for both the flat and garage."

"You've been keeping secrets, Morris my man," Caden grunted, using his hammer to lift Morris's chin. The prick's lips trembled, eyes darting between everyone before settling back on me.

"Please, you can have anything. Just don't hurt me," he said, showing no concern for the woman. It was an amusing statement considering blood was trickling down his face in a steady stream.

"How much does my father owe you?" the little rabbit in my hands asked, her voice strong compared to her pulse, which continued to give her away. I returned my attention to her, enjoying how her eyes narrowed with just a taste of insolence.

She hadn't made any attempt to free her wrists, which were both caught in one of my hands and pressed hard against her breast. She was soaking wet, the white T-shirt slick to her skin and showing every single detail of her nude lace bra. Her nipples pebbled, pushing at the fabric as if an invitation.

I decided to reach up and close my fingers around her throat, feeling the shallowness of her breaths. She tried to swallow, the motion brushing against my palm like a caress.

"How much does he owe you?" she asked again.

"Ara, shut the fuck up!" Morris hissed until Caden hit him in the stomach.

The *oomph* of air was satisfying, as was the wheeze he made as he fell forward. The scent of piss was much stronger now, obscuring Ara's faint scent of fresh rain, stale beer, and jasmine.

She was a pretty little thing, beautiful even with

animosity burning her gaze. "How much?" she repeated once more, the question more stern.

It was Caden who answered. "100k."

She flinched, those plump lips parting, and I took the opportunity to brush my thumb across the bottom one, pressing hard against her cut. She bit me, so I tightened my grip until I controlled her every breath.

"Lang," I began, keeping my eyes trained on the woman in my grasp, "prepare Mr Grey for transport. Looks like he's going to have to come with us."

She finally began to struggle, taking in a gasp when I finally relaxed my fingers.

"Please," she begged, the word like music to my ears. I wanted to hear her say it over and over, ideally seconds before she submitted to me in the most primal way.

"Please, what?" I pressed my thumb against her pulse, savouring the rapid beat.

"Don't do this. We'll find the money."

"And how exactly will you do that?" I was conscious of the sirens in the background, slowly growing louder. I wasn't worried about the police turning up, not when almost every copper was under my payroll. And those that weren't... well, they went missing.

She let out an exhale, her hot breath feathering across my skin. She didn't look away from my gaze, not even when I dipped my head closer to her height. Not many people had the backbone to challenge me in such a way, especially with my fingers around their throat.

I wanted nothing more to push her further and see whether she continued to fight. But reluctantly, I let her go. "Mr Grey," I said, speaking to her father, "as of now, your life is forfeit."

Morris was a sickly shade of grey, the whites around his

eyes only emphasising his panic. "You can take anything you want. Sir... please. Anything."

His eyes snapped to his daughter, and then back again.

I raised a brow, but those sirens were going to start causing a scene. A scene I didn't have the patience to deal with. So, nodding to Caden, I waited for him to grab Morris by his collar.

"Where are you taking him?" Ara cried, trying and failing to block my exit. "Stop, you fucking monster!"

"Monster?" I paused at the door while Morris's screams echoed around us. "Oh *belle*, you have no fucking idea."

Chapter 6
Sebastian

"You need anything else, Sir?" Mrs Pritchard, my head housekeeper, asked as she laid down a silver tray on my desk. I glanced over at the glass of whisky, immediately dismissing her with a wave of my hand.

"That's all. Please lock down the lift on your way out."

"Of course, Sir." Mrs Pritchard bowed her head.

My gaze followed her figure as she made her way through my home on the cameras, confirming she'd obeyed the order, and I had the entire place to myself. Cracking my neck, I sat back in my chair, reaching over to the ice-cold whisky and taking a sip.

I'd designed my two-story penthouse as an impenetrable stronghold capable of withstanding any type of attack. Caden and Langdon owned luxury flats below, and only because I trusted them like brothers. The floors below them were empty, gutted and reinforced with the strongest materials money could buy. I had cameras across almost every inch, and as my fingers flexed on the glass of my drink, I flicked through the twenty-or-so screens until I found my club, The Thorn.

Just as fortified as my home, The Thorn was the face to

everything. A place to entertain rich and influential guests, as well as hide my... other activities.

I became known for my fights, but it wasn't the fights or the subsequent betting where I made my fortune. No, my empire was in cocaine, the powder designed to give you the perfect euphoric high. Synthetically adapted to lessen the risk of adverse effects, my product was the cleanest on the market.

Nobody could match the quality, and anybody who tried suffered unfortunate accidents.

The leather seat creaked as I rested back, but I couldn't relax. Recently it had been like ants itching beneath my skin, making me unsettled, and not even the burn of alcohol seemed to help.

Three overdoses in two weeks. Overdoses were going to happen; it was part of the industry. But three in *two weeks?* No, there was a reason my product dominated the market, and it wasn't because my clients fucking died. At first, I was sceptical, but the men I had constantly tracking all the other players confirmed it was the Cursed Rose. My fucking powder.

Clicking a button on the mouse, I flicked through the feed until I found something to distract me. The ice clinked in my glass as I raised the whiskey to my lips, savouring the taste as I watched Morris Grey pace his cell in frantic strides. It had only been a few hours, and he already looked like shit.

You can take anything you want, Sir... please. Anything.

It wasn't unusual for weak men to make desperate pleas. I've had many offer me their wives, daughters, and sons in exchange for their lives, and I'd never been tempted.

Instead, I drew out their punishments, making each second before death agonising. Letting them wallow in their guilt just a little bit longer until I finally grew bored or lost my temper. Whichever came first.

This was the first time I'd thought about accepting.

His daughter's fearful pulse thrumming against my fingers while animosity burned in those pretty brown eyes had been... interesting. She was so loyal to her father, all while he was willing to give her over like some common whore.

In the grand scheme of things, 100k was nothing to me. I made more than that as a fighter, but this wasn't about the money. It was about someone stealing from me. I was known for being brutal well before I even stepped inside a ring.

Which was why I planned to keep Morris a little longer, pacing in his concrete cell, devoid of a window and only his own mind and a few spiders to keep him company. I wanted him to break, so I could then parade him around as a warning to others not to fuck with what was mine.

Chapter 7
Arabella

I couldn't seem to shake my nervous energy as I sat in my boss's office.

Chase was clearly picking up on it, because his surprise at seeing my face on my day off was quickly replaced with disappointment.

"Money's missing from the float. You wanna tell me about that?"

I swallowed, my hands restless in my lap. "I'm sorry–"

"Fucking hell, doll. I didn't actually think you had anything to do with it." He slouched back, his chair letting out a wheeze as if straining beneath his weight. "So, you're stealing from me now?"

"I have some of the money." Reaching into the back of my jeans, I pulled out around £230. It wasn't all of it, but it was everything I'd managed to scrape together from what I'd found in Dad's garage. "I'm so sorry, I was cornered and didn't know what else to do. I'll pay you back, I promise."

Chase's hand snapped out faster than I expected, making me flinch. "You know I have to let you go, right? You can't go around stealing from me."

My eyes widened. "No, please, I really love this job." And I needed it more than ever. "I was just desperate."

Chase scraped his teeth over his bottom lip. "What kind of trouble have you gotten yourself into?"

"I need to borrow 100k."

Chase blinked at me for a moment, then burst into a loud bark of a laugh. "Wait, you're serious?" he asked once he'd sobered. "You're fucking crazy if you think I'll lend you anything. Not even if you bent over this desk for me."

Heat prickled my cheeks, and I curled my fingers into my thighs. If I wasn't wearing jeans, I was pretty sure my nails would've sliced through the skin of my legs. "Do you know anyone who would lend me it?" I asked, deciding to ignore his previous comment.

He eyed me for a moment. "That's a lot of money. You in some kind of trouble?"

"My father is."

Chase shook his head. "Who the fuck does he owe that much to?"

"I... I don't know."

Shaking his head, he stood, towering over me. "Doll, take my advice. I don't want to turn on the news and see your pretty face as just another statistic. Your dad's business is his own, and you should run while you still can."

I was quiet as I left, that ice in my gut having melted until I felt numb everywhere. I was grateful Suzy was too busy to notice me, because I really didn't feel like arguing who would give the best orgasm from the *Lord of the Rings* franchise when I felt like my entire life had been turned upside down.

Rachael spotted me from behind the bar, her smile gentle when I gave her a small wave and quickly hurried to the staff room. It was small, consisting of just a sink, a tiny table with two chairs, and space to store our stuff while on shift.

Going over to the cubby hole, I grabbed everything that was mine, which was only a hairbrush and my notebook.

"There you are," Suzy exclaimed, sweeping in with the energy of a golden retriever. "Rachael said you were here. So, that pretty boy who was here the other night is waiting for you at the..." Her eyes dipped to the book in my bag. "Wait, are you leaving?"

I tugged the bag tighter against me. "Yeah, I... I was offered another job," I lied. "Better pay. Shorter hours. Even covers my dental, and... stuff."

Suzy's bottom lip trembled, and she blinked a few times.

Oh no. Please, for the love of God, don't cry.

"You were going to leave without saying goodbye?" A sob broke out from her throat, and then the tears came as she threw herself across the short space and wrapped me in a hug.

Jesus Christ.

"I can't believe you're leaving us! Who else am I going to discuss who's hotter with?"

I was pretty confident I resembled a statue in her arms, and even the awkward pat on her back felt strange. I had zero skills when it came to people crying. I was an emotional wreck, so I couldn't mentally deal with other people's drama when I could barely handle my own. "You have Rachael," I offered.

"We both know she's vapid. Like, come on, who hasn't watched *Game of Thrones*? Is she living under a rock?" Suzy sniffled. "And she chose *Gimli* as her favourite. Gimli! Clearly *Legolas* has far superior skills in making a woman come. Rachael has no taste, Ara."

Her tears had dried while she'd grumbled, nothing

remaining but a slight blotchiness to her cheeks. "You'll be fine," I said, trying to break free from her hold.

"What about you helping me find a date?"

I didn't do anything except swipe a few times on an app. I literally stayed with a man who gaslit me just because I was lonely. Who was I to give dating advice?

I smiled at her. "I'll miss you, too."

Suzy would forget about me within a week, her attention bright but fleeting. It was probably the reason why she went through so many boyfriends.

But other than knowing my personal preference was *Aragorn*—because of course it fucking was—she knew very little about my personal life. That was the way I preferred it, not getting too attached to people. Just in case something were to happen, and I'd have to leave again. So I kept to myself as much as possible, instead getting lost in my books.

She perked up, sniffling her nose. "Oh, yeah, don't forget your boyfriend's waiting for you at the bar. Has he come to pick you up?"

"I don't have a..." Wait, what was Gabriel doing here?

I found him leaning against the bar, a blushing Rachael beside him. I intended to walk out and not look back, but he turned at the last second and spotted me. *Shit*.

"Baby, there you are." He waltzed across the space, looking out of place in his neatly pressed suit and trench coat, which was his statement detective uniform apparently. His dark hair was swept to one side, which made his eyes pop. "Are you okay? That waitress just told me you're leaving."

He went to pull me against him, but I quickly shook him off. He didn't try to hug me again, but the look of concern seemed almost genuine.

"What are you doing here?" I demanded, gently tugging

him towards the wall where there were a few empty tables. I could feel eyes on me, and it made me want to squirm.

"Can't I come and see my girl?"

"I'm too tired to do this right now."

"I spoke to Lennon." He cupped my jaw, and all I wanted was to press myself against his palm and seek comfort. But I didn't.

"Of course you did." I tried to pull back, but Gabriel only pinched his fingers to stop me. What luck that Lennon was the responding officer, the one who had to take my statement all while snickering at me. It hadn't even occurred to me that he'd tell Gabriel, not when I was so distracted with everything.

"You should've called me," Gabriel chided.

"What good would that have done?"

"I work for the fucking Met," he snapped before clearing his throat. "I have contacts, Ara. This is what I do. Now, tell me everything that's happened. Your dad gambling again?"

My stomach recoiled with how cold he asked the question. Hours I'd spent telling Gabriel about my dad, and the demons that haunted him. He was the only person I'd opened up to, and when I thought he was listening because he cared, in reality he only listened so he could weaponise the knowledge in our fights.

I nodded, not trusting my voice for a moment even as I stepped back, putting some space between us. I needed to remind myself that Gabriel only cared about himself, even if I ached for him to care about me right now.

"Who took Morris, Ara?"

I shrugged, blowing out a frustrated breath. "I don't know. He was really tall, built large and wore this skull mask on the bottom of his—"

"A mask?" Gabriel nodded to himself, as if confirming a suspicion. "That sounds like the Beast."

I frowned at him. "The Beast?"

Gabriel clenched his jaw, that viciousness that I'd witnessed so many times in our relationship darkening his eyes. "I thought Lennon was crazy when he called," he said with such a pompous tone that I was actually grateful, because it shattered his carefully constructed façade. "Like why would someone like him be interested in someone as small as you or your father? It doesn't match his profile."

And there it was. The realisation that I was never good enough. He always wanted me to change to his idea of the perfect woman. Someone silent and pretty on his arm. Who wouldn't argue back, and simply laid flat on her back, spreading her legs and giving him babies.

I laughed, the sound slightly hysterical, and if I were a therapist, I'd probably be concerned. "You're such an arsehole, Gabe."

Taking a deep breath, I turned away before I made a scene and embarrassed myself.

"Baby, come on, you don't understand how ridiculous it sounds." Gabriel caught up to me in two strides. "Sebastian Devereaux's a big name in certain circles within the underworld. Fucking untouchable, and notoriously a ghost. The bastard's ruthless, and known to be cruel."

Jostling my shoulder when he went to grab it, I shoved myself through the door and out into the cool air.

"Look, if Morris isn't already dead, he will be. Soon."

I paused, turning to face him. "I need to find him. I can't..." *Be all alone,* I finished inside my head. I already held the guilt of one parent's death on my shoulders; I couldn't handle having another when I could prevent it.

Soft fingers along my jaw forced me to look up. "Don't worry, baby, we'll get him back."

"You know where to find Sebastian?" I asked, a pressure on my chest growing.

Gabe pulled me until I was against him, and this time I didn't fight. "Of course. He's been involved in more than one of my investigations over the years. I personally know him; he owns *The Thorn* over in Soho."

"I've never heard of it."

"That's because you don't fit there," he said. "You don't fit their... aesthetic." A smirk curled his lips, mocking, and all I wanted to do was push him away. But clearly, I needed him. "But that's okay, because I can get you inside."

Chapter 8
Sebastian

The punching bag swung beneath my fists, the leather cracking and groaning. I practiced my hits, the strikes repetitive and perfectly timed. I kept going until my arms began to ache, and my knuckles threatened to split beneath the impact.

Tension pulled my skin tight, the need to hit something an almost violent impulse that I barely caged. So after lifting weights, I used the bag, the chain clinking as it rocked. Blinking past the sweat dripping from my brow, I pushed past the pain, unable to stop until my muscles strained and exhaustion finally took over.

If I didn't, I couldn't rest, sleep eluding me as nightmares haunted.

Memories threatened.

With a last hit the bag crumpled, my breathing heavy as it collapsed to the wooden floor with an audible *thwack*. Sand poured out from where it had split, the grains pale against the dark wood.

Taking in a deep breath, I unwrapped the fabric from my knuckles before tossing it onto the sand and stepping over the mess.

"That's the second bag this month," Chip commented, appearing in the doorway. He didn't flinch when I turned my glare towards him, his demeanour almost as frosty as mine.

"Then order a new one."

Chip nodded, folding his arms. "It's your turn to play," he said, not waiting for a reply before he disappeared.

I gave myself a moment, the sand finally settling into the grooves. Chip and I had an ongoing game of chess, and it had first started as a way to teach him strategy and discipline as a favour to his mother. He was young and brash, and if he ever wanted to survive amongst the corruption of the underworld, he'd have to learn.

Until then, he wasn't ready for more responsibility.

Stretching out my muscles, I took the stairs down and made my way to my bedroom, the dark colours comforting as I walked straight into my attached ensuite. My knuckles were pink when I raised them, but not broken or bruised. It had been Caden's idea to practice with them bound, especially when I'd frequently get carried away.

Pulling off my shorts, I stepped into the shower, turning the water on and ducking my head even as it was freezing. I kept myself beneath the stream, only allowing myself to move once the water had heated. I made it quick, just enough to remove the sweat before I padded naked back into my bedroom, my eyes resting on the screen on the wall.

Reaching for the remote, I flicked through the feeds until I found the CCTV facing the garage, but she wasn't there. The woman with her messy brunette hair and eyes that held fragments of gold.

Something twisted in my gut, and I wondered if it was disappointment. It had been a few days, and still I haven't caught a single peek of her. I was almost tempted to ask Langdon to sneak into the flat above and plant a camera, hoping to catch just another glimpse of the woman who'd bitten me and then left me with the biggest fucking hard-on.

Defiance wasn't my kink, but my cock didn't seem to care.

Not when it came to her, at least.

Clicking the remote, I filtered through the feed until I came to Morris, his arms frantic as he tried to shoo the tarantulas that sometimes called his cell home.

He was standing on his makeshift bed, clearly terrified of the eight-legged creatures I was so fascinated with. He was lucky; the cell's last occupant had nothing but a bucket. The fact I gave him a bed made me a goddamn fucking saint, and he should be more grateful.

I returned to flicking through the screens, only for my eyes to immediately settle on a familiar face. Reaching for my phone, I called Caden.

He answered immediately.

"What the fuck is Detective Graves doing here?" Conniving little cunt wasn't welcome since he was caught sticking his nose into places he didn't belong. It didn't matter that he found nothing. No one, not even the police, moved in my territory without my permission.

"Oh, hi Caden, how are you? Oh, I'm great Bas, you know, chilling and—"

"Cade," I growled.

A chuckle echoed through the line. "Did you say Graves? I haven't seen him, but Miles is working the door. I'll go check."

I watched Gabriel a little longer, his posture at ease in a place he knew he didn't belong. He hadn't risked stepping foot inside any of my establishments since the last time he'd been warned. So what has changed? Why now would he risk his life?

He was a fool, but he wasn't stupid.

Phone in hand, I pulled on my black shirt and trousers, pairing it with the matching jacket. I fucking hated it, but I forced myself to look civilised because it put people on edge when they first meet me and realised I was anything but.

The fabric felt tough, brushing against the scars that sliced across my back and shoulders akin to sandpaper. They were the thickest and most irritating. But unlike Langdon, mine were made from blades and whips, not flames.

The ones on my face were nothing compared to his, mere scratches that disappeared beneath my beard. The one that sliced down my eye was harder to hide, as was the one through my upper lip. Not that I cared about hiding them. My uncle once tried to convince me to seek treatment, but I'd always refused.

Why hide from my past? The scars and the memories attached made me who I was.

Tugging at the collar, I glanced back at the screen, only to still. Because there, looking completely out of place in her pale blue summer dress compared to the surrounding elegance, was *her*.

"Bas?" Caden's voice jolted me out of my stasis. "He came in with someone on your personal pre-approved list. Want me to deal with it?"

I blinked, finding Graves tugging her to his side as if he had the right to. From the camera's angle I couldn't see her entire expression, but her shoulders tensed. Her spine rigid.

"Bas?"

"Don't worry, I'm coming in," I said, reaching for my mask. "I'll deal with it myself."

Chapter 9
Arabella

I was two seconds away from slapping Gabriel across the face, but that would draw even more attention to me. I was trying to ignore the stares, but they were starting to become obvious.

"Don't worry, baby. You look fine," Gabriel crooned, clearly ignoring my 'don't touch me' vibe when he pulled me to his side.

I forced a smile, warily glancing around the interior of the notorious *Thorn*. It wasn't what I expected for a nightclub, at least, it wasn't like anywhere I've been before.

Fitted Savile Row suits and elegant dresses more at home on the runway than a club where the music was live, and the lights were dimmed. Crystal chandeliers adorned the high ceilings, and at the edge of the dance floor were tables and chairs with personal staff.

Gabriel vibrated beside me, his knee bouncing as he tried to gain the bartender's attention. It had taken us an hour to get inside, the queue surprisingly long considering I didn't even know the place existed. The bouncers were turning people away with no reason, only letting in those they deemed appropriate. We were initially denied, and as

Gabriel had begun to argue, one of the bouncers whispered to the other before finally lifting the velvet rope.

I don't know how or why we passed their secretive criteria, because I didn't belong in here, and as soon as I'd spoken to Sebastian, I was gone.

Ignoring Gabriel's increasing frustration with being ignored by the bartender, I glanced around the room, searching for a man with eyes of midnight. But there was no one that matched his description. No unnecessarily large men, and definitely no masks. I kept checking the corner, frowning at the private bar and booth that seemed hidden within the shadows and cordoned off with rope.

Standing, I took a step away, only for Gabriel to snake his fingers around my wrist. "Where do you think you're going?" he asked, pulling me back much harsher than he needed. "We haven't even got our drinks yet."

"I need to find Sebastian." I kept my tone calm, but I felt anything but. From the way the bouncers had treated Gabe, I didn't doubt he'd lied about knowing Sebastian. Which shouldn't come as a surprise, as Gabriel was the master at bullshit. "Isn't that why we're here? Not to get drinks."

"I'm fucking working on it." His eyes shuttered, lip lifting into a familiar snarl. "This attitude of yours will need to go once we're married."

I swallowed hard, pushing past the lump in my throat as he pulled me closer.

"I never agreed to marry you," I said, my voice low but steady even as I felt my panic growing the longer we stood there doing nothing.

His eyes didn't flinch. "So you'd rather be alone? What then when we find your dad's body?" he challenged.

My palm prickled, heat rushing to my fingertips. I

didn't think, I just moved. But before my hand could connect, he caught my wrist mid-air.

I expected him to react, but instead his voice calmed.

"I'm sorry, I shouldn't have said that." He sounded sincere, but I knew better, and it had taken me way too long to realise it. He pressed forward, but I turned my head so he kissed my cheek instead.

My stomach recoiled at the thought that he was right, and I could end up alone.

"I need to use the bathroom," I whispered, finding it harder to breathe amongst the stuffy air and thumping music.

His lips pursed before he finally let me go. "Fine. I'll order you a glass of wine for when you're back."

"No, I–"

"You'll take what I give you," he warned. "Now, don't be long. Without me, you look ridiculous. You clearly don't fit in here, but that's okay. That'll change once we're married." His eyes dragged down my body, only emphasising the point that I was clearly underdressed.

Obviously, if I'd known the dress code, I would've worn something nicer. Even though my dress was cute, it was just more summer picnic than a dance club where you were required to have a bank account with a gazillion zeros. It would've been fine for a normal club because of its length, but not here. No, here I stuck out.

Crossing the room, I tried to ignore the curious and somewhat hostile stares even as the music pounded against my skull, each beat tightening my chest. I didn't bother looking towards the dance floor, not really getting a dancer vibe from what little I knew about Sebastian Devereaux.

Looking back over my shoulder, I checked to make sure Gabriel was distracted, but I shouldn't have worried. He was surrounded by three different women, all giggling as he smirked and flirted in return. Passing through an archway I found the bathrooms, the corridor dimly lit, almost intimate as I passed the doors and continued. It was empty, but there was a *click, snap, click* that was drawing me further down.

The blond from dad's garage casually leaned against the end wall, knee bent and foot flat. He didn't react, not even looking up as I approached, just continuing to play with his lighter.

Click, snap, click.

His hair had been brushed back, the strands looking almost wet. After a moment his foot hit the carpet, and still without looking at me he turned down the corridor.

"Wait!" My breath quickened, heart pressing against my ribs. "Hello?"

Looking back, I realised I was still alone, so I did the only thing I could, and I followed. He didn't look back at me once, walking with such assurance as he passed a mirrored wall. That wall opened as I approached, and without a pause in his stride he disappeared around the corner.

I hesitated, the inside of what must be a lift appearing opulent, golden. Each of the panels were reflective, so when the blond suddenly appeared behind me, I jumped.

"Hi, I'm looking for–"

He didn't let me finish, shoving me just as the doors began to close. His smirk stretched between the closing gap, blowing me a kiss just as the doors sealed shut.

"Shit." I pressed my hand to one of the panels, but there were no buttons, just my reflection repeated at me in an almost mocking way.

What kind of idiot follows a dangerous man into a secluded corridor?

Oh, that's right. Me.

Without any instruction, the lift began to descend, coming to a halt as quickly as it had started. It couldn't be more than a single floor, or maybe two. Pressing myself back, the doors opened silently to reveal solid concrete walls. After a heartbeat, I peeked my head out, the same concrete wrapping around for as far as I could see.

Light penetrated the ominous dark, the strangely elegant sconces placed every few feet covered in thick cobwebs.

"Hello?" I said, but only my voice echoed back. "Hello?" I called louder, and this time there was a response.

"Arabella? Is that you?"

Following the sound, I almost burst into tears, dropping to my knees to try and reach through the bars. "Dad?" I couldn't believe where he'd been kept, the cell so small he could stretch his arms out and touch both sides. It was just wide enough for the bed, and a bucket.

A foul-smelling tray sat on the floor beside the door, only crumbs remaining of the meal, and I swore something scurried across the floor when I'd approached.

There was barely any light this far down, but even in the darkness I could see how sick he looked after only a few days. There were bruises beneath his eyes, and his skin seemed sunken. Pale, with a slight sheen.

"Ara, how did you find me?" Dad wrapped his fingers around the bars, the skin broken and bleeding, as if he'd tried to claw his way out.

"Gabriel—"

"Did you find the money?" He licked along his dry lips, wincing a little when they cracked. "Please, you have to get me out of here." His eyes darted around the room, as if searching for something in the shadows.

"What? No, I can't find that much in such a—"

"Then why the fuck are you here? You're just going to make everything worse!" his voice thundered, making me flinch.

"I'm trying to—"

"You need to leave. Unless..." He tried to stretch through the bars. "Yes, you'll survive so much better than me."

My fingers brushed along the lock, even as my stomach twisted.

"You'd do anything for me, wouldn't you, Ara?" Dad's eyes turned wild. "You wouldn't leave me like Mum did, would you? You can fix this."

"Evening, Morris. I see you're trying to escape again." A man stepped out from the shadows, a dark brow raised. I recognised him immediately as the other man from the garage, the brunet with the hammer.

Dad shrank back in his cell. "No... of course not."

I stood, putting myself between Dad and the man. "I'm here to speak to Sebastian."

The stranger nodded. "Good, because he's waiting for you."

Chapter 10
Sebastian

I watched her on her knees, Morris's distress clear even without sound.

"Is there a reason you showed her to his cell?" I asked Langdon, who lounged against the wall of my office with a grin. I didn't even need to look up to know his expression, Lang having a more peculiar taste for anarchy and chaos.

A sharp whistle forced my head up.

"She must be really interesting if you're silencing me," Lang signed, a rough sound escaping from his lips. "Is there a reason she's on the pre-approved list?"

"That's none of your business," I commented in French.

"Yeah, fuck you, Bas," Langdon replied before flipping me his middle finger.

A laugh caught in my chest, easing some of the tension that had been growing these past few weeks. Another regular had just been found dead, likely an overdose, and it was starting to build whispers of a tainted batch. Except my stuff was pristine, clean. Either manufacturing had made an error, which was unheard of, or someone has been fucking with my supply.

Either way, someone was going to pay for it.

"You need a fight," Langdon signed after a pause, his hands slowing slightly when he realised I wasn't giving him my full concentration.

I thought about it a moment, knowing releasing some of my pent-up aggression was probably a good idea. Nodding, I agreed. "Set it up."

Langdon bowed dramatically, more at home in some royal court rather than as my enforcer. His flamboyant, flirtatious personality was a stark contrast to mine. But that was the point; people saw his pretty face and charm before they felt his dagger in their back.

Although Lang preferred to play with his prey a little beforehand, while I preferred getting to the point. My eyes dipped to the collar of his shirt, to the scars that you could only just see hidden beneath the fabric. Rather than fear the flames that had almost killed him, he embraced them.

Another whistle, and I looked up to find concern darkening Langdon's eyes. "When did you last sleep?" he asked.

A buzz drew my attention back to my phone. Caden was escorting her this way, her bag held tightly in his fist. "I sleep enough." A lie, but I wasn't exactly feeling conversational with the man who held a parallel trauma.

Langdon and I were both kids when we were hurt, almost killed. Him by being trapped in my family's home while it was set aflame, and me by the woman who'd lit the match.

Opening my desk drawer, I lifted the mask to my face, snapping it in place. Only seconds later there was a knock, and Caden opened it up to sweep the girl inside. She was hesitant, her eyes darting around, as if memorising everything about the room before finally settling on me. I expected fear, maybe a little apprehension. Not stubborn determination.

She may look like a delicate little rabbit, but she had

some steel in her spine that fascinated me. I almost smiled, but then I remembered she came with Graves, and that strange warmth in my chest chilled to ice.

"You have him in a cell," she said, her tone acerbic.

I shrugged. "He owes me money."

"How can you be so cruel? You've already taken everything else from him. At least let him have some dignity." Her hands fisted, but she made no move to approach.

Cocking my head, I relaxed back in my chair. *"Get our prisoner,"* I directed to Langdon, purposely changing the language to put her on edge. Langdon left without argument, leaving Caden to lean against the wall where he once was.

"Well?" she continued, losing some of her confidence the longer I left her question unanswered.

I decided to make her a little more uncomfortable, taking my time to appraise her from head to toe. Her dress was a pale blue, fitted around the middle to flare out slightly at her hips in a tease. It finished at her knees, revealing her curvy legs and dainty feet.

When I finally dragged my eyes back up to her face, I found her skin had pinked beneath my scrutiny.

Good.

"Why are you here, *belle*?" I asked, watching how the flush on her cheeks deepened even further at the nickname.

"It's Ara."

I allowed myself to smirk this time, but only because my mask hid it. I knew her name; Morris immediately gave me everything I wanted to know about his not-so-precious daughter.

"I've come for my father," she said, her earlier bravado lessening. I was almost disappointed, craving more of a fight. Which was unusual for me considering I usually required full obedience. "Please, I'll do anything."

"He's my prisoner. What good will it do allowing a man who owes me so much free?" Both warning and amusement laced my tone. "I have a reputation to uphold, Miss Grey."

She lifted her chin, a flash of resolve burning across her features. "He's sick."

"An addict," Caden added, and Arabella's head jerked to him with such renewed fervour that I had to suppress a demand for her to return her attention to me. It was irrational, but I wanted those pretty eyes of whisky and gold on me alone, and no one else.

"Please," she said, her glare not matching the way she begged. We'd have to work on that. "There must be some way."

"Do you have my money?" I was just teasing at this point. Of course she didn't have the money, but I was enjoying watching her try and reason with a man with no morals.

"No... I can't." Ara paused, frustration simmering in the tense set of her jaw. "Surely there's something else you want?"

I sat forward, her eyes widening a little when they darted to my mask even as I kept my voice disinterested. But there was nothing disinterested in the way my muscles tensed, or the electricity that charged the air.

"Be specific, Miss Grey. What exactly are you offering me?" My skin felt tight, anticipation thrumming through my veins at the possibility of having her.

Arabella swallowed, and I watched the delicate roll of her throat. "I–"

The door crashed open without warning, and Morris was thrown to his knees beside her. She immediately went to help him stand, only for him to shove her away.

"Ara, what are you doing?" Morris snarled, climbing to his feet unassisted. "I told you you'll only make it worse!"

Lifting his hand, he slapped her hard enough that the sound reverberated around my office.

Before I even realised I'd moved I was across the room, slamming Morris against the wall. A delicate gasp brushed my arm, Arabella reacting to the shock of violence. "Touch her again, and I'll kill you where you stand," I hissed, a dangerous edge bleeding into my tone.

Morris gulped, keeping his body pressed to the wall even as I stepped back. His eyes rounded further when he felt Langdon's pistol pressed to the side of his skull. "Has she offered to take my place?" he whispered.

Arabella jerked as if she'd been electrocuted, her eyes rounded as she stared at her father. He hasn't so much as looked in her direction.

"You think she's worth what you owe me?" I asked, keeping my body slightly angled between them. Arabella was an overwhelming presence beside me, her spine and shoulders so stiff I was pretty sure she'd break something if she wasn't careful.

Morris met my eyes, a sick hope filling his. It had only been a few days, and already he looked like shit. Which went perfectly with his personality.

Licking along his bottom lip, he nodded. "If she takes my place, will you let me go?"

Arabella said nothing, the handprint prominent on her cheek. Unlike the last time, she wore little makeup, her fair skin bare, with only the smallest amount of black high-lighting her eyes.

I nodded to Lang, who forced Morris back onto the floor. "Hmm. Maybe she should be the one on her knees before me, rather than you?" I rested back on the lip of my desk, and even like this I was taller, bigger against her smaller frame.

"She'll do anything you ask," Morris said, still not looking at his daughter. "Won't you, Ara?"

There was a beat of silence, her chest heaving with a staggered breath.

Finally, she said, "I'll work to pay off his debt." Her voice held a quiver that hadn't been there before. But she didn't look away from my gaze when I turned to her. Others would've cowered beneath my attention, and yet she refused to even blink. "I'll take his place."

Caden laughed, and even Langdon let out a little husky sound.

"Done."

The laughter cut off, and my closest friends turned to me with a shared look of disbelief.

"You can't be serious?" Caden asked in French, while Langdon's hands moved too fast for me to read while my concentration remained on her.

"Go," I told Morris, who didn't have to be asked twice. He didn't even spare his daughter a cursory glance, shooting out the door like there was a firework up his arse. I finally looked over at Langdon.

"I'll make sure he leaves," he signed, following him out.

Arabella waited in silence, standing there with nothing but fisted hands and rigid shoulders.

"Make sure Graves doesn't make a scene," I directed to Caden, purposely changing to French once more.

Wouldn't want Arabella to get *too* comfortable in her situation.

She was my new toy, after all.

Caden seemed to hesitate, his brows pulled low before he finally left, closing the door behind him. I waited, Arabella coiled so tight with tension that I wondered if she was ready to snap.

I watched her for a moment, memorising each ragged breath. "Get on your knees."

Chapter 11
Arabella

"Get on your knees." Sebastian's husky command washed over me, and my immediate reaction was to run from the man who was nothing more than a predator in human skin. He made my palms slick, fear a sour taste at the back of my tongue.

"You didn't even let me say goodbye," I whispered, staying perfectly still when he straightened to his full height. He seemed to possess the aura of some great tyrant, one that began to walk slowly around me like I was his fresh sacrifice. Which, I guess I kind of was.

What the hell was I thinking?

Why did I ever agree to this?

His attention burned, the silence stretching until I couldn't take it any longer. Closing my eyes, I begged for my own breathing to settle down, to not give away my apprehension. Everything about him was intimidating. From his presence, his sheer size, to the way he watched me with such focus it was unnerving.

"Ten seconds in, and you're already disobeying me."

Shit. I literally had one job, and I'd already screwed it up.

Opening my eyes, I found Sebastian standing directly in front of me. He was so tall I had to tip my head back to study the beautiful design of his mask.

It was a matte black skull, the jaw and hollow of the nose intricate in its detail. It curved up the side of his face and across the bridge of his nose, leaving only his eyes on full display. A thick scar marked down his right eye, like some great creature had tried to blind him but failed. It curled up through his brow, disappearing into his hairline.

You'd think it would make him seem barbaric, but the scar only drew attention to the stunning midnight shade of his iris, and the sadism that glistened in its dark depths.

"Are you always going to hide behind that mask? Be weird if we're going to spend a lot of time together." *Oh my God. What am I saying?* "Strange kink to have." *Fuck. Me. Sideways. Stop!*

I think I was having an episode. Or a stroke. Or something equally as nefarious.

Sebastian cocked his head, his eyes narrowing on me for a moment before he slowly reached up to the straps behind his ears. I held my breath as he revealed his face, memorising the sharp contours of his cheekbones and the sheer angle of his jaw.

He had a beard, too long to be stubble, but too short to do anything but keep it trimmed in the same dark shade as his long, shaggy hair. He revealed more scars, the skin rougher compared to his natural golden tan. One sliced through his upper lip, and a few fainter marks slashed across his forehead and cheeks.

It was the first time I was able to really study him, and for some reason he was letting me with a patience I didn't expect. He stood with the self-assurance of a king, his intensity almost a physical vibration between us. His suit was crisp, with the collar open to reveal tattooed black and grey thorns wrapping around his throat. A few rings adorned his large hands, the metal dark and chunky. The sophisticated image didn't match the feral glint in his eyes, like a wolf pretending to be a sheep.

"You finished?" he asked, his voice a deep gruff that sounded more like a growl than not. "It's too late to back out now. Once you're mine, you're mine, *belle*." The last part was whispered against my skin, his breath intimate as he dipped his head towards mine.

I swallowed past the lump in my throat. "It's Ara."

He wasn't even using Bella, which was a nickname I despised and refused to acknowledge. Belle was arguably worse, because *he'd* come up with it.

His upper lip quirked up in a smirk, as if reading my thoughts.

Get on your knees.

His velvet command echoed in my mind. I knew what I'd agreed, my life for my father's. I was waiting for Sebastian to demand it again, my legs locked to keep me from shaking. Getting on my knees was probably the least of my worries, and yet I stood as still as a statue. My pulse was erratic, and if I didn't calm down soon, I may end up passing out or something else equally dramatic.

"Are you going to kill me?" I finally asked, proud that my voice sounded strong and not at all scared shitless.

I watched as Sebastian reattached his mask, making him seem even more vicious.

"Is that what you want?"

"Of course not," I said without hesitation, but there wasn't much conviction behind the words. Wait, I didn't want him to kill me. Did I? No, I was definitely having an out-of-body experience right now. I'll blame the highly stressful situation.

Sebastian didn't seem convinced. Which wasn't great a start, and oh God, I think I might cry.

"Let me take you to your room." His arm brushed mine as he headed towards the door, leaving me to look after him.

"Room? But I thought..."

"You want to stay in the dungeon?" he asked over his shoulder. "I like to keep some of my spiders there."

"No." Wiping the traitorous tear from my cheek, I followed, the corridor a labyrinth before we came to the golden lift as before. At least, I think it was the same lift.

The doors opened at his approach, his shoulders eating up the space before he turned and waited. Steeling my spine, I joined him, ignoring the way he seemed to steal all the surrounding oxygen. He didn't look at me as he pressed his palm to one of the panels, and the lift began to descend.

It wasn't lost on me that he never actually answered my question. Which meant there was a very good chance that he may just kill me.

Sebastian

I fisted my hands at my sides, refraining from touching her. What I really wanted was to hit something, to expel the charge building in my body that I had no hope of concealing, but I'd restrict myself until I could get into the ring.

Fear almost had an aura, an intensity that radiated. Arabella held a faint tremor, her eyes facing forward and refusing to look at me. Fear was good, important. It meant she wasn't a fool who'd offered herself up to me on a silver platter. But someone who was loyal enough to risk herself, even if that loyalty wasn't deserved.

The doors opened, and I stepped out, and after only a second of hesitation, she joined me. Her eyes burned into my back, and I knew she was curious as to why I'd re-attached my mask.

The only time I didn't wear it in public was when I was fighting. I didn't care that people saw my scars; I'd come to use them to my advantage, a reminder that beneath the suits I'd survived more than what most could. To not fuck with me.

The mask was nothing more than a symbol of my power.

Of the Beast that I'd been unceremoniously named.

The familiar scent of perfume assaulted my nose almost immediately, those in attendance knowing not to let their gaze linger for too long. There were hushed whispers as I strode across the carpet, and quiet murmurs as people stepped out of my way.

I found Caden and Graves arguing quietly by the door, Miles, the doorman on duty standing patiently to the side. Again, he was just for show, because Caden was by far more dangerous.

Everything looked a certain way. Played a part. Power wasn't just about being the boss. You had to look right and react expectantly. Otherwise, those beneath you believed they could overthrow you, when in reality they would never be in the same league. Miles looked the part, his height only an inch shy of my six foot five, and his arms were thicker, making him unnecessarily bulky. Not great if he needed to cross his arms, but perfect for standing around and looking strong.

Grave's eyes widened when he realised I was there, sweat coating his brow.

"Detective. You were warned last time that if you stepped foot on my territory again, you wouldn't be walking away."

"My badge lets me go wherever the hell I want!" he snapped, but the fire in his voice was all bark, no bite. He could posture all he liked, but underneath that badge and bravado he feared me like the rest of them. "Ara, get over here. We're leaving."

Arabella tensed beside me but didn't make a move. *Good girl.*

"Who let you in?" I asked, keeping my voice dangerously low.

I first met Graves six years ago when he was part of the task force trying to take me down. At the time I specialised in pills before moving to cocaine because I could make it cleaner, cheaper, and even sell it at a premium to pharmaceutical companies wanting anaesthetic. Off the record, of course.

Graves was young, reckless, and dumb enough to start popping the same pills he was supposed to be nicking me for. Last I'd heard, they'd kicked him off the task force, disgraced, demoted, and barely clinging to a badge. The only reason I hadn't made him vanish was because he never got close enough to make anything stick.

Detective Graves was a pain in my arse, but if he disappeared it would've drawn more attention to me. So, I let him live. A mistake I'd happily rectify.

"Arabella's mine," he answered instead, gnashing his teeth together.

I shook my head, noticing the way his pupils were blown. Seemed he was still out partying too hard. "Not anymore," I said.

Rage coloured his cheeks. "That's it, take my sloppy seconds," he taunted, but I didn't rise to the bait. Grave's attention shifted to Arabella. "You turned me down for him?" he spat at her. "If you come with me now, I'll forgive you."

I smirked beneath my mask when she simply lifted her chin and remained silent. There was strength in her spine, in the way she'd just faced me with defiance, and now how she responded to Grave's venom. It called to the darker side of me, rousing my demons who wanted to taunt that little spark until I eventually ruined her.

Grave's hand snapped out, snagging her wrist in an iron grip.

I moved before anyone else, my large palm cuffing the back of his neck. "Last warning," I whispered, dropping my voice. "Touch what's mine again, and I'll slit your throat in front of the entire room."

I released him as abruptly as I'd grabbed him, causing him to stagger slightly to the side. Grave's face glowed crimson, his eyes darting around for help that didn't exist.

After a moment he leaned in, voice low and trembling with fury. "Enjoy her while you can, because a storm's coming," he hissed, lips curling into a twisted grin. "And when it hits, and you've lost everything, your status, your money and empire—it'll be my cuffs locking around your wrists."

Chapter 12
Arabella

Everything moved as if in slow motion, the bouncer grabbing Gabriel and the collective gasps from those close enough to witness the conversation. Even the look Gabriel shot me, so full of malice and retribution, held such a weight that my muscles automatically tensed as if preparing to be struck.

"Remember who you belong to," Gabriel snarled as he was escorted out.

I waited a breath, my lungs struggling to take in enough air before I finally turned to face Sebastian, only to find him looking down at me with an empty expression. Seemingly so unaffected by Gabriel's words, while I was here trying not to have a full-on breakdown.

I swallowed, finding myself unable to look away from his gaze.

"Car," he said, and it took a full minute for me to realise he was speaking to the one with the annoying watch. The brunet with the posh yet east-end accent, and a preference for large, blunt objects.

"Coming round now," he responded, looking down at his phone.

Sebastian nodded, sweeping out his arm for me to go before him. Which was ridiculous, because I had no idea where I was going. Except, I shouldn't have worried, because the black car with equally black windows that pulled up on the curb directly outside *The Thorn* was very clearly for him.

A hush came over the large queue, as if the sight of Sebastian in his mask out in the open was a rarity. I ignored the glares when they turned their attention to me, almost happy to climb inside the car.

But then Sebastian climbed in behind, and we were suddenly side by side in a tight, confined space. He was just so *big*. Unnecessarily so, like his mother had fed him raw eggs from a toddler just so he could become a human mountain.

The air was tense, with an almost violent undercurrent that didn't go with how relaxed Sebastian sat. His frame took up the majority of the space, his shoulder brushing mine and his legs spread as if he wanted to impose himself in what little area I had.

I refused to look over, instead counting the streetlights as they whizzed by. The car was nice, black leather interior with a little console in front of us that looked to hold two crystal glasses. There was a partition that was currently down, and I realised that the blond with the lighter fetish was in the passenger side.

He and the brunet seemed to be Sebastian's personal... men? Guards? Friends? Although, the concept of friendship was pretty far-fetched for a man like Sebastian.

I didn't recognise this part of the city, which wasn't surprising because it wasn't like I knew every inch of London. Nerves fluttered in my stomach when the car turned, and Sebastian pressed a little harder against the side of my thigh. A thousand toxic butterflies prepared me for what was to come. *I can do this.*

I hadn't realised I'd closed my eyes until a finger brushed along my cheek, catching the single tear that had dared to escape. Honestly, I needed to get it together until I was in private. Sebastian looked at the tear for a second, the drop hanging from his fingertip before he closed his hand.

I studied his face, seeing he'd lost his mask somewhere between getting in the car and when I closed my eyes.

"We should probably discuss the details," I said.

He raised a single brow at my statement, seeming to wait for me to continue with a stoic expression.

I cleared my throat. "Of your expectations of me." My eyes dropped to the thorns that wrapped around his throat, the tattoo both realistic and harsh against his skin.

"To pay off your father's debt." In the small confines of the car, his deep voice brushed over me like velvet. His accent was slight, only pronounced on certain words and letters. He was like a lion, his long hair a mane that swept forward when he tilted his head towards me. The strands were dark with a few brown highlights. "How far will you go?" he asked.

He watched me like a lion too, a predator ready to devour his prey.

"Will you suck my cock if I demand you get on your knees right now?" he whispered.

My cheeks burned, and my breathing picked up as Sebastian continued to watch me with eyes of midnight that had gotten impossibly darker, losing what little light they once held. What was left was savage. Brutal.

His fingers brushed over my collarbone until he encircled my throat, his thumb pressing against my pulse. "Will you bend over so I can fuck you any time and any place I wish?"

I swallowed, unable to find my voice.

"Will you let me ruin you for anyone else?" he whispered, pulling me closer until his breath feathered over my lips. "All to protect your father?"

You don't want a repeat of Mum, do you?

Guilt twisted inside me, memories of the woman who'd birthed me threatening to make this entire situation so much worse.

Another tear rolled down my face. "Yes."

He released me so suddenly, cold swept in to prickle along my skin.

"I have no interest in reluctance."

The rejection burned hotter than I expected, before twisting into panic. "Then what do you want from me?" I asked, but he'd already turned to the window, giving me his profile.

He said nothing else as the car rolled, finally coming to a stop once we'd driven into an underground garage. His door opened, and he stepped out without acknowledging me. I waited a second, trying and failing to calm my nerves before I followed.

There were rows of cars, each more ostentatious than the last. A yellow Lamborghini, a red Ferrari and something *James Bond* would drive. A huge SUV was parked at the end, the brand something I didn't recognise, as well as several Harley Davidson motorbikes.

Sebastian waited until I was beside him before he moved toward the lift at the back, the door opening at his approach. Much like the one at *The Thorn*, there were no buttons, just a state-of-the-art pad where he placed his hand. I didn't know what to expect as we ascended the floors, but definitely not the warm and welcoming living room that was decorated in dark woods, blues and grey.

Sebastian didn't stop to check whether I was following,

his longer strides taking him across the room before I'd even stepped out of the lift.

Scampering after him I quickly looked around, finding beautiful rugs on the hard floors, top of the range gadgets, and expensive-looking paintings that brought in bursts of colour to the otherwise masculine design.

Finally, Sebastian stopped at a door down a corridor, opening it without a single glance towards me. Stepping to the side, he waited, even as I hesitated.

"Wait, will I be able to go and get my stuff?" I wondered.

His smile was cruel, just a slow twist of his lips, and maybe I'd made the wrong decision. "No," he said, shutting me inside and then locking the door behind me.

Sebastian

Arabella hadn't moved for the past two hours, sitting in the corner of her new room with her head on her knees. I knew, because I'd been watching her the entire time on my phone.

She'd essentially offered herself to me, and my cock had been eager to take her up on it. But despite the fire in her eyes, fear wasn't a turn on when it wasn't mixed with anticipation. I'd give her a day to wallow in self-pity, and then I'd figure out what the fuck I'd do with her.

My tarantula, Raven, crawled up my arm, content to just sit on my skin while I watched my new plaything.

The lift clicked to my right, and I didn't bother to turn to know it was Caden and Langdon. They were the only ones to have access this late, as I'd sent my staff home for the evening a while ago.

"Bas, what the fuck?" Caden muttered, throwing himself down beside me before tossing Arabella's bag onto the coffee table. He eyed Raven, even reaching over to see whether she'd move over to him. She didn't, instead crawling further up my body until she nestled against my neck.

"I knew I should've locked the code," I muttered. "What are you doing here?"

Langdon shrugged, standing with his signature smirk. "How's your princess?" he signed, raising an eyebrow. "Locked away in her tower?"

I suppressed a growl, instead giving him my middle finger, which earned me a silent laugh in return. "I don't remember inviting either of you over," I grumbled.

Caden crossed his arms. "We're making sure you're okay. What you did with her was out of character."

"Impulsive," I added, and he nodded in agreement. I was violent. Uncivilised, and chaos personified. But I was never impulsive because that meant I wasn't in control.

"So, what, you planning to keep her as your personal fuck toy?" Caden shook his head, clearly disapproving.

Yes. "No."

"Then why?" Langdon asked, moving around so he could sit on the table facing us. He was wary of Raven, but not afraid. Probably because she'd bit him once when he was being a prick.

My lips parted, but for once I didn't have an answer.

I didn't know why I made the deal. She was beautiful, but I'd seen and fucked women just as beautiful, if not more so before. So why her?

Tension pulled at me, the need to destroy an impulse I soon would no longer be able to avoid. I'd always had a monster inside me, one that only relented once I purged my darker desires through either fucking or fighting. Sometimes painting, but only if I destroyed everything afterwards.

It was a compulsion I no longer contested, although fucking hadn't been as satisfying recently.

"You sort the fight?" I asked, directing my question to Langdon.

He nodded. "Saturday night," he signed.

"Good." I really needed to feel knuckles against my cheeks and blood against my skin.

"You wanna hit Atlantis?" Caden asked. "I'm sure Aeris can sort you something to take the edge off."

I reached for my whisky, the glass cold beneath my fingers. "No." The movement jostled the tarantula, who made her way down my stretched arm to the table where Caden scooped her up.

The women I usually fucked were faceless. Picked out specifically to fulfil a need and nothing more. Yet sex had become... predictable. Even when I went to Atlantis and let my monster out, it was never anything more than a physical release.

Sex and desire were not mutually exclusive, and the thrill of wearing my mask, making demands that were fulfilled without hesitation, had lost its appeal. My cock hadn't twitched for anyone in a while. Not until a certain little rabbit looked up at me with such disobedience while my hand had encircled her throat.

Reaching for Arabella's bag, I emptied the contents onto the table beside Caden, immediately reaching for her phone. Only for it to be pin locked.

"She's twenty-five, by the way," he commented, putting Raven in her box before grabbing the only other thing in the bag, her driver's licence. "Moved seven times in the past ten years, all across the country. Morris has kept them under the radar, and her mum died when she was just a kid."

He held the license out, and I ignored the text to concentrate on the picture. It was generic, her expression soft, unsmiling.

"Morris was supposed to be used to make a statement. Are you going to do the same with her?" Caden asked quietly, his eyes boring into me.

The question created a weight on my chest, my glare sharp when I looked towards my cousin. He didn't react to my frosty response. Maybe I should try and convince Raven to bite him too.

"She fascinates me," I settled on, and Caden raised a judgmental brow. I didn't elaborate that this fascination had dug its claws into me and was bordering on obsession. "Don't worry, I'll get rid of her once I'm bored."

Until then, I'd just play with her a little.

That thought was still prominent an hour later once I'd kicked them out, much to Langdon's disappointment. My muscles were tight, my demons howling at me as I walked down the west wing.

My studio was my personal space, and no one was allowed past the threshold unless exclusively invited by me. Which was usually zero, because my art wasn't meant for anyone else.

Needing to get rid of some of the excess energy before I did something else impulsive, I picked up a clean canvas and moved it to an easel. If I couldn't fight, or fuck, that left me with only one option.

Rolling up my sleeves, I grabbed the closest paint and got to work. The strokes were rough, aggressive as I pushed all my frustration and anger onto the canvas. The colours I'd chosen were dark, blending together like a bottomless night that held no hope. Twisted lines and grotesque bodies. Warped trees and broken horizons.

I painted until my hand ached, and I'd gone through eight different images. The violent pictures in my head were nothing compared to the colours I pushed on the canvas, the expression wrong. The scene was wrong. Everything was *wrong*.

The demons in my head howled for me to destroy it.

With the paint still wet, I rubbed my fingers across the canvas, hoping that I'd be able to feel something other than rage. But of course I didn't, not even when I grabbed my knife and started slicing, cutting the painting into ribbons. Not even when I started to break the frame, ignoring how splinters dug into my knuckles, or how my blood added to the already fierce imagery.

Memories threatened to consume me, my breath coming in pants, and only when my entire studio was shattered, broken, did I finally feel that sense of calm I craved so much, pulling me back from the edge.

Cracking my knuckles, I brushed my bloody and painted fingers against the punching bag I hung to the side. It was already ruined, repaired so many times it had a distinctive crisscross pattern from when I'd lost my temper and stabbed the thing. Unlike the one in my gym, this one was full of rags rather than sand.

Then what do you want from me?

Her words echoed around my mind.

My own thoughts answered, *I don't know.*

Chapter 13
Sebastian

My bike rolled to a stop, the night air brisk as I stared up at the flat above the garage. The surrounding street lamps were off, which wasn't unexpected considering the time. It was late, the heaviness of the night shrouding me in shadows.

The local council tried to save money by turning the lights off after midnight, and then they wondered why the crime rate had skyrocketed. Debauchery and terror thrived beneath the veil that was darkness, but who gave a shit if the government saved a few pennies?

Tugging off my helmet, I placed it on the seat, and despite the area not being the best, I dared anyone to take it. Not only was the Harley a luxurious matte black, but it also had my emblem engraved on the side. A rose strangled by thorns. My face may not be recognisable, and not even my mask unless you were in certain circles. But the rose was usually enough to deter a thief. And if it didn't, then I'd just have to introduce myself.

Not bothering with the garage, I headed straight to the side to find the door that must lead to the flat above. The stairs creaked beneath my weight, even as my heavy boots were silent. The front door opened with one quick swift kick to the lock, and as soon as I stepped inside a gun was pressed to my side.

Without hesitation I disarmed the assailant, turning the gun back on him.

Morris spluttered, face red and sweaty. "What are you doing here?" he gasped, winded from where I'd hit him. "I thought... I thought my debt was paid."

Without turning away, I released the cartridge and then removed the bullet from the chamber before tossing it all to the floor. "Your debt's not paid," I said, amused with how he wouldn't meet my eyes. "Just transferred."

"So, she's still alive?" he asked, finally looking at me.

His attention roamed over my face, hesitating on the scars. I didn't bother with my mask, because I didn't expect Morris to still be here. A mistake on my part.

He swallowed. "I thought you'd fuck her and then kill her like all the others."

I wasn't surprised by his words, but I was disgusted all the same. Rumours were fickle things, and this one I let grow because it would only benefit me for people to believe it. Morris clearly considered it to be true and still hadn't argued when his only daughter agreed to be put on a silver fucking platter.

I had to clench my fists to stop myself from killing him right then and there.

"If I kill her, you'd have to take her place," I said simply.

Morris picked at his bottom lip, the skin cracked and bleeding. Bottles of opened beer littered the place, and the stench of rotten food and general uncleanliness was strong.

"Then why are you here?" he asked, his indignation clear from the sharpness in his tone. The kind of edge that came from too much alcohol and too little self-awareness. "If she's still alive, you don't need me anymore. You've already taken everything. There's nothing left for you to destroy."

Morris sounded like a perpetual victim, despite putting himself in this position in the first place. Honestly, I'd have thought he'd have run far away like the coward he was, not hung around until his next fuckup came knocking down his door.

It was almost impressive, the way he managed to twist his own guilt into something pitiful.

I stepped closer, letting the silence press against him before I asked, "Do you even feel guilty?"

"Guilty for what? Arabella made her own bed." Morris tipped his head back, a weak attempt at bravado, though his eyes couldn't hold mine for more than a second. "It's the least she can do after everything she's done."

The words hit like a force, not because they were unexpected, but because he meant them. Every syllable was laced with that same smug self-pity he wore like rusted armour.

"And what exactly has she done?"

He scoffed. "Does it matter? She's yours now."

I'd expected deflection, and yet my chest still tightened with a raw, burning fury that settled behind my ribs like fire. "Where's her room?" I asked before I reacted and killed him.

I wasn't here for any other reason than I couldn't sleep. Finding out a little more about my new toy was a somewhat productive use of my time.

Morris frowned, gesturing to the stairs. I paused at the threshold of her bedroom, taking in the sweet, feminine smell and colourful decor. I couldn't actually stand up straight, having to duck my head even at the tallest section. It was clearly a loft conversion, and not a good one at that. There were gaps in the ceiling, and the floor hadn't been completely boarded properly. Her bed was pressed right to the back, the roof so sloped she'd have had to crawl across.

Arabella clearly liked pastels, all the clothes in her clothing rack similar to the pretty blue dress she'd worn earlier. Nothing like the women in my world. Grabbing a few of her clothes, I threw them on the bed. I eyed her charger, deciding she wasn't allowed a phone and making a mental note to ensure she hadn't snuck another one in.

I paused at the makeshift bookshelves, hundreds of paperbacks lovingly read and displayed as if they were trophies. The spines blurred together, so grabbing the one from her nightstand, I added it to the pile before turning toward the last piece of furniture in the room, her desk. It was well worn, held up awkwardly by a wedged box.

On top were more books, but these were different. There were no words on the front, and I decided they must be journals, or maybe even notebooks. Not that I knew the distinction.

Flicking one open, I stared at the pen marks, brow furrowed as I flipped through the pages until I found one she'd started but hadn't finished. Pulling off my backpack, I shoved everything inside, zipping it tight before throwing it over my shoulder.

Chapter 14
Arabella

My stomach woke me, the angry sound a deep rumble that almost vibrated the silent air. Groaning, I sat up, my cheek stinging from where I'd fallen asleep against the carpet. I'd kept to the corner of the room, my back aching from the horrible angle. I eyed the bed, a beautiful king with soft sheets and even softer pillows. Yet I decided to sleep on the floor.

I wasn't any less safe in the bed than I was here, and yet I couldn't bring myself to sleep there. Here I was tucked away, hidden from the door at first glance.

Not that it would take much effort to find me. I debated whether to sleep in the tub, but the bathroom had no lock, and the bath would've been cold and just as uncomfortable. But at least I had my own private bathroom.

A prisoner with her own toilet, how lucky was I?

Rubbing at my cheek, my eyes burned from where I'd fallen asleep crying. Not my best moment, I'd admit. But now that was out of my system, and I could get myself together and not wallow in self-pity.

Standing, my stomach decided to play the entire orchestra, strings, percussions, brass and all. I actually couldn't remember the last time I ate.

A nice older lady with a warm smile had brought me tea hours ago, but that sat untouched on the bedside table. She hadn't said anything more than a polite hello before leaving, as if Sebastian locking crying women in his guest bedroom was a regular occurrence. I wouldn't be surprised.

The size of the room was bigger than my entire flat, decorated just as tastefully as the other rooms I'd been marched through. The drawers were empty, as were the cupboards in the ensuite. There were no toiletries. No shampoo or body wash. Not even a bar of soap for me to clean up with.

My stomach pulled me towards the door, and to my surprise, it was unlocked.

Holy shit. Was I hallucinating? Nope, the door was indeed unlocked, but I kept my happy dance to myself for now. It wasn't like I could just run away.

You wouldn't leave me like Mum did, would you? You can fix this.

My mind echoed the words, *You can fix this.*

I wanted to believe it, but even in my head it sounded like a lie, because the truth was that I didn't know what fixing anything looked like anymore. It didn't matter how many times I tried to convince myself Dad would change, that he'd get better and finally *see* me, it never seemed to happen.

If I weren't so hollowed out by disappointment, I might've laughed.

The kind of broken laugh that scraped its way out from somewhere deep, where memory still clung to the ghost of a man who once tucked his daughter in at night. Read her bedtime stories and kissed her cut knee.

Before Mum left.

Before everything turned to shit.

The hall was dark when I peeked out, the air deceptively still. I expected to be ambushed as I took my first step, my bare feet silent as I padded back down the hallway towards what I hoped was the living room. The place was huge, the centre a large open space with tall windows that revealed a stunning view of the city at night. Light filtered in from outside, allowing me to quietly look around until I finally found the kitchen.

It was just as expensive-looking as the living room, if not more so. Pristine marble with golden veins and dark accents. The cabinets themselves were black—what a surprise—the entire aesthetic giving off ultra luxury.

I took a single step inside, intending to head towards the large fridge when I heard a wispy cry break through the night. Pausing, I concentrated on the sound, slowly moving back so I could peek around the corner. A woman arched her back against the wall, her legs wrapped around the waist of the blond man. He was fully dressed, while her breasts bounced with every rough thrust, her dress bunched up around her waist.

He didn't make a single sound while she moaned and groaned, her eyes closed and lips parted. His hands held her thighs, gripping so tight there were indents in her flesh.

I couldn't seem to tear my eyes away, rooted to the spot and caught somewhere between disbelief and embarrassment. I wasn't exactly a prude, but I hadn't been expecting *that*.

The moans grew louder, echoing off the walls in a rhythm that was almost obscene until the blond released one thigh, only to press his hand against her mouth. The woman didn't seem to care, her hips tilting to better meet his almost violent thrusts.

She came with a muffled scream, and seconds later the blond stilled with his own release.

Holy shit.

Another second or so passed before he dropped her, and the woman immediately began to adjust her clothes. *A cleaner,* I thought, noticing the feather duster by her feet. Well. At least someone was keeping things... hygienic.

I stepped back before I could be seen, heart thudding, and hurried across the kitchen to the fridge. A burst of cool air hit my face when I opened it, sharp against the heat still burning in my cheeks. This thing was loaded, and my stomach rumbled again.

A knock on the fridge door startled me, my head hitting the side when I jumped at the sudden sound. Pulling back, the blond smirked down at me, the light from the fridge washing over him in a sickly glow.

"Sorry," I stammered, closing the door. "I didn't mean to..." *Watch you have sex.* I was conscious of my cheeks continuing to tingle but decided to ignore it like an adult. "I'll just go back to my room."

His smile was friendly as he lifted his hands, and I was thankful to any god that was listening that he couldn't read my mind. But then he realised that I couldn't read his hands, his brows drawing together before he pulled his phone from his pocket and quickly typed something before turning it to face me.

Hungry? it read, and looking up, I nodded.

His smile widened, which only highlighted how handsome he was. His hair was fair, with random darker strands that went well with his naturally golden skin. His eyes were a light brown and seemed to flicker like candlelight.

Weirdly he smelt like something burning, and I was pretty sure that was soot smeared on his cheekbone. **I'm Langdon. The other prick's Caden.**

"I'm Arabella, but people call me Ara."

Langdon gave me a silent laugh, head tipping back to reveal the burns along his throat. **Oh, I know who you are.** His smile twisted, and maybe he wasn't as friendly as I first thought. **What's so special about you then, ay?**

"Go home, Lang," came a dark, familiar voice. *"Je vois que vous la surveillez bien."*

I flinched, my eyes immediately finding Sebastian standing in the doorway.

But he didn't look at me, his attention entirely on the other man. Langdon peered back over his shoulder, only for his penetrating gaze to return to me. With a wink he stepped back, passing Sebastian without another exchanged word.

Sebastian closed the distance between us, and I braced myself against the kitchen cabinet. His hands curled onto the marble counter behind me, not touching but close enough that he stole all my oxygen. "What are you doing out here, *belle*?" he asked. He was like a cat toying with a mouse seconds before it was to be eaten. "Who let you out of your room?"

I tipped my head back, because apparently, I had a death wish. "It was unlocked."

"Was it now?"

The dim light put him entirely in the shadows, his expression hidden. But I could feel his eyes on me, tension twisting between us like a noose, so abrasive I could almost see the marks left on my skin.

His head dipped closer to mine, and I held my breath.

"Just a warning," he said, voice dropping to a husky whisper. "Stay out of my way, or you'll really find out why they call me the Beast." With that he pushed off the counter, leaving me alone in his kitchen.

It took a moment for me to move, and fisting my hands I

turned away from the fridge, realising I was no longer hungry. Instead, I searched the drawers, not stopping until I found something I could use to defend myself. Something fucking sharp.

Chapter 15
Arabella

Twenty-four hours and I still wasn't dead. Yet.

I should celebrate by going back to sleep, because there was nothing else for me to do. I hadn't risked checking the door again, and no one had come in with unwanted cups of tea.

Knock. Knock.

Never mind.

Pressing my back against the wall, I used it to stand. Sebastian had said he wasn't interested in reluctance, and I was definitely in team reluctance. But that didn't mean my heart didn't race as another knock resonated around the silent room.

It was smart not to trust his word.

"Oh, there you are, dear." The same older lady as last night walked in, carrying a silver tray with her statement cup of tea. I eyed it cautiously.

He wouldn't drug me. Would he?

"You must be starving. Dinner will be in ten minutes, and he expects you to attend." She placed the teacup and saucer on the side table, clicking her tongue when she realised I'd left the drawers partially open. "Your new toiletries will be delivered shortly. Now, let me get a good look at you."

She was smaller than me, and plump. But she radiated a warmth that could only be genuine.

Smiling kindly, she said, "Don't worry, everything's going to be okay."

Okay for you to say, I thought. She hadn't offered herself up to a man affectionately called *Beast.*

"My father..."

"Oh, don't even think about him. It'll be easier that way." Her smile faltered, and a sadness swept over her expression before disappearing beneath a bubble of excitement. "Remember, dinner's in ten. I'll send my son to come get you."

As quickly as she swept in, she left.

I eyed the tea once more, the scent sweet and honestly, my mouth watered a little, but I couldn't bring myself to drink it. Setting back in my corner, I closed my eyes and rested forward until my head hit my bent knees.

"Hello?"

I jerked, looking up to find a much younger man wearing a pristine suit standing in the doorway. I hadn't even heard the door open. Had I fallen back asleep?

"I'm here to escort you to dinner," he said, his smile gentle but not quite reaching his dark eyes. With his light blond hair he gave me a deadly angel vibe. "I'm Charlie, but everyone calls me Chip." A frown marked his brow at my continued silence.

Was he the butler? Did people actually have butlers?

Bloody hell, how rich was Sebastian?

"Did my mum not come and warn you?" He eyed the untouched tea, which was no longer billowing steam.

I averted my gaze and let out a breath. "I'm not coming to dinner."

"I don't think that's an option." He studied me like you would a bug beneath a telescope. It was a little unnerving, and honestly a little rude.

"Tell him I'm not feeling well." Okay, so clearly, I wasn't finished with my wallowing. I just needed another day, one more to treat myself to a nice, healthy breakdown before I finally accepted my fate.

Chip dipped his head in a nod. "As you wish."

Sebastian

"What do you mean she *isn't coming*?" my voice boomed.

Chip tensed at my words, but other than that he gave no indication that he was affected by my anger. His mother, Mrs Pritchard, whistled a cheery tune as if I wasn't imagining all the ways I could slaughter her son.

His eyes were dead, which was the only reason I'd agreed to hire him when Mrs Pritchard had begged. Apparently, he had some antisocial issues, and for anyone else I would've told them to fuck off. But Mrs Pritchard had been with my uncle for several decades, and once I'd established myself, I'd offered her a job as my head housekeeper. She'd been with me for close to eight years and came in four times a week.

Chip, on the other hand, had been with me for around three years, and didn't bat an eye at the more vicious side of my business. For a man of twenty-two, he held himself with an assurance that was unusual for someone so young.

But then again, cocky men regularly got themselves

killed. Which was the reason behind his slow but steady training.

Clearly not picking up on the acerbic atmosphere, Mrs Pritchard placed the meal onto the table while I continued to stare coldly at her son. He stared back, unblinking.

"Get her," I snapped.

"She said she wasn't feeling well," Chip replied, his tone monotonous.

"Don't worry, she'll come around, dear," Mrs Pritchard assured me, her cheeks red from how much she smiled. "She's pretty, too. Try not to growl too much and scare her."

"You're dismissed," I said, noting how her lips pursed slightly.

"Fine, but don't say I didn't warn you." Grabbing her son, they disappeared back into the kitchen.

There were only a small number of staff allowed in my home, and they were heavily vetted before receiving an access card. Mrs Pritchard had earned her place, and kept the other workers to a strict schedule that didn't overlap in my presence.

The only exception was Chip, who answered directly to me. His unique personality would be wasted as just a footman, but he wasn't yet ready to fully immerse himself into my world. So he'd have to settle for running errands, being a competent chess player, and assisting me when needed.

I glared at the plate opposite, the food already getting cold.

This was the second time she'd ignored a direct order, and it made my pulse spike.

Will you suck my cock if I demand you get on your knees right now?

Will you bend over so I can fuck you any time and any place I wish?

90

Will you let me ruin you for anyone else? All to protect your father?

Yes.

Gritting my teeth, I jolted to my feet. I didn't bother knocking on Arabella's door, instead shoving it open with the force of a hurricane.

My eyes narrowed on the untouched bed, an unfamiliar feeling knotting my stomach until I realised she was curled up on the floor in the corner. I paused for a second, taking a moment to calm myself. There was bruising beneath her eyes while exhaustion lined her face.

Her breathing was even, and I used the gentle motion to slow my own, ragged breaths. I didn't know why I'd accepted her as a replacement, but I was more interested in why she agreed to it in the first place.

It was twisted, that interest.

An obsession I wanted to break into tiny pieces just to understand.

Reaching down, I expected her to wake, bracing myself for a burst of violence and then my own volatile reaction. Yet she barely murmured when I slipped my arms beneath her body, lifting her before throwing her down on the bed.

But when she bounced in the centre, she squealed in surprise.

With little patience I grabbed her ankle, pulling her to the end, only for her to kick out. She managed a hit on my side, followed by an arm swinging wildly before I yanked her up by her wrists.

"This is the one and only time I'll allow you to refuse an order." My tone was as hard as granite, the earlier anger still burning beneath the surface. "You eat with me, or not at all."

Arabella swallowed, her breathing heavy as she blinked up at me with those fucking doe eyes. They'd widened with initial panic, but now they'd darkened, the gold flecks glistening with defiance and a touch of loathing. She was a fascinating little thing, her emotions filtering across her expression so easily.

The way I held her forced her back to arch awkwardly, her weight held entirely by the way I locked her wrists in one of my hands. I released her without warning, her body falling against the thousand-pound sheets.

She glared at me through her hair, but didn't make another move.

Leaning down, I made sure to hover my body over hers. "Disobey me again, and I'll carry you out here on my shoulder, kicking and screaming. Have I made myself clear?"

A flush darkened the flesh of her throat, sweeping down over the top of her breasts. "Crystal."

Chapter 16
Arabella

I must've been exhausted, because I didn't wake again until Sebastian opened my door the next afternoon. Sunlight streamed inside the large window, washing the room in a warm glow that would've been nice if eyes of ice weren't glaring down at me.

Disobey me again, and I'll carry you out here on my shoulder, kicking and screaming. Have I made myself clear?

I reached beneath the pillow and palmed the knife.

His eyes narrowed on the movement, head cocking to the side. With a few powerful strides he closed his distance, and I pulled out the knife with barely enough time. I nicked him, but not even a second later his hand had encircled my fingers.

But rather than breaking my hold, he straightened my arm and held the blade to his throat.

He showed no fear at death, his eyes clashing with mine. My arm would've shook if he wasn't holding it with an iron grip. If he was dead, my father's debt would cease to exist, and I could go home. Return to...

Okay, I hadn't thought this through.

"You think killing me will fix everything?" He pressed

closer to his skin, and I tried to yank my hand back, my fingers loose on the handle.

"Stop it." I tried to pull away again, a sliver of red dripping down the tattooed thorns wrapping around his skin. He twisted my wrist, my hand spasming open, ready for him to catch the knife. My heart raced, blood rushing in my ears as the adrenaline vanished.

"Never pull a weapon you're not willing to use," he scolded. "Because trust me, *belle*, there are many that would use it against you."

He almost looked down at me with disgust, as if he was disappointed I hadn't taken it further. I'd never wanted to kill anyone before, but the temptation of it had been overwhelming. Because while it would fix some of my problems, it would also create others.

But now that I no longer held the knife I was... horrified. And a little pissed off at his disapproval.

"Do you need me for anything?" I asked, my voice more of a croak.

A muscle twitched in his jaw. "Come to dinner." His sharp gaze didn't lessen as he tossed a bag at the end of the bed. Without another word he left, taking the knife with him.

It took me a few minutes to gather the enthusiasm to get up, leaning over to reach for the bag. Relief was sudden and swift, the familiar clothes, makeup, and new bottle of shampoo enough to make me want to weep like a baby. I didn't, because I'd hit my quota of tears for the remainder of the year. So I'd settle for carefully pulling out every object and placing them in a neat line on my bed.

I grinned at the paperback, thankful I'd be able to finish the story, but my fingers automatically reached for the notebook. Clutching it close, I inhaled sharply.

When I was around thirteen, I was advised by the

school councillor–who was definitely overpaid because her advice was usually terrible–that writing things down would help me deal with my emotions by concentrating on the good things rather than the bad.

She'd given me my first notebook, and I was initially excited to write down all the things I was grateful for, to remind me to keep going when the world looked bleak.

But the bad seemed to outweigh the good, and the feeling quickly passed. Now I used the notebooks to make up dramatic situations and stories, because that was one hundred percent a healthier coping mechanism.

What better way to deal with my emotions than making them so much worse, but fictionally?

Grabbing the shampoo, conditioner and body wash, I jumped into the shower. The hot water caressed my skin, and I would've happily stayed there forever if I didn't know Sebastian was waiting. The thought of him barging in on my shower time dulled my somewhat pleasant mood, so quickly washing my hair, I grabbed a towel and walked back into the bedroom.

He'd only given me three dresses and a pair of jeans. No tops. There wasn't even any underwear, so with a sigh I washed mine in the sink, and had no choice but to go to dinner bare. Luckily the dress I'd chosen reached my thighs and shouldn't be too bad if I sat with my legs crossed.

A knock sounded at the door, and I tensed when Chip came in dressed in his sharp suit. His gaze was pointed, but his lips tipped up in what I guessed was supposed to be a friendly smile.

"Ready?" he asked, waiting expectantly.

At my nod, he guided me down the hallway, past the kitchen where the older woman, his mum, was humming to herself, and to the dining room with a table that could easily sit ten. A golden candelabra sat in the centre, all three candles lit. Sebastian was seated at the head, and Chip came around and pulled out the chair directly beside him.

"Sit," Sebastian demanded, his eyes scanning my dress with a frown.

What was his problem? He, or one of his cronies, were the ones who picked out the bloody thing. Thanking Chip, I sat down on the chair, keeping my gaze on the plate in front of me. It was salmon with couscous, and my stomach growled so violently I was confident not only Sebastian had heard it, but so had the King of England and his entire guard.

"Eat," he ordered.

I automatically tensed at the command but still picked up my fork and proceeded to devour the entire meal because *holy shit*, it was delicious. So I get to sleep all day, use a shower that was made by the gods themselves, and be served meals like this?

Sebastian was definitely the right decision.

"It's time we discussed my expectations of you."

Okay, never mind.

I put down my fork, leaning back in my chair to look at him expectantly.

"It's simple," he continued. "You'll do what I say, when I say it."

I inwardly recoiled. "So you want me as a slave?"

"Isn't that what you offered?" He raised his brow, and I remained silent because I couldn't think of a compelling argument that didn't result in me or my father getting killed.

Dessert was served, and rather than gobble the slice of Victoria sponge cake like a barbarian, I picked at it, stealing glances at him every now and then.

Sebastian was easier to look at when he didn't have his full, frosty attention on me. He wore his black shirt, the collar slightly more open to reveal a ragged scar across his collarbone, right beside the thinnest cut that no longer oozed blood.

An apology touched the tip of my tongue, but I swallowed it down.

His cuffs were pulled up, revealing his forearms covered in a dusting of dark hair and tattooed thorns. They dipped onto his hands, encircling some of his fingers where he wore heavy rings.

The candlelight flickered, bringing out his scars in darkened slashes across his skin. His cheekbones were envious, as was the angle of his jaw. His lips were sensual, the top slightly rougher where the scar had split it, and in this light his beard was a shade darker than his hair, which he'd pulled up into a messy bun.

"You'll be coming with me to the club tonight," he said, his gaze brushing mine before I realised he'd caught me staring. *Shit*, I clearly wasn't as subtle as I'd thought. "There's a fight."

"Does me attending count towards my debt?"

"Do you really believe you have a choice either way?" His eyes dropped once more to my dress, his scowl deepening.

"Would you like me to change?" The pale pink dress had the longest hem, and with the whole no underwear situation, it was the safest option considering I had jeans but no shirt. I was a huge fan of no bras, but I would rather die than go out with my actual breasts on display.

"I'll have someone bring you some more suitable clothes."

Okay, rude.

"You'll also be wearing this." Sebastian gestured behind me, and Chip appeared with a wooden box. He placed it on the table between us. "You're to wear it every time we're in public. No exceptions."

Licking along my bottom lip, I reached across to lift the lid. It was a choker, black, with a red rose pendant in the centre. "A collar? What am I, your dog?" I scoffed before I could stop myself.

"That's exactly what you are." His fingers moved to pick up the choker from the box.

I stilled when he stood, walking around until he was behind me. He brushed my damp hair away from my neck so he could lock the choker into place. It wasn't as heavy as I expected, but it was tight.

Sebastian didn't say anything else, his hand hot as it hovered on the exposed skin of my collarbone. His fingers were rough, calloused as they stroked with a gentleness I didn't expect. His breath suddenly feathered across my neck, and my lips parted to try and take in more oxygen.

"*Tu vas bien te comporter, n'est-ce pas Arabella?*"

It took a moment for me to realise I couldn't understand him, his presence distracting. Overwhelming. "I don't speak French."

He chuckled darkly, the sound tightening the air around us until it crackled. A shiver wound its way down my spine. Part fear, and part...

Nope.

Not happening.

Team reluctance.

"Who's fighting?" I asked, pointedly ignoring the heat left by his touch. It was just a natural physical reaction. Nothing more.

Sebastian didn't answer me, instead pulling out my chair before walking over to the lift. A car was already waiting for us in the underground garage, with Chip as the driver, and before long we arrived outside *The Thorn*.

Sebastian placed his mask on, his shoulders straightening and his body more rigid as he stepped out of the car.

He waited at the door, and after a beat I followed him towards the entrance. The street was already busy, the crowd hushing once they'd spotted Sebastian.

The late afternoon air chilled my skin, and I couldn't control the tremble as I tried wrapping my arms around myself. Sebastian grabbed my hand, pulling me tighter against his side. I would've usually recoiled, but considering he was the size of a door, if not bigger, he was a good block for the wind.

The same bouncer as before lifted the rope, and Sebastian paused at the entrance.

"You let anyone else in you're not supposed to tonight, Miles?" he asked, an acerbic edge to his tone that was sharp enough to cut.

Miles the bouncer dipped his head, a flush appearing along his face. His eyes darted to me, as if I could help get him out of the conversation. I would've laughed if I wasn't attached to a man who seemed to terrify everyone.

Sebastian continued, "You were made aware Detective Graves wasn't allowed in, and yet you were on the door."

"Sneaky fucker got past us," Miles said with a visible wince, his eyes now dipping to me accusingly. What did I do? "Sorry, boss."

Sebastian stiffened a little, his temper swift but quickly cooling. Without another word he pressed his palm against the bottom of my back, escorting me inside.

I'd forgotten how electric the atmosphere was, too nervous the first time I was here to really appreciate the sensual music and tempting darkness that greeted you inside. The dance floor was thriving, bodies moving to the music that was pumped through the strategically placed speakers. Guests were talking, mingling, and I was pretty sure we just walked past someone enjoying some caviar with their champagne.

I spotted Langdon on the far side, a burst of light every now and then as he played with his lighter.

More pressure against my spine, Sebastian's hand forcing me to step faster. He guided me to where two men, clearly twins if I went by their creepily identical images, stood guarding the entrance to a booth tucked away in the corner.

Neither of the guards acknowledged me at all, simply nodding at Sebastian before returning to staring straight forward. They were hard to tell apart with their dark skin, dark eyes, and dark suits.

Before I could take a seat, Sebastian grabbed my wrist and tugged, forcing me onto his lap. "Sit," he ordered.

I awkwardly sat, conscious that my skirt had risen up, and of course Sebastian had chosen to sit at the edge where the table didn't cover us. Luckily not many people were looking our way, too absorbed with their own lives. If people did glance in this direction, their gazes were fleeting as if not wanting to risk being caught.

Sebastian never relaxed beneath me, his body like stone. After a while I found myself soaking the warmth radiating from him, because it wasn't like I had anything else to do.

"Am I to just... sit here?" I asked quietly, not really expecting him to speak considering he hadn't said anything other than the single command.

"Yes."

"Why?" I tried to turn in his lap, but his hands on my thighs stopped me.

I froze, his thumbs rubbing little circles on my skin.

"Because they see you as my pet," he replied, and I bit back a retort. "As my whore."

"You said you're not into reluctance."

His thumbs never stopped moving, but I was achingly

aware of them. "I have enough women throwing themselves at my feet. I don't need to seek sex elsewhere."

"And yet I sit on your lap."

"The word '*no*' doesn't get me hard, but you see everyone watching? They need me to be the monster that goes bump in the night. And I'm happy to perform if need be."

My pulse did the foxtrot at the silent threat, my stomach cramping as if I'd swallowed ice.

Sebastian leaned forward, his voice dropping beneath his mask. "But what does get me fucking excited is your submission. So continue to fight me, *ma belle petite lapine*. Keep telling me no, because it'll be that much sweeter when I finally have you begging for my cock."

It took me a moment to understand the words, distracted by how his accent deepened when he spoke in French, more throaty. Only then did the skin of my cheeks prickle, followed by a strange warmth spreading through that ice that I pointedly ignored.

"And trust me, you will. I can already imagine the way your cunt will drip for me," he whispered against my heated skin. "Taking every inch of my cock like the good girl you are."

"Never." The word was barely audible above the pounding of my heart.

His thumb stoked higher, and I could almost hear the smirk that curled his lips as he spoke next. "I can't wait to fuck this defiance out of you."

Chapter 17
Sebastian

Arabella sat so obediently on my lap, my cock twitching at her compliance. I expected a little push back, but other than a slight darkening of her eyes and venom on her tongue, she did exactly what she was told.

I continued to stroke her soft thighs, hyper focused on how her breathing picked up, and her pulse raced on the side of her throat. But then her breasts pushed at the bodice of her dress, obscenely displayed for my eyes.

I should've made her change, because now she was pure seduction. A distraction. The fabric was tight, a pale pink that flared out at her hips and stopped mid-thigh. Usually, I only touched women with the intent of sex, and they were definitely not allowed to touch me in return. But with Arabella I wanted to touch, to see whether she'd grip my wrist with the intention of stopping me, or not. Not that she *could* stop me.

Most women flinched beneath my attention, reacting to my scars and cruelty. Those that didn't, I had no interest in. They chased thinking they could tame the great Beast, and then cried when they were bitten.

Arabella hadn't flinched, but she hadn't exactly chased me, either.

I moved my hands higher on her thighs, and again I was pushing, seeing whether I could get that fire I saw the first night. She believed she was so unaffected by me, but I could feel how her body responded. The way her pulse quickened and her legs trembled even as she fought it.

She may not like me, but her body clearly didn't care.

She believed she was working off her debt, but she was mine until I grew bored. Until then, I had no intention of letting her go.

As she wriggled in my lap, I bit back a curse as my cock twitched. If she could feel me hardening beneath her, she didn't react. Seemingly distracted with being put on display. It wasn't something she seemed to enjoy, and the feeling was mutual.

I rarely used my personal booth, preferring the comfort of my office where I could watch everything from afar. I could feel eyes glancing our way, but not lingering even as fear danced with excitement at my presence.

No, I was a rare sight. And that was what I preferred, to be the devil hiding amongst the shadows. My name may be known, but my face wasn't as common, even as distinctive as it was. Not unless you were a regular at my fights, but then again only a certain type of person attended those. People that were already familiar with how the underworld operated.

But tonight, I'd decided to come early, to sit and watch the rich and influential lose their inhibitions under the veil of privacy.

There were two rules once you'd stepped inside my club, the first being there were no recording devices. That included phones, cameras, or anything else that could record picture or sound. The second was what happened in *The Thorn* stayed in *The Thorn*.

Break a rule once, and you were permanently expelled. No exceptions.

So people danced, spilled secrets, and cheated believing no one was watching, when in reality there were cameras across every inch. Ready to be used against anyone who dared deceive me.

"Boss?"

Arabella stiffened in my lap, my thumbs having moved even further up to the point her skirt was almost revealing too much. I slipped my hands out from beneath the fabric before turning towards Micah.

"Caden has asked for your assistance." He dipped his head, immediately returning to his position by the ropes.

Reluctantly I helped Arabella off, only to lean down to whisper against her ear. "Behave."

She looked over her shoulder at me, eyes glittering with that spark, ready to ignite. I find I wanted it to burn, just so I could put her back in her place.

"Be a good girl," I whispered closer, her eyes dilating at my words. "If you try to run, I'll take the payment in your father's skin, and then I'll take joy in putting you over my knee."

She blinked, that earlier flush sweeping back across her cheekbones and down her throat. "Yes, Sir," she whispered, and I noted the sarcasm in the reply.

For some reason it sent a thrill through me. Which was strange, because I fucking hated brats. Leaving her by the booth, I crossed the carpet in powerful strides. The dancers parted, as if I was surrounded by an invisible force.

I took the private lift down a floor, the scent of puke and piss evident as soon as the doors slipped open. I came to the interrogation room, finding one man sprawled on the table, vomit smeared across his face and his eyes dulled in death. Another man sat on the floor, tears streaming down his cheeks.

"Another OD," Caden muttered, shaking his head. Tossing a packet over, I caught it.

"Please... please..." the man sobbed. "I don't know... I don't know."

I ignored him for the moment, frowning down at the emblem that represented everything I'd worked for. The rose strangled by thorns was correct, but the colour of the product was off.

Opening the pack, I dipped the tip of my finger before rubbing it across my gums. There was no numbing, just a slight tingling. Immediately I spat, getting rid of any powder.

"That shit's not ours," Caden growled, an edge to his words.

No, the product definitely wasn't ours, which meant someone was either using my name to shift their own shit, or someone had been tampering with the supply.

The man on the floor continued to sob, his eyes unfocused. It took me a moment, but I finally recognised him. The mayor's youngest son, Jonathan Smithers. A nepo child that barely looked old enough to wipe his own arse, but he must be at least twenty-one to get past the doormen.

He hadn't even realised I was there, lost in his bawling.

Caden sighed, his favourite sledgehammer scraping against the concrete when he dragged it over. The man flinched, looking up.

"I don't know," he simply repeated.

"Well, I need you to remember where you bought it from," Caden said, his voice much calmer than his expression, which looked like he was seconds away from beating the kid so hard brain splattered across the walls.

"Is Chris okay?" Jonathan asked instead.

Caden stood over, forcing Jonathan to crane his neck back. "No, Jonathan. He's not fucking okay. He's clearly dead, you muppet."

"Dead?" Jonathan squeaked. "But he was okay a minute ago."

"That was before he snorted his weight in poor grade cocaine, wasn't it? Now, who's your dealer?" Caden demanded.

What Jonathan clearly wasn't picking up on was that Caden took the product personally, as he should, considering he was an integral part behind the design. He had a weird hard-on for the science side and declared he'd been the one to perfect the product quality.

My chemist, T, disagreed, but I didn't get involved in their bickering so long as they refrained from killing one another.

"Please, I don't... I don't remember."

Patience wasn't exactly one of my virtues, so taking a step forward I crouched closer to his height. His eyes widened when he realised I was there, his sob turning into a full-on wail.

My hand snaked out, holding his jaw. "Now, we're going to start this again," I said, letting my voice deepen into a growl. "Who bought the coke?"

Jonathan's eyes flicked up to Caden, and I held back a laugh if he believed Caden would save him. My fingers tightened until he returned his attention to me, which got me a wince in return.

"I... I did," he answered.

"Good. So who was your dealer?" My hand itched to close, to break his jaw. But the fallout wasn't worth it. The London Mayor was in my pocket just as much as any other politician, but I wasn't stupid enough to take out his youngest without cause.

Suppressing my slightly more feral side, I released him.

"I don't know his name," he stammered. "He goes by Eight."

Now that I was closer, I could see the Rolex he wore on his wrist and the diamond-encrusted necklace he had tucked inside his shirt. Pompous prick born into money, with hands so soft they'd likely never see a hard day's work.

"Eight? Like the number?" Caden frowned. "How can we get hold of him?"

Jonathan seemed to calm once he'd realised we weren't going to hurt him. Probably.

"I have his contact details," he said, his voice not so pathetic this time. Arm shaking, he pulled out his phone from his pocket, holding it out to me. I immediately looked down at the screen, unable to decipher the words before Caden took it. "He's not my usual guy, but he was the one that turned up."

That got my attention, and glancing over to Caden I realised he'd raised his brow at that little bit of information too. I turned back to Jonathan, who baulked at the expression on my face.

"What can you tell me about this Eight?"

Chapter 18
Arabella

Now that people had realised Sebastian was gone, it seemed fair game to stare. People openly looked, their curiosity almost hostile as I tried not to recoil, instead meeting the gazes head on. I recognised a few politicians, socialites, and even an actor that had been in the highest grossing movie this year.

I didn't know what I expected when I agreed to take my father's place, but a toy for Sebastian to display wasn't it. Especially amongst the designer clothes, diamond jewels, and I was pretty confident a guy over by the bar was wearing a watch that cost more than my entire year's wage. I was very much in a different tax bracket.

"Where do you think you're going?" one of the twins asked when I went to lift the rope, and I froze.

Sebastian never explicitly said I had to stay by the booth. "I'll be back in a minute."

Both men nodded in unison, their eyes laser focused on me. Stepping out, I pushed through the dancers to wander over to the bar.

"What can I get you?" the bartender asked, arching a dark brow with two silver rings through it.

My lips snapped open to reply, but then I realised I didn't have any money. And drinking away my sorrows when I didn't usually drink alcohol probably wasn't a good decision. But then again, I did agree to be Sebastian's toy, so I wasn't exactly someone who made good decisions in the first place.

"Is there a phone I could borrow?"

Her eyes slipped over my shoulder, and I stiffened when I turned, realising not one, but both of the twins were hovering behind me. They were far enough away not to hear my words, but close enough that their eyes bored into my back.

The bartender jerked her head, inviting me around the side. "You can use the staff room back here," she said loudly, her smile aimed over my shoulder.

She held the door open to the staff room, which was a spacious area with a large table, several chairs as well as a large sofa, TV, and lockers. A private bathroom was to the left, beside an emergency exit.

"My mobile's in the first locker," the bartender said, her fingers reaching up to scratch at her scalp.

"Thank you." Waiting until I was alone, I opened the locker to find the phone.

It didn't have a code, so I immediately swiped it open, only to pause. I had no one to call. Not really. Dad was likely gone, packing his stuff up and running away like we did so many times before. Every time he'd caught himself in trouble, he'd force us to leave everything behind.

New number. New address.

Which meant even after all this, after I finally managed to pay Sebastian back, I wouldn't know where to find him. I didn't have friends, not unless I counted the nice old lady I chatted with every week at the coffee shop on the corner. And I could no longer call Suzy at work.

Taking a seat on the sofa I stared at the phone, long enough it timed out, the screen going dark. It had only just hit me how truly alone I was.

That if I disappeared, no one would miss me. Not even my father.

Fucking hell. I was a twenty-five-year-old woman with the social skills of a rabid hamster. I wanted to laugh at the shitshow that was me, but that probably wasn't healthy, so I suppressed it until I could write it down in my notebook later.

To be fair to myself, I always struggled to make friends growing up. I was always called a little odd, and I was bullied for keeping to myself, preferring to read rather than play with others.

It was safer, that detachment. It was difficult as a kid to make friends and then disappear, never to see them again.

Luckily, I much preferred fictional people to real life, so I hadn't dwelled on the fact I was a social outcast until now, when I wanted nothing more than to just... talk to someone.

I dialled Dad's number from memory anyway, my chest aching as the ringing droned on before the click of his voice-mail. "Hi Dad, it's me... I just... I wanted to see whether you were safe." There was a beat of silence, and I didn't know what to say. The disappointment of him not answering was crushing, even though I expected it. "Please take care of yourself."

Putting the phone back, I re-entered behind the bar, moving around to take a stool. The twins stood closer, clearly not pleased with me disappearing into the back. Honestly, I was surprised they hadn't followed.

"Did you do what you needed to?" the bartender asked, serving one of the patrons a glass of wine.

No, because I'm a loser with no friends. But of course I

couldn't admit that out loud, so instead I simply nodded. "Thank you," I said quietly.

"Don't thank me yet," she said, dropping her voice as her eyes dipped to my choker. "If anyone asks, I'll deny it."

My hand automatically went to the rose around my throat, the metal hard beneath my fingertips.

"People will be jealous of that," she added. "Many of the girls have wanted to tame the big bad Beast. Even some of the men. But he's never been caught with anyone. So watch your back."

"That's enough, Mia." Twin number one came to stand on my left, close enough that his suit was pressed against my arm.

"I don't know what you're talking about, Micah," she lied, keeping her face perfectly composed.

"Hmm." Micah looked down at me with a touch of impatience, while his brother seemed bored. "You need to return to the booth."

I slipped from the stool. "Thank you, again," I told Mia. "I appreciate it."

"See you around." She winked before sticking her middle finger up at the twins. Micah sniggered, but the one on my left only gestured for me to step before him.

The stares hadn't died down, especially considering I had two men escorting me back to my seat. Luckily, I could scoot around to the far side, essentially hiding myself in the shadowed corner while the twins took their positions at each side of the ropes.

Maybe I could get them to stand in front of me? Become human buffers?

"Sir." The twins nodded, parting once more to let Langdon through.

Reaching into his pocket, he pulled out his phone,

typing something before turning it to face me. **Come with me.**

I handed it back as I stood, the twins' stares cutting as Langdon escorted me to the corridors where I'd first found him. "Are they staying behind?" I asked when I realised I no longer had two large shadows.

Langdon pursed his lips then nodded, his strides longer which forced me to hurry up. Passing the lift, we reached a set of black, ominous double doors that opened as we approached.

Bloody hell.

Sebastian had a fighting ring attached to his nightclub.

The space was smaller, the edges holding the same elegant design as the club, with its personal tables and high chandeliers. But in the centre was a lip where concrete met the carpet, and a ring seemingly erupting from the surface in a grand stage surrounded by lights.

Half the crowd was cheering, screaming at the fighters who currently circled one another, while the other half were drinking and chatting, seeming genuinely unbothered by the show of violence.

Two men fought bare knuckled inside the ring, their faces so swollen and covered in blood I doubted their own mothers would recognise them.

Following Langdon, he escorted me across the floor towards the front row of chairs on the right side of the ring. Coming to a stop, he glared down at the man who sat on the one at the end.

"Fuck off, mate," the man grunted.

Langdon smiled, leaning down. Seconds later, the man went white as a ghost before scrambling to his feet.

"All yours!" he hurried to say.

Langdon tracked the man with his gaze as he disappeared into the crowd before looking over his shoulder at me. His jacket rustled, as if he was putting something back inside, and I glanced a sheen of black metal.

"Was that really necessary?" I asked, taking the seat when he gestured to it. "I could have stood in the corner."

His upper lip curved into a smirk. **Stay here.** He typed out on his phone. **You'll be retrieved when he's done.**

Without waiting for me to reply, he turned on his heel, and I was left sitting on my own while the surrounding crowd whispered and pointed. *Great.*

Even the guy next to me was intentionally giving me his back.

At least the current fight had finished, both the men seeking treatment from a medical team just off to the side. I actually had a good view of the ring, unobstructed. I'd be more impressed if I cared about watching any act of gratuitous violence. The idea that people enjoyed watching people fight was honestly barbaric.

Which was a shame because a new man just slipped beneath the ropes. He grinned to the crowd, waving and winking as he waltzed along the canvas. He must have been at least six three, maybe even four, with arms and legs the size of tree trunks.

Most people cheered, some even chanting, *'Reaper.'*

The name didn't suit him; he was far too cheery. But then a hush came over the crowd, and my eyes immediately were drawn to the side. Sebastian wore nothing but black shorts, not even his mask as he calmly walked towards the centre, Caden at his side.

"In the right corner, with fifteen undefeated fights, we have the Grim Reaper!" The announcer waited a beat for the cheers to quieten before continuing. "In the left, our gracious host, and three times Styx heavyweight champion, Beast!"

If I thought the crowd was loud before, they were feral now.

"Beast!"

"Beast!"

"Beast!"

The Grim Reaper's smile vanished, his eyes narrowing on Sebastian as he slipped himself between the ropes. I sat, anxious as the two men waited. Caden stayed on the floor by the corner, Langdon joining him.

I could hear the shout of bets, of money being exchanged and arguments of who was going to win, but I couldn't seem to take my eyes off Sebastian. His demeanour was cool, expression almost bored compared to Reaper's enthusiasm.

After the initial shock of seeing Sebastian half naked, I noticed his chest seemed carved from granite, with a dusting of dark hair that arrowed down his stomach. The thorns that I'd glimpsed on his hands and throat wrapped around his entire torso, entwined with a few black and grey roses on his ribs.

He turned to speak quietly to Caden, and I realised he had even more ink. '*Vincit qui se vincit*' was written across his shoulders in beautiful calligraphy, but his scars were thicker, more prominent along his back.

Rather than hide them, Sebastian seemed to embrace them. The tattoo artist incorporated the scars beautifully into the design

And then the lights dimmed, and the fight begun.

There was no warning before Reaper launched himself forward with a roar, only for Sebastian to duck flawlessly to the side, forcing Reaper to crash into the ropes and twist with a snarl. It was like a choreographed dance, with Sebastian simply stepping away while Reaper tried and failed to land a hit.

Each of his movements were becoming more erratic, and then Sebastian hit back.

The sound of flesh hitting flesh was distinctive, the resulting grunts and then cheers of the crowd a cacophony of noise that I could barely hear over the blood rushing through my head.

Sebastian dominated the ring, powerful and self-assured. His moves were aggressive, each punch landing with a crack that had the crowd going wild. He barely made a sound when Reaper finally landed a hit to his face, seeming to roll with it rather than defend. Almost toying with his opponent, who was already becoming weaker on his feet.

Sebastian was a force to be reckoned with, his lips curving into a feral smile as another one of his giant fists hit Reaper with an audible crunch, and as soon as he looked over and met my gaze, I stood and ran.

Chapter 19
Arabella

I couldn't breathe. Shoving through the crowd, I was crushed as I struggled to pass through. Their roars and cheers, it was all too much.

An elbow jabbed into my side, followed by a cutting glare before I managed to break through and run toward the black doors. They opened without assistance, but then I found the noise of the nightclub was worse, the music vibrating through my legs as I gasped.

My lungs felt like they were made of cement, my hands shaking when I made them into fists.

I needed air, space to breathe.

My feet were moving, and I crossed the floor without even thinking. Mia looked up from serving her customer, her frown concerning.

"Hey, are you..."

Her voice was lost as I shoved myself into the staff room, and then through the emergency exit and out into the open night. I gasped, the wind whipping across my skin, anchoring me to reality.

My chest was still tight, but I could breathe now that everything was quiet, and heat didn't prickle my skin.

Clawing at my throat, I tugged at the choker. But it wouldn't come off. I couldn't even feel the fastening.

"There she is," a familiar voice called out, and I immediately straightened to find Lennon standing a few feet away, flanked by two other men I didn't recognise. "I'd never in a million years think you'd whore yourself out, *Bella*."

"Lennon?" My voice came out scratchy.

"So you turn down Gabriel but shag Sebastian fucking Devereaux?" He closed the distance faster than I could react, his hand snapping out to grab my wrist. He was only a few inches taller than me, but his grip was like iron.

"What are you doing here?" I asked, failing to pull away.

Lennon smirked, watching me with unblinking clarity. "I'm here to give you Gabriel's offer." There was a predatory gleam in his eyes, one that always twisted my stomach.

Gabriel could be cruel, but Lennon was always a step further. He didn't seem to just enjoy the misfortune of others; he revelled in it. I always thought he became a police officer not for the justice, but for the domination. It was as if the law gave him permission to be spiteful.

Yanking me harshly, he pulled me against his chest. The other two men moved closer, circling like wolves waiting for the kill.

"Don't," I warned, only for Lennon to smirk.

"Don't what?" Pulling out a blade, he pressed it beneath my choker. It snapped, falling to the ground before he pressed the flat of the knife against my cheek. "Now, Gabe's ready to forgive you, but only if you beg. He'll settle your father's debt with the Beast, and then you'll crawl back to him like the pathetic whore you are."

"And you needed two babysitters to help deliver that message?" I hissed. "How can Gabriel find that sort of money?"

Lennon's eyes darkened, the knife pressing firmer against my skin. "Careful, I wouldn't want to cut up this face before I take you back. I never really understood the appeal, if I'm honest." His voice dropped to a mocking whisper. "You must really have a magic pussy, because I've always said you were nothing but a charity case with daddy issues."

"Fuck you," I sneered at him, only for him to grip me tighter.

"Is that what you're doing with Sebastian? Spreading your legs for money?"

Hands on my dress lifted the fabric until a breeze was against my skin. One of the men pawed at me with a groan. "Fucking bitch isn't even wearing underwear."

"Get off me!" I snarled over my shoulder before Lennon turned the knife and threatened to cut. I stilled, those hands pressing into my thighs and wanting me to spread my legs.

Lennon sneered, "Stop fighting. We both know how you like it rough. Gabe's even invited me to join..."

I threw my head back, jerking my entire weight to the side at the same time. The press of the blade was instant, but I managed to punch the guy on the left, blood erupting beneath my fist. He howled in pain, my elbow hitting the other in his stomach before Lennon managed to kick me to the floor. My palms and knees scraped against stone, the sting quick before I was pulled back to my feet by my hair.

Lennon snarled, rage tightening his expression. "You really shouldn't have fucking done that."

Reaper fought with an arrogance that made him sloppy. His footwork was slacking, and he preferred to entertain the crowd rather than concentrate his attention on me. Either he'd won his titles through pure luck, or he truly believed he was a superior fighter.

I didn't even bother blocking his hits after a while, wanting the pain and the resulting afterburn.

My punch landed with a crack on Reaper's jaw, so hard his head snapped to the side. Blood splattered from his parted lips, his eyes glazing for a moment before he regained his composure and snarled. I didn't dodge his jab, which barely grazed my cheek, but the move left him open for my fist to land straight on his ribs.

With a puff of air, Reaper sucked in a rattled breath. But he stayed standing. Even after another right hook, his legs kept him upright.

I craved the blood that smeared across both our bodies. It was so fucking satisfying, the ache of my knuckles and the fresh bruise on my chest. It fed my monster, calming the restless buzz that was a constant beneath my skin.

I circled, my eyes immediately drawn to the crowd until they landed on Arabella. Even through the glare of the lights I found her, and I watched as she ran at what she saw on my face.

A hit landed on my jaw, my teeth knocking together from the impact. I returned my attention to Reaper as I spat blood. He should've made that move ten minutes ago, creating a more interesting fight for me. But now I was bored, especially compared to the idea of chasing my new pretty toy.

I was going to find her while adrenaline still pulsed

through my veins, and then make her fucking beg for defying an order yet again.

My cock twitched at the thought.

I didn't hold back my next hit, my right hook landing with such force that Reaper collapsed. Not bothering to check whether he stayed down, I jumped over the ropes to land in a slight crouch. The crowd scrambled to get out of my way, climbing over one another as I stormed towards the black doors that separated the clubs.

Caden appeared at my side, but I ignored him as I stalked forward. The door almost crumbled beneath my shove, and it wasn't long before I was scanning every fucking person for familiar brunette hair.

Mia caught my eye, her chin gesturing towards the staff room with a slight guilty expression. She'd be dealt with later.

The back door was open, and stepping outside I froze as the wind whipped at my sweat-coated skin. Her voice called out, the cadence panicked, but also full of resilience as I turned the corner of the alley, and found her struggling with not one, but three men.

Blood seeped down her cheek, her skirt lifted to show off far too much skin while the man in front pressed a forearm against her throat. Her teeth were gritted, the men straining to keep her pressed against the wall as she fought.

I didn't think, simply reacting to the rage that burned through me at the scene.

How dare they touch what was fucking mine.

Arabella's eyes landed on me over his shoulder, her gasp a siren's call as I reached the man on her left—the one with his fingers on her thighs—and promptly smashed his skull against the brick beside her.

His head split from the impact, and if he wasn't dead

already, I made sure to slam my foot down on his throat just to be sure.

Arabella screamed, recoiling while also trying to fight against the other hands holding her down. A blade swiped across my chest, my bare skin unable to resist the sharp edge.

I sucked in a hiss, ignoring the burn as I reached the second man. Another blade, this time slicing across my arm. They weren't deep, more like panicked swipes rather than lunges. I grabbed the second guy by the throat, his neck breaking so easily beneath my strength. The crack echoed around us, as did the sound of his body dropping like deadweight at my feet.

The last man faced me with the knife, the end tipped red. He wasn't much bigger than Arabella, his arm shaking as he faced me.

Fucking pathetic.

He was the one who had his forearm pressed against her, and my rage darkened into something worse. It was like a haze, my instincts calling for me not only to kill but to maim. Destroy. The other two had died far too quickly to sate my cruelty, which had left me unsatisfied.

Another swipe of the knife, and rather than backing away I stepped into it, allowing my skin to split. For the sharp pain to register before embracing the heat of my blood against my cool skin. The man gasped, and I smirked, allowing my expression to take a more feral edge. His arm continued to shake, and as swift as a viper I snapped his wrist, catching the knife as it fell.

He screeched, cradling his arm to his chest while his wails echoed around us. I could easily finish this, but I wanted to drag it out a little longer. For him to fucking suffer.

"Stop!" A soft voice caused me to pause.

I looked over at Arabella, my breathing coming in pants.

"Please don't," she whispered, her fingers nervously tugging at the hem of her ruined dress.

"You care so much about him?" I asked, my tone so dark she flinched.

The man whimpered, and before he could run, I grabbed him, sinking his own blade straight into the centre of his chest. I didn't take my eyes off Arabella, her face so open with her expressions that I drowned in her emotions, the fear, shock, and then the horror at what I'd done.

I pulled at the knife, blood raining across us both in a splash of red. I wanted to paint with it, smear my canvas with the colour.

Dropping the body, I stepped over him and closed the distance between us.

She never looked away, which made that twisted fascination inside me burn hotter. As if she was unknowingly fanning the flames to my new fucking obsession.

Where others would've cowered, she watched me as if I was a wild animal. It was what fascinated me in the first place, when I had her father on his knees begging for his life. She was terrified, but she refused to look away. Refused to submit.

She was either stupid, or she didn't think much of her own mortality.

"Take care of this," I said, and it took her a moment to realise I'd spoken to Caden, who'd followed on my heel and waited on the side while I'd dealt with the situation.

Her eyes darted to my cousin until I reached up and gripped her chin, forcing her attention back to me. She shook, her face pale, made paler by the blood that dripped like an invitation down her cheek. Reaching out, I brushed it away with my thumb. She flinched but didn't attempt to break my grip.

"You really shouldn't have run from me, *belle*."

Chapter 20
Arabella

"I didn't run," I whispered, the cold causing shivers to erupt over my exposed skin now that my adrenaline had waned. Sebastian stood there shirtless, blood seeping from his wounds. He showed no signs of goosebumps or discomfort, as if the cold meant nothing.

His head tilted to the side, dark hair escaping from the band to frame his face. A bruise was already darkening on his cheek, and there was a small cut on his forehead. There was no expression on his face, but his eyes showed barely contained rage. He vibrated with it, but there was also something else there. Like he got excited by the anger and pain.

Taking the bloodied knife he'd just used to kill someone, he dragged it over the centre of my dress, the edge threatening to cut the fabric. My lips parted, and my pulse danced against my skin.

"I didn't run," I whispered once again. "I just needed some air."

I wasn't sure if he believed me, and I prepared myself for pain, or maybe even death. He'd warned me, and before I thought I'd just accept it without a fight. But now I wasn't so sure, tightening my fists in preparation to defend myself with everything I had.

Sebastian looked down, and I was pretty sure amusement lightened his eyes, as well as a touch of sadism. Dropping the knife, he stepped closer, until my breasts pressed against his bare chest.

With his free hand he touched my cheek again, and this time I didn't flinch. I hissed as he touched the scratch, but I knew that was all it was. A scratch.

"Get in the car," he demanded, his voice dangerously low.

I nodded, glancing over at Caden who was talking into his phone. He glared at me when he realised, and I quickly dragged my eyes forward until I came to the car waiting by the curb.

Sebastian was a heavy presence at my back, the tension between us stretching in the silence until it was pulled so taut it wrapped around me like a noose. He remained silent the entire drive, his body coiled so tightly beside mine. He still hadn't said another word even when we ascended the lift to his penthouse, or when he guided me down the side corridor I had yet to explore. I panicked slightly at the sight of the large bed, but he didn't pause, guiding me into the connecting bathroom.

If I thought my bathroom was big, this one was ridiculous. A large double shower was in the corner, and the bath was big enough to fit several people. Or maybe just someone as big as him.

Still no words were spoken as he pulled at the hem of my dress, and unable to control my shaking, I let him. I wore nothing beneath, the cool air pebbling my nipples.

He didn't even look at me, instead reaching over to turn on the shower until steam billowed. Moving almost mechanically, he removed his shorts, and I couldn't help but look down. Only to immediately jerk my eyes up to his chest as he stepped us back, closing the shower door around us.

Fucking hell.

He was clearly well proportioned, and if that wasn't an inappropriate thought right now, I didn't know what was. A blush prickled my cheeks, and I dipped my head in hopes he hadn't noticed.

I didn't need him thinking I was checking out his dick while we were both naked in the shower. After I'd just been attacked and he'd just been sliced with a knife.

What the fuck was wrong with me? Because no way should I still be thinking about his dick, or my own body's reaction to it, while fear still coated my tongue. Worse was the way heat curled low in my stomach, seemingly awakened by the danger.

It was wrong. Completely messed up.

There was me, trying to ignore the sudden throbbing between my legs while Sebastian was clearly having a moment. His breathing was heavy, uneven.

His muscles were rigid as he placed both his palms on the tiles on either side of my head. It was as if he was trying to steady himself, to drag his emotions back under control. A perfectly reasonable response, given the circumstances.

Unlike me who, despite everything, couldn't stop wondering what it would feel like if he directed all that anger into something else.

Fuck. Me. Sideways.

Was I having a trauma response? Or was I just unwell?

Hesitantly, I reached up, only for his hands to encircle my wrists so fast I gave an undignified squeak. There was a beat, a moment where he tightened his fingers, and my bones strained beneath the pressure. But then he released me.

His eyes darkened, and I knew not to try and touch him again.

Confident I understood, his muscles seemed to finally relax, the hot water hitting his back until the pool at our feet was no longer a rusty red.

He pulled me beneath the stream, and my shivers immediately stopped. I tipped my head back, letting the warm water wash everything away. Sebastian pulled the band from my hair until the strands fell heavily against my shoulders.

Unable to look at him, I closed my eyes, which was arguably worse, because now I could only concentrate on the way he touched me. On his fingers in my hair, stroking, brushing as he washed.

There was a scratch against my skin, and my eyes flew open to find him washing me with a cloth. His fingers kept going back to my cheek, and then to my ribs just beneath my left breast where I was sure there would be a bruise. One of the men had hit me, but I didn't remember who.

It didn't matter now, considering they were all dead.

"I'm sorry," I said, not even sure what I was apologising for.

His dark blue eyes met mine, but he still didn't say anything.

The silence kept stretching, vibrating with an unacknowledged awareness. My body was still too warm, my thighs pressing together in a subtle, futile attempt to ease some of the pressure building there. A slow, pulsing ache that had no right and made no sense given the circumstance.

Why the hell was I turned on?

I was confused, frustrated with my body because this definitely wasn't the right time. It would never be the right time. And yet, my body didn't seem to care. It responded like it had a mind of its own, completely at odds with the tension tightening in my chest.

"I didn't... I didn't know they were—"

"Give me your hands." Sebastian reached for my arm.

I was weirdly relieved to hear his voice, because then maybe he wasn't as furious as he was earlier. Holding up my hands, I tensed when he carefully cleaned the grazes with the cloth. I tried to hold back my grimace, the pain stinging.

Sebastian nodded to himself, then finished washing us both before he turned the shower off and reached for a towel. He dried me first, far gentler than I expected of him before he dried himself. His cuts looked worse, still seeping as he left me standing in his bathroom while he returned to his room.

Wiping across the condensation on the mirror, I checked my face and the small scratch that would likely be gone within the week. My body was a little bruised, but otherwise okay. I didn't actually think Lennon would've done anything, his friends there as nothing more than a threat.

Gabriel's ready to forgive you, but only if you beg.

Gabriel could go fuck himself.

Sebastian appeared in the reflection behind me wearing a pair of grey jogging bottoms and nothing else. Before I could react he handed me a T-shirt. I put it on, realising from its size that it must be his. It was long enough to reach my knees, the fabric smelling faintly like him.

Sebastian stalked back out of the bathroom, and I followed, finding he'd lit the fire at the foot of his bed, a great leather armchair facing it. A table had been set up beside him, as well as two cups of steaming tea. Did that mean I was supposed to stay?

The smiley older lady must have been in, because her silver tray was there, as was a medical kit. Sebastian had already taken a seat in the great armchair, using an antiseptic wipe to dab at the largest slice across his chest.

I hesitantly approached, but he didn't even look up.

"Let me." I slowly reached for the wipe, but he pulled it away with a slight grumble. He didn't seem to like touch, not unless he initiated it. "Please, let me help."

His eyes narrowed, but he finally relented when I dropped to my knees beside him. But then he watched me like a hawk, his body like granite as if he was forcing himself to remain still. I gently cleaned the slice, careful not to touch anywhere else.

"Thank you," I whispered against the crackling of the flames. "You know, for helping me."

"You shouldn't have run." Sebastian's voice was deeper, his anger still evident.

"I don't like violence." The way he'd found me in the crowd had caught me off guard, and I'd panicked. "But I wasn't running away."

Sebastian still hasn't relaxed, his fingers curling onto the armchair so hard I wouldn't be surprised if he left indents. His muscles tensed, causing one of the other cuts to bleed.

"You should call a doctor," I murmured.

"No."

"Are you telling me the great Sebastian Devereaux doesn't have a doctor on retainer?" I clicked my tongue, looking up to find him unamused.

No sense of humour. Noted.

"The cuts aren't deep enough to need stitches, and another scar isn't going to make much of a difference." He delivered the statement with such a lack of emotion, I froze.

He continued to stare down at me, his lashes low, but his expression was now calm.

Shaking my head, I returned to cleaning his skin. There were a few fresh bruises darkening his ribs, so I was careful not to add any pressure when I placed a bandage on the longest slice and taped it in place.

"Why do you fight?" I asked, covering the second cut lower across his abs.

He didn't answer. Not that I expected him to.

Doing the same to the cut on his arm, I sat back on my heels, tossing the bloody wipes onto the table before I stood. There was a slight tension in his jaw when he pulled me forward, forcing me to straddle his thighs. Luckily the armchair was big enough that I could push both my knees into the cushion beside his hips.

The T-shirt rode up, and I was suddenly conscious I wore nothing beneath the fabric. Sebastian's hands came down on my hips when I went to scramble off, his fingers pressing into my bare skin.

"You asked me to stop." He said it like it was a question.

"I did," I replied carefully. "I didn't want you to kill him."

There wasn't even a pause before he continued. "Why? Because you cared for him?"

I wanted to laugh, but that would look like I was losing it—I was—but I couldn't show weakness while in the enemy's lap. "I hate him, but that doesn't mean I wanted him dead." I didn't think so, anyway.

"Who was he?" he growled, the sound straining the air between us. His hand came up to collar the back of my neck, thumb reaching around to stroke along the bottom of my jaw.

"Lennon. Gabriel sent him to offer me a deal."

Sebastian stilled beneath me, his palm rigid against my skin. "What was the deal?"

"Does it matter? I refused, and Lennon got angry. Now he's dead."

Sebastian's fingers tightened enough to bruise. "What was the deal, Arabella?"

My voice was quiet when I answered. "For me to go back to him."

Sebastian's nostrils flared, and a muscle ticked in his jaw. "Is that what you want?"

"No."

His attention was like a weight along my skin, overwhelming to the point of intimidation. Internally I was terrified, but externally I tried to keep myself as calm so as not to agitate him any further.

"Have you decided if you're going to kill me?" I asked before I'd even realised the question had passed my lips, because fuck me, I didn't actually want to know the answer.

Sebastian leaned forward, and I carefully moved my hands away so I didn't accidentally touch him. "Keep testing me and find out."

Chapter 21
Arabella

I couldn't sleep. The sheets kept getting tangled around my legs, and while the bed was arguably better than the floor, I couldn't relax. Not with Gabriel's offer keeping me awake.

My notebook remained open on the bedside table. Fictionally creating a villain and naming him after my ex should've been therapeutic, especially once I'd planned his suspicious and somewhat dramatic disappearance. But it hadn't helped calm the maelstrom of emotions festering inside me.

Despair and panic. Anger and guilt.

I couldn't get Lennon out of my head, the way he'd gurgled, blood splattering from his lips before he'd collapsed. The crack of his head hitting the ground, and then the stillness of his body. He hadn't breathed. Hadn't moved. Completely motionless while Sebastian stood vibrating with barely contained rage.

I was at the mercy of a man who killed three armed men with an ease that was horrifying. And I hadn't done a single thing to stop him.

Throwing the sheets off, I silently padded to the door, finding it unlocked. I couldn't sleep, and I couldn't spend another minute staring at the ceiling. Artificial light streamed through the living room windows, London very much awake amongst the street below.

The kitchen to the side was silent, and there was no movement up on the mezzanine above. It seemed only I was up.

Keep testing me and find out.

Sebastian's warning was just another cinch in the rope around my lungs, simply emphasising my lack of control and the cage I'd put myself in. And yet deep down there was this relief that left me feeling weightless. That I no longer had to barely survive and worry about what Dad would do next to put us in danger.

It wasn't lost on me the dichotomy that I was both relieved and absolutely fucking terrified.

A groan broke through my trance, and I suddenly realised I was standing outside Sebastian's bedroom.

Bloody hell.

There was a whispered curse, and I froze, worried that I'd been caught wandering around when I was supposed to be in my room. But I was alone in the hallway, the sound coming from the gap in Sebastian's door.

Moving closer I peeked inside, finding him still in his armchair that I'd left over an hour ago, his head tipped back as he stretched his legs forward. His eyes were closed, the thick column of this throat moving as he let out another guttural groan.

There was movement at his hips, and I was drawn to his fist grasping his thick erection, stroking languorously from the base to the tip.

My mouth dried, and I sucked in a breath at the sheer size of him fully erect. His erotic grunt seared through the air towards me, and I found my thighs pressing together, trying to find relief just from the sound. Sebastian looked like he was a god, the embers from the dying flames throwing shadows across a body honed from the finest marble.

Even his cock was glorious, the surrounding skin just as scarred as the rest of him. But rather than make him grotesque, it made him almost brutally beautiful. Like a piece of broken art.

Sebastian's hand moved faster, rougher, and my body heated just like it had in the shower, responding as if he was touching me. My skin tightened, seeming to stretch over my bones as my lungs began to match his shallowed breaths.

His thumb teased the pre-cum on the head of his cock, his legs parting as much as he could with his joggers pushed roughly down his hips. His abs tensed, and I couldn't look away as thick ropes of cum covered his stomach and hand.

It was mesmerising. It was...

Sebastian's eyes slipped open, and I quickly darted past, my heart racing as I waited a second to make sure he hadn't heard me.

Shit.

There was a rustle of fabric, and then slight movement. I hurried further down the hallway, not realising just how big the penthouse was. I knew it was over two floors, but I'd only really seen a few rooms.

I heard shuffling behind me, but turning back I found myself still alone. There were no more sounds, no groans, or grunts. No rustling of fabrics or muffled footsteps.

Waiting another beat I continued to look, checking one of the doors until I realised it was locked. Wanting to give it a little longer before I risked going anywhere near Sebastian's room, I continued forward, walking down the hallway before stopping at a set of stairs leading up to the threshold of a studio.

The back was made entirely of windows, the city lights

illuminating the canvases stacked against one another on the floor. A painting of men clawing at their skin, the image shocking, but at the same time beautiful in its detail. Another of a fallen angel, his wings ripped violently from his back. A screaming woman fighting against demons.

Some of the canvases were broken, others slashed into ribbons to leave gaping holes in the violent images. There were dents in the walls, as well as the paint splattered floor. A well-worn punching bag hung on the left, beside mounts and bottles of paints that looked crushed and deformed.

Walking over I touched the picture displayed on the easel, taking a moment to push back the strips of the canvas, only to realise that it was a portrait of me.

Sebastian

My cock twitched, wanting to play with the pretty rabbit who stood in the doorway. I knew she was watching, her breath hitching with every stroke.

Fuck. I imagined it was her hand, her mouth strangling my cock. Keeping my eyes open only slightly, I made my movements rougher, harsher, just to see how she'd react. My thumb brushed over the slit on the head, and I groaned, letting the noise travel across the room to her flushed cheeks.

Her eyes burned, and the orgasm hit like a bolt of lightning. I grunted, feeling the hot pulses land on my stomach and hand. The force squeezed my eyes shut, and when I opened them again, she was gone.

The urge to follow her so she could see the results of what she'd started was almost overwhelming. Instead, I cleaned up my cum, wiping it away before pulling up my jogging bottoms.

When in the throes of such rage the noises in my head were manic, and normally not much could calm me down. But her voice had grounded me, calming the demons that were roaring in my ears.

Even now they were telling me to chase, so I stalked after her, knowing she was too curious to simply go back to her room.

"What the fuck are you doing here?" I growled, reaching up to lean against the doorjamb to my studio.

She gasped, the sound caught short when she twisted on the spot to find me standing there. A flush coloured her face, and I wasn't sure if it was because she'd just been caught, or because she was still affected from watching me.

I wonder what she'd say if I told her I was thinking about her the entire time. How I imagined how soft her skin would feel beneath my hands, and how much I wanted to mark it. How I planned to make her cry as I fucked her throat and then stretched her tight little cunt until she could take the entire length of me.

As I stalked closer, she stumbled back, her arm knocking the portrait in her panic. Arabella tried to catch it before it fell, but I was there, grabbing her wrist as it clattered to our feet, enjoying how her pulse spiked and her lips parted with a gasp.

Those fucking lips.

I'd spent hours painting them, only to not get them right. I scowled down at her, and a flash of fear settled in those large, brown eyes. It sent a jolt down my cock, and I swear the prick was already prepping for round two.

But not yet.

So I dipped my head forward, forcing her to lean back at an awkward angle. "Get out," I whispered, and her entire body jerked as if she'd been electrocuted.

I released her wrist suddenly, and she barely caught herself from falling before she twisted past me, her hair a flurry as she ran. My blood heated at the possibility of a hunt, of catching her as she screamed and fought, and then finally surrendering as I sunk my cock into her willing body.

But I held back, violence still too close to the surface.

If I fucked her now, I could end up hurting her. And while hurting my partners made my cock hard, I didn't want to break her just yet. She needed to beg first.

My cock twitched, but ignoring it I headed towards the canvas she'd been touching. Picking it up I placed it back on the easel, brushing my fingers over the frayed edges where I sliced it diagonally three times.

It had been a stunning piece, her face painted in various shades of grey and red, only for me to lose my temper and destroy it. Just like I destroyed everything that was breakable. Pulling out my phone, I placed it on a ledge, flicking up the app for the cameras and swiping until I found her room.

She was already there, laying across her bed in my fucking T-shirt. Her dark hair was sprayed out across the pale sheets, her eyes closed and her cheeks still that pretty pink colour.

Looking away I grabbed a pack of cigarettes, lifting one to my lips before lighting the tip. Throwing the portrait against the others, I grabbed a fresh canvas, the oil paints still scattered on the floor where I'd left them.

Normally after a fight I could sleep, but for some reason my demons were howling, the nightmares threatening to tear at my control.

So I'd paint. Until I was too exhausted to dream, or until morning light broke. Whichever came first.

Taking a drag, I released a billow of smoke before returning to my phone, only to pause. Arabella was still there, but her back was arched, her legs bent up on the mattress. Taking the cigarette out of my mouth, I balanced it beside my phone, leaning closer to get a better look.

Her eyes were squeezed shut, lips open in a silent cry. The hem of the T-shirt had risen, and her fingers were stroking between her thighs.

I immediately brought my phone closer to my canvas, the paintbrush moving in my hand while my eyes remained glued to the image. Her fingers rubbed, diving inside her pussy as she writhed against the sheets, the black T-shirt rising up until her other hand could brush across her breast.

Fuck.

My Arabella was a fucking temptress, and it made me want to mark her soul in the same darkness that stained mine.

Because until I grew bored, she was mine to use.

Mine to own.

Mine to fucking destroy.

Chapter 22
Sebastian

Leaning against my bike, I took a moment to glance up at the building, the dark brick three stories high. *Baron Financial Consultancy and Accountancy* was nestled in the heart of Kensington, polished to perfection and as 'legit' as any business built on corruption could be.

What pretentious prick uses his title as part of the name of his business? Oh, that would be my uncle. He seemed to forget the Baron title was hereditary and was given to him just because he was the eldest and only son.

It wasn't earned, and it meant nothing in a modern time where royalty and aristocracy had almost zero power, and contributed nothing meaningful to society other than to a small circle of elite. So his title was pointless.

But Alexander Ackworth still paraded around like he was more important than he actually was, just because he'd been the only male sibling.

Along with the title, he'd inherited the family fortune, my grandfather purposely leaving my mum nothing. Not that there was any fortune left, as my grandfather was a notorious drunk who used every last penny on sex workers and any drugs he could get his old, wrinkled hands on.

I hadn't spent much time with him before his somewhat dramatic demise—crushed to death in a sex act gone wrong—my mother having given up everything to move to Paris to be with my father not long after I was born.

"Hello, how can I help you?" the receptionist asked as I took a step inside.

I hadn't bothered with my mask, and she showed no reaction to my scars other than a slight tightening of her smile. Ignoring her entirely, I moved down the corridor and past the glass conference room towards the offices at the back.

"Excuse me! You can't just go down there!"

Baron Financial Consultancy and Accountancy was just a fancy name for a financial advisor, or wealth manager. My uncle, as well as his partners, provided advice and services to those with a significant bank account.

I couldn't speak for his other clients, but I was a somewhat unusual case in the fact that the majority of my money wasn't made legally, and it was the firm's job to deal with it. They made sure everything looked above board for His Majesty's Revenue and Customs, as well as making sure all my money was accounted for. Every single penny.

Finding his door, I opened it without knocking. *"Hello Uncle,"* I greeted in French.

Alexander sat behind his desk, his eyes widening when he looked up to find me standing there. "Sebastian?" Jumping to his feet, he caused some of his paperwork to scatter to the floor. "What are you doing here? We don't have a meeting."

"I'm so sorry, Mr Ackworth, he just barged in," the receptionist explained, her words a little flustered as she'd tried to match my longer strides.

Alexander's nostrils flared, his smile strained. "Please cancel my next appointment."

"You seem nervous. Why would that be?" I drawled.

"What have I told you about speaking that language in my presence?" he sneered, waiting until we were alone and the door was closed. "What are you doing here, Sebastian? Does Caden know you're here alone?"

Of course he mentioned my cousin, because we both knew Caden wasn't aware that I'd come for a little friendly visit. "Why, need him as a buffer?"

My uncle and I clashed more often than not, so we kept in-person meetings to a minimum.

"You know you're supposed to have a guard."

"I don't need a guard, Uncle."

"Say that to a bullet between your eyes. You wanted all this power, Sebastian. But it comes at a cost when it makes you a target." Alexander sniffed, as if displeased with my company. "You should've just called rather than turning up uninvited."

"But then you wouldn't get to see my pretty face." Crossing my arms, I leaned against the wall. Alexander stood rigid, and I knew he wouldn't return to his seat because he wouldn't want to feel less superior in the dynamic. It didn't matter that I was several inches taller regardless of whether we were sitting or not.

His stare was sharp. "Get to the point, Sebastian. I'm a very busy man, and you're already disrupting my next meeting," he seethed.

"What happened with my money?" I asked, eyeing his office, the certificates and photographs of notable people adorning the walls, and all the books with legal jargon lining his shelves. Closing the distance, I reached for the frame he had on his desk, unsurprised to see him and my mother. He may dislike me, but it was because of her that he'd bothered to pull me from a burning building.

Placing the picture face-down on the desk, I looked up,

amused with how Alexander flinched beneath my gaze. Apparently, I reminded him of her, and the resulting guilt of being too late.

"You seem to be more volatile recently. Have you been taking your medication?" he said, and I barely suppressed smashing him in the face. "You know what the doctor said."

Alexander wanted me on pills that numbed my mind and made me feel hollow. Langdon had thrown a fit when he'd seen the medication, chucking them in the toilet and laughing silently as he'd flushed them.

"I'll take your silence as a no. Seriously Sebastian, you function because you're in control, and right now I'm worried," Uncle said lowly, voice dropping in concern.

"Answer the fucking question."

Alexander sighed. "Does it matter?" He adjusted his lapels, tugging them into place. "I've heard you've dealt with the situation just fine and even came out of it with a pretty plaything, too."

I clenched my teeth, having to force myself to relax.

"Don't look so surprised. I have eyes and ears everywhere."

I knew it wasn't Caden who was gossiping, which meant he'd found out about Arabella from her visit to *The Thorn* last night.

"It's poor etiquette to keep toys for too long," he continued, clearly not smart enough to sense my spike in anger. "Dispose of her sooner rather than later."

The last of my patience was waning. "What happened with my money, Uncle?"

I wasn't asking out of curiosity anymore, it was annoyance. Alexander *knew* he'd done wrong. I could see it in the way his fingers twitched, and the vein pulsed in his forehead.

"I trusted you," I continued, the words cutting harder than I intended. "Was that a mistake?"

"You can be so dramatic," Alexander muttered. "Just like your mother." Finally taking a seat, he gestured to the one opposite his desk. I continued to stand, and he sighed once more. "I see your decorum hasn't improved."

"Stop deflecting."

Alexander cocked his head, his eyes hard when they held mine. "There was someone here that was purposely miscalculating, hiding money when it should've been flagged."

"How long was this going on?"

"I tracked it back for almost eight months," he admitted, clearly just as annoyed as I was. "She was taking a cut of the profits."

"You didn't notice for *eight months?*"

Alexander's gaze was pointed when he looked at me. "I had no reason not to trust her work. When I checked, every penny was accounted for, so she was smart in covering her tracks. Once it came to my attention, I dealt with it."

My lips tugged up into a smirk. "You dealt with it?"

Uncle always played the part: polished cufflinks, bespoke suits with the faint cologne of money and control. But underneath the elegance was the same rot that ran through the underworld. He was the one who first intro-duced me to the big names and connections, the gangs, cartels and organisations that kept the trades open and the corrupt money moving.

"Did you get your hands dirty, Uncle?" I commented, voice smooth but laced with challenge.

He scoffed, lips curling into something just short of a sneer. "Of course not. I have people for that." He flicked a hand toward the door, trying to dismiss me. "Now, if you'll excuse me."

There was a beat of silence, long enough for his arrogance to settle. Then I took a slow step back toward his desk, letting the tension stretch taut.

"I don't take orders from men I bankroll," I said, my voice quiet, but harsh. "I'll cut you off." I let the words sink in, each syllable deliberate. "You'll become just another moneyless baron with a crumbling social standing, clinging to tailored suits you'll no longer be able to afford."

Alexander's jaw tightened, red spreading across his cheekbones before he smirked. "You finished?" he grated out.

This was why we kept in-person meetings to a minimum. We were too alike, carved from the same cold ambition and sharp edges.

I leaned in slightly, just enough to let him know I wasn't in the mood for games.

"Don't fuck with my money, and I won't make another impromptu visit."

"Always a pleasure, Sebastian," he grunted, already reaching for the papers on his desk. "Next time, bring my son. At least *he's* more civilised."

I didn't bother with a reply, turning to give him my back.

"Oh, and Sebastian."

I paused, looking over my shoulder to meet his flat, calculating gaze.

"Remember what I said. You can have your fun, but that girl's still nothing more than a toy. Dispose of her before she becomes a problem. Or I will."

Chapter 23
Arabella

Sebastian was actively avoiding me.

Okay, so I didn't know that for sure, but it had been almost a week, and we hadn't exchanged a single word.

We had dinner in silence, which wasn't as awkward as I thought it would be, and that was it. During the day he was gone, and I only saw him briefly at the table every evening. I itched to speak, to break the silence, but I knew if I did I'd probably admit I'd watched him masturbate, and I didn't think I could survive the embarrassment.

He hadn't even given me anymore demands, and I definitely hadn't risked looking inside his bedroom again. You know, because just in case.

But every night I found myself sneaking into the west wing, finding he never slept. He either worked out with his punching bag and weights, or he painted at all hours. Then he'd destroy the work in a fit of rage that caused me to run back to the safety of my room.

I hadn't found the right time to bring up the debt again, but I itched to know how much I'd worked off, if any at all. The not knowing gnawed at me, leaving me stranded in a kind of purgatory, caught between hope and helplessness.

"You need to knead it harder, dear," Beatrice said, adding a little more flour to my bread dough.

Punching it instead, I began to follow her instructions. Beatrice Pritchard was a lovely woman who seemed far too gentle to be working for someone like Sebastian.

She smiled so easily, and I kept catching her looking at me with the softest expression. It was hard not to warm to her, especially when she treated me so nicely. She must be in her late fifties, with dyed blonde hair and wisps of grey that suited her rounder face. She had it in a perfect bun, not a strand out of place while mine was tossed on my head like a nest. But at least it was out of my face.

No hair in my fresh bread, thank you very much.

"So, how long have you known Sebastian?" I asked, wanting to learn a little bit more about him.

Beatrice stilled. "How's that dough coming along?" She changed the subject.

I frowned, turning to find her humming to herself.

When she noticed me looking, she sighed. "I've known him since he was a little boy. He used to spend his summers here before..." she paused, clearing her throat.

"Before what?"

Beatrice shook her head, her smile a little more forced. "Nothing, nothing," she continued in her unnecessarily cheery voice. "So, to properly knead the dough you must..."

I nodded at the appropriate times and even added my own comments every now and then. But my mind kept going back to Sebastian, as if I was disappointed he wasn't there, breathing down my neck.

I should be grateful he'd left me alone, but having no sense of purpose was starting to grate. At least when I wore his collar at the club I was doing *something*, even if it was simply being his doll. It had been less than a week since I gave over my life, and already I was thankful I was being treated like an object.

There were so many things wrong with me.

Beatrice was a nice distraction, coming in to cook and organise the cleaners that sometimes came in during the day. They refused to acknowledge me, which at first I'd been a little offended by, but I decided to be the bigger person and just ignore them back.

I'd asked to help clean, just for something to do, but Beatrice had refused and invited me into the kitchen instead.

Which was why I was currently taking out my frustrations on the poor bread dough.

Beatrice made a disgruntled noise, and I turned to find Chip standing beside her. She rubbed at his white collar, where there were little splashes of red.

"Do you play chess?" he asked when I looked over at him.

"Chess?" I punched the dough once more.

His pale eyebrow cocked. "You know, the checkered board with the little–"

"Chip, haven't you got errands?" Beatrice interrupted. "Surely, you're far too busy to hang around here with us."

Chip's brows drew together, and a shadow darkened his eyes when he looked down at her. "I have time."

"Sure, I can play chess." It wasn't like I had anything else planned other than reading, writing and my daily session of wallowing in self-pity. But I was sure I could move that to later.

Double checking my dough, I give it one last punch. Honestly, making bread should be part of therapy. Highly recommend.

"Is this ready to proof?" I asked.

Beatrice's earlier light seemed to have diminished, but

still she nodded with her signature smile. "Arabella, why don't you go set the board up in the drawing room? Chip will follow with a nice cup of tea."

Taking a paper towel, I cleaned my hands before leaving the kitchen. The drawing room was just a smaller living room without the TV up on the mezzanine. The chessboard was already set up on the side, the wooden figurines hand carved.

"Hi, sorry about that," Chip said, unrepentant when he appeared at the top of the spiral staircase, his black tie loosened around his neck. Holding a silver tray, he set down the single China cup and saucer. Steam from the tea rose, the scent sweet.

I didn't touch it.

"So, you play a lot of chess?" I asked, unsure how to take him.

Chip was younger than me by a couple years, and other than inviting me to dinner most evenings, we didn't speak.

"This is my favourite game," Chip said. "Not many games have a queen willing to die for her king."

"And yet the king is nothing without the most powerful piece on the board."

His eyes brightened at my reply, a small smile tugging his lips. "Touché."

The board was already mid play, the pieces positioned. I wasn't sure whether I was allowed to touch them, so I didn't.

"It's fine, Mr Devereaux won't mind." Chip began to reset the board.

My gaze snapped up. "Sebastian plays?"

Chip nodded, turning the board so he was the dark and I was the light. "Chess is a strategy game. It teaches you to anticipate your opponent's move several turns in advance.

The aim is to control the centre of the board, which gives you more power and options."

"So it's not too dissimilar to life then," I laughed.

"Exactly." Chip waited until I moved my first pawn before mirroring the exact same move. "It teaches you to protect your pieces and to know when to sacrifice."

"So less like life." I laughed more awkwardly this time, especially when Chip didn't react with the expected smile. "So, how long have you worked for Sebastian?" I asked, moving my next pawn.

He glanced up briefly before looking down. "A few years. My mum thought I was acting out and hoped Mr Devereaux would be able to help."

I knew he and Beatrice were mother and son, but it took me a while to notice the resemblance. Their light hair and darker eyes. "That's nice, to be able to work with your mum."

"She's overbearing," he commented, his gaze remaining on the board. "I hate that she watches me like I'm still five, waiting for me to fuck up so she can prove herself right."

"At least she's here," I whispered, immediately regretting the words as soon as they'd spilled. I looked up, finding Chip watching me with an unidentifiable emotion.

"What about your mum?" he asked, moving his next piece.

Stop crying like a baby, Bella.

I hadn't thought of my mum in so long, the memory of her voice made me jerk.

"Ara?"

"She's not like yours," I said, clearing my throat. "She wasn't... there for me."

Why are you even here, Bella?

Go in the other room. Why can't you just leave me alone?

You're always in the way.

I struggled to remember the good times, when she cared that I even existed. It was hard because what little memories of her I had were tainted, and I hated her for it.

"She died when I was a kid," I continued, moving my next pawn. "When I was really young, she was present, but as I got older she seemed to sink into herself."

It was better before you were born.

Dad and I were happy until you showed up.

This is all your fault.

I now understood she had severe depressive episodes, but as an eight-year-old I couldn't understand why Mum didn't want to play with me anymore. Then she wouldn't cook or clean for extended periods of time. She'd argue with Dad all night and then ignore me all day when he was either working, or gambling away what little money we had.

"You can't pick your family," Chip muttered, moving his bishop to take out my pawn.

My smile was forced. "I guess not."

"So, how long do you plan to be here?"

I moved another chess piece, not really paying attention. "I don't know," I said carefully, not sure how much to share. For all I knew, Sebastian regularly kept women here to pay off their father's debts. "Until I'm told to leave, I suppose."

"You think you'll be able to leave?"

I flinched at his words, looking up to find Chip watching me once more. There hadn't been any hostility in his voice, and he looked almost fascinated by my reaction.

You think he could keep me? I wanted to say, knowing once the debt was paid, I'd fight until my last breath to be free.

"Well," I began, trying to make light of the situation, "I'm sure I'll die of boredom then. I've already finished my book, and it's not like I can casually leave to get a new one."

Chip continued to watch me, not even sparing the board a single glance as he made his moves. "I'll bring you some new books," he said after a few minutes of silence. "Let me know what you want, and I'll sort it."

My grin stretched, and his returning smile was cute. "Seriously? Thanks. Being left alone with my thoughts can be dangerous."

Chip finally looked down. "Checkmate."

I blinked, realising he'd tricked me into giving up my king. "How?" I flicked over the piece, shaking my head to find him grinning, leaning back in his chair. "That's bullshit. I thought I had you."

I didn't, but he didn't know that.

Chip began to reset the board, standing slightly to reach across. The movement opened his jacket, revealing a pistol on his hip. He followed my gaze. "Don't be nervous. I'm armed so I can protect the penthouse."

"Why would the penthouse need protecting?" I wondered.

Chip shrugged, moving his first pawn for the second game. "Mr Devereaux has many enemies."

My brows furrowed. "What exactly do you do for Sebastian again?"

His smile was friendly, but there was an edge to his gaze that I couldn't put my finger on. "Anything I'm asked."

I lost three times in a row.

I was almost thankful when Chip excused himself, because then I could deal with what was left of my self-esteem.

I didn't ask him for details on what he actually did for Sebastian, especially considering the red specs on his collar had definitely been blood. I realised I didn't want to know, happy in my ignorance.

My hands ached from how hard I gripped the pen, the words flowing across my notebook as I poured my thoughts onto the page. I was running out of space, so I kept my handwriting small and using as much of the page as possible. It didn't matter if it was neat, or even legible. No one was going to read it anyway.

The lift dinged, and standing, I leaned over the banister to gaze at the living room below. Caden stepped out, followed by a shorter woman with sunshine blonde hair.

"Come down," he demanded, and clearly, he was my number one fan because his glare could cut glass.

The brat in me wanted to ignore him just because it was the only thing within my control, but I was curious about the woman with the soft smile. She clutched a large suitcase, and even though Caden tried more than once to take it from her, she casually turned away with a tut.

"Hi, you must be Arabella," she greeted after I descended the spiral stairs, her smile widening. "I'm Elena."

"Ara," I said, stopping a few steps away.

"Can you show me to your bedroom?" she asked, clearly struggling with the weight of the suitcase but refusing to let Caden help, much to his increasing distress. "I think you'll prefer this if we had more privacy."

"Elena..." he growled, and she was unable to hide her flinch when he reached over. Stepping back, he gave her a little more space. "This way," he said, his voice gentler.

I looked at Caden, who'd clenched his jaw so tight I wasn't sure whether he was about to break a tooth. I followed them both towards my room, watching how Caden always kept a gap of air between himself and Elena.

As soon as we reached my bedroom he paused, allowing Elena to move forward. She stepped inside and immediately dropped her suitcase with a thump.

"Perfect," she hummed, the earlier commotion seemingly forgotten. Bending down, she unzipped the suitcase to reveal folded fabrics, a sewing machine, and other strange instruments I couldn't name. "I've brought you some underwear."

That was it. Elena was my new best friend.

Reaching for the bag she held out, I checked through the numerous lace pieces in my size, and of course all in black. "Thank you."

"Elena's here to make you a new wardrobe," Caden said, leaning against the door. His tone clearly indicated his displeasure of playing babysitter, and I took some sick amusement in that. But he still kept his voice quiet.

"Thanks for the escort," Elena said, smiling over at Caden. When he remained where he was, she pursed her lips. "I'm going to ask Ara to undress."

"I'll be out here if you need me," he grumbled, disappearing down the hallway.

Elena closed the door anyway, her smile still in place once she'd turned back to me.

"Do you and Caden have a history?" I asked, sensing a warmth between them despite her flinching. Pulling off my dress, I held it to my front. Luckily I'd handwashed my underwear, so I wasn't completely nude with a woman I'd only met a few minutes ago. I had some standards.

"With Caden?" Elena laughed, reaching out for my dress so she could place it neatly on my bed. "No, definitely not. I don't think my husband would be too pleased."

Elena would be around the same height as me if not for her heels. She held herself with such elegance, every movement as delicate as her. Taking some measuring tape, she held it across my body.

"Do you need help?" she whispered, her expression serious when she met my eyes.

"Help?"

"I can get you out of here," she added carefully.

I laughed, the sound a little on edge. "I can't leave."

"Seriously, I know they're scary, but I can ask–"

"No," I cut in, ignoring the way my stomach twisted. I couldn't leave. Not yet. Not until I figured out what I really wanted. This damn debt still hung over me like a noose, and the truth was, I was scared.

Scared that if I ran, Sebastian would follow.

And I wasn't sure what terrified me more. The thought of him chasing me, or the part of me that *wanted* him to just because he made me feel less... hollow.

Elena gently touched the bruise on my ribs, the colour a lovely yellow.

"Sebastian didn't do that." In fact, he hadn't really hurt me at all.

For such a gentle woman, her eyes of pale blue had hardened to ice. "Then who?"

I swallowed, surprised with the change. "They're dead."

After a moment she nodded, as if approving. "Even bad guys need to fear someone. I hope he made it hurt."

Okay, bloodthirsty was not a character trait I'd expected from her.

"How do you know Sebastian?" I asked, holding out my arms when asked so she could measure. "He doesn't seem the person to have many friends." Not that I really knew him more than the man who wore a mask. Even without his mask he spoke very little, his eyes always watching me with an intensity I didn't know how to deal with.

"He was acquaintances with my stepbrothers." Her skin

paled a little, the colour draining from her face. "They weren't good guys, so I went to Sebastian."

"You asked Sebastian for help?" I clarified.

"Well, technically I first spoke to Hendrix, because he wasn't as terrifying." Her upper lip twitched, her colour returning as she took in a deep breath. "But with his help I contacted Sebastian, and he dealt with the situation, and even set me up to start a new life."

"Does Hendrix work for Sebastian?" I asked, smiling at the way she blushed.

"God no, that's a somewhat complicated story," she laughed, her cheeks becoming a deeper shade. She was acting like we were talking about a schoolgirl crush, and from her reaction, I'd guess it was Hendrix who was her husband. "Sometimes," Elena said after a few beats, "you need a monster to take out other monsters."

I wanted to ask her more, but I knew the conversation was closed.

"So, do you want to tell me why I've been dragged from my shop to come dress you?" The change of subject was a whiplash. "Caden wasn't very forthcoming as to why you couldn't come to me. I've known the guys for a few years now, and they always pop in to make sure I'm okay." Elena rolled her eyes. "But I've never seen Sebastian with anyone."

"It's complicated," I replied, distracted by Elena's words.

You need a monster to take out other monsters.

Sebastian didn't bend to society standards, twisting the rules to suit his needs regardless of expectations and consequences. That was why he wore his mask, so people could see just how uncivilised he truly was.

A monster that scared other monsters, almost crudely honest in his persona. And yet, he'd helped Elena escape. I wonder what he'd asked in return?

"I'm only temporary," I decided on.

"I wouldn't be so sure." Elena stepped back, pulling out various clothes from her suitcase. "Okay, so I've brought some stuff with me that I'll need to alter, and Sebastian has also given me a list which I can get to you by next week. Is that okay?"

I reached for the pair of jeans, my smile strained. "They're perfect, thank you."

Chapter 24
Sebastian

Eight, real name John Carp, was a nondescript man with a face and build that would blend in with the crowd. It made him generic, boring, and the ideal drug dealer.

He was anything but generic right now, though. His eyes bulged, tears and snot smearing his reddened face as he tried to jostle the tarantulas that were crawling freely over his chest. His screams were muffled by the rag shoved through broken teeth, and bruises were already appearing along with fresh welts.

Clearly, he wasn't a fan of spiders as Caden added another–this time to his face–considering Eight just pissed himself, much to the amusement of the twins, who were standing to the side. Micah laughed out loud, the sound a harsh bark while his brother, Malik, simply smirked. The twins have been with me for a few years, and like all my guards were ex special forces that were paid for their skills and discretion.

"Now, keep still, or I'll break your fucking knee," Caden ordered, forcing Eight to freeze as the spider explored his face before eventually crawling down his body.

It was always humorous to watch people fear the

spiders rather than Caden or myself. Yes, the tarantula could deliver a nasty bite of venom, but that bite wasn't what was going to kill them. I was.

Langdon appeared bored, the *click, snap, click* of his lighter the only sound other than the muffled screams in the cold, concrete room.

"You're a hard man to track down," I said, riffling through the black rucksack that had been on Eight's person. I pulled out several packets of cocaine, all marked as my product. But it wasn't, the colour was off, as well as the quality.

Walking over, Lang yanked out Eight's gag, then affectionately patted him on the cheek with a wink.

"Where did you get this?" I asked, holding up a packet.

Langdon whistled at Eight's silence, and when I nodded, he gripped Eight by his hair, wrenching his head back before holding the lighter beneath his jaw.

"I got it from the usual drop off!" he screamed, his skin splitting beneath the concentrated flame. Langdon pulled back but didn't release his grip. "By the docks. Hook, man, I swear."

I cocked my head. Hook, which wasn't his real name, owned the docks, as well as the surrounding sea. Nothing was smuggled across the water without him knowing about it, and that was how I procured my raw materials without alarming the authorities. Not to mention providing me unrestricted access to the rest of the continent.

"Hook's distributing now?" I moved closer, my sheer size shadowing him.

"One of his men, Smithy. I swear, that's where I got it all."

Tipping the rest of the contents of his bag out, I glanced at what remained. "What the fuck is this?" I kneeled, picking up another packet.

Eight squealed like a child, and the scent of burnt flesh infected the air. "That's the new stuff on the market. It's what we're supposed to be pushing. The other... the Cursed Rose is rumoured to be corked."

I clenched my jaw. "Says who?"

"I don't know, the other dealers. Come on, man, please don't—" His words ended with a scream, the skin of his jaw peeling back beneath the heat.

I studied the packet, not recognising the symbol of a stained-glass window. "What's it called?"

The cries died down, but I didn't bother looking up.

"They... they call it Enchanted Dust."

"Hmm." Nodding to Langdon, I let him have his fun.

I had a more apathetic reaction to the resulting chaos and death, which apparently wasn't normal according to both the psychologist and therapist Alexander took me to at sixteen. That lasted a whole three sessions before I threatened to kill them.

Langdon, being several years older, had gone only once, somehow sweet talking his way between the psychologist's legs even without the ability to speak.

He liked to seduce people before watching them burn beneath his flames, unlike me, who was more blunt. Caden, despite sharing blood, was by far the most rational. Unless he was bored, then he really liked to smash things with that hammer of his.

I guess Eight would've preferred Caden to be his interrogator, because after breaking a few bones, Caden would've probably put the fucker out of his misery.

Langdon, on the other hand, was still playing with his food.

Another scream, the sound causing my limited patience to wear thin.

I'd slept only a few hours, but even with painting, the

fight, and *her*, it still wasn't enough to calm this fucking current inside me. It was like I'd been struck by lightning, and my body didn't know how to deal with this excess energy.

I needed an outlet, something *more*. Something violent, preferably with my toy.

I'd been busy with tracking this prick the last week, but that didn't mean I wasn't aware of her every moment. Lounging around my home reading her book and befriending my staff. She didn't think I knew that every night she'd come looking for me, sneaking into the west wing to watch me paint from the shadows.

My beautiful little rabbit, so curious even in her fear.

It took a lot for me to cool my constant rage, but she had this calming presence that spoke to my demons. It made me want to crush her, just to see what would happen. Whether she would break or fucking embrace it.

I turned to the twins. "Deal with this once he's done."

"Sir," they said in unison, dipping their heads.

Leaving Langdon to his game, I made my way to my office.

The club was created as a place to launder money, as well as a beacon of my influence across the city. I ran it along with a group of trusted staff. Sitting at my desk I glanced down at the paperwork, the words meddling together, even moving until they blurred into something I had no hope of reading. So I didn't bother to try.

Pulling out my phone, I unlocked it, frowning at the pictures until I found the one of the phone, and then the contact with the antique clock.

I trusted Caden with my life, which was the only reason I left him alone with Arabella. I knew blood meant nothing in my world, but he'd proven his loyalty to me over and over, taking a bullet more than once.

Caden was a year younger than me, but we grew up together between my home in Paris, and his in London. It was him and my uncle who came and found Lang and I almost dead. They were the ones who'd brought us back to England, and protected us until we'd recovered.

"*Bas?*" Caden answered on the first ring.

"Meet me at the container."

I could hear his frown. "*The container? What've you heard?*"

In five years I haven't had a single problem with the quality. Designed specifically to be as clean as possible, giving off the best possible high and assuring a returning customer.

"I think someone's fucking with our powder. We've just heard a rumour that our stuff's corked and not being pushed." I made the most money keeping the entire pyramid under my thumb. But I also sold to third parties, which widened my pool of customers.

Langdon came in then, an almost peaceful gleam in his eyes that was a juxtaposition to the scent of scorched flesh. He raised a brow but said nothing as I put Caden on speaker.

"*You think someone got past T? You know how anal she is about shit down there.*"

"Meet us in thirty," I ordered. "We should check it out anyway."

"*What do you want me to do about Arabella? Elena's still here.*"

"Send Elena home and tell Arabella to wait for me."

Langdon smirked, shaking his head while Caden gave a dark chuckle.

"*Fine. See you fuckheads soon.*"

The King's Forest was under a conservation covenant agreement and preservation order. The status protected the entire belt from those wishing to disturb the area. One of those old British laws that had way too many hoops to jump through to change and essentially meant construction companies couldn't get permission to dig up the earth, which was a perfect place to hide an entire drug manufacturing unit.

My feet crunched the dried leaves, critters scattering as I walked the path towards the large, ancient tree. Staring up at its great size, I brushed my hand over the bark before finding the fingerprint scanner concealed within one of the trunk's hollows.

With a click, the forest floor opened to reveal a set of metal stairs. There was only the single access, and every person who passed the doors had to present their palm to the screen. Along with the constant camera feed throughout the forest, as well as inside the container, it allowed me to monitor who was inside at all times.

"The log's clean," Caden said, clicking through lists on the panel. "No one unauthorised has come in, Bas."

Nodding, I reached towards the metal lockers, pulling out the required PPE before pulling it on. The plastic strained, but held enough as I passed the locked door into the main section of the lab.

A few heads turned, eyes widening when I stood to observe them.

Caden went off, his knowledge of the production much

better than mine while Langdon headed towards the office, intending to check the notes.

"Sir, you're unexpected," T said when she spotted me, passing Lang as he made his way to her office.

Her nervous energy would've indicated deceit on anyone else, but she was good at her job because she was notoriously rigid in her routine. Us showing up without warning was breaking her carefully constructed day.

"Please be careful. You'll contaminate everything," she called over to Caden, who'd lifted a large white bag on one of the long desks and was currently intimidating one of the packers.

"Do you think we've been infiltrated?" I asked Caden, not taking my eyes off the small woman in front of me. There was no point speaking French, or even signing to keep my conversation private. Not when I wanted to see her reaction.

T's eyes rounded behind her goggles. "Ridiculous," she exclaimed, her voice direct, even if it was slightly muffled beneath her face mask. "Nothing passes or leaves these walls without me checking."

For a woman of barely five feet tall, she held herself with the confidence of a rugby player three times her size.

"It seems tight," Caden commented, eyes flicking to me. "I'll keep looking."

"I don't appreciate the sudden disruption." There was a predatory gleam in her gaze that I recognised, and one of the reasons I allowed her to organise the lab in the way she saw fit. Under my authority, of course.

I looked down at her, her fear buried beneath frigid control. She'd first introduced herself as T, and I never asked for her real name, or cared. This was Caden's domain, and I trusted him to run it. I also paid her a fucking fortune to deal with the bastard.

A whistle sounded, and holding my arm out I gestured for her to enter the office ahead of me. Back rigid, she entered to find Langdon lounging behind her desk, legs kicked up with his head cocked. A pile of paperwork was beside him, and when I entered the room he lifted his hands.

"Everything tracks," he signed. "If she's aware, she hasn't noted anything down."

I nodded but didn't reply while T moved to the side, tugging off her mask and goggles. They left red marks across her skin, but she seemed more pissed at Langdon's feet on her papers.

"If you're accusing me of something, say it out loud," she snapped, her tone absolute. Confident, with only the faintest tremble.

"There's been evidence of tampering," Caden said, appearing in the doorway.

"Not here there hasn't." Her gaze was sharp when she turned her attention to him.

I tossed her the packet found on the newly deceased Eight.

With a frown she moved towards the desk, and turning on the lamp she held it beneath the light. Her lips pursed, eyes focused and searching. "This isn't ours. The colour is off by a shade, and the powder density is wrong," she finally said.

"And yet the rose marks the packet, sweetheart," Caden drawled. "So someone's clearly fucking with us somewhere in the chain."

T lifted her head. "My powder leaves here perfect every time. I know because I personally check every single batch without fail." She held the packet up, raising an eyebrow. "This is mass-produced."

"*Your* powder?" Caden growled.

"Yes," she snapped, pointing a finger. "*My* powder. Who has the Master's in Medicinal Chemistry, and who just likes to mix things together and watch them go boom?"

Langdon threw his head back and laughed, the sound barely a gruff of air. Caden snarled in his direction, giving Lang his middle finger.

"Get your feet off my desk," she stressed, a muscle feathering in her jaw. "You're messing everything up."

Langdon blew her a kiss before dragging his feet. They made a thump when they hit the ground, and when she continued to glower, his smile grew into a smirk. "Am I allowed to play with the tiny chemist?" he signed to me and Caden.

T frowned, her cheeks flushing. "What did he say?"

Caden clenched his jaw, lifting his hands to reply. "Stop thinking with your dick," he signed back before speaking aloud to the room. "Everything looks clean. If someone's fucking us, I doubt it's here."

T let out a sound of frustration. "I could've told you that."

"What can you tell me about the powder?" I asked, and T's shoulders went rigid when she turned to face me.

"That it's low quality, and you'll likely find it available at every club in the city. I may be able to let you know the chemical breakdown, but I can't promise it'll help track down its origin."

She handed the packet over to Langdon, who was still staring at her. Taking the cocaine, he tipped it onto her desk, much to her distress.

"Please stop messing with my things," she hissed, reaching for the papers that he'd moved. "Manufacturing is sound. Look at distribution. Now, are we done here? Or can I get back to work?"

I straightened, my hands fisting at her tone.

"You seemed to have forgotten yourself, sweetheart," Caden commented with a glower. "Who do you think you're talking to?"

She stiffened, her gaze just off to the side rather than being directed at Cade. "You've disrupted my day with no evidence that any members of my team have tampered with the powder."

Langdon's smile tightened, eyes narrowing. But before he could move, I took a step forward, and she immediately backed into the desk.

"Don't take my lenience as a sign of weakness. I'm giving you leeway because of your value as a chemist," I said, dropping my voice in warning. "But never forget, you're replaceable."

T's eyes widened impossibly further, moving to Caden in her first sign of panic. Smart woman.

"Sir," he said, his hand landing on my shoulder. His touch jerked me out of my anger, taking it from a boil to a simmer. "She's all good, aren't you, sweetheart?"

T nodded, the movement jerky. "I didn't mean any offence."

I pulled myself back, and Caden removed his hand.

"While everything's under investigation, the operation's under lockdown," he said, defusing the situation. "You'll continue as you are, but not a hint of this conversation leaves this room. Understood?"

T licked along her bottom lip, having recovered from my slight loss of control. "Understood."

Chapter 25
Arabella

So tonight was the first night Sebastian hadn't been home for dinner, which meant I've been left alone for hours. Hours of nothing but my own thoughts, worrying whether my father was okay. Whether he was still even *alive*.

Brushing my hair, I sat on the side of the bathtub, steam fluttering around me from the shower, leaving a warmth across my skin. But inside I felt cold. Empty.

I'd always felt like everyone else around me was moving at a different pace. As if I was never really living, just going through the motions of survival. And now I didn't really know what pace I was anymore.

Placing the brush on the sink, I wiped a hand across the misty mirror—and then jumped at the reflection. "Chip?" I turned, my heart thundering against the inside of my ribs.

Chip stood in the doorway, three books stacked in his arms.

"Sorry, I didn't mean to scare you," he said calmly.

"How long have you been standing there?" I eyed the books, tugging the towel tighter around me. "I didn't expect–"

"What were you thinking about?" he interrupted,

closing his distance and tilting his head. "You were frowning."

"Frowning? Oh, I was thinking about my dad."

Chip held the books tighter to his chest, brows drawing together. "Why?" He wasn't wearing the same suit as earlier but was still more dressed than I was.

"Chip, I'm in a towel, and how did you even get up here anyway? I thought the lift was locked?" He hadn't looked at my half nakedness even once, which was good because this could've been a *lot* more awkward.

"Don't worry, I have my ways." He gestured to the books. "So, why the sign language?"

I glanced at the books. I'd only asked for one, but he'd brought me three. "I don't know how long I'm going to be here for, so I thought it was fair to learn Langdon's language." It was either that or French, and this seemed easier.

How else would I figure out what they were discussing in my presence? Knowledge was power, and right now I was deliberately being kept in the dark.

"Mr Devereaux will likely kill you before you learn anything."

"Well," I said, tightening my grip on the towel and offering a faint, wry smile, "then I'd better get started."

I took the books from him carefully, the weight of them grounding me, or trying to. A chill slipped down my spine, and it wasn't from the air. Something about this felt heavier than it should. Riskier.

"Thanks," I added, my voice softer now. "I really do appreciate you doing this for me. I just... don't want you getting dragged down with me."

He looked up, shrugging. "It's fine, there are no cameras in here."

The blood drained from my face. "Wait, there's cameras?"

"Everywhere, but I was here when they were fitted so I know the black spots." His head tilted to the side, seemingly to study me. "Why were you frowning while thinking of your father? He literally gave you over to a man like Mr Devereaux."

"I offered myself," I said quietly.

Chip shook his head, brows drawn together. "Same result. And even if he didn't push you into it, which I know for a fact he did, he sure as hell didn't stop you. Why are you letting yourself be used like that?"

"You don't get it." I moved to step past him, but he blocked the hallway, his expression unreadable. I gritted my teeth. "Chip, let me through."

"I'm not trying to upset you," he said gently. "I just want to understand."

"What's there to understand? He's my father. The man who gave me life. He fed me, clothed me, raised me... maybe not well, but at least he tried." My voice cracked, but only slightly. "Regardless of what he's done, he's still my father. All we have is each other, so if I don't try to help him, who else will?"

"That's what I don't get," he said, almost to himself. "That kind of blind loyalty to someone who clearly doesn't care for you. I don't understand how you can defend him."

"I'm not defending him," I argued, swallowing down the ache in my throat. "I'm choosing me. I couldn't live with the guilt of doing nothing. Of knowing there was something I could have done and walking away instead."

I already carried that guilt from one parent, I didn't need it for the other.

With a huff, I barged past, my shoulder hitting his as I

entered my bedroom to place the books down. A learn to sign BSL book, and two cute romances.

Chip lingered in the doorway to the bathroom, his expression stoic.

"Do you have any friends looking out for him?"

I let out a short laugh and sank onto the edge of my bed. "Yeah, I'm not exactly drowning in friends." And my dad had even fewer. "I tend to trauma-dump," I added with a dry smile. "People don't usually stick around after that."

It was easier to make a joke of it rather than acknowledge the truth, that in reality I struggled to trust anyone. It was easier, especially when Dad liked to move us around a lot. Starting over again and again thanks to the endless need to outrun his own messes taught me that connections didn't last. So I stopped trying to make them.

Books made it easier, fictional worlds breaking through the loneliness. The only person who'd been a constant was my dad. He wasn't dependable or steady, but at least he was there. And when you grew up without roots, his dysfunctional chaos became home.

So yeah, he was all I had. Maybe that was why I kept choosing him, even when I shouldn't have. Even when it hurt.

"You can trauma dump on me," Chip said, his smile gentle. "You can trust me, I promise. And if it helps... I can check in on him for you, if you want."

My voice came quieter than I intended. "You'd do that?"

Chip nodded without hesitation. "Of course."

I chewed on my bottom lip. "Would you show me how to get out of here?"

Chip froze, his face that of a statue. "I don't think Mr Devereaux would like that."

"What happens if there's an emergency? Like a fire?" I

needed a plan, a way to get out if it got to be too much. I just had to wait long enough for Dad to disappear before I risked anything.

"There are stairs, but the door's locked. You'll need a keycard, like mine, or unless there's an emergency, and the lift is compromised, then the door will automatically unlock."

"There are stairs?" That knowledge settled like a weight. "Where's the door?"

He took a moment to respond, lips curling with amusement. "Beside the kitchen."

Holy shit. There was an exit, and Sebastian didn't know I knew. "Thank you, I really don't want to get you into trouble."

"Don't worry about it." Chip's smile widened. "What are friends for?"

Chapter 26
Sebastian

I was trying to purge my excess energy, but the demons that lurked inside wanted to come out, and even the harsh strokes of the brush weren't enough to keep them at bay.

Il ne m'a pas laissé le choix.

He left me no choice.

The canvas clattered to the floor, followed by the easel. I barely pulled myself back from breaking the wood into pieces, wanting the splinters to imbed themselves into my hands so I'd feel them for days.

It was so tempting, but instead I reached for my cigarette.

Placing it between my lips I took a deep drag, the smoke burning my lungs as I held it in, savouring the sensation before releasing it in a cloud in front of me. My chest felt heavy, my muscles straining beneath my skin. Sleep was alluding me as usual, and I knew nothing but the fucking pills was likely going to break me out of this episode.

The same medication that was known to knock me out cold, leaving me vulnerable against my nightmares. But at least then I could fucking sleep.

A squeak of the floorboards echoed behind me, and

looking over my shoulder I met Arabella's eyes. I knew she'd be there, just like she was the past few nights.

Stalking over to her, I didn't give her time to run from me while I was this agitated. If she ran, I'd be forced to chase her, and when she was caught, I knew I wouldn't be able to stop myself from finally breaking her.

Taking another drag of my cigarette, I blew the smoke in her face. "So fucking desperate for my attention."

Her pupils expanded at my words, but she stood there frozen, without that light of defiance I'd grown fond of. I was still waiting to grow bored, just like I was with almost everything else. The only people who didn't bore me were Langdon and Caden, and only because they enjoyed the same depraved games that I did. Normal people were far less stimulating.

Everything and everyone else seemed shackled to society's expectations, unwilling to break free and experience a little bit of destruction in their carefully constructed world. But no, she still stole my thoughts, like a poison tainting my bloodstream.

"So desperate to poke at the big, bad Beast," I whispered, watching colour darken her cheeks at my harsh tone.

It was as if she didn't know what to do, and honestly, the feeling was fucking mutual.

Taking her wrist, I pulled her further inside the room. My nightmares were howling, the demons snapping at my sanity.

"Stay," I demanded, setting up a fresh canvas and picking up my brush, only for it to be all wrong. The shape. The colour. The fucking texture.

A tightness coiled beneath my ribs, the panic trying to swallow me whole. I felt the first phantom slash of that whip across my back, my cries falling on deaf ears.

It wasn't the pain of being sliced open, it was watching

the same thing happen to my mum and brothers. I was made to watch as my mum was raped, and then her throat slit while my dad wailed in despair.

S'il vous plait!

S'il vous plait!

My brothers were next, not even in double digits as they were beaten so badly I barely recognised them, all because of my father.

S'il vous plaît, ne faites pas cela!

Please don't do this! They'd begged for their lives, even as I cried. Even as I screamed to take me instead. Then I was forced to face him, the man I blamed for it all.

I tore my thoughts away, punching at the canvas until my fist split through. Paint splattered, but I didn't care. This rage inside me couldn't be cleansed, my memories and nightmares threatening to choke me.

"It didn't have to be this way, you know," she said, stroking through my mother's hair like a lover. Mum let out a gargled whimper, the last one before death finally took her.

"Fucking bitch!" Dad screeched, fighting against the restraints. "I'll fucking kill you for this."

She tutted, her red painted lips curving into a vicious slash of a smile. "You shouldn't have chosen her, and now look at what you've made me do."

My sobs rattled, my wrists bleeding from where I tried to free myself and reach my brothers. But it was no good; the first whoosh of the whip against my back made me scream. The pain was sharp before dulling into an ache, all before another strike parted my flesh.

"I'm sorry, Sebastian," she said, kneeling in my growing pool of blood while my dad roared. "This is all your father's fault. He left me no choice."

· · ·

Soft fingers touched my shoulder, and I flinched before there was a gasp. I blinked away the image of the woman that had tried to destroy me, only to find Arabella, her lips parted and my hand tightening around her slim throat.

A little more pressure, and I could watch her light and that infuriating defiance disappear from her eyes. Forever going dark.

"Sebastian," she mouthed, drawing me back to the present.

I hadn't even known I'd moved, lost against the fight of my past.

Fuck. I relaxed my fingers so she could take in a breath, my thumb reaching out to stroke the tear glistening from the corner of her eye. I accidentally smudged her with paint, the dark red like blood across her fair skin.

It was fucking beautiful. So I did it again, smearing it straight on her cheekbone in a splash of gore that anchored me to the moment.

She was still beneath my touch, not moving even when I stepped back to grab more paint. She watched me with those fucking eyes, and I expected fear when I reached for the bottom of her pyjama vest, attempting to rip the fabric over her head. But there was nothing as she lifted her arms to help me, a doe caught in the path of a wolf.

The fabric pulled until her breasts were free, and then I was painting them too, tracing around the luscious curves that had invaded my thoughts on more than one occasion.

My thumb brushed over her nipple, and she shivered beneath the touch. So I did it again, lost against the paint on her skin.

If I'd known better, I'd say she'd been sent to me as a Trojan horse to make me fall. But clearly, I didn't care, not when her presence was bringing me back from the void of my mind.

Her breasts moved with every inhale, my paint contouring her top half until I reached the waistband of her shorts. I tugged them off her legs even as she protested, until she stood there in nothing but black lace.

Fucking beautiful.

I stalked around her like she was a living piece of art, reaching out to paint across her shoulders, and then the arch of her back. My fingers moved down, over the slope of her arse to brush between her thighs. Her breathing hitched, the softest moan escaping her lips.

A warmth spread inside my chest, replacing the panic that was slowly receding until I could think. Until those nightmares no longer threatened to destroy me.

Her delicate throat swallowed as my fingers moved closer to her centre, only to find her underwear slick. My eyes flashed up to hers in cruel pleasure.

"Is there a reason your cunt's wet for me, *belle?*"

Arabella

His touch was harsh, calloused fingers rough. And still I felt myself aching for it. There was unapologetic power in the way he moved, his painting almost manic as he smeared colour across my naked skin.

I knew the risk of coming to watch him, and I'd thought about running when I'd first been caught. But something in his expression had stopped me. He'd looked lost, broken.

But now there was fire in his gaze, burning me from the inside out.

I should be scared, absolutely terrified in the way he looked at me like a predator ready to gobble his prey. But that knowledge did nothing to diminish the strange pleasure of the rough way he was touching me.

He was an animal barely contained in human skin, the Beast as he'd been named.

And for some reason, I've never been so turned on.

Sebastian barely moved to clean his hands before his thumb purposely rubbed between my thighs, pressing against my clit hard enough I audibly moaned before I could catch the sound. A deep chuckle rumbled in his chest, and my eyes snapped up to his sardonic smile.

"Such a needy little slut." The name washed over me, humiliation prickling.

I went to reply, but he'd already stepped back to reach for a cloth to wipe his hands. It swung the loose braid in his hair, the strands coated in red. There was even a smear of paint across his cheekbone, and I itched to reach up to touch it.

But his hand caught my wrist, dragging me closer until my breasts brushed his bare chest. He looked down at me, and I stilled beneath his scrutiny.

"*Ne touchez pas, même si vous êtes un chef-d'œuvre,*" he muttered, his gaze leaving heat in his wake. Tugging me closer, I fell onto his lap as he sat back on the chaise lounge in the corner of his studio. With both my wrists caught in his large hand, I was stuck straddling him. "So eager to please, giving herself up to save her father. Was it because you're so desperate for my cock, *belle*?"

His words shattered around me, causing anger to burn to the surface. "Fuck you." I tried to wrench myself back, but I was caught by his strength.

Sebastian's eyes narrowed, a cruel edge tipping his lips. "See, you're begging for it." His free hand pinched my nipple, followed by a slap against the back of my thigh, the sting burning. "Maybe you did it because you like to be punished? Is that it?" Another slap, this time closer between my legs. "Does my little slut want it to hurt?"

A third slap, and rather than recoil I moaned even as a tear slipped down my face.

"Answer me, Arabella," he commanded.

"I don't know," I whispered, my pussy throbbing from the impact.

Maybe I did want to be punished, especially when Sebastian was making me feel so alive. My brain was fighting my body, my mind telling me to run and hide from the monster looking at me like he wanted to devour me whole.

But my body was craving the rough treatment, wanting more. *Needing* more.

My new underwear tore at my hips, and I hissed before his fingers teased through my swollen folds, only giving me a second before thrusting two fingers inside. My back bowed beneath both pain and pleasure, a moan torn from my throat even as he held me against him.

His fingers curled, thumb reaching up to brush my clit, and I found myself rocking against his hand. I barely strangled the resulting whimper, my eyes squeezing shut at the onslaught of sensation.

"Eyes on me," Sebastian growled, releasing my wrist to grip my jaw instead. "Last warning." His fingers dug in hard enough to bruise, and my eyes slipped open at his command, immediately connecting to his. "Good girl."

Fuck. I was pretty sure I've never been so turned on, my thighs aching to clench together to ease some of the building pressure. But I couldn't, not while he held me hovering over his body, my release held hostage by his fingers.

I was into his domination, the obscene sound of how turned on I was echoing around us, adding to my whimpered breaths and wanton moans.

"Please," I begged, not that I knew whether I was begging him to stop, or keep going.

"So desperate for my cock," he murmured, his eyes never leaving mine, locking me in his orbit until a bolt of lightning swept over my body. My orgasm wasn't a sensual wave, but a violent current that seized my muscles, and made me see stars.

I screamed, unable to contain the sound even as he kept his fingers moving, drawing out every single ounce of pleasure he could. And then kept going, his thumb circling my clit, torturing the oversensitive nerves with little brushes while his fingers continued to thrust.

"It's too sensitive," I cried, trying to pull away.

Every touch was bordering on pain, my body aching from how hard I'd orgasmed, and now it was happening again. Forcing another release that left me boneless. Completely at his mercy.

"Isn't this what you wanted? To be used by the monster?" His fingers finally slowed, and I felt myself sag, held up only by his grip on my jaw. He pulled his fingers free from my pussy, which immediately ached at the loss, only to press them between my lips.

My own taste burst on my tongue, and I automatically sucked. His eyes darkened, his lashes lowering as he watched with a heated expression. My core ached, and he groaned when I twirled my tongue around his fingers, just to see what he'd do. Sebastian growled, pulling his fingers out and releasing me entirely.

"On your knees," he ordered, his voice as coarse as sandpaper.

His erection pressed between us, but he'd been ignoring it up until now.

Paint crusted on my skin, slightly flaking when I slipped off his lap, only to kneel on the floor in front of him. Sebastian widened his legs, and I shivered as he released his straining cock. He gripped it in his strong, veiny hand, and my mouth watered.

His thumb teased the head, and without a word he brought it to my lips, wiping his pre-cum along my bottom one.

"Open."

I resisted, fighting the need to bite him now that I wasn't so distracted with my body.

"Pick your battles, or this really is going to hurt. You'll be covered in my cum either way." Sebastian's hand fisted my hair, my scalp screaming as he pulled back, and my mouth opened with a gasp. He thrusted, his cock forced between my lips.

My tongue licked out, taking his taste into me.

Sebastian grunted. "Suck me, or I'll fuck another one of your holes, and I'll leave it a surprise to which one I pick."

I froze at the threat, and he used that distraction to thrust a little deeper. I couldn't fit him, my jaw already straining as I continued to tease him with my tongue, using the last ounce of control I had left.

His hand tightened in my hair, angling my head as he pumped his hips so his cock entered my throat, and I choked, unable to breathe. Pulling back, he let me take in oxygen before he thrusted forward again, gagging me with his size.

Sebastian groaned, his head tipped back and desire carving harsh lines across his beautifully brutal face. I concentrated on breathing through my nose, flattening my tongue to stroke the underside with every thrust. Spit was everywhere, my scalp burning from how hard he held me, and tears dripped down my face.

But even on my knees I felt this power at being able to watch this great, terrifying man become undone because of me. It made him seem more human.

"Putain de parfait."

Sebastian's thrusts became harsher, and he didn't pull out of my throat before a grunt slipped from his lips. I gagged on his release, having to swallow or risk choking.

He held himself inside me a beat more before pulling out, and I sucked in a much-needed breath, my lungs burning. My face was covered in spit, tears, cum, and paint. I was a mess on my knees before a man more powerful than I could really comprehend. A man holding my father's debt, and life over me.

Despite that, my pussy ached, and my clit begged for more attention.

Some sick, twisted part knew he wanted to ruin me.

And I was tempted to let him.

Chapter 27
Arabella

Shit. I'd fallen asleep.

Jerking up, I realised I was still on the chaise lounge in Sebastian's studio, a thick blanket draped over me. Paint covered me in slashes, various colours expertly smeared across my skin. It looked stunning in the daylight, the early morning sun streaming in to highlight the colour.

Rubbing my eyes I glanced around, finding I was alone. Not that I was surprised. Sebastian had made me come twice more on his fingers, watching me with an intensity each time as he played with my body. As if he was memorising every twitch of my muscle and sound that he could draw my throat.

I didn't remember falling asleep, but I did remember him picking me up, my body exhausted, and laying me down before returning to his painting. Swinging my legs over, I stood, my body aching as I turned toward the canvas.

I expected it to be slashed, destroyed like all the others that decorated the floor of the studio. But this one wasn't. Hesitantly, I reached forward, my fingers brushing across the surface. It was of me, head thrown back mid orgasm in shades of red and pink, with a splash of blue. Parts of my face had been smeared, across my eyes, and my bottom lip, as if he'd used his thumb to rub across it.

Then there was the background, black, as if the endless night was trying to swallow me whole. It was both harrowing and beautiful.

Clenching my jaw I grabbed my pyjamas, shoving them on before making my way to my room. Chip stood in the hall, his attention darting to the paint on my face.

"Mum asks whether you want to join us for breakfast," he said, his tone cold.

"Thank you," I replied, wanting to cover myself up. "I'll be there soon."

His nod was polite, almost disappointed, and then he stormed past towards the direction of the kitchen. I took a moment, my heart pounding and my stomach twisting. Fighting the burning across my cheeks, I slammed my bedroom door behind me, then immediately went to the bathroom.

I caught my reflection in the mirror, staring at myself covered in colour. I thought he'd just been obsessively applying the paint, but now I realised he was using the natural curves of my body to exaggerate my silhouette.

But now it was itchy, flaking with every movement. I needed it off.

Reaching into the shower, I turned the water to scorching and stepped beneath the stream. My body protested the heat, but still I washed everything away, scrubbing along my arms, through my hair and even the stickiness between my thighs.

My pussy was sore, aching from the way he'd used me. Groaning, I pressed my forehead against the cool tile, allowing the heated water to beat my shoulders.

Maybe you did it because you like to be punished?

"Arsehole," I whispered, fisting my hands.

I'd made the choice to search for Sebastian, fully aware of the consequences. Maybe he was right, maybe some twisted part of me wanted to be caught. To be punished. At least then I'd feel *something* instead of this constant numbness pressing down on me.

All I wanted was to curl into a ball and disappear, but even that felt out of reach.

I'd gone from living on edge, constantly bracing for the next mess my father would leave me to clean up, to being locked in a gilded cage.

From chaos to control.

One extreme to another.

And still, I was stuck. Lost.

I needed to talk to Sebastian and drag this debt out into the open, lay it bare so I could finally understand what I owed and figure out how long it would be until I could breathe again.

Scrubbing the remainder of the paint, which really didn't want to come off, I stepped out to give myself a minute. To think about my choices before I was crushed beneath the guilt.

Dressing, I grabbed one of the new paperbacks and went up to the mezzanine to be greeted by a cheerful Beatrice and a stoic Chip.

"There you are, come, sit down," she chirped, excitedly showing off a tray of fresh scones she'd set up on one of the short tables. "Sebastian's had to pop out to deal with something, but he'll be home soon, I'm sure."

She began to pour some tea, humming gently to herself.

"What does Sebastian do, exactly?" I asked, taking a seat and placing my book down.

Beatrice didn't miss a beat. "He's a businessman, dear." She concentrated on the tea.

"No, I mean what does—"

"He was such a peculiar little boy, always up to mischief," she interrupted, finally looking up to smile. "Cutthroat in everything he does."

Wait, was that a threat?

Chip sat rigidly beside me, his eyes burning a hole in the side of my head.

"Now, let's talk about you," Beatrice continued, taking a seat on the sofa opposite. "Such a fascinating little addition to this family. Sebastian isn't one to bring anyone home, especially someone like you."

I was taken aback by the slight hostility in her gaze, but it was quickly hidden beneath a gentle smile. So fast I must've imagined it. "What do you mean someone like me?"

"She's here to spread her legs," Chip commented, the words delivered without an ounce of emotion.

I expected Beatrice to gasp or even scold him. But she simply sat there, waiting for me to comment. When I didn't, Chip stood, leaning down to whisper in my ear.

"Your father's fine, if you still care."

I froze for a second, blood rushing to my face. But Chip was already gone before I could reply, disappearing down the spiral staircase to the floor below.

"Ignore him, dear. He has problems communicating and expressing himself sometimes." Beatrice cleaned up Chip's space, her head dipped as she wiped excessively over the table. "You'll do Sebastian some good. He's made his inner circle impenetrable, and here's you, infiltrating it."

"Enough," Sebastian growled, and I jumped, accidentally knocking over my tea. I didn't even hear him enter the room.

"Shit." I reached for a tissue, dabbing at the spill.

Beatrice stood abruptly. "Sir, I didn't realise—"

"You're dismissed, Mrs Pritchard."

Beatrice's shoulders tightened, her lips thinning. "Of

course. I meant no harm." Picking up her cloth she held her head up, passing Sebastian, only to pause. They exchanged a few words I couldn't hear, so I returned to cleaning the spill.

I felt him hover beside me, the tension stretching taunt between us.

"Read to me," he said once we were alone, my head jerking up at the demand.

"Good morning to you, too," I muttered, tossing the tissue into the bin. "Does reading to you count toward paying off my debt?"

"Maybe." He lounged back in the chair opposite me, legs spreading wide, taking up more space than his already overwhelming presence demanded.

A frustrated sound escaped me, Chip's silent judgment enough to set my nerves on edge. "How much have I worked off?"

Sebastian didn't flinch. He just stared, eyes locked on mine. "Nothing."

"Nothing?" I sputtered in disbelief. "That's ridiculous."

"You should've set the terms when we first made the deal."

"I was under duress!" I snapped, my heart pounding hard against my ribs. "How is it possible I haven't paid off a single thing?"

Sebastian leaned in, gaze ice-cold and cruel. "You think offering your throat clears even a fraction of what your father owes? *Belle,* I decide when the debt is paid, not you. It could be next week. Next year. Or maybe not at all."

"You're such an arsehole." My pulse pounded behind my ribs, adrenaline surging through me like wildfire. "This was never a life sentence, Sebastian."

He straightened his cuffs with deliberate calm, infuriatingly composed while I wanted to scream. "I told you," he said, voice flat and cold, "I'll decide when the debt is paid. Until then, do as you're fucking told."

My hands curled into fists. "This is bullshit! I want it written down; every act of service I do should go towards the money."

His jaw twitched, just slightly as he closed the distance between us, forcing my head to lean back. "You're not in a position to demand anything."

I refused to back down. "You don't get to own me *and* keep me in the dark. That's not control... that's... that's cowardice." I winced as the word came out, expecting his anger in return.

For a second, the silence between us drew tight. I held my breath when he leaned down, his lips hovering so close to my own. "Be careful, *belle*. You're acting like you want to be punished." He took a step back, and my breath came out in a ragged exhale as he took a seat on the sofa. "Last warning, don't make me ask again."

He wore his usual armour of his black-on-black suit, his hair pushed away from his face to reveal dark circles beneath his eyes. Those tattoos that I wished I could explore in more detail peeked through the collar, as were the scars I didn't get the chance to memorise.

"You want me to read to you?" I finally asked, and Sebastian simply nodded before closing his eyes, settling himself deeper into the seat. "Why?"

"Can you ever follow an order without questioning it?"

I bit the inside of my cheek to stop myself from snapping back, because that would only prove his point. Clearing my throat, I opened my new book to the first page and started to read aloud. Sebastian relaxed, the tension along his shoulders dissipating chapter after chapter.

I couldn't even concentrate on the story, so hyperaware

of the man who sat opposite me. Something about a prince being cursed by an old woman.

I didn't know how long I read out loud, but when I looked up, his breathing was slow and gentle. He hadn't moved an inch, his head resting on his shoulder and his lips open slightly. He looked peaceful, even approachable.

I quietly closed the book, placing it on the table before leaning forward to check him, only for his hand to snap out. I squeaked as fingers wrapped around my throat, the sudden shock forcing my survival instinct to kick in. I lashed out, managing to knock his jaw before he flipped me onto my back, his body hovering above.

Panic forced me to react, and I twisted and fought with all my energy, scratching along his arms and wriggling beneath his grip.

Sebastian frowned down at me, blinking.

"Why did you stop reading?" he rumbled, his grip tightening slightly when I managed to bite him.

I took a minute to calm down, my pulse racing. "I thought you were asleep."

He chuckled, the sound low and dark. "I don't sleep."

"Everyone sleeps." I tried to wriggle, realising I was stuck. "Can you let me go?"

His frown deepened. "Why?"

"Because you're crushing me." He actually wasn't; he was clearly trying not to touch me anywhere but his fingers on my throat.

"You weren't complaining last night."

The urge to hit him again turned my muscles to stone, but I resisted because he was several times my size, and that would probably be stupid.

"Are you feeling better?" I asked instead, because I was a diplomat and would really like to not be stuck under his body for the rest of my arguably short life. Unless it was for other things.

No. What was wrong with me?

Stop thinking about his dick.

"You show all your emotions on your face," he scolded, and if I wasn't blushing before, I sure as fuck was now. "It's inconvenient."

"You're inconvenient."

Great. Honestly, I disappointed myself sometimes.

Sebastian clenched his jaw and then released me so I could ungracefully roll out from beneath him.

"So... what did Beatrice say to you?" I stood, needing to create distance.

"Beatrice?" he repeated, his voice a deep tone that caressed my skin as he followed. "You're getting too close to my staff. You'll address her as Mrs Pritchard."

"I'm just curious." And bored. "It's not like I have anything else to do around here." I pressed myself tight against the wall, his larger frame cornering me as he planted his hands on each side of my head.

"You're not here to be curious."

"No, I'm here to be your toy."

There was a pause, then Sebastian slowly leaned forward. "You're playing a dangerous game with me." The threat danced between us, and for some reason it sent a thrill through me.

I'd have to make sure I wrote this down in my notebook later. To try and figure out where in my childhood it all went wrong. Which was a joke, because my entire childhood was a mess.

"It's Ara. Not *belle*. That's not even part of my name."

"Why are you here, Arabella?" he growled, the air vibrating with tension.

"To save my father."

"The same father who doesn't give a shit about you? Who gave you over like some common whore to save his own arse? Try again. Why are you here?"

My pulse beat against the side of my throat. "I don't know what you're asking. Why else would I be here if it's not to save my father?"

"Wrong again." Sebastian stepped closer but still left a cushion of space between our bodies. "Why are you here?"

"Does it even matter?" I tried to make myself appear more confident. Clearly I failed, but at least I'd tried. "You accepted the swap. It's done, and now my father's safe and I'm here, rotting away in your—"

"Why are *you* here, Arabella?"

"Because I don't want to think anymore!" I cried out, the words a rush that I couldn't stop. "Here I don't have to be constantly on edge, waiting for when Dad inevitably fucks up."

Sebastian had taken away my autonomy, and right now I liked it. Even as the walls around me crumbled at the loss of all my control, I found peace in his demands. It was then that I could turn my mind off and finally relax. Not be constantly on edge.

And now I was disappointed in myself, because I'd chosen this to save my father, not to save myself.

I flinched when Sebastian's thumb caught a single tear down my cheek.

"God, what's wrong with you?" I recoiled, pressing further against the wall.

His hands clenched. "Many things, but right now it's because my cock isn't buried in your tight throat. Shall we change that?"

I shook my head, shrinking back.

"Then stop testing me."

"What do you want from me?" I whispered.

He scowled down at me, his voice husky when he finally answered. "Everything."

Chapter 28
Sebastian

Arabella was mine. She'd melted beneath me so beautifully, and I'd taken great pleasure in smearing her perfect lips with my paint and cum.

She was like a walking piece of art, and I was going to enjoy using her.

Reluctance did nothing for me, not when I had women throwing themselves like whores, begging to go to their knees. They wanted to tame me. Fix me like I was broken.

Arabella was different, she saw me fractured, my mind at the edge of sanity, and didn't run. Her body responded to my rough touch, begged for it as she shattered around me several times. Even if I could see a stubbornness in those golden-brown eyes that made me want to punish her.

She was like a challenge, but even as she submitted to me, she seemed to be holding a small piece of herself back. But I wanted it all, craved it.

The women I usually fucked were just a physical release, nothing more, and nothing less. I went because my body required it, but I felt just as empty after as I did before. Even those women, the ones who liked the pain, would scream seeing me at my worst, when my nightmares and demons howled too loud.

Arabella had fucking screamed too, but only because my fingers were forcing pleasure.

I glanced to my left, unable to look away from her new choker, which did a great job of hiding the marks I'd left on her throat.

She was bored, and I'd clearly neglected her by leaving her alone for too long.

You need to be more wary of her, Sir. Mrs Pritchard's words circled around my head, and I definitely should fire her. She'd become too attached, overstepping if she believed she had any right to speak to me so casually.

Arabella turned from where she'd been staring through the car window, finding me watching her. She didn't look away, instead raising an eyebrow. Clicking a button on the door, I put up the partition so I was alone with her before pulling her onto my lap.

She froze as my hand found the slit in her dress, but she didn't stop me, knowing not to touch me in return. It was different if I initiated it, and I found I enjoyed her weight because it gave me easier access to the soft skin of her thighs.

"What are you doing?" she asked, her voice reminding me of how gentle it had been earlier, how I almost fell asleep just from her reading.

I was going to make her do it often, before I painted her skin and then fucked her throat.

"Do you understand your role?" I asked instead.

"To sit still and look pretty," she muttered, and I smirked beneath my mask at the way she straightened her spine. It made my cock ache, pressing against the fabric of trousers.

If I didn't recognise that we were close to the docks, I

would've seen if I could make my new favourite doll come again. Her moans were addictive, as was the way her face twisted when she came as if she was in pain.

"Good girl," I whispered, amused with how her breath hitched.

I'd chosen her dress, Elena fitting it to her so it was slick to her body, black satin with a slit indecently high on the right side. The black matched her choker, the only colour being the red rose pendant.

She looked stunning, especially with my fingers marking her delicate skin.

"Keep your ears open and your lips sealed," I added.

She looked over her shoulder at me, meeting my gaze without fear of repercussions. That fire was there, glittering embers that reminded me she wasn't as innocent as she projected.

Mrs Pritchard had warned me that Arabella was hoarding some of my silverware underneath her bed, a few expensive pieces from the dining room set. I was also certain one of my watches had mysteriously vanished, too. I'd decided to not say a word, even telling the maids to leave them be. I'd allow her to collect the expensive trinkets and let her believe she was clever, preparing for some grand escape.

I *wanted* her to think she had the upper hand.

Breaking her wasn't the goal.

Not yet, at least. I wanted her hope alive, just enough to keep her fighting. Just enough to make it fun when she realised I was always in control.

"Hmm," she hummed as I collared the front of her throat gently, my thumb brushing along her jawline. Those embers burned hotter, glittering with just a touch of arousal.

That's right, she liked it when I dominated her, using her hair as an anchor so I could thrust faster, deeper into that mouth. My eyes traced her lips, and they parted like an invitation. So instead, I tightened my fingers, warning her.

"I told you to seal those lips."

She laughed, an almost surprised sound that shot straight to my cock. Releasing my grip, I used my forearm to keep her where she was as we pulled up outside the restaurant just at the edge of the docks.

Langdon opened my door, having been following in another car along with Caden, a pale eyebrow raising when he noticed my lap. "Do I want to ask?" he signed before smirking. Shaking his head, he held out his hand, and Arabella hesitated before taking it, allowing him to help her out of the car.

"Thank you," she whispered, her fingers moving clumsily to sign. Langdon turned towards me, that earlier smile slipping. Seemed she'd been busy in my absence.

Arabella looked between us, sensing the tension. Dropping her hands she looked over at Caden, who joined us on my other side. A gun was on his hip, visible on the belt. Langdon's was in his palm, where it would remain for the duration while mine was tucked in a holster beneath my arm.

I wasn't a fan of guns; they were too impersonal. Too fast. I much preferred my fists.

James 'Hook' Holland stood at the entrance to his restaurant, his dark hair knotted on the top of his head. "Beast," he greeted, holding out his hand, which he quickly dropped when I didn't move.

Hook's smile strained, his black circled eyes lingering on the guns before finally meeting my gaze and then my mask.

"And here I thought we were catching up like old friends." He turned his back, walking inside the three Michelin star seafood restaurant with the expectation that we would follow.

Caden went first, with Langdon coming up behind. There was a noticeable hush when I stepped inside, only breaking once we followed Hook into the private room in the back. He was flagged by his own men, five in total, all standing along the back wall with their own weapons on display.

A table had been set up for two, which he quickly clicked his fingers for another chair.

Waiting until Hook sat, I looked towards Arabella, who scooted into the corner seat. Caden and Langdon immediately took up their positions, protecting our backs.

"I'd heard you'd paraded around a pet, but I thought you'd just added to your collection of spiders. She's pretty." Hook clearly wasn't one of the smartest men as he leaned towards Arabella. "Tell me about yourself, darling," he asked her, but when she remained silent, he clicked his tongue. "Cold, that one. I hope she's warmer between the sheets than that glare she's giving me. Otherwise, she might freeze your cock off."

"Careful," I warned, but Hook simply laughed.

"So, your man with the annoying watch has filled me in," he began, pouring us both a glass of rum. "You know I have other contracts, right? I'm not at liberty to share confidential information on my other clients, the same way I don't share yours."

"I've come to believe my product's been tampered with." The rum burned down my throat, the bottle clearly from Hook's personal collection.

Hook relaxed back in his chair with a confident smirk. "Not by us."

"How confident are you on that?" Caden retorted dryly.

Narrowing his eyes at him over my shoulder, Hook returned his attention to me. "What do you know that I don't?"

Caden explained Eight's confession, while the entire time I watched Hook's reaction to see whether it was genuine.

"I wouldn't want our working relationship to end over this," I said.

"Don't fucking threaten me," he growled, his usual cocky demeanour breaking. "You need my ships to reach the rest of the continent, as well as your connections across the sea."

"You really believe you're my only option?" He wasn't, but he was the best. We held a symbiotic relationship I didn't want to burn if I could help it, but that depended on how much Hook knew about my powder being corked.

Hook gnawed on his bottom lip, head tipped back in thought.

After a moment, he took a sip of his rum. "What can you offer me for this knowledge? Your accusation comes from none other than an addict, and therefore an unreliable source."

"Would you risk my contract over it?"

Hook's nostrils flared, debating whether to trust my threat. After a moment he laughed, which made the men at his back tense. "You're such a prick, you know that?" Reaching over to one of his men, he gripped the front of his shirt and pulled him down.

Stumbling, the man followed, only for Hook to whisper in his ear.

"Of course, Captain," he said, adjusting himself before disappearing through the door.

"Now, I think we should discuss the elephant in the room. It's out of character to bring a date. Are you going soft on me, Beast?" Hook swished his rum in his glass, turning to Arabella. "Blink twice if you're being held against your will."

My hand slipped inside her dress's slit, the skin of her thigh soft and warm. "You're testing my patience."

"Trust me, he may act like the big bad wolf, but he's nothing against my kraken," Hook continued, undeterred.

Arabella's upper lip twitched. "I'll keep that in mind."

My fingers dug into her thigh, because of course she couldn't follow a fucking order. A snort came from behind us, followed by a chuckle. "Langdon called you a wet fish," Caden said, clearly translating.

Hook licked along the rim of his rum. "I'm sorry, mute. I couldn't hear you; you might want to say it louder."

"How vile of you," Arabella snapped. "He can communicate absolutely fine without his voice."

Hook choked on his rum, spitting it across the table. "You have a feisty one there, are you sure she's your taste? Because she's definitely more like mine."

Langdon stepped forward, making sure his hands were visible to Arabella. She frowned, unable to understand while I shook my head.

"He said don't bother with the tripod," I translated.

Surprise flashed across her face, and Hook grinned at her reaction. She really needed to learn to hold back her expressions. "Don't worry, darling. A croc may have taken my leg, but my cock still works like a charm."

"There are no wild crocs in Europe, you fucking muppet," Caden muttered.

"Who said it was wild?" Hook chuckled just as there was a knock. "Ah, there he is, the man of the hour."

The door opened, revealing a short, white-haired man. "Captain, you called for me?" he said, stumbling back when he noticed me at the table.

"You're not even a fucking Captain," Langdon signed beside me, face twisting in disgust. "You're scared of water."

Luckily, Hook couldn't understand sign. "Hi there,

mate, please come join us." He stood, patting what I assumed to be Smithy on the shoulder in an aggressive manner and pushing him down into his vacated seat.

"Captain?" he warily asked, eyes darting between everyone in the room.

"My friend here has a few questions to ask." Reaching over to his own glass, Hook downed the rest of his rum before topping it up again, but this time he placed it in front of Smithy. "Now, I'd suggest you answer them, because I said you were a true and honest bloke, and you know how I don't like to be called a liar."

Squeezing Smithy on the shoulder, Hook reached over to one of his other men's belt, pulling out a knife. He slammed it onto the table, the blade curved.

"Now, have you been fucking with Beast's powder?"

Chapter 29
Arabella

Sebastian was a drug lord. Holy shit.

I didn't know what I expected, because of course the owner of a club couldn't have his sort of money. Even with the fights, Sebastian showed a wealth that was extreme.

Maybe I was just ignoring the obvious, not wanting to believe I'd given myself gift-wrapped to a man with no morals. And what's worse was that I felt... disappointed that he was a man who made his money from the misfortune of others.

Which was crazy, because Sebastian never once tried to convince me he was the good guy.

Sweat dripped down Smithy's forehead, his eyes darting around the room.

"What... n-no, of course not." His stutter wasn't a great start, nor was the way his voice raised at the end. Even I could tell he was lying.

Hook clicked his tongue, a slightly manic edge to his gaze. "Hmm, bad choice, mate. I'm going to have to take a finger for that." He didn't wait, using his knife to stab down, slicing straight through Smithy's ring finger.

He screamed as blood splattered over the table.

"Stop overreacting. It's not like it's your leg!" Hook snorted at his own joke.

I found myself unable to look away, even as nausea twisted my stomach at the scene. My knee bounced beneath the table, and Sebastian's hand stroked down my thigh to try and ease it. For some reason that grounded me, even as Smithy whimpered and trembled.

"You're acting awfully suspicious here, mate," Hook said. "Honestly, you're embarrassing me in front of my friends. Now, is there something you wanted to say?"

Smithy wheezed out a cry, snot smearing his upper lip. "I'm... I'm sorry! I... I didn't mean it!"

Another finger went, and I was surprised he hadn't passed out from how pale he was.

Langdon stepped forward, as did Caden. It was as if they'd practiced the routine, with Caden holding down the hand while Langdon used his lighter to cauterise the missing fingers. The scent of scorched flesh added to the metallic copper, and if it wasn't for me concentrating on Sebastian's touch, I think I would've been sick.

Smithy continued to scream, right up until Hook covered his mouth with a cloth. "Okay, I think it's time we moved this party outside." Nodding to his men, they grabbed a whimpering Smithy and dragged him out through another door.

Sebastian stood, waiting for me to join him at his side. His hand was hot at the base of my spine, guiding me through.

The cold air feathered over me, bringing the welcoming scent of sea and salt. Hook whistled as he walked casually behind his men, who continued to drag a fighting Smithy down the side of the restaurant and towards the docks at the back.

Concrete turned to wood beneath my feet, the sea mist

clawing at my ankles as it beat against the side, trying to pull me into the waves. The jetty was short, a large fishhook hanging over the edge.

Hook paused at the end, his grin manic. "This is the fun bit."

With a wink in my direction, he grabbed a struggling Smithy and hauled him up against the hook like the catch of the day. Smithy's next scream managed to break through the fabric, the spike spearing through his shoulder.

Hook gestured to the side, and the rope was pulled taut, forcing Smithy onto his toes at the edge of the dock or risk ripping through his muscle.

"Now, where were we?" Hook traced the curved blade down Smithy's chest. It sliced through his shirt and then skin like butter.

"Wait... wait!" Smithy cried when the knife hovered over his groin. "I did it! I was paid to swap the bags out for the contaminated ones!"

"By who?" Sebastian growled, tension vibrating his skin.

"I... I don't know the name. They bring that new stuff, Enchanted Dust. They offered me a ten percent cut on everything they sell!"

Hook's lips pursed, his head tilting to the side. "She goes by the Enchantress. She's my newest contract, straight from Bordeaux. Pretty thing, but a bit old for my tastes. Pays cash up front."

Sebastian tensed beside me. "You're not supposed to be taking any other products like mine. That's the deal," he hissed.

"It's heroin, not coke." Hook shrugged, as if unbothered by Sebastian's anger.

Sebastian seemed to have lost any patience he had, his footsteps loud as he closed the distance to Smithy. "Who's the contact for Enchanted?" he demanded, his voice dripping with disdain.

Smithy flinched, barely able to speak.

"He's going into shock," Caden muttered beside me. "Pathetic."

"Different..." Smithy managed to mumble. "Different every time. I don't know... I don't know! They come to me."

Hook and Sebastian asked a few more questions, and once Sebastian nodded, Hook slashed out with his knife. The blade sliced along his lower stomach, his guts falling to splatter by his feet.

There was a moment where he didn't die, simply staring at his intestines dangling with a horrified expression. I swallowed bile, my stomach threatening to expel what little contents it had. Blood smeared the decking, so thick in the air I was forced to breathe through my mouth.

Please don't be sick.

Please don't be sick.

Please don't be sick.

"Seems I need to apologise."

Hook nodded to his man, who released the slack and swung Smithy out to the water. He dropped with a splash below the surface, the waves lapping at him greedily, eager to swallow him whole.

"Your pet's looking a little pale there." Hook smirked, walking towards me. "She's too innocent to be from our world, so where did you get her?"

Sebastian returned to my side, and I found myself turning towards him. "You've disappointed me, Hook," he said, his body blocking the wind.

"Yes, well... mistakes were made," Hook drawled, his jaw tightening. "We're only human. Well, *I'm* human. You, my friend, remain questionable." He exhaled sharply. "But I'll make it right. I'll take a five percent cut on my fee and drop Enchantress from my contracts. She won't move a single shipment by sea; I'll see to that myself. I'm not letting anyone use me as a pawn in their territorial games."

"You'll take a *ten* percent cut," Caden said flatly.

"And you won't drop Enchantress," Sebastian added, surprising me. I glanced up at him, but his focus was locked on Hook. "She needs to believe she's still in the game, at least until I'm ready to tear her apart from the inside."

Hook pressed his lips together, then gave a slow, amused smirk. "Let's call it even and shake on it?"

Chapter 30
Sebastian

There was a pressure in my chest, like fire ants crawling beneath my skin. I needed to hit something. Break something, just to ease the fucking storm swirling inside.

Grabbing Arabella, I pulled her back towards the restaurant. Chip stood beside the car outside, leaning against the driver's door. He straightened as soon as he spotted us, opening the car for us to slip inside.

Arabella went first, and before she could scoot to her side, I'd already pulled her onto my lap. She stiffened a little but didn't fight it.

Good. She was learning.

The door slammed, the tension in the air growing until a single match could ignite it. But if it did, I didn't know what I would do.

Tearing the mask from my face, I threw it on the seat beside us, pressing my face into Arabella's hair. I needed to calm down, probably take those fucking pills just so I could get a single night of sleep.

Uncle was right, I didn't seem to be in control at the moment. My anger was quicker to provoke, and it took me longer to contain it.

"So, you're a drug dealer," Arabella said, her voice breaking the heaviness that surrounded us.

"Careful…"

"You're literally selling a product that destroys people's lives."

"People tend to destroy their own lives without my assistance," I said, my tone a deep growl that caused goosebumps to pebble along her arms. She reacted so viscerally to my presence. I couldn't help but wonder if she hated the reaction as much as I enjoyed it. "If someone wants to escape their dull lives, who am I to stop them?"

She twisted to glare at me over her shoulder. "You're creating addicts."

I scoffed. "They were already addicts. I'm just providing a more sustainable powder to those already wanting it."

"Is that what you tell yourself?"

I automatically grabbed her throat, my fingers squeezing in warning. "Careful, *belle*."

"An addict is an addict," she argued, ignoring my grip. "You're supposed to help them resist, not give it to them on a silver platter."

"Just like you helped your father?"

She tried to wrench herself to the side, but I simply tightened my fingers.

"Fuck you. Don't ever speak to me about my father." She swallowed against my palm, and I released her because I didn't trust myself to not keep squeezing. "You have no idea what I've had to do to help him."

"I'm sure he's thankful that he's still alive, and you're here with me." My words were cold, hammering down the point. "Your dependency on a man who sold you is concerning."

"He didn't sell me. I agreed to this arrangement," she

hissed, but she'd lost some of her conviction, as if she was slowly realising I wasn't the only monster in her life. "Fuck you, Sebastian. You don't get to lecture me about something you know nothing about."

I laughed, the sound alien even to me. I would've killed anyone else for speaking to me in such a way, but with her I found I enjoyed her resilience. She had no idea the edge on which she walked, risking being thrown into the abyss as soon as she pushed too far.

The car stopped at a red light, the vibration rumbling the leather beneath us.

"Ask," I growled, feeling her agitation on my lap. Her head kept turning towards me, lips opening before she lost her confidence and closed them again.

"Did you have to kill Smithy? Couldn't he just be let go with a warning?"

"I didn't kill him."

"But you didn't stop it." There was another moment of silence, and I concentrated on every single one of her breaths. "Do you think he deserved it?"

"Yes," I said without hesitation, her skin soft when I stroked up her legs.

Her breath hitched as my thumb brushed higher. "You don't get to play god with people's lives."

"I don't need to. I already own yours."

I pulled her so her back pressed tighter against my chest before spreading her legs over my thighs. Her dress strained at the position, so I pulled it up to reveal black lace.

"You disobeyed an order again."

My fingers brushed the edges of her underwear, and a groan caught in her throat. "I–"

I slapped her inner thigh, her words strangled as she writhed on top of me. "See, your mouth's going to get you into trouble."

Tugging at the lace until it ripped, I tossed the ruined fabric beside my mask.

"Sebastian..." Arabella breathed, her head pressing back against my shoulder when I brushed my fingers through her centre.

"You seem pretty wet for a monster." My thumb circled her clit, teasing without touching. "Tell me, how's that reluctance going?"

Arabella gasped. "Fuck you!"

I smirked into her hair. "Sounds like an invitation." Two fingers dipped inside, her pussy clenching around me when I finally brushed across her bundle of nerves. She wriggled on my lap, rubbing against my growing erection.

Fuck, she was tight, and I'd only gotten two fingers in.

"Stop," she whispered, and of course I didn't.

"Stop what? Stop touching you?"

She whimpered, so I pinched her clit.

"Doesn't sound like you want me to stop." My fingers moved lazily, the slick sound of her arousal obscene, and utterly addictive. "No, it sounds like my slut is enjoying this."

"Sebastian," she moaned, rocking her hips.

"Use your words, *belle*. Do you want me to stop?" I whispered.

She shook her head, her breath coming out in pants as I teased her to the edge of release. But this was supposed to be a punishment, so just before she came, I stopped.

She cried out, her body tensing at the loss, but before I could comment my phone rang. Reaching over, I clicked the button that would connect it to the car's speakers.

"Answer call," I said, the following click letting me know it had connected.

I brushed my lips against Arabella's ear, my voice dropping to a whisper.

"You'd better stay quiet." I continued to languorously tease, not giving her enough pressure to come. Keeping her on the very edge even as my cock strained painfully against my zipper.

"*Bas?*" Caden's voice echoed around us. "*Who the fuck is this Enchantress?*"

"I have no idea." I answered, using Arabella's pliant body to calm my anger.

"*So what's the plan?*"

Arabella threw her head back, her lips parted as I teased a third finger and pulled her dress down.

"We need to take this slow, so we don't scare her," I said, squeezing Arabella's breast before tugging at her left nipple. Her cunt clenched, and she barely strangled her moan, so I did it again.

"*Langdon's laughing, in case you hear an old man's wheeze.*" A thump. "*Ow, what the fuck was that for? Be fucking careful, I'm driving!*" Another thump, followed by feedback through the speaker. "*Okay, don't get your knickers in a twist. Lang said it's not exactly your style.*"

Arabella finally let me in, three fingers thrusting slowly. "That's three, do you think we can fit a fourth?" I whispered, making sure my voice couldn't be picked up by the phone.

Arabella was mine, and I wouldn't share a single fucking sound.

Caden continued, "*He's not wrong. Patience isn't one of your virtues, Bas.*"

"I think if we put on too much force, we'll scare her away." The last thing I wanted was the Enchantress to run, not unless I could give chase.

"*Hmm.*" Caden switched to French, knowing he was on loud speaker. "*You think your toy's a spy? Pretty suspicious that she gave herself to you around the same time.*"

I gave my attention to Arabella's right nipple, the skin hard as I tugged it roughly.

"The thought had crossed my mind," I replied in the same language, keeping Arabella in the dark. Not that she could really concentrate while I was trying to stretch her to accept a fourth finger. *"But no."*

"You sound confident in that."

"Doesn't mean I trust her." I could feel her pulse beat in her clit, her moans getting more frustrated each time I brought her to the edge and then pulled her back.

"Yet you brought her tonight."

So I did.

"I'll allow you to take the lead on this. You're right, you have more... patience than me," I continued in English.

Caden barked out a laugh, luckily loud enough to muffle Arabella's whimper until I placed a hand over her mouth.

"We need to be subtle," I added, her cunt resisting the stretch to take the fourth. "Put feelers out for this Enchantress. I want to see how deep her influence runs in this city."

"You know where to go to ask about rumours," Caden said, clearly not aware how close Arabella was to coming apart on my lap. *"Who better to ask than the Mistress of Whispers herself?"*

"Set up a meeting." I released Arabella's mouth to click off the phone and then immediately quickened my ministrations, making sure my fingers angled to brush against her G-spot. "Couldn't even keep quiet for me, could you?"

I pinched her nipple at the same time I pressed her clit, able to feel how close she was by how she gripped me.

"Beg me, Arabella."

"Please," she whimpered, strangling my fingers. Her entire body was tensed, ready to snap.

"Please what? Use your words."

"Let me come."

I didn't stop, her cries filling the cabin of the car as I forced the pleasure from her body. "Come for me," I demanded, biting down on her throat, just above her choker.

Arabella screamed, soaking us both as she was finally allowed to orgasm. Her body rocked, and I had to pin her to me with a forearm. My cock ached, testing the zipper of my trousers as I gritted my teeth.

"Couldn't even fit four fingers," I commented, brushing my lips over the bite mark. "How disappointing."

Arabella's chest heaved, her skin coated in sweat. She was like a ragdoll on me, her body exhausted. She went to roll to the side, but not before I tightened my grip.

"Where do you think you're going? Your punishment's not finished."

Chapter 31
Arabella

I felt like I was about to be eaten, my fear edged with arousal as I was chased through the penthouse towards the studio, never taking my attention off Sebastian as he stalked closer. He was a great shadow, his expression dark as he watched me with those soulless eyes.

He stopped at the door, his presence electric as he hooked his hands on the frame and leaned forward. My pulse raced, and I found my hands slick with sweat.

Your punishment's not finished.

Being edged for an entire car ride was not on my bingo card this year. Was it torture? Yes. Did I have the biggest orgasm of my entire life? Also yes. Even now I could feel his phantom fingers, expertly touching me as if he knew all my secrets.

My eyes dipped to where his erection pressed against his trousers. I should hate it. Hate him. But no, my traitorous pussy ached at the sight.

The dance of whether he was going to cross the final barrier and take me kept me on the edge, that he'd finally take away my will. Dominate me. And I found I craved it. It was his choice not to fuck me, to wait until I was begging for it.

Ever there he had power over me, and some twisted part was enjoying our little dance. It was... exciting. Being so close to a man who saw the world as nothing but a toy.

"Take off your dress," he commanded, my body reacting to the huskiness of his tone.

My skin tightened, my nipples pebbled, and need pulsed low in my belly. Even the air between us hummed, the weight of it like anticipation seconds before a storm.

Sebastian's head tilted, his long hair brushing over his shoulder as he took a single step closer. "Don't make me ask again."

This was a warning, not a seduction as he began to slowly unbutton his shirt, the sensual movement of it setting fire to my arousal. I stood frozen, my brain and body at war. I shouldn't want this, and yet I couldn't look away as more of his skin was revealed.

He really was beautiful, even with his scars.

"For someone who chose this," he growled, closing the distance until I was forced to tip my head back, "you're fighting me every step of the way. So let me remind you of your place."

His hand cupped my throat, thumb brushing against my pulse while his other hand ripped at my dress, the fabric tearing with little effort.

"You're mine to fuck." His head dipped closer, lips impossibly close. "Mine to own."

"No," I managed to push out.

Sebastian smiled, the expression savage. "Shall we take a visit to dear old dad instead?"

I bit at his hand, using my entire weight to shove him away. I would've made more progress with hitting a brick wall. His fingers tightened, taking away my oxygen and forcing me up onto my toes. I scratched at him, fighting him off as he watched me as if I were insignificant. As nothing more than a plaything.

As quickly as he'd threatened to take my life, he released me. I took in a startled breath, and as I did a sharp pain landed on my butt. I shrieked, the skin burning before his fingers dipped between my legs from behind.

"Such a whore for me," he murmured, finding me already embarrassingly slick. "Just a needy hole."

"Fuck you," I hissed, finding myself widening my legs further.

Sebastian leaned forward. "Now that's exactly what I plan to do."

I groaned at the loss when he stepped back, removing the rest of his clothes until we were both naked. "What if I say no?"

"You won't," he said, clearly confident. He began to walk around me, my skin heating in anticipation. "You may have made me the villain inside your head, but in reality..." Sebastian reached for some paint, smearing it straight onto my stomach. "You want to be fucked by the big bad Beast."

Another smear of paint, his fingers harsh and firm. Reminding me he was the one with the power, and all I could do was bend to his will.

"*Tu es mon œuvre d'art préférée,*" he whispered, his large hand kneading my entire breast before he moved around my back. His heavy cock nudged me from behind, and I stilled, waiting for him to cross that final line.

But he didn't, and I found myself sagging forward when he stepped back. Sebastian passed me, grabbing one of the large canvases and tossing it on the floor. Looking over his shoulder, he pinned me to the spot, and then with a crooked finger called me forward.

I moved as if my body was possessed, forced into the

intensity that was his orbit. A man of pure temptation and sin.

"What am I about to do, Arabella?" he asked, lifting me as if I weighed nothing.

My voice didn't sound like my own. "You're going to fuck me." It was way too husky, throaty.

"And you're going to fucking take it like a good girl, aren't you?" He lowered us both until my back hit the cool canvas.

I nodded just as I felt his thick cock begin to spread my pussy. Reaching for my wrists, he pinned them above my head, then made me spread my legs almost painfully to accommodate his body.

He moved forward, pressing against my entrance and brushing across my clit in a tease that had me panting. I tried to angle my hips, needing him inside me. His fingers pinched my nipple, the sharp pain immediately soothed when he rubbed it with his thumb.

"Please," I whispered, my body charged with need. "Sebast—"

He didn't give me a warning, his hips pressing forward in one violent thrust that stole the air from my lungs. Paint squelched beneath me, but all I could concentrate on were his exhales that brushed across my cheek, and his grunt that sounded like ecstasy.

"Your greedy cunt is so wet." He pulled back, only to thrust deeper, harder as I struggled to stretch to his size. "You're going to let me use this hole just like I used your throat, aren't you *belle*?"

He only gave me a moment before he began to move, my body buzzing like a live wire. Rocking up to meet each of his thrusts even as he had me pinned beneath me.

My thighs trembled against the onslaught, Sebastian's thrusts rough, as if he couldn't reach deep enough. I revelled in the stretch, heightening the pleasure he was dragging from me even if I was grateful he'd prepped me for so long in the car.

It made me feel weightless, like my mind was floating as he took away my power. I could quiet the worry and chaos inside my brain, able to concentrate only on his demands of my body.

It was euphoric.

"Fuck," he groaned, releasing my wrists, only to tilt my hips up for a different angle, his body covering mine. "Look how well you're taking me."

His hand encircled my throat, keeping me pinned to the canvas while my eyes blurred with tears from taking him so deep.

Fuck.

"*Presque là.*" His thrusts came faster, his words coming out in a husky growl. "*Tu es fait pour moi.*"

Sensation rippled across my skin, overwhelming, electric, and still, he kept pushing. His fingers pinching and then caressing as he pounded into me.

I couldn't fight the orgasm that tore through me so violently I shook, my body rippling with the intensity even as Sebastian kept going, his thrusts turning animalistic. Stretching me beyond what I was used to and reaching places I didn't even know existed.

Sebastian

I didn't give her time to adapt to my size, wanting her to feel me for fucking days, even weeks once I was finally done. She was fucking perfect, her cunt squeezing me so tightly as she orgasmed with a scream.

For someone who fought me, she came so easily.

Her face was fixed with desire, lips parted as she pressed her head back, exposing her pale throat. I bit down on her shoulder, wanting to mark her anywhere. Everywhere. She still wore my choker, the contrast of her skin against the darkness of my possession enough to make me crazy. Obsessed.

Arabella's cries became louder, tears leaking from her eyes as she struggled to take the last few inches. "Please, it's too much."

"You'll take it," I whispered, purposely overstimulating her just so I could break her apart. I pushed past her muscles until I could sink every fucking inch of me inside her, her entire body shaking beneath me.

I let out a groan, and Arabella shifted her hips, taking me even deeper.

Fuck. She really was made for me.

The canvas scraped against the floor, pushed by my movements as I fucked her with harsh strokes. Hooking her legs over my hips, I reached down and pressed against her throat, keeping her in place so I could go harder, faster.

She whimpered, but the more I choked her, the wetter she became.

Arabella reached up to grip me, nails digging into my arm to anchor herself against my thrusts. I waited for a violent response, to want to push her off and hurt her for touching me. But I found I didn't mind, enjoying the slight pain as she shattered around my cock once again.

She really was a receptive little thing, her body coated

in the most beautiful smears of paint and sweat. Her thighs and pussy glistening with her cum.

She watched me through her lashes, and my eyes clashed with hers as I fucked her until she was nothing but a malleable mess. Rutting into her like an animal, smearing her cum and paint across the canvas like my greatest masterpiece.

My own orgasm tingled my lower spine, and before I came, I sat back on my heels, pulling Arabella up so I could force her to take my cum as deep as possible. My entire body tensed, my cock pulsating as I filled her with a grunt.

Arabella sagged against me, her head resting against my shoulder as she struggled to catch her breath. It took me a moment to calm my own pulse, my cock still twitching inside her. I expected rage at her touch, perhaps even panic. But instead, I wrapped my arm around her back and stood, glancing down at the paint that had transferred onto the canvas.

I'd never fucked without a condom, but with her that would never be an option. Her body was mine to use as I saw fit, without a barrier. I knew she had the implant, her medical records the first thing I asked for when she gave herself over to me. I knew she was clean. Healthy. *Mine*.

Arabella was sated in my arms, a ragdoll as I reluctantly placed her down. My cum decorated her thighs, and I immediately scooped it up with my fingers, only to press it back inside. She was the perfect distraction, taking all my anger without flinching.

This woman was quickly becoming my very own dangerous addiction, and now that I'd had a taste, I didn't know if I'd ever want to let go.

Chapter 32
Arabella

Another week passed so fast. I wasn't allowed out of the penthouse again, which meant I was back to being locked away in my figurative tower. But I was allowed free access, everywhere except the locked door in the west wing.

I spent my days writing or exploring the many rooms up the stairs in the west wing that held no purpose other than storage or to collect dust. Seriously, this place was fucking huge.

In the evenings I read to Sebastian while he painted or practiced with the punching bag. Sometimes he'd paint me, and that always ended with multiple orgasms for us both. I found my body readying itself every time he painted, excited. He was rough, but with the pain came pleasure, and I realised I loved the feeling of being claimed.

Owned.

Used.

He didn't stop until I was practically boneless, and then he'd carry me back to my bed, or lay me on the chaise lounge.

But I was still trapped, alone.

Lounging back, I bathed in the sunlight in the studio, re-reading my favourite of the three books.

"You even allowed in here?"

I jumped up, dropping my book and losing my page.

"I'm not even allowed in here," Chip continued, standing in the doorway.

"Bloody hell, you can't sneak up on me like that!" I eyed him warily, wondering whether he was blowing hot or cold today. "Are you okay? You haven't been around lately."

Chip regarded me cooly. "Do you care about me or the fact I've been checking up on your dad?"

"That's not fair." I hadn't seen Chip since the night of the docks, and he was my only connection to the outside world. "You're my only friend here."

His eyes were intense when they met mine. "He's fine. Still at the garage and living above in the flat."

"He is?" I couldn't tell if I was relieved or worried. He'd usually run as soon as things got sketchy, so what was making him stay? "Thank you for checking on him. I can't explain how much I appreciate it." It was like a weight lifted off me, and my eyes prickled with tears that he was still alive. That he'd stayed in the same city.

"Do you want me to get a message to him?" Chip asked, his tone lighter, almost eager.

"I... Just tell him I'm okay."

Chip cocked his head, still standing in the doorway. "I want to apologise about what I said before, about spreading your legs. I was angry and shouldn't have taken it out on you. I'm sorry."

The memory of his words heated my cheeks. "It's fine."

"No, seriously. It was out of line, and you didn't deserve it."

He finally took a step inside, eyes darting around the

room. Chip pushed back the ribbons of the closest canvas, staring at the distressed art.

"You do realise you're expendable, right?" he said, voice low. "We all are. Just staff. Tools. Told what to do, when to speak, and when to disappear." Without warning he shoved the canvas, and it hit the ground with a loud crack. "Nothing but pawns on his chessboard."

I tried to move past him, but his hand lashed out, gripping my upper arm like he couldn't let me walk away from the truth he was trying to force on me.

"Let go of me," I warned, surprised by his burst of violence. "Chip."

His grip didn't tighten, but he didn't release me either. "Why do you let him hurt you?"

"He doesn't hurt me." Well, he hadn't hurt me against my will. Which just showed how messed up my life had become. Even more so than it was before.

"So you actually want him to touch you?" Chip watched me, his expression empty and his eyes lacking any light.

"That's none of your business."

"You're worth so much more than a whore, Ara. You're literally in the home of one of the most powerful men in the city, and you what? Choose to read all day and then spread your legs at night?"

"That's enough." I finally pulled my arm free, anger making my face prickle with heat. "Where the hell is this coming from? I thought we were friends."

"I thought you were like me, here because you have no other choice."

"You keep painting me as some pathetic damsel, but I'm not. Yes, I chose to be here. I *chose* to take my father's place, knowing I'd be treated like a whore, just like you called me.

And you know what? I'd do it again if it meant my father lived. You have no fucking *idea* what I've endured, so don't you dare judge the choices I've made to survive."

I managed to get past, my footsteps quick as I left him behind.

"What is it about him?" Chip snapped after me, but I was already moving. "You're closer to my age than his. He's a fucking decade older, Ara."

Guilt and betrayal burned behind my eyes as I raced back to my room. It didn't matter that he could follow me; I just needed space to think. To breathe without judgment from my only friend.

Crashing through the door, I came to a halt when I found Sebastian looking through my notebook.

"What are you doing?" I snapped, panic twisting my stomach at the drawings I'd made of the penthouse. Of the possible exits and hiding spots. "That's mine."

Sebastian didn't even look up. "What is it?"

"Did you read any of it?" I asked, noticing the tension along his shoulders.

He finally met my eyes. "Would you read it to me?"

"No." There was no hesitation, and I itched to snatch it from his hand. "Give it back." I reached out, but he held it high above my head. "Sebastian..."

"What's it called?"

I gritted my teeth. "Bound by a Beast."

His upper lip twitched. "Maybe it should be called Beauty and the Beast."

I narrowed my eyes at him. "Trust me, it's not a romance."

He looked at me, his gaze intense when he finally released my notebook. I crushed it safely to my chest. No way would I want Sebastian to read it. I didn't think I wanted anyone to ever read it.

"You look... upset," he settled on.

I averted my eyes. "It's nothing."

"Does it have anything to do with Chip in my studio?"

"You were watching me?" I looked around, but I still hadn't been able to find any cameras.

"What did he say to you?"

I took too long to answer. "Nothing important."

"If you don't tell me, I'll just have to go ask him." Sebastian took a step towards the door, and I panicked.

"What? No. Look, it's nothing. He just... he called me your whore."

"You've been called my whore before."

"Yeah, but..." I sighed. "He was just reminding me how small I am, and how easily you can toss me aside once you're bored."

Sebastian's expression darkened, his footsteps silent as he moved closer.

I swallowed under his intensity, but still I lifted my chin. "He's harmless."

"Hmm." Sebastian reached up to grip my jaw, his thick rings cold and digging into my skin. "I don't like people crushing on things that are mine. I don't share my toys, *belle*."

"You've made that perfectly clear." I tried to jerk my head back, but he only held me tighter. "And he doesn't have a crush on me."

"Maybe I should reiterate." Sebastian dipped his head, and I found my pulse reacting. "Invite Chip in here so he can watch you scream my name while I make you come on my cock."

My face prickled, but my core clenched with arousal.

"Maybe I'll just cut his throat and use his blood as lube so I can finally take that last hole of yours."

"Stop it," I whispered.

"You say that like you wouldn't bend over for me will-ingly." His thumb reached up to brush my bottom lip.

"You speak about taking lives like it's nothing," I said, trying to steel my voice. "Like it doesn't take something from you."

"Death *is* life," he replied smoothly. "Someone has to be at the top of the food chain. Don't act like you've never done something selfish to protect yourself or your father."

"That's different," I snapped. "I've never had to *hurt* anyone."

He tilted his head, eyes dark with something unread-able. "You don't know that for sure." His thumb pressed harder against my mouth, relentless, always pushing. "I know how far you'll go. How much you'd risk for a man who doesn't deserve it. Did you know your dad offered you to me before you'd even agreed? How he begged, crying on his knees in my office to take you as payment instead?"

His words hit like ice water, and my lungs seized, the sudden tightness strangling the breath from me. "I don't believe you." My dad wasn't a good father, but he'd never do that. He needed me as much as I needed him. We only had each other. "Stop it."

My hand flew to Sebastian's chest, shoving weakly against him, trying to create distance. But he didn't move.

"He expected me to fuck you," he went on, his voice colder now. "Then kill you."

A tremor ran through me, but he wasn't finished.

"And still, he handed you over like you were nothing. So tell me," he whispered, eyes searching mine, "are you blindly stubborn? Or just *stupid*?"

My palm cracked across his cheek, the sound sharp and brutal in the stillness between us. The sting bloomed across my skin, and I gasped at what I'd done.

I braced for retaliation, for him to hit me back or grip

my wrist in a bruising hold. To punish me. Instead, his eyes brightened with amusement. Like he *wanted* me to fight. Like my resistance only fed whatever dark creature that lived inside him.

He smiled, his lips curling slowly, dangerously. "If it was between his life or yours... where would you aim the gun now?"

I stared at him, my breath shallow. "I could never kill anyone, and I sure as hell wouldn't enjoy it the way you do."

"That's what makes us different," he said, voice softer than before. "You still think morality is a line, when it's not."

"You speak like a monster."

"Hmm." His head cocked to the side, his hair tied up to leave only dark wisps to frame his face. "If you believed that, I'd stuff my cock down your throat right now and ignore you if you tell me no." My lips opened to protest, and he smirked. "But you wouldn't tell me no, would you *belle?*"

This was where I was messed up, because he was right. The more he made me feel helpless, out of control, the more I ached between my legs.

"There's a reason you're here, Arabella. There's a darkness inside that matches mine."

"I'm nothing like you."

"We'll see." He pressed closer, and I felt his erection dig into my stomach. It was heavy and hard, and I waited for him to demand me to my knees. To fuck me despite the animosity burning between us. "Read to me."

"You... want me to read to you?" I asked, brows knitting in confusion.

He didn't answer, just stood there watching me with that unreadable expression he wore too well. I glanced toward the books I'd carefully arranged on the dresser, all except the one I'd left behind in the studio.

I gestured toward them, trying to mask the unease threading my voice. "Which one?"

"Don't care." He didn't even look at them, his eyes trained on me. "The one you were reading last time."

"That's *Tale As Old As Time.*"

He finally glanced at the books, but a nerve feathered along his jaw.

"I'll get it." I waited for him to drop his hand, and when he did, I grabbed the right book and turned to him expectantly.

Following him to the studio, I was thankful Chip was gone as I took a seat. Sebastian began to strip, the clink of his rings hitting the dish by the window. Followed by the clang of his cufflinks. There was silence, nothing but the sound of his buttons, and then fabric brushing against skin as he removed his shirt to reveal his wide chest. He stayed in his trousers, turning to pick up a fresh canvas and paints.

Vincit qui se vincit, was beautifully written across his upper back, perfectly blended with the thorns and roses. Sebastian looked over his shoulder when I didn't start, his eyes clashing with mine.

"What does the tattoo mean?" I asked, not that I expected he would answer, especially when his jaw clenched at the question. "It's Latin, right?"

"'He conquers who conquers himself.'"

Okay. I still wasn't entirely sure what that meant. "So you're your worst enemy?"

"Essentially. It means I need to remain in control of myself." Sebastian picked up the blue, mixing it with the black straight on the canvas. It created a beautiful, dark swirl. Like a void.

"Nobody is in complete control all the time," I argued. "You're allowed to have a bad day."

His eyes slitted to mine, probably annoyed, but I

continued anyway because talking to a wall that responded with glares was better than talking to an actual wall.

"Do you know what I do when I'm having a hard time? Aside from making up an extravagant and dramatic plot specifically for the demise of my enemies?" I joked.

"So that's what's in that notebook of yours." Sebastian's upper lip twitched. "Tell me, how theatrical is my death? Or have we only just fucked in your story?"

My ears heated, and I chose to ignore him. "When I'm sad, I like to eat cake. The really expensive ones that you see in the patisserie windows that don't even look real. Specifically strawberry and cream."

Sebastian raised a single brow, but rather than continue to paint, he cleaned his hands before wrapping his knuckles in fabric. So I opened the book, found where we'd left it last time, and began to read about the cursed prince. I found my attention drifting back to him, distracted by how his muscles along his back bunched as he punched the bag.

He stopped when he realised I was watching, glaring a warning until I started reading again. His movements weren't aggressive, but they were angry. Controlled. Practiced.

It was hours later when he finally slowed, a fine layer of sweat coating his skin.

I'd just gotten to the stupid falling in love part of the story, but I stopped reading when Sebastian approached, leaning down to plant his hands on each side of my hips. He always kept a cushion of air between us, his heat radiating as the tension stretched.

"Lay back, *belle*," he said, his voice a deep, husky sound that wrapped around me. I did as I was told, his fingers bunching the fabric of my dress. "Keep reading."

His hands were rough on my thighs, shamelessly stroking my skin.

"Such a needy little slut," he whispered when he finally brushed a knuckle against my core. I suppressed a moan, trying to concentrate on the words as his fingers teased until I shattered.

And then he grabbed the paints.

Chapter 33
Sebastian

The familiar symbol of a trident glowing over the thick, metal door came into view. There was no other sign or indication of the depravities that happened within. That was why this was the most elite sex club in the Isles, with strict rules once entering, much like my own club.

I went to Atlantis for one reason: to explore the primal edges of my desire in a space where I held complete control. There, I could unleash the monster I kept caged.

Women came willingly, drawn by the promise of exactly what I offered. I craved the rawness of it, the exquisite imbalance of power. The way it twisted and surrendered beneath my hands as they broke apart, sobbing through the ecstasy only I could give.

I've always had this impulse to inflict pain, a desire I was regularly forced to purge if I wanted to keep myself contained. And having such control over someone was a high that you couldn't replicate.

But sex had become dull, mechanical, and predictable. Even Atlantis, once electric with indulgence, had become as riveting as getting a tooth pulled. A chore that sometimes resulted in a mediocre at best orgasm, if I came all.

And yet Arabella on her knees, taking my cock between those pouty lips and looking up at me with fire in her gaze, had me seeing fucking stars. Even better was the way she pretended she wasn't turned on, and I took great pleasure in watching her take every inch of me, and then her begging for more.

She was fucking beautiful in her release, her entire back bowing and her muscles tensing. Then there were her lips, which parted with a cry I wanted to catch on my tongue.

A sharp whistle sounded beside me, and I blinked over at Langdon.

"You good?" he signed, a frown marring his brow.

"Of course," I replied, pushing thoughts of Arabella to the back of my mind as I stepped out of the car. The wind and rain whipped at me instantly, like a violent maelstrom before Chip appeared with an umbrella.

"When's the last time you slept?" Langdon continued, which made Caden frown as he came from the front passenger side.

"He hasn't been sleeping again?" Caden asked Lang as if I wasn't even here. He turned to me. "Bas, you never mentioned you weren't sleeping."

I bristled. "I'm fine."

They exchanged a look, one which I ignored. Their concern dripped off me much like the rain as I walked toward the doors. They opened automatically, greeting us with darkness held back by bursts of red light.

"Sir, am I coming inside?" Chip asked, his frustration tightened his lips when I simply pinned him with a look. He nodded his head at my silence, his hand gripping the handle of the umbrella before he returned to the car.

Charlie Pritchard was becoming a pain in my arse. I knew he wanted to do more, but he was still a kid who strug-gled with boundaries and was far too trigger happy to be of assistance. His lack of empathy and emotional under-standing made him dangerous, not to mention a liability.

"You're going to have to deal with him eventually," Caden muttered. "Either initiate him or cut him loose."

"He's too unpredictable," I replied, my tone closing the conversation.

But of course, Caden didn't give a shit. "You're right, but maybe he needs to make a mistake or two. How else is he going to learn control?"

"A mistake could get him killed." It was why I humoured his chess games, to teach him you couldn't win in just a few moves. It was all about discipline. Control. A strategy that held. Chip already had issues with impulsivity, and more than once I'd had to send people to clean up his mess.

"Then cut him off or put him with his mother." Caden dropped his voice to a whisper, the red lights overhead making him look splashed with blood. "Better yet, send him to the Bratva. Sasha will sort him out."

Pursing my lips I faced the receptionist, Caden on my right and Langdon on my left. She didn't even blink at the weapons beneath our jackets, her gaze hovering over Langdon far too long to be professional.

"You're expected," she said, gesturing for us to continue on to the main floor. "Mistress has set up a table, and she will be joining you shortly."

I didn't bother to acknowledge her, passing through the thick curtains into the centre room. Each space consisted of various themes, kinks and exhibition levels. The main room, however, was created as an old 50's style piano bar. It was the place to meet people and discuss consent and boundaries before exploring the more open spaces.

I've spent very little time in this room, but I knew

exactly which table had been reserved for me, slipping into the seat that had the perfect view of the stage.

Large velvet booths and circular tables surrounded a Steinway grand piano, our host singing into the mic with a voice made from sex. Aeris wore a skin-coloured dress so tight it was as if she was naked, while her statement red hair fell in waves down her back.

She was beautiful, and she knew it.

"Sure loves the spotlight for someone who deals in secrets and rumours," Caden muttered, seemingly more uncomfortable than Langdon or myself. "She should be more careful. It wouldn't take much for someone to permanently steal her voice."

Langdon smirked, lifting his hands. "Sore spot, Cade?" he signed.

Caden gritted his teeth. "No, I don't fuck sirens who think they hold the world between their legs."

A few of the waitresses looked our way, and I met their eyes just to watch them scatter. I shook my head, reminding myself that Arabella never looked away. That she met my gaze head on, even when she was scared. Even when she'd slapped me, her eyes widening in surprise at her reaction.

She didn't run then, either, instead standing her ground and waiting for a retaliation. And fuck, I wanted that. I wanted her to bare her teeth. To fight back and show that fire I seemed to crave because it made her come alive.

"She's always listening," I warned, finding Aeris strutting towards us on long, exposed legs.

"Sebastian," she purred, folding herself gracefully into the seat opposite me. Reaching across the table, she tried to brush her index finger over my hand, only for me to grab her wrist and squeeze in warning.

Her smile strained, her laugh forced when I let go.

"Nice to see you again. It's been a while." Her voice was raspy, like scorched velvet.

"Cut the shit," Caden growled. "We're not here for that."

"Are you sure?" Aeris turned to him, pouting her red painted lips. "I can offer you any girl or guy you want. Free of charge." When Caden didn't comment, she turned to Langdon. "What about you? See anything you like?"

A nerve feathered in Langdon's jaw, and rather than respond he reached for his lighter.

Click. Snap. Click.

She smirked, returning her attention to me. "I've heard you've taken on a pretty pet, one who wears your collar. Is it true?" At my silence she laughed again, the sound grating.

"Do you have what we asked?" Caden said, and I allowed him to take the lead because I found her voice fucking annoying.

Aeris's smile tightened when she looked towards my cousin, and I noticed the tension there. Interesting. That was a weakness I could extort if need be.

"That depends," she said, her tone slightly clipped.

"On?"

"Whether Sebastian answers my questions." Aeris met my eyes once more, confident in her position of power.

I'd chosen not to wear my mask because I didn't want to draw any more attention to this than needed. Clearly that was a mistake from Aeris's reaction. She believed she had the upper hand.

"Tell me about your new pet," she purred.

My answer was immediate. "No."

"So protective," she laughed, leaning across the table. "Has the great, powerful Beast fallen for the pretty damsel in distress?" She raised a coy eyebrow.

I reached over and fisted her hair. The people behind

her stilled, not used to such blatant show of violence outside sexual acts.

"I thought you'd want to play?" she continued, smiling even as I held her head at a painful angle. "Or would you prefer I play with your toy and have you watch instead?"

"Touch her and I'll break your fucking neck," I growled, the instant rage like lava through my veins.

Aeris pouted. "Threats don't work well with me, Sebastian. Remember that."

"Don't touch what's mine, then I won't need to keep my word." I tightened my fist, making her wince before releasing her as suddenly as I'd grabbed her.

She threw her head back and laughed, and I had to clench my fists to stop myself from clamping my fingers around her throat just to throttle the sound.

"Ah, there he is," she chuckled. "The monster beneath the mask. I so wish you'd join me in my playroom. I've heard from my girls how... thrilling it is to be beneath your power."

"Last warning," Caden growled.

Aeris sniffed, her confidence waning once she realised she couldn't use her cunt to try and take control. That was one of the reasons I'd never taken her up on her offer. Her whispers were dangerous, poisonous even as she pretended to be the perfect sub.

In reality, she was sucking out your soul through your cock.

She snapped her fingers, and a waitress brought over a tray, a silver dome placed on top. Aeris thanked the woman before lifting the cloche, revealing the paperwork beneath. "These were hard rumours to decipher, Sebastian."

"It's why I came to you."

She pushed the papers towards me, but I didn't bother looking down.

When I was younger, I didn't understand why it took me so long to read compared to everyone else. The words would always blur, shift or dance across the page as if they were alive. It took one of the nannies to recognise the severe dyslexia, explaining that I simply had a different brain.

So I grew up understanding my limitations and figured out ways to thrive without being able to read with ease.

"I've tracked this notorious Enchantress, as promised," Aeris continued. "Luckily, I have spies across the continent." Her long red nails separated the pages before she tapped a photograph. I finally looked down, only to still.

Because the woman on the page was supposed to be dead.

Chapter 34
Sebastian

"I'm sorry, Sebastian," Margot said, kneeling in my growing pool of blood while my brothers whimpered in pain and dad roared. "This is all your father's fault. He left me no choice."

My back burned, as did my shoulders as I tried to wrench my wrists free. Wrapping her fingers in my hair, Margot lifted me up so I was on my knees.

"Stop this!" Dad thundered, being held back by the same two men who had just raped and then murdered his wife. "Margot, please."

"Maybe you'll grow into the man I need." Margot caressed my face, her nails lingering on my bottom lip before she leaned forward for a kiss.

I tried to jerk back, but she held me to her, her tongue teasing against mine until I bit down. Margot screeched, and as she pulled away, I spat the blood in her face.

My neck jerked to the side, her slap stinging my cheek.

"Bas?" Caden lifted his fist, his knuckles knocking me back hard enough my teeth clashed together. "I need you to stay with us. Seriously, we don't know it's her."

Langdon was frantic in my peripheral, but I couldn't concentrate on him while this energy beat inside my head. The memory calling for pain. For vengeance for my family that were nothing but ghosts.

"The photograph could be fake. Dad said she was dead, that he dealt with it himself," Caden insisted. His knuckles were red from where he'd just hit me, and I needed the pain again, because when I closed my eyes all I could see was my father's mistress holding that knife.

"You spoiled little brat," Margot snarled at me, blood trickling down her lips. Her eyes were dark when she slashed down my face, pitch black.

Pain erupted, so sharp before she did it again, then again.

"Margot, stop!" Dad cried, his voice scratchy from screaming.

Drip. Drip. Drip.

I couldn't open my eye, the skin around it already beginning to swell. I swayed on my knees, my body feeling hollow. Empty as I struggled to stay awake.

But I had to, for Noah and Beau.

"Why didn't you pick me?" Margot cried, her once beautiful face made uglier with despair. "You should've picked me, Mael. We could've ruled this empire together, but now, you're just going to watch everything you love burn."

Another blow to my jaw, forcing me back into the present. Caden swore beneath his breath, shaking his hand out with a wince. "Bas, you good?"

The rage choked me, all consuming as I tried to force the memory of the woman who destroyed my family to the back of my mind. She was once the nanny, but behind closed doors my father was promising her a life where she could run his empire beside him. When in reality she was nothing but a hole he'd toss away once bored.

He'd done it before, I knew, being the eldest. My mother knew too, and I saw how each woman he took to their bed broke her heart just a little bit more. So I'd begun to hate him long before I watched my mum be raped, and then my brothers beaten until they no longer moved. All because of him.

I felt nothing as his throat was slit, my chest hollow as the man who I'd planned to kill left his children alone to defend against his fucking mistress.

It was my brothers' cries that broke me, their smaller bodies fighting with everything in them. All while Margot watched, laughing. Then she set them alight, forcing me to watch while I bled out.

A blur flashed to my right, and I caught Caden's next hit in my hand. Dropping his fist, I turned to Langdon, who stood stiff, an edge to his eyes that worried me.

"We need to tighten everything up," I gritted out, ignoring how my palm ached along with the welt on my jaw.

His nod was stiff, his hands coming up to sign. "No mistakes."

"Agreed." Caden stepped towards us, clamping a hand on Langdon's shoulder. "And if she's back, then we take her out."

"Same page," Langdon signed.

"Same fucking word," I snarled, feeling this wrath pulsating inside my chest. "And call Alexander to meet us. I think it's time he explained what the fuck happened."

Chapter 35
Arabella

The city below carried on, oblivious to my existence. Which shouldn't surprise me, considering I was *barely* existing when I was down there anyway.

Knees pulled to my chest, I sat at the studio window and watched the world shrink into ant-sized figures, too distant to recognise. Still, I liked to imagine they were thriving, living full, vibrant lives while I remained locked in my tower.

Trapped with my books.

Once, that sounded like a dream. Reading all day with no real responsibilities. But in reality, it was suffocating. A quiet kind of madness that crept in with every passing hour of stillness.

The lift dinged, and I found myself jumping up. I was almost excited to see Sebastian, not that I would ever admit that out loud, because at least he was here.

Picking up my book, I walked out to find Chip stepping out of the lift. "Oh, hi. You're here late," I commented, pleased to see him because holy fuck someone talk to me before I start losing my mind.

I haven't seen his mum in a few days, which was leaving

me with a very small pool of people to communicate with. Especially considering the cleaners were still actively ignoring me. Seriously, I should start leaving little passive aggressive notes for them to find.

Chip's smile was a little crooked. "Good, you're still up."

"Up? What's going on?"

"You're being summoned, but first I need to do a quick security check." Before I could respond he began to walk towards the west wing, looking back over his shoulder to see whether I was following. "You coming or what?"

I fell into step beside him, unsure when he took out a keycard and slotted it into the one door that was always locked. "Chip, what are you doing?"

"I've already told you, a security check. This is Mr Devereaux's study." He unlocked the door, revealing a relatively empty room save for a wall of screens, an unnecessarily large terrarium, and a desk. On it was a computer complete with keyboard and mouse, some pieces of paper, and a strange looking pen.

Chip waved, and his image waved back across three of the screens.

"He really does have the whole place on video?" I asked, studying the wall before I moved to the terrarium. My skin crawled at the spider that sat content inside, half hidden inside its cave.

"Yep, and he records it too." Chip walked across the space to sit at the desk in the corner. "Watch," he said, clicking some buttons.

I looked over my shoulder. "Are you allowed to do that?"

"He won't know." A few more buttons, then suddenly all the screens along the wall revealed my bedroom. He began to rewind it, and I watched myself move in reverse as I wandered around with my notebook.

"Stop!" I said when I started to undress.

"Sorry." He didn't sound particularly apologetic as he continued to reverse at a faster speed that blurred the image so you couldn't see the details. After a moment a dark shadow appeared, showing me Sebastian standing in my room while I was fast asleep. He hovered by the side, his fingers gentle as he brushed hair from my face as I slept.

"You needed to see this," Chip said quietly. "He barely sleeps. A couple hours at most, then he watches you almost every night."

"Why did you show this to me?" I asked, my voice flat.

"Because we're friends," he said gently. "And I don't want you to get hurt."

The footage rolled on for a few more minutes. Sebastian lingered, motionless, before finally turning and slipping out of the room.

"Turn it off." I walked out, unsure how to feel.

Chip hurried after me. "Hey, what's wrong? I didn't mean to upset you; I just wanted to make you aware so you can–"

I spun around, stopping so fast he nearly collided with me. "Aware of what?" I snapped. "That I have no control over my own life? That I'm being watched while I sleep?" My voice shook, but I didn't back down. "Trust me, Chip. I'm *painfully* aware."

Before he could comment, the lift chimed, followed by the sound of deliberate, heavy footsteps.

"She was just freshening up," Chip said quickly, smoothing his tone just as Langdon stepped into view. "I'll meet you both at the car, Sir." Chip gave a respectful nod, slipping away.

Langdon turned his hard gaze to me, his hands signing far too fast for me to even attempt to follow.

"Erm..." Seriously, I'd only just started to learn. Give me a break. "I don't know what you're saying."

Langdon released a wispy sound of frustration before reaching for his phone.

Sebastian needs you.

I didn't think I'd ever get used to watching Sebastian fight. Every blow made my body tighten, and I knew I should simply look away, but I found I couldn't.

Neither Sebastian nor Caden seemed to notice we'd arrived, too consumed by the brutal rhythm of their brawl to care.

I felt a touch on my shoulder, and I turned to find Langdon watching me rather than his friends, a frown creasing his brows. "Has he always fought?" I asked, aching to know just a little bit more about my captor.

Bas first got his name in the underground fights. A champion, it's how he first made some real money, he typed on his phone. **He's always been good with his fists.**

I couldn't argue with that. Sebastian moved with purpose, each strike a full blow that contained barely suppressed rage. His muscles rippled from the hit, both men shirtless as they circled each other like predators. They snarled as they punched, their knuckles meeting flesh and bone in a cacophony of sound that turned my stomach.

Wanting to concentrate on anything else, I returned to

Langdon and clumsily signed, "Why is he upset?" Okay, so I didn't know if that was what I'd actually said, because I was pretty sure I got a letter or two wrong.

But Langdon seemed amused with my attempt. **You've been learning to sign?** he replied on his phone, which just proved that I'd messed up. **Why?**

"I have a lot of time on my hands," I admitted. "So it was either this or French."

Langdon laughed, his chest puffing out with no sound. **Keep trying.**

"Why am I here?" I asked, my voice a whisper so as not to disturb the fight. "Sebastian seems... distracted."

Langdon shrugged, taking his time to type. **Isn't that what you're for? To be there when called?**

"Because he's upset?"

Langdon's left brow rose, his head tilting to the side. **You sound sure he's upset?**

I pursed my lips, unsure what to say. There was always a slight tension along his shoulders when he was upset, a tell that I'd noticed when he came home some nights. His eyes were darker, his touch harsher.

Something haunted him, I just didn't know what.

The ropes stretched, with Caden thrown to the side with a crash that drew a gasp out of me. Sebastian turned, his eyes clashing against mine that he held.

There was so much rage there, his eyes nothing but a thunderous storm.

I should be terrified, especially because he'd taken a step across the ring towards me, his movements agitated. But I found I wasn't scared, instead drawn to him like a suicidal moth to an open flame.

He kneeled, closing our distance as the tension between us cinched tighter around my chest. It had only been a few weeks since I'd agreed to this arrangement, and I felt myself lost. Stuck, but also feeling more alive than I'd ever felt before.

I knew it wasn't going to last. Either I found myself a way out, or Sebastian would get bored and kill me.

Not that I would let that happen.

He'd have to catch me first.

I found myself holding my breath when he jumped down to the floor, his expression cold. Hard. He reached out to cup my jaw, and I tilted my head back to show I wasn't afraid of him. Which was of course a lie, but he didn't know that.

"Why the fuck have I been summoned so late at night?" an unfamiliar voice snapped, breaking our connection and making his fingers stiffen against my skin.

An older man walked in, his steps self-assured as the bouncer, Miles, hovered by the doors. He scowled, looking between the three men before settling on me.

"Who are you?" he asked far sharper than needed, brushing his salt and pepper hair away from his face. "What's the meaning of this, Caden?"

Caden spat blood by his feet before jumping down from the ring with an elegance that didn't match his size. "Evening, Dad, we just want a few words is all."

"So you sent a lackey to pick me up?" The older man's expression was murderous when he looked back over. "You must be Sebastian's whore."

Sebastian picked the man up by his collar, lifting so he was forced onto his toes. I hurried to stop him, holding out my hand while Langdon and Caden remained unmoving.

"Sebastian." His gaze warned me to back away, but I couldn't. "Please," I whispered, and with a clenched jaw he let the man go, only to reach for me. He gestured to Miles, who came to stand by his side.

"Be a good girl, and go wait up in my office," Sebastian whispered, lips brushing against the shell of my ear.

"But–"

"Don't make me repeat myself, Arabella."

Chapter 36
Sebastian

I was hyperaware of Arabella walking towards the lift, my body coiled so tightly as she was escorted by Miles. I should've lost interest by now, but there I was, watching until she disappeared before I could return my attention to anything else.

I'd been in the middle of one of my episodes, my demons howling so loud I'd almost knocked out my own cousin just to purge some of the fucking tension, and then I turned to her, and the roar of violence quietened. Just like that.

Langdon shouldn't have brought her, not when I was so close to the fucking abyss.

And yet rather than run, she'd tilted her head back, a flash of disobedience in those fucking eyes that had me wanting to bury my face between her legs just to hear her scream.

"So, is anyone going to tell me why I'm here?" Alexander snarled, one of few men to ever speak to me like that and survive. The only reason I hadn't killed him yet was because he was blood, and Caden had stopped me. "Caden, you were supposed to keep him under control!"

Purposely ignoring my uncle for the moment, just to calm down, I moved towards Langdon, realising his eyes were vacant.

"Lang," I whispered, nudging him slightly. There was a moment his eyes weren't so empty but instead widened and panicked as he relived the past, and then his usual, malicious spark returned.

"Let's get this party started," he signed, looking around. "Wait, where's Ara?"

I pinned him with a glare, and he simply smirked in return. Bastard knew what he was doing.

"See, this is why you need to go back to the therapist, Sebastian." Alexander touched Caden's nose, who was ignoring the fact that it was still bleeding. "Acting like animals isn't going to help your CPTSD. I'll ring him in the morning and get you a new prescription."

I wanted to laugh at the comment, Alexander yet again pushing therapy and drugs on me, believing I was like this because of my trauma. When in reality I was trained to be this bloodthirsty. First by my father, who'd been grooming me from five years old to take over his position within the Le Milieu. And then by Alexander himself, who encouraged me to carve my name amongst the powerful men of the underworld just so he didn't have to get his own hands dirty.

Caden grabbed his dad's wrist. "You want to tell us what happened to Margot?"

"Margot?" Alexander's eyes narrowed, his upper lip curling into a snarl. "She's dead."

"You sound confident in that," I said, flexing my hand to relieve some of the ache across my knuckles.

"Of course I'm confident." He turned to face me. "Do you really think I'd leave the woman who'd murdered my sister alive?"

Langdon began to sign, his hands frantic in his anger.

"He called you a lying cunt," I translated, and Caden simply dragged a hand down his face in exasperation.

Alexander's face turned red, his eyes almost bulging. "You little bastard." He pointed a finger towards Langdon, taking a step closer. "I should've left you to die in that house. You're not even my—"

His words ended with a screech when I broke the finger pointed towards Lang. My uncle grunted in pain, and rather than stop me, Caden simply snarled, "Speak to him like that again, and I'll kill you myself."

Alexander snapped his mouth closed, his anger paling against that of his son's.

"Now, let's start this again, shall we?" I continued, enjoying the way his pupils dilated. He may act like he was the big man, but in reality, he was nothing compared to me.

Caden handed his father the photograph, which showed an older woman smiling. Her hair was still a copper red, with strands of grey that showed her age. There were lines on her face that weren't there twenty years ago, but it was definitely my father's mistress.

"Impossible," Alexander whispered, curling his broken finger protectively to his chest. "She looks just like Margot Laurent."

I barely stopped myself from reacting to the name, the edges of my peripheral darkening as I fought the memories that threatened to consume me.

"She's supposed to be dead," I snapped, my voice so cold it was arctic.

"She *is* dead, I made sure of it." Alexander's head whipped up, and I believed the anger that burned his eyes. "How do you know it's even real? We all know how easy you like to make enemies, Sebastian."

"He didn't even fucking do it himself," Langdon signed,

but rather than comment at the lack of translation, Alexander simply clenched his jaw. "He lied to us."

Caden reached for his discarded shirt, using the fabric to wipe the blood and sweat from his face. "Let him speak," he signed back, his movements rigid.

"I thought this was an open conversation?" Alexander growled, a vein popping in his head. He'd had the opportunity to learn sign when the doctors first told us of the damage to Langdon's vocal cords, but he decided it was beneath him.

I saw him make Lang feel less than because he wasn't blood, which was why we left as soon as I turned eighteen, taking Caden with us.

My uncle added, "I don't know what to tell you. I was assured she was dead."

"You told us you dealt with it personally," Caden growled. "Which is it, Dad?"

He didn't answer, and a fresh wave of rage swept over me. I took a step forward, and Alexander instinctively stepped back, much to his annoyance.

"Sebastian, she murdered my sister. My nephews. If I knew she was still alive, I would've dealt with it. The fact she's still out there while my sister's..." He cleared his throat, an uncharacteristic bit of emotion shadowing his words. "I hired only the best, but clearly I failed."

I believed him, but that didn't ease any of the tension that crawled and buzzed beneath my skin like a thousand wasps. "Being blood doesn't exonerate you."

"That's where you're wrong," Alexander said, jaw tightened, shame creeping in just enough to sour his anger. "Blood is everything. Otherwise, I wouldn't have gone through hell to get you back."

"That's called guilt," Langdon signed, but neither I nor Caden bothered to translate.

"You're going to find her," Alexander demanded rather than asked, his gaze direct. "Make sure it fucking hurts. Make Margot pay for what she did to our family."

"I'll drive you back." Caden pulled on his shirt, leaving the buttons open. He nodded his goodbye, but I'd already turned to Langdon.

"Go home," I snapped. "And don't think I've forgotten you've brought Ara into this. Stay away from her."

Langdon smirked, purposely pushing me to try and play the situation for his entertainment. It was how he held control of his reality.

I didn't wait for him to respond, not when I was already storming towards the lift.

Miles should not be in my office, and his eyes widened when I walked in to find him scowling down at Arabella, and her glaring at him in return. I gestured my head to the door, dismissing him before I settled my attention back on her. She was curled up in my chair, watching the monitor with my reading pen clenched in her hand like a weapon.

"Miles giving you trouble?"

She released the pen, slipping from the seat slowly as if not to set me off. "He's just opinionated." She carefully moved around the desk while I circled it, her back rigid.

My eyes fell to the screen to find she'd been watching the security camera. "You been spying on me, *belle?*"

She didn't bother to deny it. "Why did you break his finger?"

"Because he said something I didn't like." Her voice

washed over me like a drug, calming the fury that vibrated my soul.

"You're angry," she commented, pressing herself into the corner.

I placed my palms flat to the wall, caging her in. Rather than recoil, she lifted her chin, never looking away.

"Read to me," I demanded, *needing* to hear her voice calm the demons that still howled for me to destroy. To become the man my father had trained me to be.

I'd never needed anyone before, and I hated this vulnerability with a fury I couldn't name. But I still craved her voice, her soft words and delicate laughs. She quieted the noise.

Arabella frowned, seeming confused by my demand. "You want me to read to you?"

There was a rush at having her pressed against the wall, my cock immediately waking up as I pressed my lower half against hers. A flush darkened her cheeks as she felt my reaction.

"There's... there's nothing to read," she stammered.

I gently cupped her throat, wanting to feel it move. "Make it up."

She laughed, and I was ready to drown in the sound. "I don't know what to say."

Closing my eyes, I allowed her voice to wash over me, even as phantom slices split the skin of my back.

Il ne m'a pas laissé le choix.

He left me no choice.

"Sebastian," she whispered. Fear, and something else darkening her tone. "You're okay."

I blinked, finding Arabella pressed further against the wall, pinned almost painfully with my weight. She gripped my wrist, nails digging in.

"You're okay," she repeated, her fingers moving to brush

along my arm, and I stilled beneath the touch. Fire thrummed in my blood, the anticipation of what she could possibly do to fight for her life tightening my muscles.

I didn't usually feel this alive unless I was in the ring or expressing my darker side when it came to sex. Deviant tastes that I'd since grown bored with. Nothing other than violence seemed to quench my demons these days, feeding their bloodlust just so I could fucking sleep.

Until her. I needed to mark her. Own her.

Discover why the fuck I was so infatuated with a woman not made for my world.

Arabella's fingers were light, tracing over my skin and brushing over my scars like she had the right to. Her lips pursed, so full and yet defiant in the face of my monster.

She seemed to have forgotten that I controlled her life in my hand, literally. Her pulse was violent against my palm, a little beat that revealed her sheer terror at the situation she'd found herself in.

She should be scared.

Using her throat, I pulled her against me, my lips sliding against hers until I could swallow her gasp. I bit and sucked, devouring her like I should've the first night.

I rarely kissed, finding the act unstimulating, but with her it was everything. The way she moaned and gripped me tighter. The way she tried to take control, fighting my dominance with little nips along my lips that had my cock aching.

My free hand slipped beneath her dress, rubbing between her legs to find the fabric already soaked. Pulling the underwear to the side, I thrusted two fingers into her roughly, her moan so delicious I caught it on my tongue. She was soaking wet, the slickness coating her thighs and dripping down my hand.

"Look how wet you get for me," I growled, nipping along her jaw.

She groaned, and her cunt clenched at my words. Smirking against her skin, I used the heel of my palm to add pressure to her clit.

I could feel how close I could get her, knowing it could be almost painful when it was forced so quickly. But this was a punishment for making me crave her. To show her how little control she had over her body and how easily she gave herself to me.

Arabella's hips rocked against my fingers, chasing a release to the very edge.

What a shame I wasn't going to give it to her, not yet.

Chapter 37
Arabella

My core clenched, aching with the denial of my orgasm.

Bastard.

I'd never seen his eyes so dark, like the deepest, scariest parts of the ocean. He was truly terrifying, his jaw held so tight I could make out the veins popping on his neck.

His fingers softened on my throat, but not releasing as he held me there, forcing me on my toes with his head dipped close to mine. My lips felt swollen, and I wanted nothing more than to get lost in his kiss.

It was savage, a violent claiming of tongue and teeth. He was pushing all those nightmares that I saw darkening his eyes onto me, and I was letting him.

What could possibly give a man like Sebastian Devereaux nightmares?

Hesitantly, I reached up to touch his cheekbone, and the fingers that were just inside me gripped my wrist so hard I could swear my bones creaked.

"You really do like pushing," he rasped, his voice a low growl that pulled my skin taut. "As if this is all a game."

He released my wrist, only for those same fingers to pinch my nipple above the fabric of my dress, then immediately caress it with a soft brush. His touch was a total paradox, both sensual and rough. Like he barely held back his darker side.

I'd always been sensitive, but with him it was different. As if he forced me into survival mode, so I'd notice every little detail. Making every sensation heightened.

Clearly, I was broken and had no survival instincts whatsoever because here I was at the mercy of a tyrant, and my thighs were embarrassingly slick with arousal. Even now his intensity radiated off him in possessive waves, a dominance I had no hope of fighting against.

"What, no comeback?" he asked, a cruel smirk twisting his lips.

I froze as his eyes held mine hostage, fear mixing with need in a twisted aphrodisiac that I still didn't understand. I hated this feeling, the way he held influence over me.

He was so unpredictable with his actions, his nature that of a killer. And yet anticipation tingled down my spine at the way he used my own body against me, reminding me who held all the power. Spoiler alert, it was him, and when he made me feel this good, I wasn't even mad.

Sebastian's fingers found themselves at my core again, stroking so confidently I tried to move my hips away from the sudden sensation. There was no hesitation, my stomach tightening as I was quickly pulled to the tip of my orgasm once more.

"Beg me," he whispered, standing over me like some great god as his fingers thrusted languorously. His intensity burned hotter, his gaze searing across my face. "Arabella. Beg. Me."

It was nothing short of a command, and I immediately wanted to rebel. To spit in his face and tell him to go fuck himself. I knew it wouldn't stop him, and honestly, I didn't want him to.

My pussy ached, my breaths coming out in undignified pants as he kept me on the edge, not allowing me over. But *'please'* got stuck on my tongue, just to push him a little bit more. To enjoy the little control I still had before he took that, too.

His smirk widened, as if he was enjoying this game. Tutting, he removed his fingers, and I whimpered at the loss.

"Wait..." I began, the rest of my words lost when I noticed him pull out a pocketknife. He flipped it open, and I tried to push myself harder against the wall, away from the sharp edge. "Sebastian?" I whispered.

He was spiralling and using me to try and control it. I could see it in the way he held himself, the way his muscles tensed. His irises had somehow darkened further to become the endless night. It was worse than when he was lost in the studio, because then the haunted look stopped after a few seconds. But this time it was different.

"Such a needy little slut." Lifting my skirt, the knife sliced into my underwear until it was nothing but shreds on my hips.

I gasped at the first cold touch of the blade between my legs.

"You're fucking soaking, *belle*." Lifting the knife to his lips, his tongue snaked out, licking my arousal from the metal. It sliced his tongue, but he didn't seem to notice, or care. "Si *parfait, putain*."

He stared down at me with unapologetic possessiveness surrounded in fire.

As if I was a puzzle he couldn't quite figure out, and that infuriated him.

His lips caught mine, the tang of copper on my tongue. I tensed when I felt the knife touching me again, pressing against my clit in a burst of cold steel. Sebastian held it there, slowly rubbing it back and forth while he bit my throat hard enough I knew I was going to bruise.

More pressure, and I was so close. My orgasm clawing at me with a vicious force that had the influence to push me to my knees.

"Please," I finally begged, my strangled voice alien as I rubbed against the blade. So dangerously close to the sharp edge. A rational part of me knew I should be alarmed by the situation, but she could go fuck herself because where was she when I agreed to swap with my father in the first place? "Sebastian!"

My release tore through me like a hurricane, confiscating the air from my lungs as I gasped to regain enough oxygen to survive the pleasure that twisted my insides. Sebastian kept touching me, stroking me through it while watching me with an intensity that was distinctively him.

My entire body trembled in aftershocks, my muscles languid as I clung to him to centre my equilibrium. His grip on my throat eased, allowing me to collapse against the wall.

"You wanted to play, so let's play." He pulled his knife away, only to press it against my lips. I stilled, conscious not to get cut. "Run and hide, little rabbit. Because when I catch you, I'm going to fucking ruin you."

I did the only logical thing any woman in my situation could do, and I ran.

Okay, it was more like stumbled. The remnants of my underwear twisted around my legs, as if wanting to trip me before I ripped it and left it in my wake.

I could feel his overbearing presence behind, like a

shadow I could never escape. I scrambled from his office, racing towards the lift which immediately opened at my presence. There were no buttons inside, and in my panic I slapped the walls.

The doors closed, and the lift descended with a quiet purr before opening at the corridor of the floor below. The club lights were off, almost too dark save for a single strip by the bar as I quickly manoeuvred across the dance floor. The cavernous room was silent, empty but for us. I could hear his footsteps, each thunderous stride breaking through the blood rushing in my ears as I tucked myself against a wall, trying to control my pulse while my heart dramatically threatened to break through my ribs.

Anticipation started low, spreading like wildfire despite fear being bitter on my palate. It consumed my soul, tightening my muscles until I fought for every breath.

I couldn't see him or hear him. Risking a glance, I poked my head around the corner, having to blink for my eyes to adjust to the darkness. Sebastian stood on the other side of the club, all black tailored suit, sharp lines, and broad shoulders.

He was silent as he moved through a door, and I used the opportunity to run towards the bar, ducking beneath a table to hide when I heard a sound from behind.

The lights above turned on, spotlights flickering while a heavy beat filled the air.

Boom. Boom. Boom.

The bass vibrated the floor, drowning out my senses.

Something encircled my ankle, and I screamed as I was yanked, my nails digging into the carpet. I was forced onto my back, the sudden movement knocking the air from my lungs before I managed to fight, kicking and scratching before he pinned my hands above my head.

I froze when I saw his mask, my fear doubling as Sebastian loomed over me like the grim reaper, those dark, stormy eyes reflecting nothing but primal desire.

Boom. Boom. Boom.

The club was alive around us, the lights and music disorienting.

"Don't move," he commanded, and even his voice, deep and intoxicating, was enough for my body to warm. I didn't move, especially when there was a glint of metal in his hand.

With his knees on either side of my hips, he sliced my dress down its centre with the knife, the spotlights making it glisten when they flicked on overhead. My breasts sprung free, and he immediately placed the tip of his blade to my left nipple, pressing until I felt a sharp sting, followed by a stream of liquid heat.

Fire pulsed between my legs at his erotic growl, those eyes watching the single drip of blood travel down the curve of my breast.

"Belle."

The sound of a zipper, and I risked looking down, my mouth drying as he gripped his cock in his large, veiny hand. It somehow looked bigger, thicker in the menacing light.

It wasn't going to fit, I thought, which was stupid considering it already had.

"Eyes on me," he demanded, and I automatically glanced up at the same time he thrusted forward, forcing me to try and take him to the hilt.

My back bowed under the onslaught, my body protesting, even with how wet I was. But he didn't seem to care, stretching me to the limit while staring down at me like I was his.

"Look how well you submit, *ma petite lapine.*"

I whimpered at the words, my legs automatically encircling his waist to take him deeper. I rocked up with his thrusts, absorbed with the way he used me for his benefit. It was as if I was the fuel, and he was the match ready to set me alight.

I revelled in the pleasure, chasing the pain just because it made me feel present.

Less lost in a world where I had no purpose but to survive.

His attention was an addiction, the intensity of it a stimulation I wanted to never stop. Sebastian fucked me like I was his catharsis, and I wanted it. Wanted *him* just as much as I hated him.

My orgasm was approaching at a rapid speed, making my movements more frenzied as I gripped his arms to better anchor myself against his violent thrusts. He didn't stop me when I sank my nails into his skin, wanting him to experience just a fraction of my loss of control.

The growl that vibrated his chest almost sent me over the edge, the sound sending both dread and delight across my skin.

"Wait..." I cried when he pulled out, only to flip me onto my stomach. He tore the rest of my dress away, and it wasn't lost on me that I was now entirely naked. Exposed while he was fully dressed. Just another power imbalance. "Sebastian!"

Lifting my hips so I was on my knees, he pounded into me from behind, and I let out a strangled scream at how deep he could reach. This position hit new angles, and I clenched around him when he slapped a palm against my arse.

Those same fingers pressed deeper into the skin, drawing out the sting, making me whimper and beg for more.

"My needy little slut." His fingers brushed lower,

dipping to the space where his body joined mine before moving to press against my back hole.

I gasped, jerking away until he wrapped his spare hand at the hair on my nape.

"Enough," he warned, his finger brushing, teasing. "Your mouth is mine. Your cunt is mine, and this little hole..." His thumb pressed into me. "Is mine."

My orgasm tore through my soul, my mind lightheaded as I shattered into a million fractured pieces. The sound of his thrusts and his skin on mine echoed around us until I was free falling again, my body trembling.

"Such a good fucking girl," he rasped, his thumb thrusting in rhythm with his hips. "And all mine."

I couldn't breathe, my body exhausted as I accepted every inch.

Sebastian turned frantic, his movements savage. As he released my hair, I sagged forward, the sharp threads of the carpet rubbing against my breasts with every thrust.

Boom. Boom. Boom.

He was drawing out the pleasure, his free hand reaching around to brush my clit in a way that was the opposite of how he fucked me. He was gentle but rough. Soft yet violent.

I finally felt his cock stiffen, swelling as he groaned, and that alone had me coming once more, clenching to keep him locked to me for just a little bit longer.

Chapter 38
Sebastian

I didn't get addicted. I've seen what it could do, that sickness. The obsession over your next fix. Nothing else mattered, which was why I never fucked the same girl twice or allowed myself to taste the cocaine.

But Arabella was different. A poison injected directly into my bloodstream, and I couldn't wait to take another hit.

I had planned to toss her away once I'd grown bored and then track down her father because he still needed to pay. But she'd somehow brought me back from the abyss, *again*, her sunshine and light in the most dire situations calling to my demons.

Hunting had been euphoric, stalking her through the darkness only for her to fight and then submit so beautifully. She'd been scared of the knife, and yet when I touched the sharp edge to her skin she'd moaned, her cunt pulsating.

Greedy. Perfect. *Mine*.

Her weight was sleight in my arms, her head resting against my shoulder as I walked her towards her room. I knew I should simply put her to bed and leave so I could figure out my next step. But I found I didn't want to go, not yet.

Things were happening outside my control, but with Arabella she was a constant. Something that anchored me when everything else was fracturing.

Setting her down on her sheets, I ached to touch her. To rouse her from her sleep just so I could watch her shatter around me again. Hear her cries of pleasure and unrestrained moans.

She'd pretty much passed out once I'd finished with her, her skin decorated in my marks. Covering her in my shirt, I'd carried her to the car where Chip drove us both back to the penthouse. I snarled at him, as well as the guards trailing me, warning them that if they dared to look at her in this state, I'd kill them.

The bed dipped as I put my knee on it, and her eyes fluttered open.

I expected panic, or even fear. Not a lazy blink and a slight frown.

She sat up in bed, and my eyes dipped down to where her pussy was still pink, swollen, and had the biggest urge to make sure all my come remained inside. *Fuck.* I imagined her swelling with my child, and this strange possessiveness shot down my spine.

"Were you just watching me?" she asked, peering at the room.

She really was cute while freshly fucked, wearing my shirt and a little dishevelled.

"You talk in your sleep," I commented, just because I wanted to see colour flush her cheeks.

I was rewarded with exactly what I'd wanted. "I do not."

I smiled, unable to stop my lips curving. "You do. You whisper and moan my name."

Arabella jerked up further in bed. "I do fucking not."

She did, and the first time I'd heard it I thought I was

manifesting. But she did talk in her sleep, which was why I liked to come listen. Her voice was calming, soft and lyrical with just the perfect amount of husky bite.

"Do you need me to read?" she asked, as if reading my mind.

I raised a brow in question.

"You always ask me to read when you're in a mood." She pulled the sheets to cover her lower half, and I had to clench my fist to not rip it from her.

I stilled, my eyes clashing with hers. "You're not here to notice my moods, you're here to be a warm, wet hole," I said, delivering the statement cold. "That's what you agreed to, wasn't it?"

An angry flush burned across her chest, and her eyes narrowed on me.

"Fine, read to yourself then." She went to swing her legs over the side of the bed, but my hand on her thigh stopped her. "I didn't agree to be your prisoner."

"You did. You wanted an escape for your pathetic life, and that's exactly what I gave you. Don't come crying to me now that you've decided this isn't what you want."

"I agreed to pay off my father's debt," she bit back.

"You agreed to do whatever I wanted in return for his life," I pulled her a little down the bed, the motion moving the sheets and revealing what was mine. "That includes where you spend your time."

"Can I at least go out?"

"No."

"Not even for a walk?"

"No."

She sucked her bottom lip between her teeth, her usual defiance hidden beneath a streak of stubbornness. "Please?"

"Please only works when you're on your knees about to suck my cock." I pulled her closer, until I felt her staggered breath brush against my chest. "Stop painting me as your prince."

That fire I craved so much danced in her irises. "Trust me, I stopped believing in fairytales the moment I met you."

"And yet you screamed my name only an hour ago."

A sound of frustration left her plump lips. "I hate you."

I leaned closer, noting how her pulse jumped against her delicate throat. "Your cunt clearly disagrees." I went to stand, the movement jerking her slightly on the bed, and she winced.

The sheets pooled, the swell of her breasts showing in the gape of my shirt. Without thinking I turned to the bathroom, grabbing a washcloth and running it under warm water.

She eyed me like I was a snake, flinching when I pulled the sheets off entirely to leave her mostly exposed.

"What are you doing?" she demanded, but I ignored her, gently washing her inner thighs and then her pussy. She hissed but didn't stop me.

"Don't look so concerned. I'm not going to fuck you again because I know you're sore." She didn't seem to believe me. "Don't get me wrong, I am this monster you're picturing in your head. I do what I have to do to keep my position. But I don't intentionally hurt women or children if I can help it."

"You hurt me," she pointed out.

"You wanted me to hurt you." I dared her to argue, but of course she didn't.

"Why not women and children?" she asked, moving away so she could curl her legs beneath her.

My hand clutched the now cold cloth. "Because they're always used as pawns in someone else's game."

"Am I not a pawn in your game?"

"A willing one." I pinned her with my stare, loving how she never looked away.

"What happened to make you so angry earlier?"

She was so fucking curious. It was going to get her killed. "Were you scared?"

"Not of you."

Such honesty. "Then what were you scared of?" I asked.

Her jaw clenched. "Is Caden okay?"

My knuckles cracked from how hard I clenched my fist. "You were scared for Caden?" I was definitely going to have to pay him a little visit later. Maybe hit him a little harder.

She shook her head, which eased some of the anger that sparkled with jealousy. "I was scared you were going to hurt yourself."

I searched her face for deception, almost sickened to find the comment genuine. "You care about everyone you hate, *belle*?"

"Only those who keep me locked in a tower, and it's Ara."

I let out a puff of air, which was as close to a laugh as she was going to get. "I found out the woman I thought was dead may actually be alive."

"Why is it important that she's dead?" she asked gently.

"Because she was the one to give me my scars."

Chapter 39
Arabella

I was sore, the ache between my legs both delicious and frustrating. I'd never admit it to his face, but I've never orgasmed so hard. I was pretty sure I'd passed out, because I had zero memory of leaving the club, never mind waking up with Sebastian glowering over me.

He was like a cornered animal when pushed for his feelings, and in my professional opinion, had the emotional maturity of a rock. Not even a pretty rock, but a boring grey one that had been smoothed by the vicious waves of the sea, but if broken open it would be jagged and sharp.

It was as if he made the conscious decision to repress himself. Hide his emotions in the same way he wore that mask.

But he wasn't hiding when he chased me through the club, his eyes alight with pure sadism and desire. They'd brightened further when he'd caught me, hurt me. Except, he wasn't hurting me. His bruises weren't out of pain, but out of possession. Need. Desire.

I wasn't surprised to wake up alone, Sebastian having left my room early in the morning. Pulling on a pair of jeans and a T-shirt, I came out expecting to be greeted by Beatrice, except I was alone. Not even Chip or any of the cleaners were present.

The place always seemed achily empty when I was the only one here.

Disappointed, I grabbed my notebook and a pen but found myself outside his bedroom. The door was closed, and I almost lifted my fist to knock. To see whether he was...

Shit. What the hell was I doing?

Turning on my heel, I went to the kitchen, grabbing one of the muffins waiting on the counter before sitting on a stool so I could comfortably write.

The story in my head flowed so easily onto the page. It was just a first draft and would likely always remain a first draft. But it was cathartic, putting all my feelings in black and white. Putting the fictional characters through trials and heartbreak. Making them suffer and then succeed.

I don't know how long I wrote for, my hand aching when I came to the final page, and the muffin nothing but annoying crumbs beside me. I stared at the words, a hollow feeling inside my chest that the story wasn't finished, and there was no more paper.

That *my* story wasn't finished.

"What are you writing about?"

I jumped from the stool, catching it before it clattered to the floor. "Bloody hell."

Sebastian stood in the doorway, dressed in his statement black-on-black. The suit stretched across his broad shoulders, perfectly tailored to his large frame.

I huffed, "Remind me to put a bell on you."

His upper lip twitched, but other than that his face remained in his usual scowl.

"It's nothing." I closed my notebook, freezing when something moved across his chest. "Sebastian..."

He brought up his hand, allowing the giant fucking

spider to scramble over his fingers before skittering further up his arm. "So scared of something so small," he mused, closing the distance between us.

"Don't you dare." I moved around the island, keeping it between us at all times.

Lazy amusement glistened in his eyes. "Come here, *belle*."

"I swear if you come near me, I won't be held accountable for my actions."

"Raven won't hurt you."

I almost scoffed. "You *named* your spider?"

"Come here." The lethal tone of his voice reminded me who held control of the situation. Hint, it clearly wasn't me. And still my gaze strayed sideways, looking for a way out. "Arabella…"

He caught my wrist, tugging me back until I bent awkwardly against the counter. I stilled, unable to look away from the spider perched on his shoulder.

"I could kill you so easily," he mused, his hand sliding around my throat. "And yet you're more scared of Raven."

I swallowed against his palm, trying to bury myself against the countertop. Sebastian cocked his head to the side, staring down at me. After a moment he released his fingers, and I released a shaky breath.

"Put your choker on," he ordered.

I eyed him warily as he pulled the spider from his shoulder and held it in his palm. "Where are we going?"

"You said you wanted to go for a walk, so let's walk."

"You said we were walking," I commented, but there was no agitation behind it because at least I was outside. Sort of, anyway. In the passenger seat of Sebastian's car counted because I'd opened the window and had a breeze. Honestly, I was feeling spoiled.

He didn't reply–what a surprise–so I snuck a peak at him beside me. It was weird to see him drive, something so ordinary, and yet he looked at ease. Almost relaxed, if Sebastian could ever actually remove that stick up his arse and do such a thing.

"That spider thing wasn't funny," I muttered beneath my breath.

"It was," he said without a change in his expression. "She wouldn't have hurt you."

"You don't know that."

He glanced at me from the corner of his eye before returning his attention to the road. "Don't worry, she lives in a terrarium in my home office."

"Why do you even have a pet spider?" I wondered.

"Because arachnophobia is a very common yet irrational fear."

"So you keep her because the majority of people are scared? That's... horrible."

Sebastian let out a puff of air, almost like a laugh.

"Also, it's not an irrational fear. They're creepy. Who needs eight legs?"

Sebastian pulled over, turning in his seat to raise a brow. "Are you finished?"

I pursed my lips, looking out the window to realise we were in part of the city known to the locals as the Graveyard. He didn't seem bothered about leaving his expensive-looking car in an area notorious for theft, rape, and homicides.

Another car pulled in behind us, a 4x4 that looked to be built like a tank.

"Stay here," Sebastian said, and before I could reply he was out of the door and stalking to the car behind. I watched in the mirror, seeing him lean down to the driver's side to speak to the twins that were trailing us the entire time.

After what looked to be a tense conversation, the twins drove away, and Sebastian reappeared to open my door.

"What was that about?" I asked, and Sebastian's jaw clenched.

"Caden's overprotective."

"Of you?" I accepted his hand as he held it out.

He looked at me from the corner of his eye. "You seem amused."

"Maybe a little," I teased. "Is it because of that woman?"

"No. He's always been overprotective."

He was right; I was pleasantly amused that someone as powerful as Sebastian had people caring for him enough to be overprotective. "That's nice, that you have people looking out for you like that."

Sebastian frowned, his fingertips tracing my hand. "And you don't?"

I laughed, but there was no humour in it. "So, you going to share why we're here?" I looked down the street, at the broken windows and abandoned buildings. This part of the city seemed to have been forgotten by the council, leaving it to become derelict and desperate.

"I have someone I need to meet, and you said you wanted some fresh air." He looked down at me, his expression cold even as he held my hand.

It was a strange contrast, especially when he pulled me closer.

"So... no mask?"

"Not unless I want to start a war."

The Fluffy Duckling looked completely out of place amongst the rest of the street, with its adorable theme and old, Tudor-style building.

The outside was untouched, unlike the surrounding businesses that looked worse for wear. There wasn't a scratch on the windows or a dent in the door. Inside was warm, with a few patrons turning to glare before quickly returning to their drinks once Sebastian turned his attention to them. Luckily it was quiet, considering it was early.

Everything seemed made from the same type of wood, from the tables and chairs, to the long, worn bar and decorations adorning the panelled walls. It was rustic and incredibly hostile if I went by the bartender's scowl. Nothing "fluffy" about this place. Not to mention I didn't see any ducks anywhere.

"Ty zdés' nezelánnyy," the bartender muttered, shaking his head. "Sasha won't like this," he continued in English, his Russian accent thick enough it took me a moment to understand.

"We have a truce." Sebastian's hand tightened in mine. "I'm looking for a man named Ryder."

The bartender's thick brows practically rose to his hairline. Without another word he nodded to a man at the end of the bar, his dark hair around shoulder length as he spoke animatedly with another patron.

Although, he clearly wasn't reading the vibes, because his friend was looking at him like he was debating whether he'd get away with murder.

"And I was like... of course it'll fit, love," Ryder said, ending the comment with a chuckle. "As if... Hey, are you okay, mate?"

The unnamed man paled, eyes widening on Sebastian who'd moved to stand behind Ryder. With a single jerk of his chin from Sebastian, he scrambled from his seat, and Ryder frowned, watching his companion leave in a rush.

"What the fu…"

Sebastian gestured towards the vacant stool, moving behind me like he was death personified. Ryder blinked, barely giving Sebastian a courtesy acknowledgement before settling those warm brown eyes on me.

"Why, hello there, love," he purred. "What's a pretty girl like you doing in a shithole like this?" He was typically handsome, with straight features and a sharp jawline that held the faintest stubble. From the way he stretched his legs beneath the bar, I would also guess he was almost as tall as Sebastian, just not as broad.

"Are you Ryder?" Sebastian asked, his tone so icy I was surprised frost didn't appear.

Ryder grinned, finally looking up at him. "Never heard of him." Taking a long drink from his glass bottle, Ryder slammed it onto the bar. "Now, if you'll excuse me…" He went to stand.

"Sit. Down." Sebastian's tone left no room for argument. "Or you won't like what happens."

Ryder's smile turned fake, revealing dimples. "Do you know who owns this pub?" He looked around, as if manifesting help from the surrounding wood. "I don't think he'll be too pleased that you're threatening his loyal customers, now, would he?"

"I have a proposition for you," Sebastian said. "I need you to find something for me."

"Mate, I think you've got me mixed up with someone else. I'm just trying to enjoy my drink after a hard day's work."

"I'll pay 50k."

"Fuck me." Ryder coughed, choking on his own spit.

"Now, I'm clearly at a bit of a disadvantage. You seem to know who I am, but I have no idea who you are."

"He owns *The Thorn*," I said, noting how his smile didn't tighten or slip. Only the slight narrowing of his eyes gave away his understanding. He knew exactly who Sebastian was.

"Thought you were supposed to wear a mask?" Ryder hummed, but when he didn't get a response, he continued. "*The Thorn*'s supposed to be a nice place. Not that I know personally, considering I've never been allowed in. Bit elitist if you ask me." He raised a sly eyebrow.

"I need you to find this." Sebastian pulled out a photograph from his breast pocket, the older woman in it beautiful.

He pointed to the brooch on her chest, a white crystal rose that looked like it cost more than my entire life. Which amusingly wasn't true, considering I sold myself for double what Sebastian was paying for the brooch. Clearly, I knew my worth.

Ryder studied the photograph. "By find, I assume you mean steal?" Sebastian remained silent, and Ryder smirked at me. "Is your boyfriend always this intense?" he asked.

"Yes," I answered honestly, and Sebastian curled a hand around the back of my neck in a loose grip. He squeezed a little, and I understood the silent *'behave.'*

"Speak to her again, and I'll cut out your tongue," Sebastian warned, and Ryder laughed, throwing his head back.

"Alright, don't get your knickers in a twist." He studied the photograph once more. "When do you need it by?"

"As soon as possible."

A single nod, his teasing expression turning serious. "Give me everything you have on the owner, and I'll get it to you within the week."

Chapter 40
Sebastian

The brooch had been one of my mother's, a gift on her wedding anniversary.

That was what had made me almost lose control, my mind giving into the darkness that I had to purge regularly if I didn't want to lose myself entirely. Not Margot's face, but the fucking brooch that I went with my father to choose only a month or so before my life turned to ash.

Ryder was a prick, but he was known for his skills. Luckily, I didn't have to retaliate because he didn't speak directly to Arabella again, but I forced myself not to react when he shot her a wink as he stood to leave. Which was fine, because I'd just wait for him to finish the job, then carve out his fucking eyeball.

"Speak to her again, and I'll cut out your tongue," Arabella mocked, making her tone deeper. "Honestly, you're like a barbarian." She turned on her stool to smirk up at me, those golden brown eyes dancing with amusement.

I leaned down to whisper my next words, my hand curving around the side of her throat to feel her pulse. *"Belle,* if I was a barbarian, I would've sat you on this bar and eaten out your pretty cunt in front of everyone."

She sucked in a breath, her pulse rapid against my palm. She wore my collar, as well as my bruises. Her lips were no longer swollen, and I wanted to bite them so everyone could see who she belonged to. As if the collar just wasn't enough.

But I didn't, if only because of our audience. No one deserved to see how Arabella reacted so viscerally to me. She liked to fight it, and when she did, her submission was that much sweeter.

"I would spread your legs, use my tongue and fingers to make you scream my name just so every man here knew you belonged to me. Want to know why I don't?" I brushed my lips on the opposite side of her throat. "Because I don't share."

She swallowed, and I reluctantly released her. "Noted," she muttered, a flush darkening her cheekbones, and I knew she was currently imagining me doing just that. It was tempting to get the privacy of a side room, but it was true I didn't share. She may not be in the view of the patrons, but they'd hear her cries, and that just wasn't acceptable.

Maybe I could make her come on my face just like I'd promised, and then simply kill everyone who'd overheard? Tempting.

"Are you okay?" she asked, warily watching me as I imagined her spread out before me like a feast.

Her hair had been pulled into a high ponytail, with only a few strands framing her makeup-free face. She was beautiful, made more so by the choker, as well as my teeth marks along her delicate throat. She didn't seem to care for my grip on her neck, at ease with my hand there.

"Was that her?" she continued. "The woman in the photograph?"

I could feel eyes along my back, prickling with awareness. I'd never stepped foot in the Fluffy Duckling, a somewhat amusing front for the Russian Bratva within London.

Many of the patrons were members of various criminal organisations and firms, dangerous men and women who knew not to approach without risking a territorial war.

"Margot Laurent," I answered, keeping my voice low. "My father's mistress."

Arabella tipped her head back to better meet my gaze. "I'm sorry."

"Why? You didn't ask him to fuck her."

"For what she did. Nobody deserved that."

My thumb reached up to brush along her bottom lip. Arabella knew nothing of what had happened, and yet her words were achingly sincere. People like her would be eaten alive in my world.

"You can't choose your family," she added, her eyes holding mine with utmost sincerity. "I would know."

"Hmm," I hummed, dipping my head until my lips almost brushed hers. "Careful, you're going to make me believe you actually like me."

A gentle laugh escaped her lips, and I stiffened knowing I didn't want to share that sound with anyone else, either. "We can't have that now, can we?" she teased.

"What the fuck is this?" a voice snarled, and I turned to find Graves standing there dressed in a cheap suit.

"Detective," I greeted, coldly. "To what do we owe the pleasure?"

Arabella tried to stand, face paling. "What are you doing here?"

"I didn't believe it when someone tipped me off that you were out in public," Graves sneered, his badge flashing just enough to remind us of his role, even if his authority behind it was rotten to the core. "Yet here you both are, slumming it with the plebeians."

"Have you been following me?" she demanded, staying by my side.

"You haven't been answering your phone." His eyes flicked between us, restless and alert, clearly aware of the growing attention from nearby patrons.

The Fluffy Duckling wasn't exactly a place frequented by law enforcement, and everything about Graves, from the stiff posture to the barely concealed arrogance, screamed *cop*.

"Have you even spoken to your dad lately?" he asked, tone darkening. "Or have you been too busy screwing Sebastian to remember who you're supposed to be protecting?"

I lunged forward, grabbing Gabriel by the lapels and yanking him up until he was forced onto the balls of his feet. His breath hitched, but then he laughed, sharp and unsteady, the sound just a little too wild for someone who pretended to be in control of the situation.

"That's right," he goaded, eyes gleaming. "Go on. Give me a reason to put you in cuffs."

A slap of a palm on the bar echoed through the room. "*Dostátochno!* Take this outside or use the back room," the bartender growled in our direction. "I mean it."

I clenched my jaw, noting how Graves stared over my shoulder at Arabella with a viciousness I didn't appreciate. I already knew they were once an item, but from his expression he saw her as nothing but a possession that he'd lost. A strange lump formed in my gut at their history, but then I remembered that she was now mine.

Reluctantly, I dropped him, and he staggered back, a flush darkening his expression before he wiped where I'd gripped him with disgust. "Touch me again, and that's assault on an officer."

I swept out my arm, allowing Graves to go first so I didn't have him at my back. Arabella was a flurry of anxiety beside me, but she remained uncharacteristically quiet as she kept to my side. Like Graves was able to steal her light.

"Gabriel, what are you doing?" Arabella asked, her voice low and strained once we had privacy. "You shouldn't be here."

His eyes didn't leave mine, his smile tight. "I was checking to see if you were okay, baby."

I arched a brow. "Is *that* why you've been skulking around outside my club?"

Langdon had mentioned it days ago that he'd caught Graves lurking in the alley, loitering like a dog looking for scraps. I hadn't thought he was worth the effort, not until he'd been spotted outside a few of my other clubs too, ones not as publicly tied to me, which told me he wasn't just aimlessly watching. He was *digging*.

"Where's Lennon?" he demanded, suddenly turning to Arabella. "I know he spoke to you, but he never came back."

Arabella stiffened beside me, and I didn't need to glance down to know her expression. She was an open book, with every emotion etched across her features whether she meant it or not.

"I told him no," she said quietly. "I wasn't interested in your offer."

Graves didn't react immediately, instead his eyes hardening as he stared at her a beat too long. "You sure about that?" he asked, voice softening just enough to make it sinister. "I want to protect you, baby. You have to let me before you're caught up in everything. Because if you're lying to me, I can't help you when things turn ugly."

There it was, his ulterior motive. This wasn't about her safety. It was about leverage.

"Careful, Detective. The last time we did this, you almost lost your badge, and I walked away with an apology," I drawled, my face twisted into a sneer.

"You really think you're untouchable, don't you?" Graves hissed, something desperate flickering in his eyes before he shifted his gaze back to Arabella. "You wouldn't have anything to do with his disappearance, would you, baby?" he asked, reaching across the narrow room like he could still touch her.

But I was already there, pulling Arabella to my side before he got too close.

"We both know how you have this little vicious side when pushed," he continued.

"Your friend hasn't been seen since he cornered Arabella at my fight weeks ago," I growled.

Graves's nostrils flared. "Where did he go after?"

"That isn't my concern," I replied, voice like ice. "Maybe check the Thames. I've heard it's pretty busy this time of year."

Graves whipped his eyes to mine, violence thickening the air. "My offer still stands," he said to her, despite his attention remaining on me. "I can save you, all you have to do is—"

"I don't need saving," she cut in sharply. "Now just go. Please."

His features hardened, but before he could comment further, I warned, "Careful, otherwise you may meet your friend sooner than you think."

Something sinister flashed in Graves's eyes, and a smile cut across his face, cruel and devoid of civility. "Just so we're clear, baby, you're really choosing to stay with a known murderer and drug lord instead of coming home with me?"

"As opposed to a dirty cop?" I said, my voice low and steady.

Graves chuckled, the sound mocking. "This isn't over," he murmured, his eyes lingering on Arabella before he turned to leave without another word.

As the door shut behind him, Arabella pulled away from me, crossing the room to create distance. "Was that really necessary?" There was a bite to her words, her lips pressed into a stern line when she looked up at me.

"Why? Care about him?" Seemed I wasn't quite over the jealousy of her being with Graves first. It wasn't something I was used to, and it made me step closer until she was forced against the wall. Still, she jerked her chin up, her eyes narrowed.

"Stop acting like a caveman," she snapped.

"Is that what I am, *belle*?"

"It's Ara," she growled, and I bit back a laugh.

"You can't be benevolent to everyone in this world, especially pricks who've caused you harm."

"Stop acting like being kind is a weakness." Her hands clenched at her sides, and I kept myself from smirking at her little show of frustration.

"It is in my world." I dipped my head but purposely kept a cushion of air between us.

She kept pushing, and the only reason I wasn't punishing her against this wall was because I was patiently waiting until we were alone. Where she'd take her punishment where no one else could witness.

"There was no need to tell him Lennon was dead. It was cruel."

"I never said he was dead."

"You implied it."

This time I did smile, dipping my head closer to feel her breath feather across my lips before my phone vibrated in my pocket.

I ignored it, my attention entirely on her.

Arabella let out another sign of frustration. "Gabriel means nothing to me. He asked me to marry him last year, and I said no."

Rage boiled through me at the idea of this fucker claiming her. "Why?"

"Because he wasn't the guy I thought he was." Her voice was quiet. "My dad was furious. Gabriel offered him money, which was obviously taken away when I declined."

"He ever hit you?" The thought sent white-hot fury through my core.

Arabella frowned. "My dad?"

"Gabriel," I gritted out.

"Oh... no."

"Your answer isn't convincing."

She met my eyes, her jaw set. "I would never have let him hit me."

"Hmm." I wanted to know why she flinched in his presence, or why the light in her eyes dimmed whenever he was near. "Graves is up to something."

She blinked, looking up at me like the observation had caught her off guard. "He's always up to something," she muttered. "When he gets an itch, he doesn't stop. He becomes—"

"Obsessive," I finished for her. "Impulsive." That was how he'd fucked up the first time he tried to investigate my empire. He got caught up in the thrill, too blinded by his own ego to be patient. Instead, he wanted to be the hero, and failed, even when he tried to play it dirty.

He'd fail again, too. I'd make fucking sure of it.

My phone started to vibrate once more, which I ignored until it stopped, only for it to immediately start up again.

"You going to get that?" Arabella asked, and I found I was amused with the indignation in her gaze. "Or are you just going to interrogate me on my ex all day?"

"Your mouth's going to get you into trouble," I muttered, knowing who was calling before I'd even answered.

"What the fuck, Bas? You dismissed the guards?" Caden exclaimed on the other end of the line.

"What do you want?" I snapped. "I'm busy." And by busy I meant getting Arabella worked up so I could take her home and do exactly what I'd described earlier.

Caden snorted. *"I want you to not be a cunt, but I think it's impossible."*

Arabella burst into laughter before she caught the sound, and I stared down at her to stay quiet.

"Lang's burning shit again. I'm worried," Caden added, and my expression darkened.

Fuck. Lang burning shit wasn't uncommon, but if Caden was concerned it meant Langdon was pushing it. "He hurt anyone?"

"Other than what's been approved, no, I don't think so."

Arabella frowned, and I smoothed the line between her eyes with my thumb. "I'll speak to him, but for now let's just keep a closer eye. Make sure he sticks to reality rather than getting lost in his own mind."

Chapter 41
Sebastian

As soon as I stepped into Lang's place, I was assaulted by the scent of perfume, weed, and sex. Three naked women lay together on the sofa, all fast asleep from a long night of partying.

"Fuck off," I growled, waking them up.

All three of them squeaked in surprise before running to the lift, naked. Candles were lit everywhere, forgotten as they melted to encrust the floor. The brunette knocked one in passing, sending them scattering before I managed to pick them up. Luckily the fall extinguished their flames, but wax had already scalded the wood.

Discarded bottles lay on the table, beside Lang's golden lighter and a couple of used condoms. *Shit*. Langdon didn't drink unless he was in a downer.

Making my way to his bedroom, I found him lying on his back in bed, the black silk sheets fallen to reveal a busty blonde riding him with vigour. Lang, as usual, was fully dressed but for his cock, his fingers clamping onto her hips as she put on a performance.

I didn't wait. "Times up. Get out."

The woman didn't stop, instead turning her head to pout at me. "There's room for one more," she purred, reaching back to try and touch me. Lang reacted before I could, throwing her off so she bounced ungracefully beside him.

His hands lifted, his movements angry as he signed, "Don't touch him."

But the woman didn't understand, instead fluffing her hair and reaching for her discarded clothes. "Arsehole," she muttered, glaring at him as she passed. "Don't call me."

She slammed the bedroom door behind her, and I leaned back against it as I waited for Langdon to tuck himself away.

"What the fuck, Bas?" he signed, brows furrowed in annoyance. "It's like six in the morning. You could've waited for me to finish."

"You fucked with me by involving Ara. This was just payback."

A slow smirk curved Lang's lips. "Don't tell me you didn't enjoy her. I know you sent all the guards outside just so you could chase her around. I've had to delete all the fucking footage."

"Hmm." I nudged a glass bottle that was placed on the carpet beside the bed, letting it *cling* into another. "You want to talk about why you're burning shit again?"

Lang's smile strained. "Don't know what you're talking about."

"You're self-destructing," I commented, watching how his nostrils flared, and he wouldn't look me in the eye. Lang was impulsive, while I was just destructive. But my destructive tendencies were usually thought out beforehand.

"What do you want me to do? Sit around until she comes after us again?" He finally looked at me, his eyes wild as he signed. Glinting like the fire he was so obsessed with. It had taken Caden and I years to try to calm that look.

"We're not kids anymore." I closed the distance between us until I could grab him, pulling him until we were forehead to forehead. Unlike me, Langdon craved touch. "If it's true, and she's back. We'll get our revenge."

Langdon couldn't sign this close, but he simply breathed. Each inhale as haggard as the exhale. After a moment he punched my shoulder, stepping back. "Where's your Ara?"

I searched his eyes for any signs of a breakdown, but he seemed calmer. Less on the edge. "Doesn't matter. She's mine, so keep her the fuck out of your games."

"Or what?" he signed.

"Fuck around and find out."

Arabella

"Sebastian has people watching me inside the penthouse now?" I asked Langdon, who casually leaned against the kitchen counter when I got up. "I thought you were Beatrice." It had been a few days since the Fluffy Duckling, and I was used to waking up to find Sebastian had already left. Also, I really missed Beatrice. And her baking.

Lang smirked, bringing out his phone to type a message. **Thought you'd want the company.**

Opening one of the kitchen drawers, I sighed when my notebook didn't immediately appear out of thin air. "Where's Sebastian?"

Langdon shrugged, beginning to sign before reverting back to his phone. **Probably dealing with things.**

"Things like what?" I glanced at him, finding him watching me with an intensity that was different to Sebastian. His gaze was charged, as if he was a child doing something he wasn't supposed to do.

He smirked, tilting his head to the side. **What are you looking for?**

I slanted a sideways glance at him. "My notebook. I left it in the kitchen the other day, but it's disappeared." I hadn't been able to find one of the cleaners to ask where they'd put it.

That's boring. Want to run some errands with me? he typed, turning his phone around. **I've already called Chip to drive us.**

I frowned at the text, unease prickling at the back of my neck. "Does Sebastian know?"

Langdon shrugged, that smug smile of his stretching wider. **Does it matter? I'll have you back before he even notices. Promise.**

"I'm not some toy for you to use in whatever twisted game you two are playing."

I was almost certain this was his way of getting under Sebastian's skin, a quiet act of retaliation, dressed in charm. Reaching past him, I grabbed a bottle of water from the fridge, resisting the urge to slam the door.

A sharp whistle cut through the air, stopping me mid-step.

I turned to see Langdon signing something with exaggerated flair, then rolling his eyes when he remembered I couldn't understand. **It's not like that.**

"Then what is it?"

He didn't answer, a frown developing as he crossed his

arms and simply stared at me. He'd essentially silenced himself rather than reply. Very mature.

I sighed and started to turn away, but another sharp whistle followed me.

Just come keep me company. I promise to answer any questions you have about Bas.

Chapter 42
Arabella

The familiar scent of books and coffee surrounded me, the gentle hush of excited whispers and rustle of paper. The little bookshop wasn't somewhere I'd been before, with its rows of antique-looking shelves and a little corner café that served hot drinks and cake.

"What about Chip? Is he not allowed inside?"

Langdon shook his head. **He knows his place. And so do you. Don't leave the shop,** Langdon typed, pointing at his eyes, then pointing at me dramatically. **You can grab one book and then meet me at the table.**

I grinned, already knowing it was worth Sebastian growling at me for leaving the penthouse. He'd never explicitly said I *couldn't* leave, and it wasn't like I'd wandered outside alone. Scanning the shelves, my fingers trailed over the spines as I debated which book might give me the escape I was craving. Something that could pull me out of my head and into someone else's mess for a while.

Then my eyes landed on it, a Mafia romance, and I couldn't help but grin. The idea of reading it aloud to Sebastian, just to watch him smirk, was too tempting to resist.

Grabbing the first in the series, I turned back and spotted Langdon already waiting with two drinks and a generous slice of cake. He waved, and I took the seat across from him, book in hand.

"How come you don't have guards like Sebastian?" I asked, taking a sip of my coffee. "Or does Chip count?" Langdon had a hot chocolate complete with cream and marshmallows, and even had a chocolate moustache that I refused to tell him about.

I *am* Bas's guard. He smacked his chest with an open palm. He began to sign slowly, and I watched every movement before he typed the sentence out. **He's the man at the top, and Caden and I are his enforcers.**

I couldn't help but raise an eyebrow. "Enforcers?"

Langdon sliced the cake in half, shoving his half in his mouth before pushing the rest towards me. I took a bite, taking my time to chew.

"How long have you known Sebastian?" I asked when he wouldn't elaborate.

Langdon held up his hand, his fingers spread.

"Five years? Or since you were five?"

He was five, I was seven. Means I'm the more mature one. He grinned, tapping the screen while I read it. **Our fathers were rivals. Really pissed them off that we were friends. We'd sneak over each other's houses, and then when my dad croaked, I moved in permanently.**

"I'm sorry."

Don't be, he was a cunt who beat me. Mael treated me better, even if Bas hated him. He downed the rest of his drink, eyeing mine until I did the same.

Picking up the book, he walked over to the counter and

paid before gesturing for me to stand. Taking one last bite of the cake, I placed it on the tissue, following him outside. The breeze was gentle, breaking up the heat from the sun as I waved to Chip, who was leaning against the car.

I handed over the tissue, Chip frowning down at the small chunk of cake nestled inside. "Thanks," he said quietly, glancing at Langdon as if seeking permission.

"So, what errands do you need?" I asked over my shoulder as Langdon watched the exchange with a strange expression. With his chin, he gestured towards the Chinese takeaway across the road called *Wok & Roll*.

"Did you need assistance inside? Or would you like me to stay here, Sir?" Chip asked, almost eager to tag along.

Langdon pointed to the car, and Chip's face tightened.

"Of course. I'll be out here if you need me."

Taking my arm, Langdon crossed the road, banging on the shutters of the restaurant three times. It didn't look open, the shutter down and covered in obscene graffiti that really emphasised the male appendage. I'd never thought I'd witness two cartoon men having a sword fight with their penises, but here we are.

After a moment, the shutter began to rise with a squeal, and a short, elderly Chinese woman greeted him with a wide, toothy grin.

"Mr Langdon, how lovely to see you. We were expecting Mr Caden," she gushed with a thick accent. "My granddaughter's looking for a husband, you know."

Langdon shook his head, then bent gently at the waist while she chuckled.

"Come, come. Everything's arrived and ready to be processed. My grandson's currently checking to make sure nothing's been compromised. Just as instructed." She gestured her arm for us to go forward, and after Langdon made sure I was following, he walked through the charming takeout, past the counter and into the kitchen at the back.

"It's too early for food," the woman said, the top of her head barely reaching my nose. "But take these." She handed me and Langdon a fortune cookie each, and Lang immediately cracked his and crumpled up the paper in his hand.

"What did it say?" I reached out for his fortune, smoothing out the wrinkles. "It says to 'Seek help from professionals trained in mental health care.'" I laughed, and Langdon rolled his eyes before pointing to my cookie. I broke it open, and read, "*The fortune you seek is in the other cookie.*"

Langdon smirked before tugging at a large metal door, the air icing as he continued through the walk-in freezer. Making sure I was still following, he placed his palm on a strange looking panel hidden partially by a box of frozen meat. The wall clicked, opening up with a waft of smoke.

Noise assaulted me, male voices arguing followed by laughter. Hidden behind the freezer was a large warehouse storage room piled high with plastic-wrapped cubes. Two men with sweat-stained vests moved cubes of powder from the shelves to the table in the centre, a cigarette hanging from their mouths. Face masks hung from their necks, and the plastic overalls that clearly were supposed to be worn were tied around their waists, leaving their legs protected but their arms bare.

They didn't acknowledge us, instead continuing to check over each cube before carefully breaking the powder into individual packets and placing them in takeout boxes.

A third man stepped into the room from the only other doorway, snapping something in Chinese. The two men replied with a panicked tone before quickly removing their cigarettes and pulling up their masks.

Langdon turned to the woman, who was angrily glaring at the men.

"Yes, yes, it won't happen again," she said before stepping inside.

"So, this is where you package it all?" I asked, wrapping my arms around my waist to protect myself from the cold.

Lang looked down at me with a raised brow. After a moment, he lifted a single finger.

"One of them?"

He nodded, seeming to wait for me to react at the knowledge. To be honest, I didn't really know how to react. I knew Sebastian ran a business, and I knew it was to do with cocaine. I just wasn't sure how in-depth the operation was, or whether I really wanted to know.

Wait here, Langdon typed, showing me his phone.

"Sure, don't worry about me. I'll just casually freeze to death," I muttered to his back. One of the men eyed me cautiously but didn't approach as Langdon disappeared into the side room.

I decided to step further into the space, the cold behind me biting at my skin.

The men continued to inspect each cube, chatting away while I waited for Langdon to return. The room was reasonably large, with exposed concrete walls and metal beams. Shelves lined both sides, mostly holding supplies for the takeaway restaurant, as well as wooden pallets and cooking equipment easily large enough to hide anything if need be.

I debated whether to wait in the front of the restaurant, but as I turned there was a loud bang, followed by an intense wave of heat. A shove to my side nearly knocked me off balance, the two men running past me hard enough that I was crushed against the wall.

With my ears ringing I shouted for Langdon, coughing as smoke erupted and got trapped against the concrete.

Moving quickly, I ran further inside, skidding to a halt at the flames eating up the far wall. "Lang!" I shouted, finding him on his knees on the floor, staring at the fire. Awake but unresponsive. "Langdon?"

A wail drew my attention to the elderly woman crying. The third man was trying and failing to lift a heavy desk that had been overturned, with her crushed beneath it. She sobbed, blood trickling from her lips as tears left a clean line down her dust-smeared cheeks. Rushing over I tried to lift the desk, but even with my help it wouldn't budge.

"It's pinned!" I said, realising part of the brick wall had collapsed on top. The entire room was a mess, my brain unable to understand the chunks of debris and warped metal. The holes in the walls and the strange whirring sounds.

Then there was the crackling of the flames, which continued to move closer, the heat stinging.

I pushed at some of the rubble, realising the woman's foot was caught by the corner, her bone protruding from her ankle.

"Over here!" I called, realising each time the man tried to lift he was just crushing her further. I caught his attention above the roar, waving him over.

As he began to lift from this side I knelt, pulling the woman out from beneath the desk. As soon as she was free, the man scooped her up.

"Go get help!" I screamed, having to duck beneath the growing smoke.

My lungs burned with every breath, Langdon almost lost as he continued to stare.

"Lang!" I fell to my knees beside him, relieved to see he was unhurt but for a cut along his cheek. "I need you to get up!" But there was no response, not even as I shook him.

Gripping his chin, I forced him to face me. "Look at

me!" His eyes stared blankly, as if I wasn't even there. "You're okay, but we need to get out of here right now."

A slow blink, a little of his earlier light finally reaching his eyes. With a jerky nod, he gripped my hand and pulled us both to our feet. I tugged him towards the freezer, only for a fresh wall of heat to hit us, throwing us both back against something solid. It knocked the air from my lungs, the smoke forcing me to struggle to replenish the oxygen.

Langdon sat beside me, his eyes open but once again vacant as the flames ate away at the surrounding space.

"Please! You're too heavy for me to drag!" I tried to shove him and pull his arm, but he wouldn't budge. Cursing, I searched his pockets, my hands shaking when I found his phone. I almost cried at the single bar of signal, quickly scrolling through his contact until I found Sebastian.

Except he didn't answer.

"Fuck!" The flames were getting closer, almost kissing his outstretched legs. I managed to pull him back an inch, but it wouldn't be enough. Scrambling through the contacts once more, I found Caden.

He answered on the first ring. *"Lang, remember you can't speak you fucking—"*

"We're at Wok and Roll, and there's been an accident!"

A pause, the ceiling above us cracking beneath the heat.

"Ara, why the fuck are you on Langdon's phone?" he growled. *"What the fuck have you done? Where's Lang?"*

Honestly, if I survived this shitshow, I was going to smack him for the unnecessary attitude in this stressful situation.

"It exploded, and I can't get Langdon to move." I tugged him once more with all my strength, but he barely stirred. "Cade, the flames are coming, and I can't move him!"

"Hit him."

I froze. "What?"

"Hit him. Hard."

I slapped him, his head jerking to the side. "It didn't work!" I cried, Lang simply continuing to stare into the fire.

"Fucking hell, Ara, hit him harder!"

This time I punched him, my knuckles aching from the blow. It knocked him to the side, closer to the flames that were threatening to consume us both.

Chapter 43
Sebastian

I couldn't relieve the pressure on my chest, the nurses shouting as I ran through the corridors as fast I could move. I'd never felt panic like when Caden had called. His voice had been tight, urgent, barely holding it together as he'd explained what had happened. By the time I'd hung up, the ambulance had already arrived, and I diverted towards the hospital.

I couldn't lose Langdon. Not when he'd been with me through every dark corner of my life, and I sure as hell couldn't lose Arabella. Not now. Not yet.

She didn't have my fucking permission to leave.

I quickly located the room, Arabella immediately jumping to stand from where she'd been perched on Langdon's hospital bed, and just like that the crushing weight in my chest eased. My lungs able to take in a breath at seeing her unharmed.

"Are you okay?" I asked, already crossing the space so I could just touch her. Reassure myself that she was here. That she was whole.

"Langdon's fine," she whispered as I smeared my thumb

through the soot on her cheek. "There was an explosion, but he's okay."

It took me a moment to realise I'd barely given Langdon a glance, my concentration on her. "I was asking about you."

Her brows drew together, a flicker of confusion crossing her face at the weight of my concern. "I'm okay," she said softly, like she wasn't sure why it mattered so much to me. But it did. She did.

I'd already been informed about the restaurant, but I didn't give a shit about the loss of my powder. It was replaceable, whereas Lang and Arabella were not. I finally tore my attention away to check on my longest friend, who was much cleaner and had a small cut across his cheek, as well as a fresh black eye.

"Your girl has a nasty right hook," he signed, winking at me before wincing.

I checked her hands, finding her right red and swollen.

"It's not broken," she explained, wincing slightly. "I've already been checked. It's just bruised."

"Remind me to teach you how to throw a punch," I muttered.

She laughed, the sound huskier than normal. Scratchier, and that pressure renewed beneath my ribs, but it was no longer just panic. It was something else.

Something just as crushing.

Just as consuming.

"Bas?"

I turned towards Caden, reluctantly dropping Arabella's hand. "How bad?" I asked, finding she'd returned to sitting on Langdon's bed.

"It's gutted."

I nodded, expecting as much.

"Then there's this." Caden threw something on the table, and Lang stiffened, his eyes glazing as he recognised one of his lighters. It was slightly warped, the gold tarnished. "A firefighter found it tossed where they suspect the fire started."

"Langdon didn't do this," Arabella commented, her chin lifting as she glared at Caden. "I was with him."

"We know," Caden said without hesitation. "Someone is going out of their way to frame him."

I grunted, watching Langdon as he began to dissociate. Arabella placed her hand on his arm, talking quietly as he stared blankly at the lighter.

"Was anyone hurt?" I asked Caden, who was watching Arabella try and bring Lang back with an unreadable expression.

"One of the runners was killed in the initial explosion, and Mrs Zhao has sustained some serious injuries. She's currently in surgery."

"She going to survive?"

He shook his head slightly. "They're not sure."

I nodded once, forcing a slow breath into my lungs to keep the pressure from tightening further across my chest. "Make sure the deceased's family gets a generous condolence package, and let Feng know we will cover everything until she recovers."

Caden agreed, exhaustion lining his face. "If Ara hadn't been there..." he hesitated, swallowing. "We could've lost him, Bas."

I didn't reply, not wanting to acknowledge the possibility. "When's the next fight?" I asked instead, knowing Lang would need a different way to anchor himself to reality rather than flames and destruction.

"In a couple nights, why?"

"Put him down."

Caden nodded. "I've already called in a private team to investigate the incident," he continued quietly. "Feng mentioned a ticking noise before the explosion. He said he also heard a second bang but was already outside at that point."

A whistle, Langdon lifting his hands to sign. "It was a bomb?"

When Arabella turned with a frown, I translated.

"So, it planned to go off for when Langdon arrived?" Her eyes widened, horrified.

"We don't know yet," Caden said quickly, clearly only just realising the possibility. "Langdon wasn't even supposed to be there. *I* was."

"Make sure they prioritise this investigation," I growled. "We need to know who the fuck was able to get in and plant those explosives."

"And what?" Arabella asked, her tone uncharacteristically harsh. "Kill them?"

I moved closer, cupping her jaw when she tilted her chin up to look at me. Even as she glared, I took my time to let my eyes trace over her, grounding myself in the fact that she was okay.

"Does it bother you?" I finally asked.

She swallowed, her eyes searching mine. "I... I don't know."

"Tell me, what would you do?" Her lips parted to answer, but there was no reply. "There's no mercy here, Ara. They made that choice when they attacked. That bomb killed one of mine, maybe more. Do they not deserve justice?"

"Justice is not the same as vengeance," she whispered, fear a fine thread through her words. "You'll start a war."

I wanted to laugh, but found the sound stuck in my throat. "*My beautiful little rabbit,* the war has already begun."

Chapter 44
Sebastian

The whoosh of the match made my heart stop, my brothers unable to cry as Margot set their crumbled bodies alight. I tried to pull at my binds, but every second I felt myself weakening. Bleeding out against the polished floor.

"Please!" I begged, my wrists caught behind my back as the ropes cinched tighter and tighter the more I struggled.

Margot frowned, looking back over her shoulder. My voice was barely a whisper, broken from screaming and crying. From cursing my father even as he'd pleaded for her to let us live. But Margot had been relentless, enjoying watching his pain as she'd destroyed everything he supposedly loved before finally ending his life.

"We need to leave," one of her men said, stopping her from approaching.

Margot's smile was manic, her eyes bright as she laughed above the growing flames as I continued to fight. They clawed at the walls and climbed the curtains. I was helpless as the fire ate everything in its path.

Without another word, she left, escorted out while there was a distant pop, the floor beneath me rumbling.

Heat licked at my skin, the ropes tightening, squeezing what little breath I had left.

"Get up!" Lang screeched, his movements frantic as he appeared behind me, having snuck inside. His arm was broken, held awkwardly at his side as he tried desperately to untie the knots at my back with a single hand. "You don't get to fucking die on me. Not after everything."

Blood dripped slowly down his face, smearing when he wiped up to clean it from his eyes.

"You need to go," I managed to push out, my voice as strangled as my body. "Leave!"

"Not without you." The ropes loosened, just enough for me to free my arms and climb to my feet.

The ceiling creaked beneath the intense heat, followed by a violent screech. Langdon pushed me just as a beam fell in the space we once stood, staring at me through the flames that had finally reached us.

"Sebastian!"

I jerked awake, my hand immediately tightening on Arabella that I had somehow trapped beneath me.

"You're okay," she whispered, reaching up to brush my cheeks, her fingers coming away wet.

I frowned down at her, my lungs aching as I tried to control my body's reaction. She wore a long T-shirt, and the window told me it was still dark. Late.

"You were screaming," she explained, and that reminded me I'd taken a pill. Just to help me calm down and actually sleep. Except it hadn't fucking helped me sleep, and instead trapped me in memories I'd rather forget.

Rage burned beneath my skin, turning my breathing harsh and my muscles to stone. Jumping up, I stalked out of the room, needing to create space. To calm down as my demons all but tore at my mind.

I needed to remove these memories from my head.

Arabella followed, keeping a wary step behind. I ignored her entirely, my attention on the canvas I set up and the paints that splashed onto the surface.

The flames I created were violent shades of orange and red, shadowed with vicious faces. Monsters that clawed at the figure in the centre. Langdon. I painted him with his mouth open in a silent scream, unable to be heard above the roar and crackles as everything around us was ruined. Destroyed. I painted him with sorrow in his eyes, accepting his death but mourning his life.

The flames slashed at him with sharp talons, the monsters burning, ripping away his skin while I watched at just fourteen. Bleeding out.

Unable to move.

Unable to help.

Tears burned my eyes, scoring down my face much the same as they did all those years ago. But I wasn't that same kid anymore. The one that was too small, too scared, too powerless to fight back.

Arabella stepped closer, watching me paint, her sadness thankfully silent as I poured my soul onto the canvas. Needing to purge this fucking ache that haunted me. She was patient as she waited for me to finish and then slash the piece with a knife. Tearing through the canvas as if I could that particular memory.

But I didn't want her silence. I wanted her moans, and her whimpers and cries.

I wanted her pliant beneath me so I could use her body to anchor me to the present.

"Sebastian," she whispered, my movements agitated,

rough as I grabbed her. Smearing her with the remnants of paint.

Except that was wrong, the vicious red and orange too much. So I tore at her T-shirt, using the fabric to remove the colour before my past engulfed my present. Ruining my future.

"Sebastian?" Her fingers were soft, her movements gentle.

I silenced her tears with my lips, needing her in that moment. Her hands gripped me, tearing at my clothes with a heat I revelled in. Deep down I loved how she saw past my cruelty and scars. How she seemed to want me as much as I wanted her.

She audibly swallowed when I released my aching cock, her eyes darting up to hold mine. Without a smile I lifted her naked in my arms, walking back until her skin hit the coolness of the window. Her thighs tightened around my hips, her moan caressing my face when I fucked into her in one thrust. Her body was always ready, allowing me to sink deep.

Tangling a fist in her hair, I pulled it to the side, biting and teasing her throat. Needing to mark as her inner walls clenched the rougher I thrusted. I bit to bruise, to bleed before using my tongue to ease the sting.

"Look how well you take me, *belle*." Her head hit the glass, hair framing her beautiful face as I reached between us to press against her clit. "Like you were always meant for me."

She came in a gush, and I went fucking savage. My hips pistoned into her until I knew she'd feel me for days, and I didn't stop when she tightened around my cock again, her scream echoing around me. Her voice keeping my demons away as I finally found my release.

Chapter 45
Sebastian

I needed this fight. Needed to feel flesh split and bones break beneath my fists. But I wasn't fighting, instead I was forced to watch because Langdon needed it more.

He didn't fight often, but when he did he was quick, his movements like dancing. If he had working vocal cords, his taunts and chuckles would be heard above the violence. Instead, he'd settle for frantically signing, knowing usually only I and Caden could understand his words.

Arabella watched beside me, reacting to every hit as if it had been personal. A particularly hard blow knocked Lang into the ropes, and Arabella flinched, as if she'd felt it.

"He's playing," I assured her. "Pretending he's weaker than he is, so he can draw his opponent into a false sense of security before he strikes."

Arabella didn't seem particularly pleased with my explanation. "Is this safe for him to do this so soon? He looks like he's losing." She wore a new dress, a deep gold colour that framed her curves perfectly and kept drawing my attention to her rather than the fight.

I returned my attention to the ring, able to read Langdon's enjoyment from his movements. Even if he lost, he would've been able to release some of his frustrations. He never cared whether he won or not, and often asked to go against men twice his size just for the thrill.

The bell dinged to finish the round, and Langdon grinned, his teeth red with blood.

"He just called his opponent the 'syphilitic remains of a gangbang.'"

"A what?" Arabella snorted.

She looked stunning beside me, and I glared at the men whose eyes hovered on her for far too long. "Come here," I said, waiting to see whether she'd follow the order.

She pursed her lips, sliding across until she could settle with her back against my chest. I didn't understand what made me feel so anchored with her weight on my lap, when anyone else would've turned me violent.

"Are you fighting?" she asked, always so full of questions.

"Not tonight." Despite losing a chunk of product in the fire, in the past few days there had been two more OD's, and each one pointed to my powder. We may have stopped anymore from being tainted, but I didn't know how long Margot had been fucking with my existing supply.

"Why do you do it?" Arabella asked quietly. "Langdon said you got your name in the underground fights."

"Langdon has a big fucking mouth."

"So that's how you gained the name Beast?" she wondered, seeming quietly excited by my answer.

"Among other reasons," I said, brushing my fingers down her exposed arms. "I fight because I enjoy it." When I didn't elaborate, she wrinkled her nose. "I find it calming."

"Calming?"

"Hmm," I hummed. "When I'm in the ring, I can ignore the outside noise. Nothing else matters other than my opponent." I've always found it hard to shut everything else off, when my demons howled and my nightmares threatened. It was constant, like a violent buzz beneath my skin. Until I met her, at least.

"Is that why you don't sleep? Because of the noise in your head?"

"You been watching me, *belle*?" She rolled her eyes, laughing when I pulled her tighter against me. "You going to behave tonight?"

"Do I have a choice?"

I pressed my mask against her ear. "We all have a choice, and you made yours by sitting on my lap." My erection ached, throbbing against my zipper. It was a fucking nuisance, and if I had my way, I'd already be home painting her skin in various shades before making her come repeatedly.

But other than supporting Lang, there was another reason I had to be seen tonight. I needed to appear unaffected by those fucking rumours. As not to be seen as weak.

At the moment they were somewhat contained, but I knew how quickly those devious whispers could spread.

"So if I so *choose*, I could walk out that door and never come back?"

"Yes, if you want your father's blood on your hands." I pinched her chin, forcing her gaze to mine. "I've told you before, *belle*. You're mine."

"Until the debt is paid," she shot back. "So tell me, how much have I actually paid off?"

"Nothing."

Annoyance darkened her eyes, and I smiled slow and cruel beneath my mask.

"You're not even pretending there's a way out, are you?" she huffed.

"You made a choice. You knew exactly what you were

agreeing to when you took his place." I brushed a thumb along her jaw.

"I agreed to pay off his debt." She jerked her head away. "How can I if you won't let me?"

"You don't get to play the victim, *belle*." There was no arrogancy in my words, just the truth. "You gave yourself to save him. Which makes you mine until I decide otherwise."

Arabella

An ember of anger sparked to life beneath my skin, but before I could make everything worse Caden appeared at our side, kneeling beside Sebastian. His words were lost against the general noise of the room, but his face was severe. Angry, which was his generic expression if I was being honest.

With a nod Sebastian went to stand, sliding me off his thighs before pinning me with his gaze.

"I'll behave," I whispered, ignoring how my lungs tightened behind my ribs.

What was even more frustrating was that I found myself tracking him across the floor, his presence like a hurricane tearing through my soul. There were moments of calm, when he revealed a little bit about himself, making him seem almost human. At the way he showed little bits of vulnerability through his art, something I was sure he'd never shown anyone else.

He'd been more than human the other night, the fear in his expression real before he'd blinked and replaced it with black rage. He'd painted for hours, and each second I'd been there, silently watching the pain he was pushing onto the canvas.

Then the moment would pass, and his eyes would hold me hostage, reminding me how little control I had. It was made worse by the ache between my thighs, at how warmth spread through me when he held me in a bruising grip. How he seemed to centre himself just by touch.

At first, I believed I was giving up my control entirely, but I'd come to realise that there was power in that loss. That by trusting Sebastian with my body, trusting him to know whether to push or when to pull, was a type of control in itself. It was an illusion that gave me peace, the not needing to think or worry about day to day because Sebastian would deal with it, and in return he used that need for dominance to calm his emotions. The ones he'd buried so deep, they came back to haunt him.

I found myself no longer swiping expensive trinkets to hide beneath my bed or sketching every possible exit in my notebook of the penthouse. And when he spoke of retaliation against the people who'd nearly killed Langdon and me, I wasn't as horrified as I should've been.

Before, I would have protested, even begged him not to choose violence. Now... I wasn't so sure. Because when he spoke of vengeance, his reasoning made sense in a way that unsettled me.

We seemed to be existing in this strange, shifting balance. Dark and intimate. Yet somehow it made me feel... whole. Like I fit into a space I hadn't known I'd been searching for. And that scared the hell out of me.

Fear rippled through the crowd as Sebastian walked amongst them, and I watched him until he disappeared through a door on the other side.

"I wouldn't recommend running this time, Miss Grey," Miles warned, coming to stand guard beside me.

"Don't have on the right trainers tonight, Miles?"

He blinked at me, clearly unamused with my joke. "I'll be your shadow until Mr Devereaux comes back."

"Ah, so you're my latest prison guard. There's me thinking you're here to just keep me company."

Miles's expression tightened, his eyes darting to the side before returning to me. "I'm whatever Mr Devereaux asks me to be."

I didn't grace him with a reply, instead trying to distract myself from the vicious fight in the centre by studying the crowd instead. I really didn't understand how people could get joy out of watching two grown men scrap at each other.

Clearly, I was in the minority, because the audience became fevered the more blood that spilled, even if it soaked against Langdon's long-sleeved shirt. He was beautiful in the way he moved, but he was a tease. Egging his opponent on with little skips and smirks. Twisting out the way at the last minute before rapidly signing what I assumed were creative insults.

Despite reading through the BSL book twice, I couldn't understand a single hand gesture.

Langdon took a particularly hard hit, his head whipping violently to the side. Unable to watch any longer I jumped to my feet.

Miles caught my upper arm in a bruising grip. "Where the fuck do you think you're going?"

"I need to pee, or is that not allowed?"

"Careful with the attitude," he growled.

"Get off my arm, Miles," I warned, the urge to lash out curling my fingers into a fist. Except my knuckles still ached from where I'd struck Lang. "Sebastian gets jealous."

"Of course, wouldn't want to upset your owner." He

released me, my skin pulsing as blood rushed back. "You'll have to use the other bathroom; this one is out of order."

"Sure." He was my shadow as I passed through the doors into the main club. The atmosphere was electric, the lights dimmed and the music loud. I wasn't so out of place this time, my dress fitting in with the others. But I could still feel curious eyes tracking me as I made my way towards the bathroom at the back of the room.

Something grabbed my arm, and before I could react, I was pulled to the side. I turned, ready to fight.

All the blood left my face. "Dad?" It took me a moment for my muscles to unlock before I threw myself at him. "How are you? Are you okay?" A thousand questions bubbled, and then my stomach dipped. "You shouldn't be here."

"Easy..." Miles warned before Dad untangled himself from my arms.

"Just give us a minute." I expected him to haul me away, but Miles simply nodded before stepping to the side. "Please."

Miles pursed his lips. "Two minutes."

Dad waited until Miles had stepped away, pulling me closer to his table. "We don't have much time." Picking up a drink, he handed it over. "Here, drink and smile before we draw attention."

I gripped the glass hard enough to break. "Why are you here? This isn't safe."

"I've worked out protection for us," he continued quietly. "I have a plan."

"What do you mean you have a plan?" Dad looked unwell, his eyes sunken, and he'd definitely lost some weight. There was even a yellowed bruise along his jaw, turning his skin a sickly shade. "Dad?"

"Trust me, Ara, we'll never have to worry about anything ever again. I promise, I can fix this."

Dad's eyes moved behind me, and I knew it wouldn't be long until Miles's patience ran out. I pushed us further into the shadowed corner.

"Smile," he hissed, clinking his glass against mine. "Drink, pretend you're enjoying yourself."

I took a mouthful, the alcohol burning as it went down. "What are you talking about?"

He leaned in, voice low and razor-sharp. "You're going to kill him."

My blood froze, and a tightness gripped my chest. "What? No. Absolutely not."

Dad's brows pulled together, his jaw locked in a hard line. "You agreed to take my place."

"I never agreed to *hurt* him," I snapped, the glass shaking slightly in my hand.

"Keep your fucking voice down," he snarled, dipping his head closer. "Stop acting like a saint. You'll do what you need for us. All you have to do is gain his trust before you can strike. I've set up–"

"No, stop it."

"You'll do this for me," he said, voice cracking in desperation. "And then we'll have no debt. The money we've been offered for his head is life changing, Ara. We'll finally be free."

I tried to place the drink down, but Dad gripped my wrist. "For how long, Dad? You might be free, until the next time you lose big. My entire life has always been fixing your addiction; even before Mum died you'd borrow money from bad people, and then leave it for us to suffer the consequences."

I'd witnessed him be beaten up for not paying on time

since I was little, and when he wasn't home, the men that came to our house took it out on my mum instead.

Years I'd had to hide, clamping my hands over my ears to dampen the screams. Every time he'd come home with gifts, begging for forgiveness. Saying he'd never do it again, only for him to go out the next day.

This was your fault, Bella.

My mum's voice in my memory was always harsh, cutting as if she'd swallowed broken glass.

He's like this because of you.

Why did you have to be born?

"You spoilt bitch. Everything I've ever done is for you. Every tournament, every fucking game was so you had food on the table, clothes on your back and a goddamn roof over your head." His fingers tightened, nails digging in. "You owe me."

"No." My voice croaked, and I tried tugging my wrist free. "I don't. Not anymore. Not since I gave over my life to save yours."

His expression turned vicious. "You think you're worth anything more than a whore who spreads her legs?"

I flinched, tears burning until I rapidly blinked them away.

"You're exactly like your mother. So fucking weak, and when I get–"

"I wouldn't finish that sentence," Caden cut in coldly, stepping in from behind.

Before my father could react, Caden grabbed him by the collar, yanking him back. The sudden movement jerked me forward with them until my father finally let go of my wrist, only for the rest of my drink to tip down my front.

You're only good as payment.

My chest heaved, soaked and shaking, but not from the cold.

Dad stumbled backward and would've gone straight to the floor if Caden hadn't caught him. "Get off me!" he snarled, trying to wrench himself free.

"Yeah, I don't think I will." Caden snapped Dad's finger, his wail a high-pitched screech. "Bit stupid to touch Beast's property, Morris."

"Dad, just go." My voice came out cold, detached. I set the empty glass down, my hand shaking. "Please."

"I'll handle this," Caden said to me, his eyes dipping to where the alcohol had darkened the gold of my dress. "You go clean up before Sebastian gets back."

I nodded, feeling numb. "Please don't hurt him."

Caden grinned. "Don't worry, we're just going to have a friendly chat." He turned to Dad. "Isn't that right, mate?"

Chapter 46
Arabella

The music quietened when the bathroom's door swung closed behind me. I ignored the empty three stalls, choosing the mirror furthest away above the sink. Picking up one of the towels I dabbed at my dress, fighting the tears that threatened to fall.

Throwing the towel to the side, I swayed a little. I didn't give a shit about the fucking dress. "Shit." Closing my eyes, I breathed through the sudden dizziness. It had been so many weeks, and Dad didn't seem to care about anything other than money.

I shouldn't be surprised, but still it hurt.

I'd wasted years of guilt, making sure he survived his stupid decisions. Years of sacrifice, all for him to want me to kill one of the most powerful men in the city. I would laugh if my stomach wasn't cramping.

"So, this is Beast's little pet."

My eyes snapped open, and in the reflection a man wearing a blue suit snickered behind me.

"I've heard he's pretty possessive over you."

His hand reached out, and I immediately reacted. My elbow swung, hitting the man in the face before he slapped me hard. I tasted blood, the momentum throwing my body to the side. My head cracked against the tiles, pain shooting across the front of my skull.

But I didn't have long, my movements sluggish as I managed to duck under his arm.

The man snarled, grabbing me as I tried to reach for the door. But he was stronger, easily throwing me back against one of the mirrors that shattered around me.

"Fucking bitch," he spat, the shards cutting into my back.

I scrambled against his hold, my nails scratching against his arm. Something snapped in the sink below me, freezing cold water spraying across us both. The man pulled me back, only to slam me once more against the fractured glass.

"I'm really going to enjoy this," he said, his voice barely a whisper against the thumping inside my head. Releasing his grip, I collapsed to the floor, my body feeling heavy. My limbs holding a weight I couldn't lift.

I was dragged across the tiles, the man's hand clawing at my dress until it ripped.

"Pretty thing, aren't you?" he crooned. My breasts came free, exposing me further before moving down.

I didn't feel the fabric of my knickers snap, only noticing the black lace being tossed amongst the mirrored shards and leaking water. I managed to reach for the largest shard, fingers barely able to hold it as I tried to stab him.

But my arm was too slow, my muscles not responding. It only sliced across his shoulder, barely cutting, and with a snarl he slapped me again.

Water splashed against my face, and the thought of drowning passed through my mind when I struggled for a breath. I clawed at the floor, trying to pull away, but fingers held me tightly before there was something hard pressed between my legs.

The man's grin was malicious as he reached for his belt, pulling it through the loops quickly before he moved on to his zipper.

No.

I tried to throw myself to the side, do anything to dislodge him from between my legs. But my body wasn't responding. The belt was looped behind my neck, using it to lift me against him.

Please. Stop.

"Don't worry," he muttered, his left hand bruising as he held me in place. "You're going to like it."

I wanted to close my eyes, to be anywhere else. But I couldn't even do that. The pressure increased, and not even a whimper could escape my–

There was a crash, the man jerking up before he was gone.

"Fuck!" Caden knelt beside me, but I couldn't move. "You're going to be okay." He removed his jacket, draping it over my front before Sebastian appeared above me like the God of Death.

His eyes narrowed when they landed on me, his anger so vivid I imagined it lashing against my exposed skin. I would probably physically flinch at the storm darkening his eyes if I could actually move my body.

"I think she's been drugged," Caden said, stepping back so Sebastian could take the space beside me. I tried to turn my head, a whimper barely passing my lips.

"I'm sorry," he whispered, pinching my jaw and opening my mouth. He thrust two fingers into the back of my throat, and just before I vomited he turned me on my side, his hand warm against my spine. *"Tout ira bien, je te le promets."*

He repeated this twice more, and then finally he lifted me into his arms.

My head rolled, and I was able to see the man knocked out in the corner, blood dripping from his temple with Miles and Caden glowering beside him.

"D...dad?" I managed to ask, my body shivering against my will.

Caden pursed his lips, eyes moving to Sebastian, who simply pulled me tighter against him.

Chapter 47
Arabella

The doctor helped me sit up against the pillows, my back stinging slightly from the coolness of the silk.

"Luckily the cuts are superficial, and won't need any stitches," the doctor said, her voice gentle as she double checked my forehead. "You're going to bruise, so I'll advise Mr Devereaux on an ointment that'll help."

"What about whatever I ingested?" I asked, tugging the sheets higher.

Sebastian had carried me to his room, ignoring my protests. He'd only left my side when the doctor asked him for privacy, and honestly, I thought he was going to bite her head off. But he'd gritted his teeth and nodded. Only after threatening her, of course.

"Luckily it wasn't in your system long, and I've taken your blood to be tested just to make sure. If it's my guess, it seems to be a generic date rape drug, and shouldn't have any lasting effects."

I swallowed, the relief so swift it took me a moment to reply, and even then my voice shook. "Thank you."

"You're very welcome." The doctor's smile was gentle, but her eyes darkened with concern. "Are you sure you want to refuse? I highly suggest I assess if there's any bruising–"

"I don't need it," I repeated for the third time. "I'm fine."

"Miss Grey..."

"Thank you, but no." I made sure my tone was stern, ignoring how my head pounded.

Her smile tightened, but she simply nodded. "The painkillers I've given you should kick in soon, but I suggest some rest. I'll update Mr Devereaux."

Collecting her things, she finally left to give me some privacy. I knew I wouldn't have long, so I immediately swung my legs off the side of the bed, ignoring the twinge from the fresh bruises on my hips.

My muscles felt tired, but at least I could feel them. Pulling the sheets I wrapped them around my body, only to look up and notice the painting on the wall.

"Where do you think you're going?" Sebastian asked, and I turned to find him closing the bedroom door behind him.

"Returning to my own room." I looked back over at the painting, frowning until I recognised the shadow of my own naked body amongst the smears of colour. Sebastian had hung the canvas he'd first fucked me on opposite his bed.

"You're not leaving." Sebastian came to my side, glancing up at the painting. He'd removed his black jacket and had pulled up his sleeves to reveal his arms. Blood splattered across his skin from where he'd held me.

I was too tired to argue, and those painkillers had yet to kill the dancer currently tapping away across my brain. "Sebastian–"

"The doctor said you refused an internal exam," he commented, his voice far gentler than I expected. I finally looked at him, holding the sheets tighter to my breasts. "Arabella, you need–"

"My body, my rules," I interrupted. "I don't need the exam."

Sebastian cocked his head, reaching down to cup my jaw. "How far did he get?"

"Why? Because you don't play with broken toys?"

His eyes narrowed a fraction. "Answer the question, Arabella."

"He didn't." I swallowed, frustrated with the way my eyes burned. "Caden interrupted just before he..." I couldn't finish the sentence, the words getting stuck.

His thumb brushed along my cheek in a gentle caress. "Come with me."

I went to protest, but he didn't give me a choice before he picked me up and carried me into his bathroom. He sat me at the edge of the tub, reaching over to turn on the taps. The heat was instant, the steam comforting as he added a sweet-smelling liquid to the quickly rising water.

I stared at the bubbles forming, my hand clutching the sheet until my knuckles had whitened. I didn't notice Sebastian leaving, the light above me dimming, or the candles that had suddenly appeared. Only reacting once he gently tugged the sheet from me.

"*Ça va aller, belle,*" he whispered when I flinched. "*Je ne laisserai rien te blesser.*"

"It's Ara," I muttered.

"Hmm." Sebastian's upper lip curved. "I've never called you *belle* because of your name."

"No?" I frowned, hooking my arm over the back of his neck when he lifted me once more, only to gently lay me down into the water.

"*Belle* means beautiful."

Oh.

"You're going to get wet," I whispered, unsure what to say.

Sebastian smirked, pulling out his arms to find he was indeed soaked. Tucking my knees to my chest, I watched as he unbuttoned his shirt before removing it entirely.

He stood with his chest bare, the flames from the candles creating harsher lines across his skin. Reaching for a cloth, he wet it in the water before gently washing it along my arm.

"Is my dad okay?" I asked, the words so quiet I didn't think he'd heard them.

His movements paused for a beat, and after the moment he continued to gently wash me. "He's alive, if that's what you're asking."

I pulled my bottom lip between my teeth. "I didn't know he would be there. I wasn't running. I didn't–"

"I know."

A lump formed in my throat, as if I'd swallowed frost, and I shivered despite the heat from the water. "Please don't hurt him," I whispered.

Sebastian washed across my shoulders. "Did he give you the drink?"

That frost shattered into a million icicles, cramping my stomach and turning my blood to ice. "Sebas–"

"Did he give you the drink?" he repeated, his voice stern yet somehow still gentle.

I couldn't look at him, simply hugging my legs tighter to my chest. "Yes."

"Do you think he knew what waited for you in that bathroom?"

Now, all you have to do is gain his trust before you can strike. I've set up...

"He wouldn't..." My voice cracked, unable to understand that the man who'd fathered me could do such a thing. That he thought so little of his only daughter that he could hurt her in such a way. Yes, he'd pushed me to take his place, to carry his debt.

But this was different. This was calculated. Deliberate.

The sobs finally broke free, tearing through my ribs as if each one came directly from my heart. It didn't matter that I tried to calm myself; I couldn't seem to stop them.

"Arabella..."

Pain tore through me, my head pounding and my heart breaking. "Why... why would he do that?"

A muttered curse, followed by a splash. Sebastian had stepped into the bath, trousers and all. Slipping his much larger body behind mine, he pulled me against him.

"Tout va bien se passer," he whispered against the top of my head. *"Cela ne se reproduira plus, je le promets."*

I closed my eyes, calming myself with his heat at my back. I don't know how much time passed with him simply holding me, long enough for the water to cool and the bubbles to pretty much disappear.

"I grew up in Paris," Sebastian said after a while, his voice deep, and yet soft as it brushed over me. "With two brothers."

Laying my head against his shoulder, I looked up at him. "There were two more of you?"

"Hmm." He brushed his fingers down my arms, his chest vibrating against my back. "Noah and Beau."

I could hear the sorrow in his words. "What happened to them?"

There was silence, stretching for so long I didn't expect him to answer.

"Tip your head back," he said quietly, the tension there beneath the huskiness of his tone. I hesitantly followed the command, and water poured carefully over my hair. "They were killed. Murdered when I was fourteen."

My heart ached for him. "Sebastian..."

"They were just six and nine."

I swallowed, my tears renewing, but this time they were for him. "Just babies."

"Hmm." He took his time with the shampoo and then the conditioner despite the angle being awkward. He didn't ask me to move forward to make this easier, seemingly content to hold me against him. "I couldn't save them."

"Is that how you were hurt?"

He didn't answer, instead gently washing my hair. I wanted to push, to understand one of the most dangerous men I hadn't even known existed. He rarely offered anything personal, but when he did, I longed to know more.

"What about your parents?" I asked softly, his fingers weaving slowly through my damp hair.

I couldn't see him, but I felt Sebastian smile. "My mother was like sunshine," he said. "Petite and delicate. She left everything for him, giving up her inheritance and family to move to Paris when she fell pregnant with me."

"And your father?"

He exhaled, a breath laced with old weight. "It was a whirlwind romance. He promised her the world, and for a while, I think he meant it." A pause. "But he was already tangled in the Le Milieu, quickly rising in ranks until he held a prominent position within the heroin trade over on the continent. With that came money, status, and power."

I listened, Sebastian's voice hollow, as if recalling everything without emotion.

"He trusted the wrong people, invited a viper into our home, and because of him I lost everything." Sebastian's fingers brushed through my hair, cautious of the cut on my forehead. "I despise him for it."

"Would he have invited her if he'd have known?" I asked.

"Does it matter?"

I didn't respond, just leaned into the quiet, Sebastian's heartbeat a steady rhythm against my back as he finished washing my hair.

"Why did you leave the arena?" he asked after a moment, his voice softer than before.

My cheeks burned from where my tears had dried, my eyes heavy with exhaustion. "I didn't like seeing Langdon fight, so I was going to wait in the bathroom until you came back."

"So why didn't you use the bathroom in the arena?"

"Because Miles said it was out of order."

Sebastian stiffened, his body rigid beneath me. I could almost feel the anger spiking from him in waves, and I waited for him to explode. To jump from the bath so he could break something and release this violent energy he always seemed to harbour, but never quite expel.

"What's going to happen to that man?" I asked, stroking down his arms to help calm his storm. I expected him to push me away, but he didn't.

"I'm going to kill him for daring to touch what's mine."

Chapter 48
Sebastian

Arabella stiffened at my words, turning in the water until she faced me with those eyes that seemed empty. Numb. I didn't fucking want her eyes to show nothing; I wanted that spirit that had burned me the first time we'd met.

I've never quite felt such rage at seeing Arabella on that bathroom floor, her blood smeared with her dress torn. It was as if something had possessed me, and at first I'd stepped closer to the man that had hurt her, but then decided she was more important. That my vengeance could wait until I could reassure myself that she was okay.

She made no sound as I lifted her from the water, carefully wrapping her in a towel despite me leaving a trail behind. The fire in my bedroom was already alight, and settling her on the edge of the bed I got rid of my soaking trousers before placing her back on my lap facing the hearth. The armchair squeaked beneath me, the towel separating our bodies.

At first, she was tense, her eyes fixed to the dancing flames.

"If you want to be alone, I'll leave," I said, fighting my

own selfish need to use her to calm those voices that called for me to react. To kill.

She swallowed, still facing forward. "Stay," she whispered, the word barely audible as she finally relaxed against me.

Her answer eased some of the weight on my chest, allowing me to breathe a little easier. I'd never found anything that would relieve this energy, and the thought that she'd been hurt...

Arabella turned, those eyes blinking up at me. "Promise me you won't kill him."

I knew she wasn't talking about the man who had tried to rape her, because nothing would stop me from taking his last breath. Her dad deserved the same fate. "Why shouldn't I?"

"Because if you do, I'll never forgive you."

"You think I care?"

Her eyes searched mine. "Please, I'll do anything. Double the debt."

I gently cupped her jaw, keeping her in place so I could press my lips to hers. *"Belle, la paix que je trouve en ta présence vaut la peine d'être le méchant de ton histoire."*

Beautiful, the peace I find in your presence is worth being the villain of your story.

"Sebastian..." She was frustrated at the lack of translation, but she was too exhausted to fight me, her adrenaline waning. So I simply pulled her tighter against my chest, letting the crackling of the flames lull her to sleep. Only when I was confident she wouldn't wake did I finally place her in my bed. Where I planned to keep her forever.

Each step towards the dungeon sent a bolt of lightning through my muscles, my knuckles aching from how hard they were tensed.

Regarde de l'autre côté, bébé!

Look the other way, baby!

I couldn't have looked away if I'd wanted, my head forced up so I had to watch the numerous men assault my mother violently. It was part of the torture, that we all had to witness each family member be hurt, one after another. My mother was first, then my brothers, then me, and then finally my father.

But while my mother was killed quickly, Margot had wanted my brothers and I alive just a little bit longer. All so we could witness my father sob, begging as we lay there broken.

The twins stood in their positions by the door, their expressions identically sober when they nodded in my direction. "Boss, they're waiting for you."

I took a deep breath, trying to calm the rage festering in my soul. "Nobody comes inside until I'm done."

It was Micah who answered. "Understood."

Stepping inside the concrete room, I glanced at Caden, who was leaning casually against the wall with a cigarette hanging out his mouth.

"His name's Anton Hill," he said in French, his own anger palpable as he straightened to his full height. *"Where's Lang?"*

"Watching over Arabella," I replied in the same

language, noting how Anton and Morris's eyes widened at my presence. I'd made sure I presented myself in what they'd expect, including my mask. My suit was fresh, and the rings I'd chosen the heaviest I own. Specifically designed to leave a print when I likely lost my temper and resorted to fists.

Caden had tied Anton naked to a chair, the thick rope grazing the cunt's bare skin. His cock could barely be seen between his slightly spread legs, shrivelled up and hiding in the purposely kept cold room.

Morris was beside him, his left eye already swelling shut and his shoulders hunched forward. He was clothed, but that would change depending on his explanation.

"How is she?" Caden asked, taking a drag from his cigarette before flicking it towards Anton. Anton screeched into the rag between his lips, the tip burning his side before falling to the floor.

"She's strong." I cracked my neck, the two men flinching at the sound. Crossing the room, I knelt in front of Anton, purposely ignoring Morris for the moment. "Do you know who I am?" I asked in English, Anton's eyes widening before he gave me a jerky nod.

Good.

"You're going to die here today," I said calmly, enjoying the panic rising at my words. "How quickly will be up to you."

"Interesting torture technique," Caden commented, returning to French. *"You're supposed to lull them into a false sense of security so they answer your questions, and then you kill them."*

"I want him to be terrified the entire time, until all he can feel is his heart beating as violently as I'm sure Arabella's was," I replied, yanking out the cloth from Anton's mouth.

He coughed, almost retching as he tried to lean forward. Except the ropes kept him in place. "Please, I didn't—"

My fist hit him in the jaw, all my anger and rage coming out in the force. Even his voice made me see red, my imagination conjuring up all the vile words he'd likely whispered to her as she'd laid there vulnerable. Unable to fight back.

The second hit knocked several teeth out, the third caused the entire chair to topple, blood spraying as his skin split from the impact.

"If you break his jaw, he won't be able to tell us anything," Caden said calmly, his presence anchoring as I tried to control the maelstrom inside me. It was a pressure, tightening my lungs and stiffening my muscles.

I swallowed past this black rage, nodding for him to lift Anton back up from the floor.

"Right, mate, shall we get this party started?" Caden said. "You're going to tell us everything we want to know, otherwise it's really going to hurt. Understood?"

As Anton opened his mouth to reply, Caden shoved in several blue pills. He gagged, but Cade kept his hand over his mouth, stroking down his throat until he swallowed.

"There you go, princess. Give them a minute to kick in, don't be shy. Now, why don't you start from the beginning for us?"

"I... I was paid to... hurt her."

"Rape," I added, my tone dangerously quiet. "You were paid to rape her."

He licked along his bottom lip, tears and snot smearing across his face. "I was paid to rape her."

"By who?" Caden asked.

"I don't know... some older woman. She paid in cash and told me she'd call me with the time and day."

"*I'll see if we can trace the call,*" Caden said, nodding towards the pile of clothes on the metal table beside the wall. *"But it'll likely be a burner phone. You thinking Margot?"*

"What the fuck is he saying?" Anton cried, eyes darting between us. "Please, I swear I don't know anything else. I've never met her before, but she called and told me I had to be at *The Thorn* within the hour."

He glanced at Morris, who was aggressively shaking his head and trying to escape his bonds.

"How did you get inside?" Caden asked. When Anton didn't immediately answer, he grabbed a small hammer from the table and then brought it down on Anton's left knee. "Don't be a muppet, answer the fucking question."

"The bouncer!" Anton screeched. "I was told to meet the bouncer, who let me in."

"What about old Morris here?"

Anton let out a sob, his cock hardening despite the pain thanks to the extra strength Viagra. "Please..."

Caden brought down the hammer on his right knee, and Anton's scream echoed around us like the greatest symphony. I was going to paint this later, this exact scene while remembering his pathetic wails.

And then I was going to carve it up because he didn't deserve to be remembered.

"I don't know him!" Anton's eyes bulged, his chest rising with rapid breaths. "I've never seen him before!" he blubbered.

Caden clicked his tongue, stepping back with his bloodied hammer. I decided it was enough, reaching for the blade kept neatly on the table.

"Please... don't," Anton cried, but I'd already turned to Morris. I cut his ropes, pulling him up by his throat before thrusting the knife in his hand.

"Cut off his cock," I growled, squeezing his fingers tightly around the handle.

"W...what?"

Caden laughed, even as the colour drained from Morris's face, his movements jerky as I forced him over to where Anton was trying to pull himself free from the ropes. His legs were a mess of flesh and bone, and yet his pathetic cock stood proud between his thighs.

Still holding Morris, I guided his hand. He fought, but he was no match for me as I forced him to hold Anton's straining cock and then slice it off. Unfortunately, it wasn't a clean slice, so we had to repeat it a second time.

Morris wrenched himself to the side as Anton screamed, blood sprouting violently from between his legs. The sharp scent of puke erupted as Morris vomited on the concrete, and the sound of Anton's shrieks ended suddenly when he finally passed out.

Shame I wasn't finished. Holding the bloodied knife out to Caden, I reached into my inner jacket pocket and grabbed the smelling salts.

Cracking the capsule, I shoved it inside Anton's nose. He came awake with a jerk.

"Tell me about the bouncer," I demanded, holding his jaw in a bruising grip. I didn't care that I was being coated with blood, the coppery tang mingling with ammonia and puke. "Was he named Miles?"

Caden's gaze burned, but I refused to look away from Anton.

A frantic nod. "He helped me get inside and then told me he'd get her there. That's it, man, I've never met him before tonight," he swore, voice fraught with desperation.

I nodded, reaching down to grab the withering remains of his dick. "You really shouldn't have touched what's mine." I shoved the cock down his throat, letting him choke.

Caden winced, shaking his head. "That means it's our man Morris's turn."

Morris was still on his hands and knees, his head hanging between his arms. On hearing his name he scrambled onto his arse, sliding back until he hit the wall.

"Please... don't do this." He held up his hands, as if that would stop Caden from yanking him up and holding the same knife that had just cut Anton's cock off to his throat.

"Why did you give Arabella a drug-laced drink?" I asked, my muscles aching from how tight I held myself back.

"Because that's all she's good for," he sneered, a drop of blood dripping down the column of his throat.

"You're such a weird cunt," Caden sneered. "Honestly, who the fuck would set up their own daughter?"

"People have been talking, saying you've been a little possessive." Morris tried to swallow, but struggled. "I thought her being hurt might bring you closer, that's all."

"*How much of this do you believe?*" Caden asked, reverting back to French when he wanted the conversation to be private.

"*I believe she would do anything to help her father.*" The thought angered me.

"*You think she knew of his plan?*"

Her pain at the realisation of what Morris had done had been real. "*No.*"

Caden nodded, pressing the blade deeper.

"Wait, wait!" Morris cried. "If you do this, she'll never forgive you."

I'll never forgive you.

Her threat meant little to me, and yet I stopped Caden.

"What the fuck, Bas?" He kicked at Morris, who collapsed back on his knees.

"Come near Arabella again," I warned, reaching for the discarded hammer. "And I'll make sure your screams will be remembered." I brought it down on his right hand, the same hand that likely poured the drug into her drink.

Morris screamed, but I kept bringing it down until his hand was nothing. Each finger shattered beyond repair.

I left him there, needing to return home and make sure Arabella was safe. Caden chased me into the hall, the twins moving in to clean up behind. "Bas, stop!"

I turned, grabbing Caden and shoving him against the wall. "If you have something to say, say it."

"You should've killed him. He publicly insulted you by hurting Ara." Caden's eyes darkened with frustration. "She really influences you this much?"

I pushed away from the wall before I did something volatile, like hit him.

"What the fuck are you doing with her, Bas? Is she really just your toy, or is she more?"

"More." There was no hesitation. She'd been more to me since the first time I set my eyes on her. It just took me a while to realise.

Caden's nostrils flared, the skin on his cheeks a little flushed. "Does she agree?"

"She will." She wasn't going to be given a choice. "She quiets the noise, Cade."

"Jesus, you sound whipped. Lang isn't going to believe it." Caden pursed his lips, but there was still anger there. "What do you want to do about Miles?"

"Put out a price on his head. Alive."

"He's been with us a decade." Caden dragged his palm down his face. "Fuck."

"I don't care." Arabella was the first time I'd ever wanted to keep something, rather than destroy it. "I've decided. She's mine."

Chapter 49
Arabella

I was pressed to something hard and deliciously warm. Opening my eyes to slits, I found myself wrapped around Sebastian like ivy. My leg was hooked over his hip, and my palm was placed directly above his heart.

Sebastian's face was turned towards me, features completely relaxed. I'd never seen him so calm, even if his hand was holding me against him at the bottom of my back.

My naked back. Even in sleep his fingers pressed, pinning me exactly where he wanted me. This was the most I'd ever touched him, and I needed to carefully twist out of his hold before he woke and realised. Gently reaching back for his arm, I tried to wiggle myself under it when he pulled me even tighter against his side.

It was then I realised he wasn't asleep.

I stiffened, and it took me a moment to relax into his embrace. To frown because his fingers had started to rub gentle circles rather than push me away.

Sebastian just laid there, his breathing even as he watched me. His chest was bare, and the sheets were pooled low on his hips. I took my time to look for injuries or evidence of blood. But all I noticed were the split knuckles on his right hand.

"Did you kill him?" I whispered, my heart aching as I waited for an answer.

Sebastian said nothing, his eyes of midnight cold. Frozen.

My chest tightened. "He was all I had."

I sucked in a staggered breath, unable to get in enough air. I shoved into his side, knowing I only managed to get out of his grasp and climb to my feet because he'd let me.

Ripping the sheets off the bed, I wrapped them around myself, trying and failing to use them to keep this pressure from escaping my body. Sebastian sat up slowly, eyes following me as I began to pace.

"How could you do that?" My voice hitched, my breathing rapid.

"Why does he matter so much to you?"

"Because he never left me!" I screamed, my walls crumbling.

Sebastian stepped closer, and I couldn't help but shove him back with all my strength. It was like trying to hit a mountain. So I hit him again, and again, each blow landing on his chest.

He encircled my wrists, tugging me until I was flush against him with my head tipped back. "Stop before you hurt yourself."

I wanted to fight, to scratch and claw until he was as messed up on the outside as I felt on the inside.

"He was a rotten father, but at least he stayed." I sucked in another breath, trying to control the way my lungs squeezed. "My mum couldn't even do that."

The air rippled with tension, and I found myself caught by my own anger. It perforated the air like smoke, suffocating as I dragged up memories I'd rather forget.

"She left us, and it *destroyed* him!" I choked out, my voice barely more than a ragged whisper. "It shattered something in him so completely that he stopped being a father. He couldn't even look at me without seeing everything she took with her."

I'd come home late from school, the rain soaking through my uniform as I walked, wondering how they could forget me again. The house was dark when I arrived, shadows pooling behind the windows. I fumbled for the spare key beneath the loose rock, the metal cold in my hand, my fingers trembling against the cold.

I expected to find Mum inside, either crying at the kitchen table or frantically throwing pans around, halfway through some manic attempt at dinner. But when I stepped through the door, the silence hit me first.

There were no lights. No voices. Just the faint, steady sound of running water.

It seeped down the stairs, saturating the carpet and making each of my steps squelch.

I'd found her in the overflowing bath, the knife on the floor and her wrists slit. At eight I didn't understand why she wouldn't respond. Even when I shook her or called her name.

"I'm so fucking angry," I whispered to Sebastian, my eyes burning with tears I refused to let fall. "Why was she so selfish to take her own life?"

Dad had found me in the bathroom, and rather than offer comfort, he'd broken down. Sobbed for a wife who didn't want her life with us. A woman who didn't want *him*. Didn't want *me*.

It was the first time he'd looked at me like I was the reason she'd chosen to die, as if it was my fault. And that look never faded. Not when I cried. Not when I tried harder. Not when I did everything for him to feel something towards me other than obligation.

That blame was a weight I could never seem to shift. But Dad had never thought about taking the same exit as Mum, and despite his faults, he was still here. *Was.*

I choked down a sob, captured by Sebastian's hard, unrelenting gaze. "He was all I had left, and you took that away."

"I didn't kill him."

I began to shake, and it was only Sebastian's grip that kept me on my feet. "You didn't?"

He shook his head, the movement slow and his jaw clenched.

The crushing wave of grief subsided as I concentrated on the weight of his words. "Why?" I had felt his rage, the savage rise and fall of his chest as he'd held me in his arms while I'd broken into pieces.

Sebastian reacted; that was what made him the Beast. He was volatile and didn't allow anyone to challenge him. And yet he didn't kill the man who had hurt his toy.

"Because now you owe me." He stared down at me, and I made sure I tipped my chin in return.

"How could I possibly owe you anymore than I already do?"

His upper lip twitched, those eyes I was so obsessed with darkening with desire. Or it could be that I was projecting, because now I knew my father was well and alive, I was somewhat aware of how close Sebastian held me. One hand gripping my wrists against his chest, and the other spreading on the small of my back.

"You'll stay."

It took me a moment for his statement to register. "Wait... what?"

The sheet had draped low, and he made quick work of

removing it until I stood naked. I didn't feel exposed, or cold. Not when he watched me with such heat, and something else. Something that sent a thrill through me. It was like he wanted me to defy him, just for the sick game of crushing me beneath his power.

"You'll stay with me," he repeated. "You'll never try to run."

"I told you to double my debt if you didn't hurt him."

"Then it's doubled." His fingers grazed my jaw, gentle and possessive. "And now, *belle*, you owe me a lifetime."

"Sebastian..."

His head dipped, his lips gentle as he swallowed my protest. "You'll let me take everything, won't you, *belle*?"

He nipped along my jawline, teasing the skin, and I found myself arching to the side, giving him a better angle as he moved down my neck. He had the ability to steal my thoughts. My breath. Even my heart.

But this wasn't something I would bend to.

"No." My answer was a whisper, and I winced as he grabbed the hair at my nape and tugged my head back painfully. His lips found mine again, and this time there was no gentleness to the way he claimed them. It was aggressive. Possessive.

And I was drowning in his intensity. Aching for it, even.

I met his aggressiveness with my own, but I should've known I could never be in his league. Picking me up he laid me back down on the bed, his body hovering over mine as he devoured me as if I was his lifeline.

As if this was real.

"You like when I take control," he said, his fingers rubbing between my legs. "Look how wet you get when you're at my mercy."

I caught the whimper before he could hear it, trying and failing to stop myself moaning when he thrusted a single finger inside. Anticipation slithered down my spine at the way he always pushed. Taking what he wanted, distracting me from my thoughts and making me crave his chaotic energy.

"See, you're fucking soaking." Sebastian added a second finger, his beard scratching down my stomach. "And all mine." Throwing my legs over his shoulders, he dived between my thighs, his tongue lapping at me with powerful strokes that had my back bowing immediately off the bed.

"Sebastian..." I cried out, and he slapped my thigh with an open palm, the sting making electricity dance across my skin. There was no teasing or gentle nips of his teeth. He devoured me as if I was a feast, sucking my clit between his lips in such a way that my orgasm teetered on the edge within seconds.

I could feel it, the sensation growing until I found my fingers scratching at his scalp. My hips rocking up against his tongue. He groaned into my pussy, the vibration about to push me over...

"*Tu n'as pas encore le droit de venir.*"

I cried out in frustration, my fingers unwinding from his hair. Sweat coated my skin, my pussy clenching at the loss of my release. He blew a hot breath, and I noticed his smirk at my returning whimper.

His rough hands shaped my body, stroking over those new bruises on my hips, followed by his lips. I froze at the gentleness, at how he was erasing what had happened and replacing it with himself.

"*Tu es à moi.*"

My nipples were hard, aching for attention. "Sebastian, please," I begged, needing more. Needing him.

He made his way up my body, hesitating at my breasts. "Only if you agree to stay."

Chapter 50
Sebastian

Arabella pressed her lips into a stubborn line, her face flushed with arousal. "No, I can't."

I wanted to chuckle at her response, even as she moaned at how hard I tugged on her nipples. She was panting beneath me, trying to rub her clit against my heavy thigh between her legs like a cat in heat.

Except she wasn't allowed to come, not yet. Not until I decided she'd had enough, and the attack in the bathroom was fucking erased from her memory. Replaced with only me.

Only I was allowed to bruise her, mark her as my own. I have never been gentle in sex, needing that control over their bodies. Making them come over and over, or not at all. It was fucking euphoric, and Arabella gave herself to me so easily, even after last night.

But I needed to replace them, press my fingers into those exact bruises so I could make them mine. So I did, her resulting cry not of pain, even though I knew it hurt.

"You're so fucking pretty when you scream," I growled, diving back between her thighs to eat out her cunt like it was my last meal. She tasted fucking perfect. She tasted like she was mine.

My fingers dug harder, deepening those bruises as I lapped at her faster, teasing her throbbing clit with my tongue until her entire body tensed beneath me. This time I didn't stop, not even when she tugged at my hair or tried to scramble from my hold. I devoured her until she came, squirting all over my face with the power of her orgasm.

And still I continued, not giving her a reprieve so I could force another orgasm out of her within seconds. Her cries echoed around me, and I was thankful no one was here to hear her because I didn't share.

She was almost hyperventilating when I finally pulled back, my cock aching as I pressed it against the mattress to try and ease the throbbing. I wanted to demand her onto her knees, so I could fuck that throat and paint her face with my cum.

But I wasn't done with her just yet.

"Stay with me."

Arabella swallowed, her eyes only open to slits. But I could still see that fire there, and fuck I wanted to be burned.

"I can't."

I smiled, because her answer didn't matter.

Standing, I moved my armchair until it was beside the foot of the bed, perfectly angled for what I planned to do next. Taking a seat, I watched her in my bed, the dark sheets perfect against her pale skin. Her lips were parted, and her hair was a tangled mess.

She'd never looked more beautiful.

Fisting my cock I gave it a tight squeeze, amused with how her eyes immediately darted to the way I rubbed pre-cum along the head.

"Come here," I demanded, and her eyes snapped to

mine. I was obsessed with how she was unable to hide her emotions. With her flushed cheeks and parted lips. Lust battled with defiance in her gaze, a war in which I knew what side she would fall.

She took a tentative step forward, and I groaned as a reward, squeezing my cock harder. Arabella was all but panting, her entire body flushed with arousal. As soon as she was within arm's reach, I grabbed her waist, pulling her to my side.

"You're going to sit on my cock," I whispered against her skin.

I turned her around until she faced away before lifting her onto my lap. She moaned as I settled her on me, her pussy clenching as I pulled her tightly against my chest. She sunk an inch, her groan vibrating through us both.

"Sebastian..."

"You can take it," I murmured, knowing this angle put me deeper.

With one hand I pinched her nipple painfully, the other I wrapped in her hair so I could angle her head towards the mirror. I watched as her eyes widened at the sight, her cunt stretching obscenely to take my entire length.

"Look how pretty you look, *my little rabbit.*"

I thrusted up from below, the movement violent as I sunk the last few inches inside her. Her lips parted on a cry, but I didn't give her time to adjust before I started moving harder, faster. Her breasts bounced, so I released her nipple, only to sink my fingers down her stomach to flick at her clit.

Arabella clenched around me, her orgasm tearing through her body. I was able to watch her cunt pulsate. Watch her release soak us both. But I wasn't finished.

I wanted her a mess. To beg as I overstimulated her to the point of pain. To make her understand that she belonged only to me.

"Up," I demanded, her legs barely holding her weight when she climbed off. "Hands on the mirror, and arse in the air." I pressed her forward, placing her palms on the glass and bending her a little. I groaned at the sight, her pretty cunt pink and swollen, but it wasn't her pussy I wanted.

She panted into the mirror, eyes wide as she watched me move behind her.

"Remember, *belle*. Your mouth is mine." I slipped two fingers between her lips, pressing them against her tongue. "Your cunt is mine." They dipped between her legs next, coating them in arousal. "And this little hole..." I dragged them up, a whimper escaping her throat when I slowly pressed one inside her back hole. "Is also mine."

"Sebastian..." she groaned, her head dropping low between her shoulder blades as she slowly opened for me.

With my free hand I tangled my fingers in her hair, forcing her eyes up to mine as I worked the second finger inside. Another whimper broke free from her lips, her face flushed as I slowly stretched her last hole.

I thrusted my hips forward, coating myself in her arousal as I pulled my fingers out, only to replace them with my cock. "I told you I wanted everything."

She let out a strangled sound, my cock spreading her further.

"Relax for me; it'll only hurt for a minute." I didn't thrust inside in one go, knowing I had to take it slow the first time so I could feel her entire body shudder through the pain.

But I knew my Arabella liked the pain, so I laced it with pleasure, my fingers circling her clit as I gave her a moment to stretch to my size before I pulled out, only to thrust back inside. This time harder.

She let out a cry, but I felt arousal dripping from

between her legs and saw the way her eyes darkened with pleasure in the reflection.

"Fuck," I cursed, having to clench my jaw from the way she strangled my cock. Pulling her up until her back hit my chest, I dropped my lips to her ear. "Your arse almost feels as good as your cunt."

Arabella swallowed, her eyes wide as she watched me fuck her from behind, one hand on her clit, the other I wrapped in her hair.

"Look how perfectly you fit me," I said to her as I continued to thrust.

"It's too much," she cried, a tear dripping down her cheek as my movements turned animalistic. "Sebastian, please. I need..."

I pinched her clit, forcing another orgasm that strangled my cock so tightly I almost lost it myself. "Next time you tell me no, remember how you looked when you came, my cock deep inside your tight hole, stretching you open while you begged for more."

I had to concentrate on the words, keeping them English rather than French. Arabella had the ability to make me forget myself, especially when she wiggled back, meeting my thrusts with her cute little whimpers.

"One more, *belle*. You can do it for me, can't you?" I whispered in shallowed breaths. "Such a good girl."

She moaned, her head held painfully by my fist, forcing her eyes on me as I played with her clit. "Please, Sebastian," she begged.

"You're so fucking beautiful." *Thrust.* "Addicting." *Thrust.* "Mine."

She was like a vice as she shattered again, and I caught her scream with my lips, my own release following with a vicious intensity.

Arabella was like a missing piece of my soul, not just

someone who could endure me at my worst, but someone who stood her ground against it. She didn't flinch in the face of my demons; she made them hers.

Arabella sagged against me, her body limp with exhaustion as I gathered her in my arms. She reached for my neck, her lips brushing mine so tentatively it stole the breath from my chest. It was the first time she'd initiated anything, and I felt it like a spark beneath my skin. I took it as her silent agreement.

Her unspoken surrender.

Chapter 51
Arabella

This was the first time I'd spent an extended period alone in Sebastian's bedroom. I would've escaped to my own, except Sebastian had scowled and demanded I rest specifically in his bed. I would have protested more if he hadn't placed the gentlest kiss on my lips before leaving. And now even after returning to my own room to get dressed, I found myself back here unsure why my heart was thudding so harshly, or why my chest felt tight.

My hips ached, the bruises throbbing. But when I thought of them, I didn't think of the man, I thought of Sebastian, and how he'd made them his own.

I'm not calling you belle *because of your name.*

I refused to acknowledge this change between us, as if the dynamic had shifted into something more... intimate. So instead of sitting with the weight of it, I pushed it aside and reached for his drawers, letting curiosity get the better of me.

There were no hidden weapons, or something else equally as nefarious tucked away. It was almost a little disappointing.

Ignoring the art on the wall entirely because I didn't have the mental capacity to deal with the sex print just yet, I looked over his side of the bed in his nightstand, pausing when I realised he had a row of books tucked neatly away in the little cubby hole.

Slipping to my knees beside the bed, I picked up the closest one and flipped through it. They were mainly thrillers, a little fantasy, and even some fiction in French that I barely glanced at. But what caught my attention was the large black device that had been placed down beside them, the word '*C-pen*' written across it. I'd noticed something similar in his office, and frowning, I held the power key and clicked 'reader.'

"Scan text," a small robotic voice came from the device.

Picking up one of Sebastian's books, I followed the instructions, delighted when the device started reading out loud the same text I'd just scanned.

Placing it back where I'd found it, I opened another drawer, pausing when I realised that was where he'd put my phone. Turning it on I placed it on the bed beside me, the battery flashing red, but still the screen filled with missed texts ranging from several weeks to days old.

GABRIEL:

You have no idea what you've done, baby.

You should've just agreed to stay mine, and then this wouldn't have happened.

Your dad misses you. I miss you.

Let me handle this, okay? I'll save you.

Why aren't you answering your fucking phone?

Three hours ago.

My finger hovered over his contact, my chest tightening at just the thought of talking to him. Swallowing the sudden metallic taste, I clicked call, expecting to go straight to voicemail.

"*Ara?*"

I breathed through my nostrils, trying–and failing–to stop the panic growing at just his voice. "Dad?"

"*Why the fuck has it taken you this long to call me?*" he seethed, but panic underlined his tone. "*That monster destroyed my hand. He's a fucking animal!*"

I couldn't bring myself to respond, deciding to concentrate on the anger that was burning beneath my ribs rather than the growing pain.

"*Ara, are you not even going to say anything? He broke my hand with a hammer!*"

"Is that all you have to say? After what you tried to do to me?" I hissed. "You're lucky that was all he did."

"*What do you want me to say? I fucked up, Ara. I panicked, and everything's gone to shit.*" There was a pause, a heavy exhale. "*I shouldn't have said you were like mum.*

You're nothing like her, I know that. You were always the strong one. You always did what was right for us."

"Dad–"

"You have to fix this, Ara," he said quickly, desperation spilling through the phone. *"Be my brave girl. You've always been that. Just get through this, gain his trust, and then we can set it all right. We'll get our payback, just like I've planned. After what you made Mum do, you owe me that–"*

I hung up, turning the phone off as soon as Dad tried to call back. I wanted to laugh and then cry until every single one of my tears were spent. The man who'd raised me couldn't care less that he'd orchestrated his own daughter's rape. He only cared about what he could get from it. He dared to use Mum as an excuse, like her death could somehow justify the choices he'd made, that he'd traded his daughter's safety for his own survival.

It made my stomach twist and my heart clench. He'd always done that. Weaponised the past, using my guilt to manipulate the situation in his favour.

And I'd let him. For *years* I'd let him pull my strings, hoping that maybe one day he'd look at me and see something worth loving. Hoping that if I was just good enough, quiet enough, strong enough... he'd finally forgive me for something that was never my fault.

But now it hit me. The brutal, suffocating truth.

He didn't love me, not since Mum had taken her life. I reminded him too much of what he'd lost, so instead of protecting me like any other parent, he'd used me.

I never knew I could hate someone so much, and yet still love them because he was all I knew. All I had.

"Ara?"

My head jerked up, finding Chip standing in the doorway with a frown. "Oh, hi." I rubbed at my cheeks, expecting them to be wet. But they weren't, and for some reason that eased the pain inside my chest.

"Are you okay?" His eyes scanned my body. "I'd heard you'd been–"

"I'm fine," I interrupted, giving him a strained smile. "Seriously, I'm okay."

He eyed me warily, clearly unconvinced. "I didn't expect to see you," he admitted. "I thought maybe the attack would've scared you off. I was worried."

It probably should've, except Sebastian hadn't initiated it. And he'd been the one to hold me while I'd broken apart and then pieced myself together. Except I didn't say that out loud, because even in my own head it sounded too raw. Too honest.

"Is your mum around?" I asked, scanning the space behind him. "I'd really like to talk to her."

It had been over a week since I last saw her, and honestly, the idea of kneading bread dough until my arms ached while she told me stories sounded like the healthiest way to deal with my emotions right now.

"Oh, no. She was fired a while ago," he said carefully, waiting for my reaction.

"Wait, she was fired?"

He nodded, even his movements cautious. As if he was expecting me to break. "Mr Devereaux's currently interviewing for a new head of household. Until then I've taken over when I'm available. If not, Mr Devereaux has been getting all the meals ordered in."

"Oh." The word came out small, flickering with disappointment.

Chip's smile was soft, almost awkward. "Also, Mr Alexander Ackworth's waiting for you up in the drawing room."

I frowned, because I'd never had a guest since no one really knew I was here. "Who?"

"The uncle. Mr Ackworth's insistent on seeing you without Mr Devereaux present." His eyes searched mine before he dropped his voice to a whisper. "Want me to ask him to leave? I can make up an excuse that you're sick or something."

I swallowed past the unease. "No, it's fine. I'll see what he wants."

"Are you sure about this?" Chip frowned, expression etched with concern. "You should be resting, not wasting your energy on *him*." His voice sharpened on the last word, as if even saying it left a bad taste in his mouth.

"Is Sebastian's uncle that bad?"

Chip pursed his lips, turning to the hall. "You have no idea."

Following, he walked me over to where Sebastian's uncle stood over the chessboard, frowning at the pieces from when Chip and I had last played.

"Charlie, how... quaint of you to be working for my nephew. I assume that's your mother's doing?" Alexander barely glanced in my direction. "Where is Mrs Pritchard?"

Chip's shoulders tightened. "Here's Arabella, as you'd asked."

"Hmm." Alexander finally turned his attention to me, his gaze sweeping over with a glint of displeasure. *Rude.* "Charlie, please bring up some tea. Your mother knows how I like it." He dismissed him with a sweep of his hand, while simultaneously gesturing for me to take a seat opposite him. "Miss Grey—"

"Please, call me Arabella."

His smile was forced, almost fake. "I'm very busy, so I'll make this quick," he said, sitting back in his chair with an aura of superiority in his expensive suit and shiny shoes. "You're a problem."

"Excuse me?"

"I told my nephew to get rid of you." His eyes narrowed. "And yet, here you are. Still clinging to Sebastian like a leech."

"You seem to think it was my choice to be here."

"Oh, but you do," Alexander replied, his smile curving with quiet cruelty. "You could've asked anyone for help, and I have it under good authority that a certain Detective Graves has been sniffing around. Rather persistently, in fact. So forgive me if I suspect your presence here isn't as helpless or innocent as you pretend."

My nails dug into my palms. "I have nothing to do with Gabriel."

"And yet ever since you've arrived, he's taken a sudden and *very* personal interest in matters well outside his jurisdiction as a detective. Sebastian's business, the club, the accounts. Even the supply routes." Alexander's gaze sharpened, his tone cool and deliberate. "Quite the coincidence, wouldn't you say?"

"Is there anything else?" I asked coldly. "Or did you come all this way just to insult me?"

"I've come to offer you a deal." Alexander paused, a muscle feathering in his jaw. "I've prepared everything you'll need to... escape, shall we say. I have a driver waiting to take you to the airport, and I'll pay for you to travel anywhere in the world."

He pressed a single finger to the pile of papers on the table between us, ones I hadn't even realised were there.

"I've already organised a replacement passport," he continued. "And I'll provide you with enough money for you to survive for the next several years, maybe even longer if you live within your means. All you have to do is leave."

I glanced down at the papers before returning my attention to him. "Why would you offer me that?"

Alexander's eyes, the same colour as Caden's, stared at me coldly. "I'm going to be honest with you, Miss Grey. I may have a... strained relationship with my nephew, but he is blood. Which means I will do anything to protect him."

"Protect him from what? Me?"

Alexander went to reply, but his attention flickered over my shoulder. His posture tightened as Chip placed two cups of tea on the table and then disappeared back down the stairs. "Sebastian needs control to function," he continued once we were alone. "He's been like that since he was very young, and it's only gotten worse since he lost his parents. Without control, he becomes... unruly."

"Unruly?" I echoed, and Alexander's eyes narrowed on me like I was an idiot.

"He seems very proprietorial over you, and I believe if he accidentally harms you when he's—"

"Unruly."

"Yes, Miss Grey," Alexander growled, clearly unimpressed with me interrupting him. "If he accidentally harms you, or if you turn out to be the snake I suspect you are, it could push him into a spiral none of us may be able to pull him back from. And if that happens, I won't be nearly as forgiving."

I ignored the silent threat. "You think I'm harming him by being here?"

"It's possible." Picking up one of the China teacups, he took a sip, only to immediately spit it back out. "This is ghastly. Where's Mrs Pritchard? She'd never allow such swill to be served to guests."

I didn't touch my own tea, my hands aching from where I clenched them so tight. "Let me get this straight, you're going to give me a passport and enough money so I can what... run away?"

It was what I'd wanted, wasn't it?

Except now the thought of leaving left a strange hollowness in my chest.

"Exactly, but only if you agree to never return." I watched as he set the cup down with a grimace, my nails continuing to dig into my palms.

"What if I don't want that?"

"It's your choice." Alexander picked up the paperwork, holding it out to me. "So, Miss Grey, what will it be? To continue to wilt in my nephew's shadow, or will you accept your freedom?"

Chapter 52
Sebastian

I watched as Ryder glanced around my office, his brows raised. "Fuck me, this place is nice. How do I get a membership to this *Thorn* then?"

"You don't."

"Rude," he chuckled. "But at least I get to meet you with the mask. I get to tell all my friends that I survived a meeting with the notorious Beast. Maybe they'll buy me a few drinks."

"You don't have friends," Caden muttered, leaning against the door directly behind him. Langdon silently laughed beside him.

Ryder's smile tightened, and he leaned back so he could look over at Cade. "And who the fuck are you again?"

"Do you have what I asked?" I silently glared at Cade to shut the fuck up. My cousin wrinkled his nose but continued to stand in position.

"Of course, and early, might I add." Reaching into his pocket, Ryder pulled out a piece of fabric, carefully unwrapping to reveal the brooch I'd asked for. At this point I wasn't surprised to see it, not when a few more explosives had been found in my other distributions. Venues Miles didn't even know existed, which meant there was another snake.

"Do you have the address?" I asked.

"No, I snagged that while the woman in the photograph was out on a morning stroll. She's pretty hot for someone old, by the way. I'd totally fuck her."

"Careful," Caden growled.

"What, she your mum or something?" Ryder grinned, clearly trying to piss Cade off. "I'll call her a MILF if you'd prefer?"

Langdon took a threatening step forward, only stopped by Caden's hand on his shoulder.

"Mr Finn..." I clenched my teeth to stop from crushing his head against my desk. "Where did you find her? I need an address."

He shrugged. "What am I, an estate agent? You never asked for an address, just for the brooch. I tracked it to somewhere in France. Bordeaux, or however you fucking say it." He lounged back in his chair, swinging his arm out to hook over the back. "So, I think it's time we discussed my money."

"It's already been wired over," Caden said, his hands moving suspiciously closer to his gun.

"There's more if you get me the address," I said. "Double."

Ryder whistled, his cheeks dimpling as his grin widened. "Double you say, for just an address?"

"It'll need to be verified, of course," Caden added. "Including photographic evidence before we release you any more money. You know, in case you try and fuck us over."

"You're super untrusting. Has anyone ever told you that?" Ryder chuckled. "But I'm interested. Look for an address? Easy, I'll have it with you in the next few days."

Ryder stood, his finger brushing against the diamonds of the brooch. "Pleasure doing business with you, Mr Beast." He winked at Caden as he left, my cousin stiffening.

"You want to tell us what that's about?" Langdon signed.

Caden shook his head. "Ryder's famous for sticking his dick in places it shouldn't be."

"Hmm." I glanced down at the brooch, the diamonds still as bright as I remembered. Picking it up, I felt the weight, turning it over to touch the engraving.

Langdon appeared over my shoulder, stiffening a little before signing out the words for me.

A ma Margot, de ton amour, Mael.

To my Margot, from your love, Mael.

I threw it across the room, the brooch breaking into several pieces as it hit against the wall with an audible crack.

"Bas?"

"My father bought two identical brooches." One for my mother, and one for *her*.

Caden went to pick up the pieces, reading the back for himself. "What a cunt."

"Fuck." I dragged a hand down my face. "Margot's been silent for almost two decades, so why now?"

Langdon took the brooch from Caden, barely glancing at it before tossing it onto my desk. "Maybe it's taken this long to infiltrate us?" he signed. "Miles was just a meathead. She'd have needed to find someone else who'd betray us and actually knew something important."

I leaned back, the chair squeaking beneath my weight. "Someone's sold us out. Someone important enough to know exactly where we store and distribute the powder."

Langdon managed a frustrated rasp in agreement, his

hands reflecting his agitation. "Our priority should be to find Miles."

Caden nodded, reaching into his pocket for his phone. "What the fuck? You expecting anything, Bas?"

I went to reply when a ring pierced the air. I answered on loudspeaker.

"Beast, my friend," Hook's obnoxious voice echoed in the air. *"I heard you've been having some... technical problems. I hope that that pretty girl of yours is okay?"*

I looked up at Langdon, whose expression had blackened at the mention of Arabella being hurt at his fight.

How the fuck did he–

"And before you get pissy, I can easily explain how I already know," he mused, clearly enjoying knowing this little bit of information. *"Although, it would be easier to show you."*

"Get to the point," I snapped.

"I'm sending a gift. Make sure you accept the package." With that he hung up, and Caden turned his mobile to show me the CCTV of someone dressed like a fucking pirate–fake parrot and all–leaving a box just outside *The Thorn.*

"You scan it yet?" Caden asked, arms folded as he frowned at the large cardboard box tied with a giant red bow.

"It's clean of any metal," Richard, one of the team members assigned to T, said. "If you're not in a rush, I'd advise that we take it back to the lab to test for toxins."

He'd been called in specifically because he dealt with the

security of the shipments coming in. Which literally meant he made sure they were safe before they were taken inside the container. He was the one that found the other explosives, securing them safely before they could destroy anything else.

Langdon picked up the card poking out from the bow, finding a handwritten note. He laughed, throwing his head back silently before passing it to Caden, who began to read the note aloud.

"Found this slimy fuck trying to kill me. He was very talkative when I placed a terrapin on his balls."

Click, snap, click. Lang flicked at his lighter, his eyes alight like the flames as he waited for Caden to continue.

"He was one of the Enchantress's bitches, so thought you'd appreciate his head considering he was supposed to be one of yours," Caden continued as I opened the box.

Reaching inside I grabbed a fistful of hair, pulling it out to find it was Miles. I dropped it with disgust. "What else does it say?" I asked.

"He told me what happened with Arabella, so I made sure it hurt before I took his head. You're welcome, love Hook. Kiss, kiss, kiss." Caden crushed the note in his palm. "Seriously, the guy's missing some marbles."

"There goes our lead," I grunted, watching as Langdon kicked the head. Richard flinched as it rolled with a squelch, while the twins who stood guarding the door didn't even blink. They'd probably seen worse in their careers. "I think it's time we called everyone in for a meeting."

Langdon frowned. "You think the traitor could be one of them?"

Caden sighed. "Miles was with us for what... a decade? It could be anyone."

"Exactly," I said. "So we'd better be careful how we approach this. Wouldn't want the snake to escape before we cut off its head."

Chapter 53
Sebastian

I knew Arabella was safe, but my shoulders were still tight until I was able to see for myself. Since she'd been hurt, I'd reassigned Chip to keep a watch on her.

Dismissing him as soon as I got home, I paused at the threshold of her bedroom, simply watching her practice her British Sign Language in the mirror. In front of her on the chest of drawers was a book, and she was clearly copying the hand gestures.

"You're doing it wrong," I said, making her jump and spin on the spot.

A blush darkened her cheeks before she frowned, returning her attention to the book. "How am I doing it wrong? It looks exactly the same."

"Here, let me." Placing the pastry box down beside her book, I showed her how to say *'Hello, my name is'*.

Her frown deepened as she studied my movements before attempting it herself. I carefully moved her hands into the right shapes before continuing to add her name at the end.

"You want to tell me how you got the book?" I knew exactly how she got the book, but I wanted to hear her say it.

I wasn't threatened by Charlie Pritchard, and his infatuation with Arabella was the reason I'd assigned him to her in the first place.

Not once had he ever shown interest in anyone as much as her. Keeping her safe was proving his loyalty, something he'd been wanting to do for a while.

She pouted her lips, reaching behind her to slap the book closed. "Does it matter?"

"Keeping secrets from me matters." I reached behind her for the book, glancing at the front cover before returning my attention to her. "You're learning BSL. Langdon uses *Langue des Signes Française.*"

"So I've been learning the wrong sign?" Her eyes widened with her words, and I laughed at her expression.

"Lang understands and can sign BSL fluently, but he uses LSF to communicate the majority of the time." Which Chip knew, considering as a young child Mrs Pritchard worked for my uncle. He spent the majority of his time there when he wasn't at school and watched as we all learned to adapt to Langdon's way of communication. So why did he get her a book on the wrong language?

"Oh my God, I should've learned French instead," she groaned, hiding her face with her hands. I gently gripped her wrists, pulling them back down.

"I'll teach you."

"Really?" Her voice held a cautious edge, like she wasn't sure if she could trust the offer.

"Yes. But only if you move into my room. Permanently."

"There's always a condition with you." Arabella rolled her eyes, but I tugged her closer anyway. She didn't resist, her breath hitching as I leaned in, her pupils darkening just before our lips touched. "I want to ask you something," she whispered, my breath mingling with hers. "I want my freedom."

I froze. Jaw tight. Pressure blooming hot in my chest.

"Ara–"

"I'm not leaving," she cut in, soft but steady. Determined. "Not until my debt is paid. I just don't want to feel like a prisoner anymore. I want to be here because I *choose* to be, not because I have to."

Because I choose to be.

Shit.

"Fine," I said, my voice rough. "But you'll have a guard with you whenever you're outside. That's non-negotiable."

"Sebastian–"

I silenced her with a brush of my lips, just enough to feel the catch in her breath. To remind myself she wanted this. Wanted *me*. Even when she shouldn't. "That's my condition, *belle*."

"Deal." She laughed, a delighted sound that hit me square in the gut, sharp and unexpected. "I thought I'd have to fight you on it," she admitted, eyes dancing with surprise.

"You wanted me to say no?" I arched a brow, watching her closely.

"No," she said quickly, then hesitated. "I just didn't expect you to say yes so easily."

The truth was, I didn't *want* to give her freedom. I wanted to keep her close. Locked down. Protected. But I knew that would only push her away, and as any strategist knew, control wasn't always taken by force.

"Hey, have you seen my notebook?" she asked. "It's driving me crazy that I can't find it."

"You mean the one you've been plotting your great escape with?" I replied, teasing her.

Her cheeks blossomed red, but she didn't deny it. "It's rude to go through other people's things."

"Hmm," I hummed, releasing her so I could reach for the box from the overpriced patisserie. "I haven't seen it, but

I'll make sure it's replaced." I handed it to her, feeling strangely unsure for once.

"You bought me a cake?" she asked, opening it up to reveal the strawberry and cream slice. "Because I said I liked them when I was sad?" She held the box tighter, as if it might disappear. "Thank you."

She smiled, and my chest tightened before I cleared my throat.

"You're welcome."

Chapter 54
Arabella

I needed a new hobby. Something other than reading because playing chess was not for me.

"Checkmate." Chip grinned, dramatically flicking over my king.

Groaning, I mourned my chess playing skills. It was like I was getting worse, because Chip had won every single match for the last few days with an ease that was borderline embarrassing. Maybe knitting was my thing? Although I don't think I'd have the patience to create anything more than a square.

"So, are you finally going to admit you're my new shadow?" I glanced up to find he'd already reset the pieces and moved his first pawn. I'd agreed to a guard outside, not inside.

He was dressed casually, in a buttoned-up shirt and jeans rather than his typical uniform of a black suit. His gun was on the table beside us, but I pointedly ignored its existence.

"Don't think I haven't noticed that when Sebastian isn't here, you are." I mirrored his move, blocking in his pawn. If it wasn't Chip, it was Lang, or sometimes the twins.

"Are you saying you don't enjoy my company?" he asked with a raised brow. "You know Mr Devereaux's feeling a little overprotective right now."

"So that means you're stuck babysitting me?"

He simply shrugged, playing his next move. "There are worse jobs."

"Wow, I'm feeling a little offended," I chuckled.

It had been almost a week since what happened at *Thorn*, and while I hadn't returned to the club, I haven't been left alone, either. Sebastian was home early every day, choosing to work from the office here when possible. I'd sometimes just watch him concentrate on the paperwork, using the reading pen to read aloud before he used a voice-to-text feature on his phone or computer.

Every time he'd sit with that bloody spider on his shoulder and had more than once tried to convince me to touch it. Which was a big nope.

"How's your mum?" I asked Chip, still missing her baked goods. "You never speak about her."

"That's because she isn't interesting." Chip's attention remained on the board. When I didn't make a move, he looked up. "She's fine. Taking some time off to travel, which is something she's always wanted to do. Now are you going to concentrate on the game?"

"Fine," I grumbled, not caring about the knight I moved.

"Checkmate."

I blinked at the pieces, surprised that he won so fast. Yes, I wasn't paying attention, but seriously, it had been under five minutes. "You're cheating."

"No," Chip said. "But I can read every single expression on your face, so I can predict the move before you make them." He watched me with flat, dark eyes. Much colder than when he'd first came in this morning. "Chess isn't just about strategy; it's about playing the player just as much as the game."

"So, you're playing me?" I surmised.

"Your head's not in it. You're distracted." A smile curved his lips, but the flatness never quite left his eyes. "I can tell you miss your dad. You say as such in your writing."

I paused, the piece I held hanging above the board. "Wait, you found my notebook?"

Without dropping eye contact, Chip reached into his backpack, pulling out the exact notebook I'd been searching for. "You've got an interesting writing style," he said, voice low but playful. "But pouring your emotions onto the page like that? Dangerous. Especially in the wrong hands."

I reached for it instinctively, but Chip stood, lifting it just out of reach. "Seriously, Chip. Give it back."

He raised a brow. "What's the big deal, Ara? It's just a notebook."

"Then why did you take it?"

"I didn't mean to," he said, seemingly amused with my response. "It must've ended up in the paperwork I was sorting. I didn't realise what it was until I got home. I didn't mean to upset you, and I've already replaced it with a new one."

He'd brought me a new notebook a few days ago, and I'd accepted that one of the cleaners must have tossed my old one. "I didn't want anyone else to read it," I mumbled.

"I can see why; your fixation over Mr Devereaux is a little uncomfortable. You want to tell me why the character I assume is supposed to be him is coming across as the hero?" He waited eagerly for my answer, as if we were still playing chess and he couldn't make his move until I made mine.

"I'm not writing about Sebastian," I defended, even

though it was completely a lie, one that felt sour on my tongue. "They're entirely fictional characters. Now give it back."

Chip snorted, holding the book higher. "I'm a little disappointed that I'm not mentioned. I thought we were friends?"

"Chip..."

"Even if you don't want to admit it out loud, you miss your dad." He threw me the book, and I scrambled to catch it. Some of the pages tore, and many became crumpled. "He misses you too, you know. He told me so yesterday."

"You went to see him?" I touched my words on the page, my voice dropping to an irritated whisper. "Why?"

"You never told me to stop. You know I've been visiting him for weeks, making sure he's eating and paying his bills." Chip's face sobered, his tone gentle. "I know how much you care for him, even if he doesn't deserve it. But I think you should speak to him. Let him explain."

"Explain what?" I was frustrated with the tears that threatened to spill. "You know what he tried to do."

"I know." Chip still stood, his height forcing me to look up. "He told me everything, how he became addicted to the high risk of gambling, the money on his big wins, and how he was a terrible father."

I clenched my teeth, my breath seeming to get caught in my chest. Chip noticed, crossing around the table to pull me against him.

"He's still your father, and he's asking you for forgiveness," he whispered against my hair, his arms wrapping around me in a hug. "To be the bigger person."

"Why are you saying this?" I asked, blinking away those bloody tears.

"Because I think you'll regret it if you don't."

I nodded, more to buy myself time than anything else. Just one moment to think. Dad was like a sword hanging above me, a pendulum just waiting for the right time to strike. If I didn't speak to him, there was a chance he would never stop.

Chapter 55
Sebastian

With my mask in place, I watched from the head of the table, the atmosphere in the room apprehensive as everyone felt the strain beneath my attention.

"Honestly, is this meeting really appropriate?" my uncle demanded, eyeing the rest of the table with the snobbery of someone brought up with a silver spoon. "It could've been a phone call."

Caden shot Alexander a glare, father and son holding identical expressions before Alexander finally settled grumpily into his seat.

Feng Zhao sat in the place his mother would usually sit, his grandson sitting beside him despite the burns that marked his flesh. They'd already nodded in my direction, and I'd already given my condolences to the loss of their matriarch.

The other managers of my distribution were here too, as well as a few of the more profound dealers that catered to certain high-end demographics. They held the highest hierarchy in the separate branches of my empire, employing many below them. They were men and woman I'd worked with for years, gaining trust and a mutual respect in an industry that promoted corruption.

Any one of them could be the snake, which just meant I'd been too lenient. Maybe I needed to remind them exactly why I held the largest and most successful cocaine trade on the entire continent.

"We appreciate you being able to take time to come today," Caden said, his tone demanding the attention of the room. "You've been called because a woman known as Margot Laurent, alias the Enchantress, has been actively trying to take over our territory."

I watched from my position, no longer Sebastian, but the Beast who was the judge, jury and executioner. I didn't speak, simply content to watch everyone's expressions as the information sunk in. It made people more on edge to know they were being watched, more likely to make a mistake if they're under the impression I was hunting. Waiting for them to fuck up and face the consequences.

"I've heard of her," Qian, the only grandson of the Zhao family, muttered. "I've seen that new Enchanted Dust pop up at a few places."

"You didn't think to mention it?" Caden asked, his exterior calm, but I could tell there was rage burning beneath the surface. Langdon noticed too, frowning over from his position by the wall. He never joined in with these meetings, simply watching the same as me with the *click, snap, click* of his lighter.

"I didn't realise I had to." Qian winced when his father gripped his shoulder tightly. "It wasn't on any of our guys."

"Hmm," Caden hummed, tugging at the sleeves of his jacket in a subtle gesture of frustration. "We believe she's behind the bombs."

Feng stiffened at the same time his son's complexion paled.

"We also believe she's managed to swap our product with a cheap alternative, one that has been causing these deaths."

"So the rumours of Cursed Rose being corked are true?" Alexander asked, his lips pursed into a frown. "That would explain the decrease in sales across the board."

"Which is why we need to reestablish trust in the brand," Caden added. "We'll need–"

"This is bullshit," one of the dealers snapped. "How can we reestablish trust when we're being made targets? You sit up here with protection, while we're the ones risking our lives. You're not doing anything to–*ugh!*"

I didn't bother to remain calm, simply shoving his head down so hard it knocked against the wood of the table with a crack. Before he could move, I placed the cold tip of my gun against his temple.

"I think I've seen you at parties." My uncle squinted, wrinkling his nose. "Kill him."

"Wait! Wait!" The man trembled beneath my grip. "I'm sorry! I take it back!"

"I know exactly who you are," Alexander continued with a pompous tone. "You run a small team of three, each who have proven to sell more efficiently than you. They understand the dangers of the role, and if the substantial sum of money isn't enough for you to do your job, then maybe we should look at someone else who's willing to take the risk."

Another interesting fact about my uncle is that he takes everything to do with money seriously. Considering his surname is worth nothing thanks to my grandfather, he has an investment in how well everything runs just so he can keep up his lifestyle.

It wouldn't surprise me that he had a colour coded

spreadsheet with every dealer with a rating of how competent they were.

"Anyone else care to interrupt me like this daft
muppet?" Caden asked the room.

When he was met with silence, I reluctantly let the
man's head go.

The meeting carried on without issue, and only when
everyone had left did I finally unclench my jaw. I didn't get
any suspicious vibes from anyone, but we hadn't expected
Miles to betray us, either. If someone in the meeting had
sold us out, they hid it well.

"You're looking in the wrong places," Alexander
muttered, remaining in his seat. "The dealers only know of
their distribution unit, and the distribution managers only
know of their own venue, not the others."

Caden sighed, dragging a hand down his face. "Dad..."

"You know I'm right." Alexander glanced at me. "Use
your brain, not your brawn. Unless they were all conspiring
against you, not a single one of them could be the snake.
They simply don't have the information, and that's for good
reason."

Alexander was right, but that didn't mean I wasn't
cautious. "We can't rule anything else out until we get
Margot."

A knock on the door, followed by a gentle squeak of its
opening.

Arabella's eyes widened when she looked across the
conference table, a faint blush darkening her cheeks.

"Everyone out," I demanded, ignoring the surprised
looks. "Now."

Langdon pushed the door further open, gesturing for
Arabella to step inside while everyone else left. She refused
to look at Alexander, who scowled at her in passing.

"I'm so sorry," she whispered, glancing over her shoulder. "I didn't realise..."

"What's happened, *belle*?" I reached for my mask, pulling it off. "Are you okay?"

Arabella swallowed, looking back at Chip as if he would help. I suppressed my growl, instead reaching over to cup her jaw.

"I want to see my father."

There was no hesitation in my answer. "No."

She stiffened beneath my palm. "You promised me freedom, or am I still just some toy to you?"

"Ara..."

"He's still my father."

"He tried to have you raped," I snapped, my anger as vicious as a thousand hornets. "He hurt you."

"I know." Arabella straightened, holding her head higher. "But I came to you first. I could've just gone without telling you, but I didn't."

If she thought that comment would help with my fucking resentment...

"Please," she added. "I need to see him. You keep asking me to stay, but this is what that means, Sebastian. Letting me choose. Letting me make decisions for myself. For you to *trust* me."

Her words hit harder than I liked to admit. I wasn't used to giving space, not when I'd built an empire on control. And letting her go, even for a moment, felt like loosening my grip on something I wasn't ready to lose.

I clenched my jaw, forcing back the instinct to shut it all down. To lock the world out and keep her where I could keep her safe. But she was right, I needed to trust her if I didn't want to lose her.

"You'll take the twins," I said finally, voice tight. "And Chip. No exceptions."

Her upper lip twitched. "That's a little bit overkill."

I tried to calm my voice, not wanting to growl when she'd so easily agreed to my rules. "No exceptions."

Her smile brightened her face, and I was glad that I'd removed the mask because she reached up on tiptoe to press her lips to mine.

Chapter 56
Arabella

My stomach was tight, made even more nervous with each familiar street we went down. I was almost thankful it was Malik sitting beside me, rather than his brother. Malik didn't speak much, whereas Micah seemed to need to fill the silence.

The car rumbled to a stop as the garage appeared, the shutter down and the lights off. The late evening sun did little to ease my discomfort.

Three years I'd lived above, and I hoped after so much time being away that I'd feel some sort of comfort coming home. But there was nothing other than the need to leave and never look back.

"You'll need to wait in the car," I said, turning to find Malik frowning out the window.

"That's not happening," he said, his voice a deep timbre that vibrated the air between us.

"He won't speak to me if you're there." My hand gripped the handle of the door, pushing it open before Chip could.

Micah appeared, his eyes darting between me and his twin. "We're under strict instructions to protect you."

"He's my father," I snapped, my chest aching as I glanced up at the window of the flat. The curtains were drawn, despite it being only late afternoon. "I just need to speak to him alone. He won't hurt me."

I wouldn't let him. Never again.

"They're right, Ara. I'll escort you inside," Chip said with an assurance that was unexpected.

"No, I've already said–"

"Ara, that's enough," he growled, his eyes colliding with mine. "You guys can scout the perimeter," he continued when I stayed silent. "Meet back at the front door in five once it's secured."

The twins shared a look, and in that moment if I didn't know Micah had a thin scar along his jawline that was lighter than his skin, you wouldn't have been able to tell them apart. Nodding in sync they split, each walking around the building in slow, steady strides.

"Come on," Chip said, taking my arm. "It won't be long before Mr Devereaux wants you returned."

It was like I was in a daze, my lungs filling with cement with every step I took towards the place I once called home. I needed to see Dad, to understand whether he actually wanted forgiveness or whether this was just another ploy to get what he wanted. To feed his addiction that mattered more to him than I, or even Mum, ever could.

"Don't worry, I'll wait here," Chip said, his voice far gentler than it was a minute ago. "It's against protocol, so you'll have to make this quick before the twins realise you're alone."

"You're not coming in?"

Chip shook his head. "You won't have long, so make it count."

I nodded, taking a moment to myself before I reached

up to knock. The door squeaked a little as it opened from the force, and I frowned.

"Dad?" I whispered into the darkness, stepping inside and closing the door behind me. Glass crushed beneath my feet, bottles lining the hall all the way to the living room. "Dad?" I shouted louder this time, my stomach recoiling at the stench before my brain could catch up to the smell.

He sat in his favourite armchair, his head bowed forward like I'd found him passed out so many times before with that stupid lamp alight beside him. It created an eerie glow, casting much of his features in shadow.

I crashed to my knees, ignoring the way my knees squelched in the sticky carpet, or how I finally recognised the scent of blood. It suffocated the air around me, choking my throat with every breath.

"Dad..." I reached over to him, finding his body not warm, but not exactly cold either. I frantically shoved at his arm, expecting for him to grumble a curse for waking him from his drunken slumber. But there was nothing, his body a weight that barely moved but for the springs in his seat. They squeaked, the sound so loud in the stillness that surrounded us. Surrounded me.

The front of his shirt clung to him like it was wet, his pulse vacant when I reached for his wrist. My hand shook as I reached up to brush the hair from his face, finding his eyes clouded in death.

It was then I noticed the skin around his throat was raw, the flesh bright red and open where he'd been sliced from one side to the other.

I waited for the realisation to kick in, for my grief to become so overwhelming that it confiscated the surrounding oxygen and strangled me of my words. For the tears to pour, and for the guilt to consume.

But nothing came but anger, so sharp and pure. It sliced through my chest with such vicious claws it left me winded.

He'd been taken away before I was ready. Before I had the chance to say everything I'd buried for years. I hadn't screamed or cried. I hadn't exorcised the fucking weight of a childhood spent drowning in guilt. I wanted to purge it all, every unspoken word and every desperate attempt to earn his love.

And now I didn't get that.

My breath came out ragged, like I was gasping for breath against the bonds cinching around my lungs. A single tear burned down my face, but it wasn't from sorrow for his death. It was for me. That I didn't get the closure that I deserved.

"What the fuck happened here?"

I jumped to my feet, ignoring how the blood had soaked the hem of my dress and stuck to my knees. Gabriel stood by the door, his upper lip twisted in a grimace as he glanced at my father.

Wiping the tear from my face, I stepped back, wary as Gabriel reached over to lift Dad's head up. With a sound of disgust, he let his head drop once more to his chest.

"I told you not to trust Beast," he said. "I'm sorry, baby, but I warned you."

"What are you doing here?" I whispered, my voice dangerously quiet, even as panic clawed at me. "Gabriel, you need to leave."

"What's with the attitude?" he growled. "It's not like I killed him. He's the one who embarrassed your fucking captor at his club."

"Sebastian wouldn't…"

"Of course he fucking would." Gabriel closed the distance until we stood toe to toe, his movements frantic, putting me on edge. "Sebastian's the Beast; he doesn't care about anything or anyone but himself. All he gives a shit about is power and keeping his reputation."

I glanced over his shoulder at the door, wondering where Chip or the twins were.

Gabriel followed my line of sight, his expression tightening as if he knew I was ready to make a run for it. "I wouldn't do that if I were you," he warned.

Something glinted in his hand, a gun that caused anxiety to slither beneath my skin.

"You just had to pick *him*," Gabriel snarled, taking a step forward as I instinctively stepped back. "Do you know what I've had to do, baby? I've done things I'm *ashamed* of because of you. I'm on suspension because no one believed me about Devereaux. They called me obsessive. *Crazy*. Can you believe that?"

His laugh cracked in the air like glass shattering.

"But that's fine," he whispered, the gun rising until it pointed directly at my chest. "You're here now. And soon... it'll all be over. Together we can take him down, and I'll fucking show them that I was right."

"Gabriel..." I choked, my voice barely a whisper. "What are you doing?"

"Don't worry, I'd never hurt you," he said, his tone eerily calm.

"Then why bring a gun?" I inched back again, trying to place the armchair between us.

He frowned, as if confused by the question. "Because how else am I going to get you away from that monster?"

Chapter 57
Sebastian

My phone burned in my pocket, cracked from how hard I'd held it. It hadn't been long since I received the picture of Arabella being held at gunpoint. It had been sent from a blocked number, but I didn't need to understand the accompanied text to know where it was taken.

I'm taking back what's mine.

I'd been too enraged to activate the text-to-speech, but Caden had been there to read it out. Along with the attached address. Even now I could barely keep myself caged, my anger perforating every single one of my cells until I only had a single thought.

"If you run in, you'll get her killed," Caden said calmly, sensing my intention just by the tensing of my muscles. "Wait for Lang to get into position."

I carefully released my fingers from the door handle because my prick of a cousin was right. "She's been in there for over thirty minutes."

I spotted the car directly outside the garage, the driver's side door open wide. This time I ignored my cousin, jumping out of an armoured truck to duck behind. A leg was stretched out, a growing pool of blood beneath it.

"Sir?" Chip groaned, his teeth clenched as he tried to cinch his belt tighter around his upper thigh.

"Where's Arabella?" I asked, my gun hot in my grip.

"She's still inside."

"What about the twins?" Caden demanded, coming up from behind.

Chip clenched his jaw. "I haven't seen them."

Caden's phone vibrated, his lips pursing as he read the message. "The twins are dead."

Chip's expression didn't change, his concentration on trying to stem the blood from his bullet wound. "A few guys turned up and started taking shots at us."

"Why the fuck is she inside alone?" I growled, reaching down to press my thumb into his wound. Chip hissed, looking up at me with dark eyes.

"Because she said she had permission," he replied, his voice gravelly from pain. "Why wouldn't I believe her?"

I stuck my thumb deeper, feeling the bullet wedged against bone.

"Bas..." Caden gripped my shoulder, easing me back from my rage. "Lang said the area's secured."

Chip barely swallowed his cry as I pulled my hand away and returned to my feet.

"I'm going in."

"You don't know how many men are inside," Caden growled. "At least wait until—"

But I was already moving, my gun out as I stormed towards the stairs and up towards the flat. Caden was tight on my heels, muttering quietly beneath his breath as he took point and swept the area behind.

I spotted Langdon on the other street, moving silently as he joined us.

"Volatiles inside are unknown," he signed, his face

spotted with blood. "Three were armed around the building, but I've taken care of them."

"The backup team are five minutes out," Caden replied, keeping to sign. "Including cleanup."

I nodded, my body relaxing at the thought of violence. With a heavy foot I kicked the door, taking a shot at the man guarding the entrance. He took my bullet in his vest, the momentum turning him to the side before Caden was able to place one in his skull. I moved forward, the scent of blood thickening the air.

"Get off me!" Arabella cried, her voice pulling me forward until I came to the living room. Her father was unmoving in the armchair while she fought against Graves's grip on the three-seat sofa opposite.

I lifted my gun, but there wasn't a clear shot. Fuck.

"Stop fighting me, baby," Graves grunted, trying to keep her held against him even as she fought.

Arabella scratched and bit, a feral cat trying to get free before he backhanded her hard enough that she fell to the floor, her hair creating a curtain over her face. Lifting a boot, he pressed it against her head, keeping her pinned.

"When we get home, I'm going to fucking–" His eyes widened when he spotted me in the doorway, his arm lifting as he took his shot.

Arabella screamed, but the bullet went wide, hitting the doorframe to splinter the wood.

I didn't even flinch, simply stepping forward as Graves's arm wavered, shaking. It had been a while since he'd used a gun, evident in the lack of confidence. Most people felt powerful when holding a weapon, but Graves held himself differently, his shoulders tight and his eyes bloodshot as he reached down and pulled Arabella up by her hair, using her as a shield.

"Where's your mask, Beast?" He spat the name, lifting

his gun to hold it to her head. "Or do you not wear it when you murder old men?"

I glanced at Morris, who was clearly dead. "What do you want, Detective?" I asked, hearing a scuffle behind. Either my reinforcements had arrived, or Lang and Cade were dealing with more of Graves's men.

Except Graves didn't have any fucking men. He wasn't acting under any official authority, and he sure as hell wasn't backed by law enforcement. So who the fuck did they belong to?

"You took everything from me," he snarled, tugging Arabella's hair to expose her throat. "You took my friend, my reputation, and now my fucking wife! I'm finally going to give you everything you deserve."

Arabella winced, but she remained calm. Her breathing even and her eyes calm when they met mine.

Good girl.

"So why are you pointing the gun at her and not me?"

Graves frowned for a moment, his teeth clenching as he turned it towards me. He popped another shot, the bullet skimming across my arm with a burn before Arabella reached for it. Another shot, the silencer muffling the sound into a whispered hiss.

Arabella let out a gasp, and panic seared through my chest as I rushed forward. The force of the bullet caused Graves to spin, blood coating them both.

I pulled Arabella back, her hands covered in red.

Graves choked, looking down at the growing red stain on his lower stomach before he turned and ran. I didn't bother going after him, not when Ara was frozen, her eyes a little dazed and lips parted.

"Are you hurt?" I pressed my fingers against her body, sweeping over everywhere I could to find an injury. "Ara?"

"Your arm." She blinked up at me, reaching over to where the bullet had grazed.

"It's fine." I cupped her jaw, but she simply frowned at her father.

"Did you do it?" she asked, the question hollow as if she'd resigned herself to the answer. "Did you kill him?"

"No."

She swallowed, her tears falling silently when she returned her attention to me. But she wasn't sad. No, she was angry. Furious. Her fire burning bright with a fierceness my demons revelled in.

Glancing to the side, I turned to find Caden and Langdon there, a man bleeding from a headwound on his knees before them, a gag shoved into his mouth and his arms bound.

Langdon flicked at his lighter, expression excited as he took in the bodies. His eyes collided with mine, silently asking for permission.

I grabbed Arabella's hand, tugging her to my side. "Do it."

Chapter 58

Arabella

"I didn't need to be escorted up," I said, my tears long gone, only to be replaced with this anger that lapped at me in waves. Anger was good. Anger was a much-needed distraction. "I could've come back on my own."

Sebastian eyed me, his attention firm as we ascended in the lift. He hadn't said a word, so I glared up at him, hoping he saw my frustration. But of course, a man like Sebastian didn't see, or maybe didn't even care.

"I want to help."

"Help how?" His head dipped closer, voice dropping to a husky whisper. "Help me torture one of the men who tried to take you from me?"

My breath caught in my throat at the deadly intention behind his words.

"Because if you do, then your darkness really does match mine." His fingers laced through my hair, scratching at my scalp to tilt my head back. "I'm going to remove that man's fingernails one by one, hoping he breaks quickly so I can get back to you. But if he doesn't, then I'll destroy his dominant hand, and then his kneecaps. I'll put glass beneath his skin and even hold a needle to his eye. Do you think that would be enough for him to tell me everything I want?"

I stared at his eyes, the midnight of his irises darkening to the purest shade of wrath.

"But some men don't respond to pain," he continued, his fingers tightening to emphasise his point. "They're trained to withstand it. So that's when I go through their fears, wearing them down until they finally break into a million fucking pieces. Claustrophobia, pyrophobia, thalassophobia, or maybe it's as simple as spiders."

I shivered, unable to control the reaction.

"You think you can help with that?" he asked, the lift coming to a stop at the penthouse. "Break a man so efficiently they have no hope of surviving?"

The doors opened silently, and Sebastian waited for my response.

I slowly shook my head, my heart racing and my chest aching. No, I could never do that to someone, and I wasn't sure how I felt that Sebastian could.

His eyes softened a fraction. "I'll be back as soon as I can." His lips caught mine, but it wasn't gentle, or romantic or anything sane. It was heated and rough, his emotions pouring into me with little groans and nips of his teeth.

I didn't want it to end, but before long he was gone, the lift locked down leaving me alone to finally come to terms that dad was dead, and Gabriel had tried to...

Swallowing, I looked down at my hands, finding them red. My knees too, the hem of my dress saturated with my own father's blood. Swallowing bile, I ran to my room, stripping as I went to stand beneath the shower and scrub until my skin was raw. No more tears fell, and for that I was grateful.

I don't know how long I stood there beneath the water, long enough for the temperature to cool and for my body to shake at the loss of heat. With chattering teeth, I finally stepped out, drying myself quickly before I managed to find one of Sebastian's T-shirts. I pulled it on, the cloth long enough it almost hit my knees.

A creak sounded behind me, and spinning on the spot I expected to see Sebastian, or maybe even Chip. Instead, I froze, my eyes taking in the man by the door. He wore all black, his face covered but for his eyes. I recognised those eyes, but they were no longer a warm brown, rather now hard as he stood with a needle glinting in his hand.

"Nothing personal," Ryder said, his voice shocking me out of my stasis. "It's just business."

Chapter 59
Sebastian

The man knew nothing, but that didn't stop me from using my knuckles. His flesh split at the impact, his bones crunching beneath my force.

It wasn't enough.

It would never be enough.

"He's dead," Caden commented, but he was smart enough not to try and stop me. "He's just a hired gun who's clearly shit at his job."

My knuckles ached as I pulled back, my breathing frantic as this rage surged through my veins like poison. Blood coated my skin, the heat of it a small comfort as I cracked my neck to try and relieve just some of the fucking tension. Licking along my bottom lip, I kicked the chair, sending the prick crashing to the concrete.

Of course he didn't react. I was pretty sure I'd killed him five minutes ago, but I couldn't help myself. Not when they'd come *that* close to hurting her. Graves pointed a fucking gun to her face, and the thought of losing her clawed at my ribs, leaving my lungs tight.

I wasn't used to this panic, this brutal fucking vulnerability.

It was fear, I realised, searing me from the inside out.

Turning, I found Caden standing there with his arms crossed, the sleeves of his shirt rolled up from where he'd had a turn. His watch was smeared with blood, the obnoxious ticking louder now I wasn't so focused. He usually took it off, but clearly, he'd gotten caught in the moment.

Langdon was the first to have a go but quickly grew bored, which was very unlike him. He still smelt like smoke, the soot and scorched flesh clinging to his clothes as he frowned down at the information found on the hired gun.

Which always was nothing but an agreement for money, and a number that we traced to Detective Gabriel-fucking-Graves. A soon-to-be dead man.

I couldn't calm down, this insistent energy crackling beneath my skin only increasing. Needing to get home I left Langdon there to organise the cleanup team, Caden side eyeing me as I chose to drive.

I wasn't any calmer, my grip on the steering wheel making the leather squeal. My control was fracturing, the very thing I needed to keep my demons at bay disappearing too fast for me to rebuild. It put a pressure on my chest, as if I was fourteen again watching my power be taken by someone I was told to trust.

Pulling into the underground garage, I didn't bother to park in a bay, swinging the car to a stop and stepping out before I could combust.

You're so fucking weak. They died because you weren't strong enough.

I never knew if it was actually a memory or whether it was a manifestation of my subconscious. Either way, it was always my father's voice that scolded me. Reminding me of my failures.

Caden silently stood to the side, the lift taking its sweet time to ascend before it finally opened on my floor. Except the air was too still, my eye drawn to the broken statue just a few feet away.

Caden tensed, as if sensing the same distinctive stiffness. "You think she's finally made a run for it?"

I stormed through my home, but she wasn't here, my lungs becoming heavier with every vacant room. Where the fuck was she? She wasn't allowed to leave.

With a snarl I went to my office, Raven tapping at the glass of my terrarium as if she could sense my distress. Bending over the computer I scrolled to the security log.

"Bas, maybe you should just let her go. She's just lost–"

"Shut up and read the fucking log."

Caden pursed his lips, his attention burning the side of my face. "Beatrice Pritchard used her card a few hours ago to unlock the lift." I stilled in my chair, and he glanced down at me with a raised brow. "What?"

"Mrs Pritchard was fired over a week ago."

"Jesus Christ." Caden dragged a hand down his face before clicking a few buttons on the mouse. "Unless your girl's a secret IT nerd, I don't think she has the knowledge to scramble the cameras, do you?" He pointed at the screens, showing the footage being blocked for a total of nine minutes.

There was footage of Arabella arriving with me, our kiss, and then nothing. It only started up again after a short time had passed, showing nothing for a few hours until Caden and I ascended the lift.

The security was on a separate server, protected and supposedly tamper proof.

So who the fuck managed to interfere with it?

My stomach dropped, my palms sweaty as I stared at the screen. Someone else had been here. Someone else had taken Arabella.

"Need to get someone over to check on Mrs Pritchard."

Caden clicked a few buttons on his phone before placing it face-up on the table. "Dad, there's been an incident."

"*Son, I was just about to call,*" my uncle's voice echoed through the speaker.

"I need the contact for someone able to hack the surrounding CCTV of the penthouse, all street cameras as well as private. We believe someone's broken into the penthouse."

"*Ah, that's exactly why I wanted to speak to you,*" Alexander said cooly. "*Sebastian should really take better care of his toys.*"

Heat seared through me, my rage almost blinding. "Where the fuck is she?" I snarled.

"*Oh good, you're there. It saves me from having to make a separate call.*"

"Dad, get to the point," Caden growled. "Do you know what's happened to Arabella?"

"*I suppose you should come over to my place. I have a guest you'll want to meet.*"

"Dad... what the fuck?"

"*Honestly Caden, your language is atrocious.*" Alexander swirled his glass of wine, taking a sip before turning to me with a raised brow. "It's clearly from the company you keep." He glared at Langdon, who simply responded with his middle finger.

"You want to tell me what happened?" I demanded, frowning down at Ryder tied up to a large oak dining chair. He flinched at my expression, my anger barely contained.

Alexander tutted his disappointment. "You were being

erratic, Sebastian. It was clear you weren't taking your medication, so I made sure you were keeping safe."

I narrowed my eyes at my uncle. "So you had me tailed?"

"You seem to forget I've been dabbling in this industry for far longer than you've been alive." His gaze was sharp when it met mine. "And I didn't trust you'd do something stupid, like hire this buffoon."

Ryder seemed offended, his complaint muffled by his gag.

"Which was why I hired my own tracker," Alexander continued, taking the seat opposite. "They caught a certain thief stealing something he shouldn't."

Then Ryder was dead.

I surged forward, rage boiling pitch-black in my veins. My hand closed around Ryder's throat with every intention of crushing it, only for Caden to yank me back.

"If you kill him now, he won't give us the answers we need to get Arabella back," he growled into my ear, voice low and urgent.

I heard him, but every cell in my body screamed for blood. I wanted to watch the light drain from Ryder's eyes, to feel his last breath shudder against my grip. Violence was the only thing keeping me from falling apart, the only thing louder than the terror hollowing out my chest.

But I forced myself to nod, dragging myself back under control.

"Why didn't you stop him from taking Ara?" Caden asked his father, his grip not lessening on my arm, as if worried I'd give in to my demons.

"Because I didn't get the information until much later. He was told to follow, not interfere." Alexander downed the rest of his red wine, placing the glass onto the table beside him. His home was as opulent as him, with rich wooden furniture and expensive art. He sat on his brown leather Chesterfield, having placed Ryder on the chair in his living room.

He'd pre-emptively rolled up the rug, leaving the wood between them bare.

Shrugging free from my cousin's grip, I reached over to yank Ryder's head back awkwardly before removing the gag. "Where's Arabella?" I snarled.

"Yeah." Ryder winced. "So I think we have a bit of a misunderstanding."

I released his head, only to reach down and pull his middle finger back until it dislocated. Ryder screamed, his smile turning into a sneer. I did the second finger, enjoying the way the bone cracked before reaching for the third.

"Okay, okay! Stop for just a fucking second and let me fucking answer!" He let out a wheeze when I stepped back, sweat beading down his face from the pain. "I took her to a private airfield in Upminster."

"Did she go willingly?" Alexander asked, always stirring up shit. I would've snarled at him if Ryder wasn't so responsive now that I'd dislocated and possibly broken three of his fingers.

"Fuck no. Bitch bit me." He began to smirk. "I like them fiery."

"This guy has a fucking death wish," Langdon signed, and Caden simply shook his head in response.

"Where was the plane headed?" Alexander asked, his tone tediously calm, the polar opposite of this maelstrom inside me.

Ryder licked along his bottom lip, eyes darting between all three of us. "Look, I was paid to steal and take her to the airfield. After that, I couldn't care less, so I didn't ask."

I raised my fist, ready to break his fucking jaw.

"Not the face!" Ryder tried to bend back, as far as the

chair would allow. "Look, I had a cheeky look at the flight manifesto. The plane was chartered for Paris."

"And who exactly paid you for all this?" Alexander asked, swinging his leg to hook over his knee. "Let me guess, Margot Laurent?"

"Bingo." Ryder grinned. "The same bitch I stole the brooch from. I have her address, by the way. Plus, I have details of all the fancy gadgets she has in that posh Chateaux of hers. Top of the range security stuff."

"How many men work for her?" Langdon signed.

"Mate, do I look like I can read fingers?"

"He asked how many men work for her?" Caden translated before he frowned down at his phone. Stepping back, he answered quietly, his shoulders tensed.

Ryder's eyes brightened. "Okay, let's talk payment first. What was it we agreed, 100k?"

"Payment is we don't strangle you with your own intestines," Langdon responded, and I immediately translated, if only to give myself something to do that didn't involve re-arranging Ryder's features with my fist.

"Okay, seems fair," Ryder said, clicking his tongue as he gave us the address. "If that's all, I'd like to be untied now." He wiggled his unharmed left hand, as if emphasising the ropes which I was pretty confident were from the curtains.

Caden came back, his expression tight. "Mrs Pritchard committed suicide. Our guys found her hanging over the banister in her home. Looks to be a few days old, at least."

"I have nothing to do with anyone self-exiting." Ryder strained against his restraints.

"Mrs Pritchard would never have done such a thing. They're obviously mistaken," Alexander said stiffly, clearly disturbed by this new information.

"They're not," Caden muttered, dragging a hand down his face. "Fuck, she was my nanny for almost a decade."

Ryder rocked the chair slightly to the side. "Sorry for your loss?"

I kicked at him, almost toppling him over before I caught the front of his shirt. I kept him there, on the edge of falling with his weight on the two back legs of the chair. "You entered my penthouse with a keycard."

"Yeah, yeah, it was literally left outside for me!" He sucked in a breath when I let him jolt back slightly. "Look, it's not my fault the bitch who hired me clearly didn't trust my skills, because I'm far too talented to use a simple key card. At least I got to use some of my new toys to jam the cameras. Sorry about that, by the way. I highly recommend you get someone to redo those servers; they were way too easy to hack."

He looked between us as I settled the chair back on all four legs.

Licking his lips, he drawled, "So, it looks like you guys have a lot to think about. If someone would be kind enough to untie me, I'll be on my way."

Caden held his gun to the side of his head.

"Fuck, okay there, big man. Let's talk about this first. Do you really want to mess up your dad's pretty floor?" Ryder stammered.

"Let him live," I said, Caden's eyes widening when he turned to face me.

Ryder's shoulders sagged. "Thank you."

I breathed through my nose, trying and failing to expel the relentless buzzing beneath my skin. "Don't thank me just yet."

Chapter 60
Arabella

Unfamiliar voices were arguing, my brain fuzzy as I lay against something soft. I forced myself to remain still, my breathing calm even as cotton coated my tongue.

"Shouldn't she be up by now?" Gabriel growled, and I couldn't help but flinch. "I was promised she wouldn't be harmed."

Shit.

Fingers brushed through my hair, and I jerked back. My wrist screamed in pain, metal screeching against metal as I tried to pull free from the handcuff keeping me locked tight.

"You're finally awake. Good." Gabriel sat at the edge of the bed, his torso bare other than a bandage wrapped around his waist. "I was worried."

My stomach turned cold, the handcuff around my wrist cutting painfully into my skin as I tried to press myself further against the wall. "Gabriel–"

"*Madame a dit qu'elle ne devait pas avoir d'invités,*" a man dressed all in black interrupted. "*Elle doit rester–*"

"Can't you see I'm fucking busy?" Gabriel sneered, never taking his attention off me. He had heavy circles beneath his eyes, and yet his gaze was razor sharp.

The man's lips pursed before he nodded, closing the door behind him. It did very little to muffle the loud music coming from below. Loud enough I felt the vibrations through the bed.

"Now, are you going to behave?" Gabriel asked, the lethal threat of his voice hitting me like a whip. "You know I don't want to hurt you, baby." Scratches marked his arms where I'd caught him, and a bruise darkened his jaw.

I barely managed a nod, not moving a muscle as he reached across and undid the handcuff. I immediately pulled the arm to my chest, my wrist already darkening with a bruise.

"Where am I?" I asked, the words more of a croak.

Reaching over to the nightstand, Gabriel grabbed the glass of water. When I hesitated, he smirked. "Stop being dramatic; it's not drugged."

Still, I refused. "What have you done, Gabriel?"

"I'm saving you, like I said I would." He placed the glass back on the nightstand, but it toppled, shattering against the floor. "Now look what you made me do!"

Quietly cursing, he rubbed at his jeans as the water spilled, and I quickly glanced around. I was in a bedroom, the walls painted in deep purples, with a large bed and an expensive-looking frame. The window outside showed a landscape that definitely wasn't London, the sky dark enough to see the glittering stars.

Where the fuck was I?

"You couldn't just come with me, could you?" he snapped, his movements frantic. "No, you had to fucking fight it, and now *she's* involved."

"I'm... I'm sorry," I whispered, jerking back when he jumped to his feet. "I didn't mean it."

Gabriel instantly calmed, just like he did every time I'd apologise in an argument. "It's okay, baby. I've even forgiven you for shooting me, and luckily it was a through and through, missing everything important." His smile was crooked as he knelt back on the bed, leaning over me. "Fuck, I've missed you."

His lips touched mine, and it took everything in me to remain still. To not fight and claw as revulsion swept through me. I even allowed him to deepen the kiss, for his tongue to explore my mouth as I forced myself not to bite down.

Pulling back, he pinned me with a heated look. He ripped at the T-shirt, the fabric tearing.

"Gabriel, please don't!"

"Don't?" he growled, grabbing my hands as I tried to push him away. "Do you know what I've had to do to get you here? You should be more grateful that I risked everything to save you." He straddled my waist, his weight knocking the breath from my lungs.

"Gabriel..."

He squeezed my wrists, the bruise aching as he pressed his thumb purposely into the mark.

"I am grateful!" I lied. "I'm sorry."

"Prove it." His eyes narrowed on mine.

I wriggled beneath him, trying to get him to let go. "Please Gabriel... Stop!"

His expression darkened, his hands releasing my wrists, only for one to grab my breast, and the other to dip between my legs. I kicked at him, shoving with all my strength.

"Ara..." he hissed, trying to hold me down.

I hit at his wound, my knee knocking against the bandage on his lower stomach with as much strength as I could. He screeched, rearing back. The bandage immediately spotted red, his blood growing against the white.

"You stupid bitch!" He raised his fist, my head bouncing back against the bed from the impact when he struck. "This is all your fault! Why couldn't you have just chosen me?!"

Pain shot through my skull, my arm coming up to block the next blow when a guard pulled him back.

"Madame has asked for your presence," he commented, his eyes cold when they met mine. "I suggest you both make yourselves presentable."

The borrowed black silk dress clung to my body, goosebumps prickling my skin as the night air stroked as if it could soothe my apprehension. The music had stopped, leaving a strange quiet but for the shuffling of shoes and quiet murmurs in a language I didn't understand.

I really should've learned French.

"This way," the guard said, his gravelly tone urging me forward even as he held a hand to the gun on his hip.

The house was elegant, with gold accents and large tapestries. Thick rugs decorated the tiled floors, my bare feet making no noise as we passed down several corridors to a set of glass double doors.

Gabriel waited for me there, but I refused to look at him. He'd put on a shirt, covering his bandage, but I knew he didn't have time to change it as blood had seeped through to the fabric.

The guard opened the door, his arm sweeping out to the balcony that appeared to curl around the side of the opulent house. Stepping outside, I gazed at the grounds, the house surrounded in a thick forest. The moon was high in the sky, but the way was illuminated by the warm glow of candles protected from the wind by glass. The garden lights cast a soft glow, revealing figures moving several floors below.

They were tidying up, gathering what looked like scattered napkins and empty glasses. Tables and chairs were being collected and stacked neatly against the surrounding hedges, as if clearing the remnants of a party.

Turning the corner, I noticed a woman stood with the moon as a backdrop, her gaze on those below. On hearing our steps, she turned, a cigarette to her lips. She was beautiful, with her elegant gown and pearls around her throat. Her dark red hair was dyed, but even aged her face was memorable.

Her smile barely curved her lips, a hollow gesture stripped of warmth that was almost welcoming if it wasn't for how her eyes narrowed.

They froze me in place, as if she was already debating what to do with me.

The same woman from Sebastian's photograph. Margot Laurent.

"I don't see it," she said, glancing over to Gabriel as she breathed out a line of smoke. "I don't see the obsession."

"Why the hell didn't you tell me you were grabbing her?" Gabriel snapped, his voice sharp with fury as he dragged me to the edge of the balcony, the balustrade coming to my waist. "You're supposed to keep me in the loop. *I'm* meant to know every step of the plan."

"And you were supposed to take down Sebastian, yet here we are."

"What the fuck did you want me to do? Sebastian's empire is airtight. It didn't matter how hard I looked; I couldn't find anything concrete to stick without getting caught. I've already turned someone close to them. These things take time."

One of the guards stepped closer, crowding us further

against the stone balcony until the edge dug against my back.

"*Tu peux partir*," Margot said, dismissing the guard with an elegant flick of her hand before returning to Gabriel. "*Un petit garçon si incompétent et si pathétique.* You couldn't even shoot him right."

"I was trying not to hit Arabella," Gabriel continued with a sneer, resentment vibrating from him. "Besides, you said you wanted him alive."

"Hmm." Margot turned her attention to me, her smile turning cruel. "Ah yes, Arabella. You have no idea how much you've interfered."

"Ara's mine. That's what we agreed," Gabriel growled. "I destroy Sebastian's reputation, and I get to keep her."

"Yet you failed," Margot snapped back, blowing out more smoke. "You came to me, Detective. I agreed because you weren't afraid to get your hands dirty. You told me yourself you'd do whatever it took to deliver results, take Sebastian down so long as your name stayed clean."

A muscle in Gabriel's jaw feathered, his teeth clenched tight as he grabbed my upper arm in frustration.

"But I'm sure your boss would be very interested to know how flexible your morals have become," she continued with a manipulative purr. "Oh, that's right. You've been suspended, all because of your desperation to get *her* back."

I went to step away, his anger radiating from him in waves when Gabriel's fingers dug deeper. "Where do you think you're going?" he snarled.

He pushed me slightly, the old stone crumbling at my back until my upper body hovered over the side.

"Gabriel!" I cried, my nails clinging to his wrist as he held me suspended above several stories. The wind picked up, whipping violently, almost as if it was trying to suck me over.

"This is all your fault," he spat. "All I wanted was to make you my wife. But now you'll have to settle on being just another one of my holes."

"Fuck you," I hissed, wincing at the bruises forming beneath his grip. "I've never been yours."

He pulled me back over until I was flush against his chest, my heart thumping against my ribs as I tried to twist out of his hold. "You've always been fucking mine."

I fought with everything in me, my panic at the height and the foreboding wind giving me strength to hit out. Gabriel let out a puff of air as I aimed for his wounded side once more, his grip loosening enough so I could shove him until it was his back that pressed against the edge. It creaked beneath his weight before crumbling entirely.

Gabriel fell back, his arms spreading as if to catch himself. But still he toppled backwards, straight over the balcony.

Without thinking, I lunged forward and grabbed his arm, the one barely clinging to the ledge.

"Pull me up!" Gabriel screeched as he dangled over nothing but air. "Ara!"

The stone continued to crack, spreading beneath his fingers.

"Detective, it's been... disappointing," Margot sighed, her breath hot against my nape. Without warning she pressed the end of her cigarette against Gabriel's hand. His eyes widened a fraction, his fingers scrambling to keep hold as he yelped at the pain.

The stone crumbled, disintegrating beneath his grip. He slipped through my fingers, his scream echoing as I scrambled back, only to hear a sickening thud.

Shaking, I dared to look over the side, finding Gabriel face down on the paving several stories below, blood pooling by his head.

"Je n'aurais pas dû envoyer un homme faire le travail d'une femme," Margot mused, flicking what remained of her cigarette over the side. She didn't seem concerned she'd just killed someone, or that there were people already circling the body. "You should never trust men. They can be foolish." Margot turned, her eyes piercing as she swept closer. "What about you, are you foolish?"

I moved away from the edge, the balcony uneasy beneath my feet.

"Maybe not," she chuckled, her heels tapping quietly as she followed my every step. "I still don't get it, Sebastian's obsession. But then again, I don't try to pretend to understand the minds of men."

"Margot..."

"Ah, so he's spoken about me." Her smirk was cruel, twisting her beautiful face. "Now that wasn't something I expected. It has taken me years to realise he was alive, but then again even as a child he was clever, hiding in the shadows and watching. Has he ever told you about it?"

I shook my head, wary as Margot cocked her head to the side, watching me. She was like a viper cloaked in graceful silk. Just dangerous enough to make my instincts warn me to run.

"Shame. It's a good tale," she continued, her accent only adding to her overall elegance. "About a scorned woman taking revenge on the man who promised her the world, only to treat her like his whore. It was all supposed to be mine, you know. It's what I was promised. Mael loved me–"

"But not enough to leave his wife." *Oh God, Ara, shut up!*

Her eyes were razor sharp when they collided with mine, her lips pursed as she slapped me with an open palm. My head snapped to the side, the skin stinging against Gabriel's bruise.

"Careful, or I may forget I need you alive."

I swallowed my response.

"Did you know he's never had a weakness?" Margot's voice softened, her nails scoring gentle lines along my jaw. "Until you."

"I'm not his weakness. I'm just a toy."

"You have no idea, do you? He's never been sentimental or even possessive with anything. Yet he tortured a man to death just for touching you." Margot laughed, but the sound was too calm. "Even as a child if someone else touched his things, he'd simply destroy it, then throw it away. But not you, it seems. Which can only be a good thing, *non?* Because he rarely showed his face in public, and when he did, the places were heavily armed. It was too much of a risk, but luckily my patience was rewarded because you literally fell into my lap. A pretty little weakness I could exploit."

My body locked in place, her touch crawling beneath my skin like insects. "Why do you want to hurt him so much?" I dared to ask.

The calculation in Margot's eyes was as cold as the chunk of ice in my stomach. I was trying to remain calm, my lungs tight with how controlled I made each breath.

"Because he's a Devereaux," she replied, as if it was obvious. "Because he's his father's son, which means he cannot be trusted. His empire was built on the ashes of his name, a name that was supposed to be mine."

"You're delusional," I snapped, my temper rising even as I tried to suppress it. "He was fourteen."

"Every monster was once a child. Sebastian was simply born one; he was made because that's what Mael needed in a son." Her voice rose to a scream with every word. "An heir to everything that *I* was promised! Mael showed me the life I deserved, and then he tore it all away for a woman that meant nothing, and a child that I could've given him. Years I've built on his fortune, and now I'm more powerful than Mael could've ever dreamed."

Margot's nails dug into my skin as she gripped my jaw.

"Do you know Sebastian sobbed as my men used his mother? I made them all watch too, his brothers and father because the bitch deserved it. She was the one who poisoned *mon amour* against me. The only time Sebastian didn't cry was when I had him whipped, or when I carved those pretty slices down his face."

"They were just children."

"If they'd survived, they would've been entitled to everything, and I couldn't let that happen. Not after I've worked so hard for it," Margot sneered, releasing her grip. "I was stupid not to check he was still breathing when I set that fire, and once I realised, it was too late. But don't worry, it's a mistake I won't make again."

"*Madame, un invité est arrivé.*"

We both turned to the guard who spoke, his brows drawn together.

"The party's over. Who is this guest?" Margot spat.

The guard darted his eyes to me. "The thief."

Chapter 61
Arabella

Margot's nails dug into my skin, her fingers encircling my wrist as she guided me to the large fabric sofa. The room was in the process of being cleaned, the maids scattering as soon as we'd entered.

"There was a party, and I wasn't invited?" Ryder said, grinning at me as he was escorted inside from another door. "Maybe next time."

Margot crossed her legs, the slit in her dress baring the skin. "*Cherchez des armes.*"

"Hey, easy now," Ryder chuckled as he was patted down, the guards thorough. "That's my cock, mate."

"*Clair.*" The guards stepped back, and Ryder took the opposite sofa, his arm stretching across the back and his legs spreading, giving off the aura of complete ease. A coffee table separated us, the wood covered in uneaten fresh fruit, crackers and cheese.

"Nice place, this," he said, whistling through his teeth. "Bet it cost a pretty penny."

"Hmm." Margot sat rigid beside me. "How did you find my home?"

"The same way I find everything I want." He shrugged,

nonchalant as his attention brushed around the room. "Did you get a mortgage? Or could you afford to buy this place outright?"

"Is there a reason you're here?" Margot's tone darkened with impatience. "Our business has concluded."

"Oh, of course." Ryder leant forward, his eyes holding a hard intelligence when they met mine. "Sebastian Devereaux, aka, the Beast."

Margot cocked her head, her red hair sweeping forward delicately. "What of him?"

"I just had this thought that maybe you'd want to... you know... win?"

Margot stilled, her nails clamping down on my knee. "I'm listening."

Ryder smiled, and I could see how many women would find him irresistible even if a snake lurched beneath his skin. "So, you want to tell me about this feud?"

"How is that important?"

"It's important enough that he hired me to steal your brooch, sorry about that by the way, and you hired me to steal *her*." His eyes met mine again, glittering with amusement. "You popped my cherry, love. I've never stolen a person before."

"If you're here just for gossip, then my men will escort you out." Margot snapped her fingers, and two armed men pointed their guns at Ryder.

"If you do that, then you won't know where I've hidden Sebastian."

"Hidden?" Margot held up her hand, her face twitching. "Where is he?"

"Not so fast." Ryder reached over for one of the crackers, adding cheese before munching down, seemingly unconcerned with the guns pointed in his direction. "Let's talk payment."

Margot chuckled, gesturing for her men to step back. "How much?"

"One million. That's pound sterling, not euros, by the way." He picked at a grape next, throwing it up into the air before catching it in his mouth. "Oh, plus hazard pay." He held up his right hand, showing his three middle fingers splinted together.

Margot let out a controlled breath. "Is he alive?"

"He was when I left him." Another shrug, his movements relaxed. Almost controlled.

"Deal."

"Great." Ryder jumped up like an overexcited child, brushing his hand down his dark T-shirt to get rid of any crumbs. "Then if you'd like to follow me." He went to turn but was blocked by the guards. "Look, I know I'm pretty, but I'm just not into guys. So you'll just have to back the fuck off."

Margot stood, holding out her hand for me to take. "Let him through," she said, her grip like iron when she pulled me to my feet.

Ryder grinned, patting one of the guards on the shoulder as he passed. "Good boy."

Margot yanked me along, her guards trailing behind us as we followed Ryder out the front of the house to a large SUV. He stopped at a car, sweeping out his arm dramatically.

"Ta da!"

Margot raised a single brow. "You've brought him here?"

"Yep. Tied with a bow." Ryder waited a beat, his smile straining when no one moved closer. "That's your cue," he said, pointing to one of the guards and then to the boot. "Seriously, you can't get good help these days."

Ryder stepped back, moving closer to us as the guards

finally circled the car slowly, waiting for Margot to give the order before one held a gun up, and the other reached for the latch.

I tried to peer closer, Ryder's arm brushing against mine as the boot popped, revealing nothing inside.

"Well, shit." Ryder whistled. "He was there a moment ago." He turned to wink at me, reaching over and forcing me to duck just as the first bullet soared overhead.

Chapter 62
Sebastian

I never thought I'd step foot back in France, the country of my birth holding tainted memories I'd rather forget. Yet I hadn't hesitated on getting on the plane, crossing the sea to arrive within hours of finding out Arabella was taken.

"Coming outside now, over."

I moved further around the tree, watching the car outside the front of the house. It had been a shock to see the building, an almost exact replica of the place I'd once called home.

Langdon had laughed, throwing his head back when he'd first noticed the similarities. Margot had made it a little more grand, adding decorative columns and making it five times the size of the modest home I'd grown up in.

But it was still the same. The bitch had rebuilt the house she'd burned all those years ago.

"We have visual, over."

Straightening from my crouch, I moved forward, trusting my team to protect us from the treeline. They'd already taken out the guards that were roaming the grounds, moving silently into position so the place was surrounded. Ryder had confirmed Margot had built the place like a fortress, to keep her safe inside the walls with her bullet-proof windows and reinforced doors.

Which meant we needed to bring her outside.

Arabella shivered, her face pale as a bruise darkened her cheekbone.

I waited, the early morning air burning my lungs as Ryder said something with a smirk, closing the distance just like he'd been told so he could get to Arabella, and then protect her.

It went off like clockwork, with Ryder putting his body over hers and pushing them both lower as the first shot sounded.

A splatter of blood, guard after guard falling to the ground while Margot spun, eyes wide and mouth agape. She spotted me amongst the trees, her movement calm as she bent down for one of the dropped guns. She straightened, her arm unwavering as she swung it towards me.

Langdon appeared behind her, holding up his own weapon to the back of her head.

"*You look like* him," she purred, seemingly in complete control of the chaos that surrounded her.

I tossed the brooch, and Margot remained still as it crashed to the stones by her feet. She didn't even glance at it, her attention remaining on me.

"Sebastian?" Arabella whispered, her voice drawing me to where she stood to the side, Caden pulling her slightly behind him. Ryder was nowhere to be found, but right now he didn't matter.

Margot was so much older than I remembered, but her eyes were the same. Just as pinched. Just as harsh.

Il ne m'a pas laissé le choix.

He left me no choice.

My demons roared, threatening to unravel my control. But I refused to let them.

"*Do you know how easy it was to infiltrate your little empire?*" she continued, her posture stiff as Lang pushed the muzzle of his gun harder against her head. "*All it took was a little... persuasion.*"

She laughed, her red hair coming around to brush along her bare shoulders. She didn't seem to react to the cold air, yet the wind bit harshly at my exposed skin.

"*You made a mistake, Maggie,*" I said calmly, purposely using the name my brothers and I called her when she was first introduced as the nanny. "*You were overconfident, which has made you arrogant.*"

"*You're right, I probably shouldn't have trusted a thief,*" Margot smirked, pouting her red painted lips. "*But do you really believe you have the upper hand?*"

With a gasp, blood appeared on Caden's shoulder. Arabella cried out, catching him as he fell. Another shot, this one whizzing past my head.

"*You seem to have forgotten that I was beside your father for years. Every dirty trick I have, I've learnt from him.*" Margot smirked. "*Now, there's a sniper aimed at your Arabella. I suggest you remove the mutt from the back of my head, or she'll lose hers.*"

I glanced at Arabella, who was calmly whispering to a pale Caden, unable to understand the conversation. His shoulder was a mess, his teeth gritted as she tried to put pressure on the wound. He needed medical attention, and soon.

"*Langdon, step back.*"

Langdon didn't even blink, his arm unwavering.

"*Lang!*" I barked, and he finally looked at me before glancing at Caden. "*Step back and drop the gun.*"

He followed the instruction immediately, trusting that I knew what I was doing.

Margot smiled. "*Good.*" With a wink, she turned and

pulled the trigger. The bullet hit Langdon straight in the chest, the momentum throwing him to the floor with a heavy thump.

Arabella screamed, unable to move as she kept the pressure on Caden's shoulder. I spared a quick glance at Lang, finding him limp with his eyes closed. I ignored the burning in my own chest, at the rage that perforated every single one of my cells.

A crackle in my ear. *"Those on the roof have been neutralised, Sir. Over."*

Margot laughed once more, turning to point the gun at Arabella.

I didn't hesitate, moving to put myself between them. *"You're supposed to be dead."*

"As are you, but clearly we are not, no?" Margot mused. *"Tell me, do I still haunt you? Does what happened keep you up at night?"*

My jaw tensed, the muscles twitching as I stared her down. *"You really think you have that much influence? Margot... you're nothing."* Her smirk faltered, so I stepped closer, making myself a larger target. *"An old, withered whore that my father fucked, then discarded."*

"Sir, incoming," came another crackle in my ear. *"Thirty-second warning."*

"Still your father's son, I see," she said, her voice sharp. *"Even with those scars, you wear your anger beautifully. Just like he did."*

"And I'll finish what he was too weak to," I growled, goading her as I took another step forward until I blocked her view of Ara entirely.

Margot's upper lip curled, clearly amused. *"Such fire in you, something your father lacked. It's a pity it's come to this,"* she murmured, almost regretful, though the glint in her eyes betrayed her hunger for retribution. *"But don't worry."*

She raised the gun with terrifying calm, her smile widening as her finger found the trigger.

"I'll take real good care of your little toy."

I ignored the burning when the bullet hit, instead reaching across the space for the weapon. Margot clawed at my skin, fighting as I twisted her own gun beneath her chin.

She screeched, her movements frantic as she tried to push me away. *"Guards!"* she called. *"Guards..."* Her voice cut off, my fingers tightening around her throat until she could barely draw in a breath. She looked so pathetic in my grip, the woman who haunted my nightmares.

The woman who took everything from me.

"You really believe you can do this?" she gasped when I relaxed my fingers. *"Kill me now, and you'll forever doubt everything and everyone."*

"If I'd wanted to kill you," I hissed against her face. *"I would have already."*

"ON THE GROUND, HANDS ON YOUR HEAD!"

I immediately released her and dropped to my knees, following the instructions as she stumbled back. Margot's face was pale, her lips lifting into a snarl as the Gendarmerie surrounded us.

"ON THE GROUND, HANDS ON YOUR HEAD!"

Her arm shook, dropping the gun before a gendarme immediately shoved her face-down onto the floor. Another set of hands pushed me down, and I let them, turning my head to look at Arabella. She continued to hold her weight on Caden's shoulder.

"STOP WHAT YOU'RE DOING AND PUT YOUR HANDS ON YOUR HEAD!"

Ara didn't stop, her arms shaking as she stemmed the blood that was still pumping.

"Arabella, you need to step back," I said, keeping my tone calm. "Everything's going to be okay."

She looked up then, our eyes meeting. Her hair was a mess, curling around her face, and her skin was pale. Yet determination was there. "Caden?"

"Everything's going to be okay, *belle*," I repeated, grunting when a knee was pressed into my spine. "Trust me."

She blinked, her eyes wet as she knelt back and was immediately handcuffed. A medical team began working on Caden as I was dragged to my feet, facing a combative Margot.

You couldn't simply chop the head off the snake and expect everything to disappear. No, I wanted to destroy the entire fucking nest. I wanted every piece of her empire dismantled, every lie she'd built her legacy on exposed and shredded beyond repair. So one anonymous tip later, here we are. Her estate swarmed, officers sweeping through every inch, closing in on the evidence my team had already made sure they'd find.

I watched her struggle, making sure my face was the last thing she saw before she was shoved into the van. I smiled, noting how her eyes flickered with confusion, followed by slow, dawning fear.

That was the reason I'd chosen not to wear my mask, wanting her to see the resemblance, to recognise the face of the man she once claimed to love.

To see my brothers, and my mother.

To see that I'd won.

Chapter 63
Arabella

"So let me get this straight," the inspector began, tapping his pen repeatedly on the cold, metal table. "You have no idea who Miss Laurent is?"

I remained silent, my body heavy and my bones aching. I didn't even know my bones could ache. Or my eyelids.

"She's a big name here in France. She's been on our radar for quite some time, but she's smart. Playing the rich socialite but never directly being connected to the heroin trade. So imagine my surprise when we get a tip that she's holding some Enchanted Dust in her own home. Laurent doesn't make mistakes like that."

Again, I remained silent. Debating whether it would be rude to just take a little nap here, or would that just make my situation a thousand times worse?

"Okay, tell me about a,"–he looked down at his notes–"Sebastian Devereaux. Now, that's a name I haven't seen in a long time." He glanced up, face tightening when I didn't react. Turning to his partner, he spat something in French before returning his attention to me. "He almost killed Laurent."

"He did nothing but defend himself," I said calmly,

pressing my fingers to the cool table. My body shook slightly, goosebumps prickling my skin. "If Margot was already on your radar, then you'd know how dangerous she is. I'm sure you saw the amount of manpower she'd hired."

The inspector's eyes brightened, as if he'd caught me out. "What happened this morning, *mademoiselle* Grey?"

I swallowed, returning to my comforting silence. If only to piss him off.

His shoulders tightened, and if I wasn't so tired I would have done a victory dance. "*Mademoiselle*, if you refuse to co-operate with our investigation. Then you'll only–"

"I think that's enough." Alexander burst through the door, escorted by one of the uniformed officers.

The inspector stood, knuckles white as he gripped the table's edge. "This interview isn't over."

"Oh, but it is." Alexander snapped his fingers, and the officer beside him relayed something in French.

The inspector's face turned red in response, a muscle feathering in his jaw.

"You've been interrogating a traumatised woman, one who's been kidnapped and clearly harmed," Alexander continued, helping me gently to my feet with a tut. "Look at her, she's still covered in blood." Removing his jacket, he draped it over my shoulders.

"She received the appropriate medical attention."

"Come on, Ara, let's get you out of this cesspool." Alexander held out his arm, and I took it as he escorted me out of the building to a waiting car. He let me enter first, sliding into the seat beside me. "Did you say anything?" he asked, adjusting his cuffs.

I turned to face him, my hands still crusted in his son's blood which now gripped the edge of his jacket. "Say what, exactly?"

Alexander's lips pursed for a moment before he reached

for a button on the door. "Please head to the airport." He released the button, and the car began to move.

"Airport? Is that where Sebastian is?"

"No, he's not." Alexander's attention was direct, almost uncomfortable. "You need to understand, this is the last time I will offer you your freedom. After today, my nephew will never let you go. He doesn't believe in love the way your fairytales describe it. His love is cruel, twisted... born from a trauma that will never heal."

"I don't–"

"You're an obsession that almost got him and my son killed. You would do well to leave before it gets any worse. For both your sakes."

I was so tired, but anger seemed to give me that much needed energy. So I clung to it like a lifeline. "You're such an arsehole."

His brows drew together. "Excuse me?"

"It was Margot that almost got them killed, not me." Frustration made my words sharp. "So you can stop with the blame. I can see you're trying to push me away."

"Hmm," he hummed, but there was an edge to it. "This is your last chance to run. Everything I promised still stands, a new life, anywhere you choose. But after this, the offer disappears. So make the decision."

"Oh, so it's my decision, and not yours?" I sat rigid, the silk of this fucking dress clinging to me like a second skin I didn't want. "How generous of you."

His eyes narrowed on mine, nostrils flaring as he waited.

"I think you're wrong."

He blinked, seemingly surprised with my response. "How so?"

"I understand you love him, in whichever way *you* define love to be. Whether that's because of blood, or just a sense of duty."

"I'm just saying that sometimes it doesn't matter how much you love them, or how much you try to help. They just can't be fixed."

"That's because he's not broken." I made sure to keep eye contact, for him to see the conviction behind my words.

"I–"

"No, it's my turn to speak," I interrupted.

Alexander's upper lip twitched.

"I'm in love with Sebastian. I can't tell you if it's some fairytale kind of love, or if that even exists. To be honest, I don't exactly know when it happened, but it did. I love him for who he is, and not who you think he should be. So take me to him, *now*, or I won't be held responsible for my actions."

Alexander gave me a long look, then finally smiled. But there was no happiness behind the emotion, just resignation. "His love comes at a cost. I only hope you're willing to pay it."

I ignored the grumpy-looking officer standing at the door, Alexander dealing with him when he went to stop me from entering.

My hand shook as I pushed my way inside, the obnoxious beeping sending repetitive jolts through my chest. Caden lay on his back on the bed, eyes closed and looking pale.

Bas turned from where he was standing over his cousin, and everything just stopped. The beeping became nothing but white noise as I dragged my eyes over every inch of him, my lungs aching as if I'd held my breath. Bruises decorated his chest, barely seen beneath the tattoos except for one right in the centre.

A sharp whistle forced my attention to the side where Langdon stood with a grin. He signed something with his hands, which made Sebastian smirk, and I simply burst into tears.

"I thought you were dead," I cried.

Langdon crossed the room faster than Sebastian, pulling me into his arms before he winced. I stepped back, realising he had just a single bruise, one that covered half of his chest.

I didn't get long to look before Sebastian pulled me against him, his thumb coming up to brush the tears from my cheek. "It takes more than a bullet to get Langdon down," he commented, the deep timbre of his voice washing over me.

"He was shot." I tried to free myself from his arms, but he simply tightened them. "*You* were shot."

"It's called Kevlar," Alexander explained, stepping inside the room with a stern expression. "Sebastian's simply bruised, but considering Langdon was hit at such close range he's sustained a few broken ribs."

"Which means he'll be fine," Sebastian whispered against my ear, and Langdon gave me two thumbs up.

"What about Caden?" I asked, managing to turn towards the bed. "Is he going to be okay?"

"My son was just unlucky enough to be shot in the shoulder where he wasn't protected. The surgery was a success, and he'll gain full function. Apparently, he survived the initial blood loss because of you, so I suppose you have my gratitude."

He said it with such stiffness that I laughed.

"What of our situation. Have you dealt with it?" Sebastian asked his uncle.

Alexander rolled his eyes. "Of course it's been dealt

with. Who do you think I am? Your weapons have mysteriously disappeared, as well as any evidence that put you as the aggressor."

"How many of our men were arrested?"

"Only one. The others followed protocol and managed to escape." Alexander raised a single brow. "He's an ex Royal Marine so he knows not to speak. And if he does, well, he'll just be dealt with in exactly the same way as Margot. With a suspicious, and no way related to us, death."

A sharp ring sounded through the room, and Alexander pulled out his phone to snap at the person on the other line.

Sebastian moved us to the corner, using his back to block the room from view. "You came back," he whispered, almost reverently.

I reached up to cup his jaw, my nails scratching through his unkept beard. "You came for me first."

"Always," he grumbled, his lips brushing against mine in the most gentle caress that had my toes curling. "*Belle, tu es ma lumière dans l'obscurité. Tu seras toujours la mienne.*"

Reaching up, I deepened the kiss, having control for a split second before Sebastian devoured me like the merciless monster he was, and I didn't want it to stop. He was the man who travelled across the sea, stood in front of a bullet, and faced the woman who haunted his past. All for me.

He may be the Beast.

But he was mine.

"Okay, wrap this up. As soon as Caden's stable, we're all returning to the UK and away from this godforsaken place," Alexander tutted, shooting us a look of disgust. "God bless the king."

Epilogue Part 1

Sebastian

Charlie Pritchard struggled as he was pushed down in the chair, skin bruised from where Langdon had been a little rough.

A muffled noise echoed through the room, Chip's words lost beneath the gag and black fabric bag that was ceremoniously placed on his head. I sat opposite, my mask in place as I watched him continue to struggle. The metal handcuffs bit into his wrists, hard enough for him to bleed.

With a nod, Caden moved, his arm carefully held tight to his body as his shoulder continued to heal. Luckily, he'd been shot on his left side and not his dominant right so he could drag his favourite sledgehammer against the concrete floor, the sound causing Chip to try and recoil. Except he had nowhere to go.

"Think it's time to get this party started," Caden said, and Langdon grinned, reaching over with his lighter to set the edge of the fabric bag aflame.

Chip tried to shake it off, the fire eating across the fibres quickly before he managed to awkwardly reach up, tug it off, and throw it to the floor. He blinked at the light, glancing around the concrete walls, hesitating at the display of weapons before settling on me.

He knew exactly where he was, having stood guard on numerous occasions while we'd interrogated people in this room. Yet his demeanour was calm, almost controlled despite the situation.

I didn't expect anything different. Chip had always displayed his emotions in a limited way, which had always been a concern for Mrs Pritchard. Honestly, he would've grown up to be an essential part of the team. Yet he'd fucked up, and I wanted to know why he'd thrown it all away.

Chip blinked a few times, waiting until Caden reached over to remove his gag.

"Does Ara know where I am?" he asked. "She'll be upset. Maybe even hate you if you hurt me."

"You truly believe you mean anything to her?" I leaned forward.

"We're friends," he said, eyes darting around the room. "Her *only* friend."

"Yet you organised her rape."

Chip stilled, unmoving. "That was her father," he said carefully, the earlier concern disappearing.

"Well, it's interesting because Mr Hill was real fucking chatty when we cut off his dick," Caden added. "He said he was paid by an older woman. Now, obviously, our first thought had been Margot, and that was our mistake." Caden dragged his sledgehammer until the handle rested against Chip's knee. "Once we actually looked into it, we realised it was your mother who'd paid him."

"What's that got to do with me?" Chip asked in a flat tone, his expression calm. "I can't control what Mum does. Maybe that's why she killed herself? From the guilt."

"Mrs Pritchard was found with defensive wounds on her hands," I said, his dark eyes meeting mine.

"Honestly Charlie, it was clever to get your mum to pay," Caden continued, lifting the sledgehammer until the entire weight rested on Chip's bandaged thigh until he winced. "We'd never have suspected the same woman who was my nanny for so long. So tell me, how did you convince her to do it?"

Silence followed, and Caden pressed harder against the hammer.

"No point in lying now," Langdon signed, knowing Chip understood.

Chip hissed through his teeth, and Caden eased back a little. "She didn't know anything. I asked her for a favour, and after she'd met him she realised what had happened at the club." It took a moment to break his façade, a smile curving his lips. "What gave me away?"

"Your thigh injury was self-inflicted," I said. "Innocent people don't shoot themselves."

"You think I shot myself?" Chip asked, clearly amused. "Why would I do that?"

"You staged the whole thing, knowing we'd never suspect you," Caden answered. "Hell, I'll admit it was a clever move. Almost flawless, and might have even worked if you didn't make a mistake."

A nerve twitched in Chip's jaw. "Which was?"

"You used your own gun," I said.

He blinked up at me. "That's easily explained."

"Maybe, but not that it was your gun that took out the twins, too."

A pause followed, the silence heavy. "If you believe all this, then why am I not dead?" Chip asked me. "I've watched you for years, learning how you work. I did everything you asked, and it still wasn't enough."

"Is that why you did it?"

Chip smirked. "I tied Mum's rope and pushed her off the landing because she wanted to tell you what I'd done. Can you believe that? She'd rather choose to tell on her only son rather than live with the guilt. She always said I was such a disappointment. I couldn't do anything right. I couldn't even gain your respect."

"You think hurting Arabella would gain my respect?" I growled.

His expression was cold, despite the smile. "I was fascinated with your obsession with her, so I wanted to see whether you'd still like her after she was spoiled."

"Why?" I hissed, needing to know the answer. He'd worked for me for years, and I'd known him for almost his entire life.

"Arabella's way too innocent for you," he said. "You'd have grown bored with her eventually, and honestly, I was doing her a favour. Even her father took advantage, so I thought she needed to learn the hard way."

He tried to shrug, except Langdon pressed down on his shoulders from behind, fingers digging in painfully.

Swallowing, he continued, "Morris was too easy to convince, so selfish that he'd happily have his daughter raped just for monetary gain. I actually enjoyed slitting his throat; it felt cathartic. I'm just disappointed I didn't get to see Ara's face. I hope she felt... relieved."

"You've been playing us all," Caden cursed, and Chip chuckled.

"Tricking Gabriel into meeting her there was like the perfect play, the knight coming in to defend the queen. Except he was more like my pawn."

Caden removed the sledgehammer, taking a step back as I stood.

"Are we still playing chess?" I asked.

"We're always playing," he snapped, finally showing a little bit of frustration. "We've been playing for years, except I was always a move ahead."

"Clearly." I glanced down at his handcuffs, then back up to meet his eyes.

"I thought the bombs were a clever distraction," Chip continued, his eyes empty. Resigned. "Made you believe Margot knew about all the distribution, when in reality it was just me."

"You made a mistake in coming after my Arabella. You did me a favour in taking out her father, but now it's your turn." Reaching over, I encircled my fingers around his throat, feeling his breath strain and his pulse become erratic.

Chip sealed his fate the moment he'd set his eyes on her. From the start he'd manipulated her kindness, turning her trust into a weapon against me. That betrayal I could never forgive.

Once, I might've strung him up above my ring, left him there as a warning. But things had changed. Now, Chip wouldn't bleed. He'd simply vanish, because Arabella needed more than vengeance. She needed a future where she was free to be whoever she wanted to be. To have a life that wasn't controlled by fear.

She may have never been meant for my world, but she chose me anyway.

Which made her mine to not only possess, but to protect.

"How does it feel to have the snake so close to home?" Chip managed to push out, his face becoming red the harder I squeezed. "Do I have your respect now?"

"No." I dropped my face closer to his, my words the last he'd ever hear. "Checkmate."

Epilogue Part 2

Arabella
Six months later

I didn't think it would be this hard to say goodbye to a place I never cared about. But it was once my home, a place I thought was safe. With my single cardboard box, I stared at Dad's armchair, trying to see whether I could see any stains. Which of course I couldn't, the place having been thoroughly cleaned to the point I couldn't even see the rings that were once engrained in the table from his bottles of beer.

I'd been putting off coming back for so long, and now that I was here, all I wanted to do was leave. To close this part of my story and honestly never think of it. Almost pretend it didn't exist. Which yes, was a super unhealthy way to deal with my emotions, but I'd already filled up several notebooks and had run out of space. So I think I deserved a little head burying, thank you very much.

"Are you ready?" Sebastian asked, reaching over to take my box from me. It was pretty much empty other than my books and perfume bottle collection. Everything else I'd organised a charity to come pick up.

"I think so." Taking the key, I left it on the table beside the armchair for the landlord to find. "You didn't have to come with me, you know."

"I know," he said. "But I wanted to."

I smiled up at him, finding those intense, midnight blue eyes on me. It was strange to think that nine months ago I didn't know he even existed, and now I got butterflies at the thought of this dangerous man coming with me to say goodbye to my old life.

Because *he* was my new life.

With one last look, I left the house I'd shared with my father and walked out to the car. I smiled at the driver when he noticed me approaching, his returning expression warm as he opened the passenger door.

Sebastian appeared, shoving the box aggressively into the driver's hands. I'd have rolled my eyes, but I'd already slipped into the seat, with Sebastian coming in beside me. He immediately pulled me onto his lap, spreading my legs so he could stroke my inner thighs.

"Bad girls don't get to come," he whispered against my neck.

I laughed, resting my head on his shoulder. "What makes me bad?"

He slapped my thigh, the sting lasting only a second before warmth spread across my skin towards my core. "Flirting with the driver. I'm going to have to fire him."

I sucked in a breath, his fingers teasing the lace between my legs. "He... he didn't do anything wrong."

"No?" He teased across the fabric, thumb pressing against my clit.

"Sebastian!" I groaned, trying to move, except he pinned me against him with a hand collaring the front of my neck.

"What does my *beautiful little rabbit want*, hmm?"

I shivered at his words, his voice always huskier when he spoke French. *"I want you,"* I replied in the same language, having been learning it along with sign.

Sebastian tore the lace, his fingers finally touching me. "Ask me what he did, Ara."

"What... what did he do?" I breathed, unable to concentrate while his fingers stroked, teasing.

Sebastian sunk a thick finger inside, thrusting languorously. "He looked at what's mine."

The car ride was a mixture of moans and cries, with Sebastian never letting me come but bringing me to the edge over and over.

So much had changed since I first agreed to take my father's place. I'd gone from feeling like a captive to choosing to be here. From hating Sebastian to choosing him with my entire heart.

I was no longer locked in the tower, but Sebastian's protectiveness was still a bit much, so I technically wasn't allowed out without a guard. But I was working on that, and every time I'd brought it up, he just watched me argue my point with this twisted amusement. Seriously, it was rude. So I had a guard until further notice, and that was only if Sebastian wasn't by my side anyway.

The car eventually pulled into the underground garage, and pushing away from Sebastian I opened the car door before the driver could, sprinting to the lift to press the button. I didn't need to turn to know Sebastian was there, his presence sucking all the surrounding oxygen. My body felt tight, my thighs slick with need. Sebastian pressed against my back, his erection so hard it must be painful.

I observed him in the mirror, completely cold except for his eyes, which watched me with such heat I could easily combust on the spot. He held my gaze, his breath against my nape almost enough to make me come at this point.

The lift came to a stop, my entire body on edge because of the man at my back.

The doors slipped open, and I hesitated at the darkness.

"Run, *beautiful*." Sebastian leaned down, lips brushing the shell of my ear. "You know what happens when I catch you."

My heart pounded in my chest, but my legs moved without thought. Sebastian's favourite game was to chase, to have me run and hide so he could catch me. And he always caught me.

Adrenaline surged through my veins, my breathing frantic as I tried to manoeuvre through our home with such little light. He'd drawn the curtains, making it almost pitch black save for a few candles here and there.

Stumbling over something soft, I swallowed my laughter, my movements frantic as I strained to hear him chasing behind. I couldn't, but I knew he was there, stalking me in the dark.

Another candle, then another. They drew me down the west wing, past our bedroom and the studio to the stairs in the back. Sebastian had placed a small candle on each step, and despite knowing it was a trap, I couldn't help but go up. I froze each time my foot hit the wood, not wanting to make a sound as I ascended.

Light perforated the darkness, candle after candle pulling me past the gym and towards the large, back room. It had always been empty, used as storage. But as I pushed open the door I gasped. Light came in through the large windows, illuminating the newly built shelves that stacked across every inch.

A creak of the floorboard echoed behind me, and I squealed when strong hands encircled my waist. "Caught you. Now, on your knees."

I immediately followed the instructions, anticipation

making my thighs slick with need. My mouth watered when he released his cock, my tongue coming out to lick the head. He groaned, tilting his head back to reveal the thick column of his throat.

It wasn't long before he'd lost patience, bending me over to fuck me from behind. I revelled in every feral thrust, in every slap of his palm. It was only after we'd both come, still dressed and tucked hot and sweaty against his chest, that I finally raised my head to have a good look at my surroundings.

There weren't just shelves, but also a large armchair and even a desk. Beautifully woven rugs covered the wooden floor, and Sebastian's dark art claimed the walls beside the large windows. The shelves were floor-to-ceiling, taking up all the space including above the door frame.

Jumping up, I moved to the desk, my fingers touching the beautiful rose locked beneath the glass dome. It was the single colour in the room, a stain of red amongst the wood, greys and black.

"I built you a library," Sebastian said, and I turned to find him standing.

"A library?" I asked, my voice husky. "Why?"

"I plan to gift you a new book every week, slowly building up your collection," he said, his chest rumbling when he pressed against my side.

I swallowed past the emotions, grinning when I noticed the ladder on rails. "That's going to take some time."

"Months."

"Years." My eyes traced his face, my chest aching as I smiled. "All this just so I'll read to you more."

Sebastian laughed, and I drowned in the sound. He rarely laughed, but when he did, I made sure to kiss him. So I did, going onto my tiptoes so I could press my lips gently to his.

"I love you." It wasn't the first time I'd told him, and each time it felt right.

This possessive, dangerous man had somehow filled this emptiness inside me. I was no longer just surviving. I was living. Breathing. Wanting. And for the first time I could see a future that wasn't full of seclusion and fear.

I had a life, and I couldn't wait to see where it took us, together.

"I never believed in love," he admitted, his voice low and rough, like gravel dragged across silk. "I thought it was a weakness, something that only destroyed." His hand cradled my jaw, gentle but possessive, tilting my face towards his. "But what I feel for you is beyond love. It's need. It's chaos. It's the only thing that's ever made sense. You quiet the demons in my head and keep me from falling over the edge.

"I'll never be the man from your fairytales, but if there's one thing I can offer it's this: Everything I am, everything I have, I'd give it all up just to call you my wife."

I blinked up at him, lips parting at his words. "Sebastian, are you asking me to marry you?" I whispered.

His fingers moved down, tightening on the side of my throat as he kissed me, claiming me in his own, savage way. "No, I'm telling you. It's not a question, because there isn't an answer in this lifetime where you don't belong to me."

"I want nothing more than to be your wife," I laughed against his lips. "Thank you for saving me."

His head dipped, pressing his forehead against mine. "It was you who saved me. I didn't know what I was missing until I found you. And now, I can't let you go. Not now. Not ever."

"Am I still in your debt?" I asked with a grin.

Sebastian laughed. "Always."

What's Next?

Thank you so much for reading Blood and Thorns! I hope you enjoyed Sebastian & Arabella's story, and if you liked it, please leave a review. Your support means everything!

**She's his greatest mistake…
and the one he'd risk everything for**

Next up is Locks and Lies, a stand-alone dark contemporary romance inspired by *Rapunzel*.

Not ready to say goodbye to Sebastian and Arabella? Here's a bonus Blood and Thorns scene. Visit this link: BookHip. com/QQJQBGJ

Acknowledgments

Where do I even begin? *Blood and Thorns* is different from what I usually write, but I'm endlessly grateful to those who encouraged me to explore this new genre because I've absolutely fallen in love with it.

To my husband—who hadn't read any of my work (aside from the spicy scenes, obviously)—thank you for helping me push past the fear of trying something different. Your unwavering support and belief in me means everything. You are, and always will be, my biggest cheerleader.

To Alexxi, thank you not only for helping me curate the perfect playlist, but for constantly filling my DMs with inspiration and friendship. Your presence and excitement throughout this journey is something I'll always cherish.

To my incredible beta readers: you are absolute gold. Your insights helped shape this story into what it is today, and I'm forever grateful for the time, energy, and love you poured into that chaotic early draft.

To Kat, for not only the amazing proofreading, but for always being there for me as not just a PA, but a friend.

And finally, to my readers, thank you for always showing up. You make this dream possible.

Much love,
Tay

About the Author

Taylor Aston White writes deliciously dark fantasy & romance, where tension burns, secrets break, and love always wins. Based in the UK with her childhood sweetheart and their two children, she's the author of several bestselling series and loves to explore mythology and European faerie tales to create her own, modern twists.

SOCIALS

Instagram
@taylorastonwhite
TikTok
@taylorastonwhite
Facebook
/taylorastonwhite
Website
www.taylorastonwhite.com
Bookbub
www.bookbub.com/profile/taylor-aston-white
Goodreads
www.goodreads.com/taylorastonwhite

Sign up for Taylor's newsletter mailing list to receive updates, exclusive content, giveaways, early excerpts and much more.
www.taylorastonwhite.com

www.ingramcontent.com/pod-product-compliance
Lightning Source LLC
Chambersburg PA
CBHW010314100726
47906CB00006B/990